"I should let you g   one," he muttered.

"You think?" I snapped.

His arm curled, moving me to his front and curving around me.

"Hawk…" I warned when his head dropped. I twisted my neck to try to avoid it, his arm tightened, his other one wrapping around me, and I failed to avoid his lips hitting my neck.

"You need to get caught up, baby, carve some time out for me," he murmured against my neck. I was about to say something snotty but wasn't able to when his tongue touched the skin behind my ear. I instantly forgot I was insanely pissed at him, and then he said, "We're due."

"Due?" I breathed because I could still feel his tongue behind my ear.

His head came up, he looked at me, and he repeated, "Due."

"For what?"

His black eyes warmed, the dimples popped out, and his arms got even tighter, plastering me to his long, hard body.

Oh.

Due.

Mm…

Also by Kristen Ashley

The Colorado Mountain Series

The Gamble
Sweet Dreams
Lady Luck
Jagged
Kaleidoscope

The Dream Man Series

Mystery Man
Wild Man
Law Man
Motorcycle Man

The Chaos Series

Own the Wind
Fire Inside

MYSTERY MAN

KRISTEN ASHLEY

FOREVER

NEW YORK   BOSTON

Forever
Hachette Book Group
1290 Avenue of Americas
New York, NY 10104

www.HachetteBookGroup.com

Printed in the United States of America

First Edition: August 2013

10 9 8 7 6 5 4

OPM

Forever is an imprint of Grand Central Publishing.
The Forever name and logo are trademarks of Hachette Book Group, Inc.

The Hachette Speakers Bureau provides a wide range of authors for speaking events. To find out more, go to www.hachettespeakersbureau.com or call (866) 376-6591.

The publisher is not responsible for websites (or their content) that are not owned by the publisher.

MYSTERY
MAN

PROLOGUE

Mystery Man

I FELT THE covers slide down my body then a hand light on the small of my back. It was so warm it was hot, like the blood that ran through its veins went faster than the blood of any average man.

If this was true, it wouldn't surprise me.

I opened my eyes and it was dark. It was always dark when he visited me.

I had a moment like every moment I had when he showed. A moment of sanity. A moment where my mind said to close my eyes, open my mouth and tell him to go away.

But if I did, I knew he would. He wouldn't say a word. As silently as he came, he'd leave.

And he'd never come back.

But this was the right thing to do. The smart thing to do. The *sane* thing to do.

And I was thinking of doing it. Honest to God, I was. I thought about doing it every time.

Then I felt his weight hit the bed and his body stretching out beside mine. He turned me into him. I opened my mouth to speak. Before I could do the sane thing, his mouth was on mine.

And for the next two hours, I didn't think at all.

But I felt. I felt *a lot*.

And all of it was *good*.

*   *   *

It was still dark when his shadow moved in the room.

I lay in bed and watched him move. He didn't make a noise. It was weird. There was a rustle of clothes but other than that, silence.

Even as a shadow, I saw he had masculine grace. Powerful, masculine grace. That was weird too. Just watching my Mystery Man putting on clothes was like watching a badass, macho dance if there was such a thing. Of course, there wasn't except in my bedroom when he came to visit. No, when he was getting ready to leave.

It was so fascinating I should sell tickets. But if I did, I'd have to share. I probably already shared with half of Denver, all of them getting their own private show. That already messed with my head enough, that and the fact that he came at all. I let him come then he made me come after which he came. Then, often, like tonight, repeat.

He moved to the bed and I watched that too. He bent low. I felt the heat of his hand on my knee, his fingers curling around the back. He lightly kissed my hip, his lips skimming across my skin, making it tingle. Then he slid the covers up my body to my waist, where he dropped them.

I was mostly on my belly but partly on my side. My arm was crooked, hand tucked under my face on the pillow. His body moved in that direction, his fingers slid under my hair, pulling it gently back, and his lips came to my ear.

"Later, babe," he whispered.

"Later," I whispered back.

His head moved infinitesimally and his lips skimmed the

skin at the back of my ear before his tongue touched there. That made my skin tingle too, so much my whole body shivered.

He pulled the covers up to my shoulder.

Finally, he turned and he was gone.

No noise, not even the door opening and closing. He was just gone. Like he'd never even been there.

Freaking crazy.

I stared at my bedroom door awhile. My body felt warm, sated and tired. My mind did not feel the same.

I turned onto my back and tucked the covers around my naked body. I stared at the ceiling.

I didn't even know his name.

"God," I whispered, "I am *such* a slut."

CHAPTER ONE

D-e-a-d, Dead

THE NEXT MORNING I was sitting at my computer in my home office.

I should have been working. I had three deadlines over the next two weeks and I'd barely begun the work. I was a freelance editor. I got paid by the hour and if I didn't work that hour, I didn't get paid. I had a mouth to feed, my own. I had a body to clothe, a body that liked all sorts of clothes, it craved them, so I had to feed the habit or things could get nasty. I had a cosmopolitan addiction, and cosmos didn't come cheap. And I had a house I was fixing up. Therefore, I needed to get paid.

Okay, that wasn't strictly true. I wasn't fixing up my house. My dad did some of the work. My friend Troy did the rest. So I should say that I had a house I was guilting, begging and emotionally blackmailing others into fixing up.

But still, it needed fixing up, and cabinets and tile didn't march from Cabinet and Tile Land into my house and say "We want to live with you, Gwendolyn Kidd, affix us to your walls!"

That only happened in my dreams, of which I had many, most of them daydreams.

Like right then, sitting at my computer, one heel on the

seat, my chin to my knee, my eyes staring out the window, I was thinking about my Mystery Man, the Great MM. I was daydreaming about changing our first meeting. Being smarter, funnier and more mysterious. Being more alluring and interesting.

I'd hook him instantly with my rapier wit, my flair for conversation, my ability to discuss politics and world events intelligently. I'd tell my humble stories of expansive charity work all wrapped up with enticing looks that promised a lifetime of mind-blowing orgasms, making him declare his undying love for me.

Or at least tell me his name.

Instead, I was drunk when we met, and definitely not any of that.

I heard my doorbell go, a chime then a clunk and I started out of my elaborate daydream, which was beginning to get good.

I got up and walked through my office into the upstairs hall making a mental note, again, to call Troy and see if he'd fix my doorbell for a six-pack and a homemade pizza. This might mean he'd bring his annoying, whiny, constantly bitching new girlfriend though, so I changed my mind and decided to call my dad.

I got to the bottom of my stairs and walked through my living room, ignoring the state of it, which was decorated in Fix-Up Chic. In other words dust rags, paintbrushes, power tools, not-so-power tools, cans and tubes of practically everything, all of it jumbled and covered in a layer of dust. I made it through the area without my hands going to my head, fingers clenching my hair and mouth screaming, which I counted as progress.

I got to the entryway, which was delineated by two narrow walls both fit with gorgeous stained glass.

Two years ago, that stained glass was my undoing.

Two years ago, approximately six months and two weeks prior to meeting my Mystery Man, I'd walked one single step into this ramble and wreck of a house, saw that stained glass, turned to the Realtor and announced, "I'll take it."

The Realtor's face had lit up.

My father, who hadn't even made it into the house yet, turned his eyes to the heavens. His prayer lasted a long time. His lecture longer.

I still bought the house.

As usual, I should have listened to my dad.

I looked out the narrow side window at the door and saw Darla, my sister's friend, standing out there.

Shit.

Shit, shit, *shit*.

I hated Darla and Darla hated me. What the hell was she doing there?

I searched behind her to see if my sister was lurking or perhaps hiding in the shrubbery. I wouldn't put it past Ginger and Darla to jump me, tie me to the staircase and loot my house. In my darker daydreams, this was how Ginger and Darla spent their days. I was convinced this was not far from the truth. No joke.

Darla's eyes came to me at the window. Her face scrunched up, making what could be pretty, if she used a less heavy hand with the black eyeliner and her blush, and if her lip liner wasn't an entirely different shade as her lip gloss, not so pretty.

"I see you!" she shouted.

I sighed.

Then I went to the door because Darla would shout the house down and I liked my neighbors. They didn't need a biker bitch from hell standing on my doorstep and shouting the house down at ten thirty in the morning.

I opened it but not far and moved to stand between it and the jamb, keeping my hand on the handle.

"Hey, Darla," I greeted, trying to sound friendly and pretty pleased with my effort.

"Fuck 'hey,' is Ginger here?" Darla replied.

See!

Totally spent her days looting.

It took effort but I stopped my eyes from rolling.

"No," I answered.

"She's here, you better tell me," she warned then she looked beyond me and shouted, "Ginger! Bitch, if you're in there you better come out here, right fuckin' now!"

"Darla!" I snapped. "Keep your voice down!"

She craned her neck and bounced on her toes, yelling, "Ginger! Ginger, you crazy, stupid bitch! Get your ass out here!"

I shoved out the door, forcing her back and closed it behind me, hissing, "Seriously, Darla, shut up! Ginger isn't here. Ginger is *never* here. You know that. So shut up and *go.*"

"*You* shut up," she shot back. "And *you* get smart. You're helpin' her…" She lifted her hand, pointed her finger at me, thumb extended upward and then she crooked her thumb and made a gunshot noise that puffed out her cheeks and made her lips vibrate. I would have taken a moment to reflect on how good she was with verbal sound effects if the serious as shit look in her eye wasn't scaring the crap out of me.

So, instead of congratulating her on the only real talent I suspected she had, I whispered, "What?"

She dropped her hand, got up on her motorcycle-booted toes so we were eye to eye, and said in a soft, scary voice, "D-e-a-d, *dead.* You and her, you don't get smart. You get me?"

Then I asked a stupid question because the question was

asked often and there was always only one answer. The answer being yes.

"Is Ginger in some kind of trouble?"

Darla stared at me like I had a screw loose. She lifted her hand, did the gun thing with the sound effect, finger pointed at my head. Then she turned around and walked swiftly down my front steps.

I stood on my front porch staring at her. My mind absently noted that she was wearing a tight tank top, an unzipped, black leather motorcycle jacket, a short, frayed jean skirt, the wearing of which was a crime in several states for a variety of reasons—both fashion and decency—black fishnet stockings and motorcycle boots. It was around forty degrees outside. She didn't even have on a scarf.

The rest of my head was caught up with my sister and Darla's sound effect.

Shit. Shit. *Shit*.

*   *   *

As I drove, I kept trying to tell myself this was a good plan. Knowing that my first plan, the one where, after Darla left and I went back into my house, I walked directly to the phone and called my father, was the right plan and this plan was garbage.

But my father and his wife, Meredith, had disowned Ginger a while ago. It was approximately ten seconds after they came home from a vacation to Jamaica and lost their happy, island holiday mojo when they saw their daughter. She was on her knees in the living room, her head between the legs of a bare-chested man, his jeans opened, his head lolled on the back of the couch because he was passed out. Ginger was so whacked on whatever she was taking she had no idea her activities were getting her nowhere.

And, incidentally, the living room was a disaster, as was the rest of the house.

As you can probably see from this story, I was loath to bring my father into another situation involving Ginger. Especially since this wasn't the worst story I had, it was just, for Dad and Meredith, the last. They were currently living a carefree, Ginger-free existence and I didn't want to rock that boat.

Therefore, I didn't call Dad.

Instead I thought of Ginger's boyfriend, Dog. Dog was a member of a biker gang and Dog was as rough as they come. But I'd met Dog. I liked Dog. Dog was funny and he liked my sister. She was different around him. Not a lot, but at least she was palatable.

Okay, so Dog was likely a felon. As ironic as it was, he was a good influence on Ginger and those didn't come around very often. As in *never*. Not in twenty-five years. So, since I was getting the hint from Darla, Ginger's one and only friend, that Ginger's trouble was a little worse than normal, I needed firstly to do something about it. Secondly, since this was Ginger, call in reinforcements or better yet, lay the problem on their door.

Enter Dog.

I drove to the auto supply store on Broadway and found a spot on the street. Even before I knew Dog, and thus figured out this was probably a front for a biker gang's nefarious dealings, I knew about this store.

It was called Ride, and I'd shopped there mainly because I could find an excuse for shopping anywhere. But Ride was awesome. It had cool stuff in there. I bought my windshield wiper fluid there. I bought new car mats there last year and they were the bomb, supreme car mats, the best I'd ever had. And when I was in my twenties and going through one of my many phases, in an effort to pimp my ride, I went there and bought a fluffy, pink steering wheel cover and a glittery, pink Playboy Bunny thingie to hang from my rearview mirror.

Everyone knew Ride had a triple-bayed garage in the back but it wasn't for normal cars and motorcycles. It was for custom-built cars and motorcycles, and it was world famous. They built cars and bikes and they were extremely cool. I'd read an article in *5280* magazine about the place. Movie stars and celebrities bought cars and bikes from there and, from the pictures, I could see why. I wanted one but I didn't have hundreds of thousands of dollars so that was a bit down on my List of Things I Want, right under a Tiffany's diamond bracelet, which was directly under a pair of Jimmy Choo shoes.

I got out of my car and walked down the sidewalk to Ride hoping my outfit was okay. I'd put my hair in a girlie ponytail at the top back of my head, I was wearing low-rider jeans, low-heeled boots and my biker jacket. Mine wasn't like Darla's. It was a distressed tan leather, had a bit of quilting around the high waist, was lined with short, warm fur and had a six-inch tuft of fluffy fur at the sleeves. I thought it was *hot* and the deal I got on it was hotter. However, I wasn't sure about the fluffy fur. I didn't think bikers were concerned with animal rights. I thought they'd think it was an affront to their brotherhood and they might garrote me.

Welp! Nothing ventured, nothing gained.

I straightened my shoulders, walked into the cavernous store and turned direct to the long counter at the front. It held one cash register even though sometimes the place could get packed. Since I didn't have his cell, my intention was to ask if someone there knew how I could get hold of Dog. I didn't expect to see tall, broad, inked-to-the-max, long-blond-haired Dog standing at the other side of the counter. There was one big, rough biker guy on his side of the counter, three on the outside, and all of them turned to me the minute I walked in.

"Hey, Dog," I called on a smile, walking toward him but stopping dead when his eyes sliced to me.

Uh-oh.

His eyes narrowed and his face didn't get near to hiding the fact that one look at me made him extremely pissed off.

"Do not shit me," he growled. I took the nanosecond before I peed my pants to try to remember the moves I'd learned in the one half-hour self-defense class I took.

When I made no response and didn't move, Dog repeated, "Do not come in here and fuckin' shit me."

"I'm not shitting you," I told him because, well, I wasn't.

His brows flew up. "That cunt sent *you?*"

Uh-oh again. Dog was using the c-word. I suspected that the c-word wasn't worda non grata in Biker Club Land like it was in the rest of the English-speaking world but still, it said a lot.

Before I could speak, Dog did. "She sent *you.* Jesus, Gwen. You got one warning, woman. Get your head outta your ass, turn that sweet tail a' yours and *get…outta… here.*"

Wow. Dog thought I had a sweet tail. He was scaring me but he wasn't entirely unattractive so I thought that was kind of nice.

I focused on the matter at hand, took a deep breath and walked forward. All of the bikers went on alert or, more accurately, scary biker guy alert, so I stopped moving.

Then I said to Dog, "Ginger didn't send me."

"I'm bein' cool with you, babe, go," Dog replied.

"No, really, she didn't. Darla came around this morning

and she freaked me out. She did this." I lifted my hand up and did the gun thing with the sound effect thing and my gun blast was nowhere near as good as hers but I forged ahead. "She seemed serious so I thought I'd check in with you, make sure Ginger is all right."

"Ginger is not all right," Dog returned instantly. "Ginger is *far* from all right."

I closed my eyes. Then I sighed. I did the sigh thing loudly. I was good at that since my sister made me sigh a lot and I had practice. Then I opened my eyes.

"I take it you two aren't together anymore," I surmised.

"No, babe, we are *not*," Dog confirmed.

Damn.

"What'd she do now?" I asked.

"You don't wanna know," Dog answered.

"Are the police after her?"

"Probably."

I studied him. Then I asked, "But that's not why she's in trouble?"

"Ginger's got all kinds 'a trouble, babe. But if the cops are after her, that's the least of her worries."

"Oh boy," I whispered.

"That's about right," Dog remarked then his eyes shifted over my shoulder.

I was turning to see what he was looking at when I heard a deep, gravelly voice ask, "Who's this?"

Then I saw him.

I wasn't into biker dudes but I could seriously make a turn to the Harley side for *this* guy.

He was tallish. He was broad and ripped and there was no "ish" about either of those. He had a lot of tattoos up his arms and neck that I instantly wanted to examine, up close, to the point of cataloguing them and maybe writing books about them. He had salt-and-pepper hair, mainly pepper, *black* pepper, and it was long with a bit of wave but not too long or too wavy. Ditto with the pepper in his salt-and-pepper goatee that hung a bit long at his chin in a biker way that was mammoth cool. His cheeks were a couple days' past needing a shave, which looked good on him too. He had spikes of pale radiating in the tan skin around his blue eyes.

There were only two words to describe all that was him: *Biker Yummy.*

"Hey," I whispered, and his eyes went from over my shoulder, looking at Dog, to me and my whole body did a shiver.

Then his blue eyes did a body scan and it shivered again.

They locked on mine and his gravelly voice growled, "Hey."

Another shiver.

Yowza!

"Tack, she's cool. She's with me," Dog stated. My body did a lurch and I turned to see he was around the counter and heading my way.

"I am?" I asked, and Dog's gaze pinned me to the spot and said without words, "Shut the fuck up!"

I shut the fuck up and turned back to Biker Hottie.

"Sheila know about her?" Biker Hottie asked.

I turned to look at Dog who was standing next to me. "Sheila?"

"How many bitches you need?" Biker Hottie went on.

"She's not my woman, brother, she's a friend. She's cool," Dog answered.

"All right. So who is she?" Biker Hottie, otherwise known as Tack, pushed.

"Her name's Gwen," Dog answered. Tack looked at me and I froze.

Then I watched his lips move to form my name softly.

"Gwen."

Another shiver.

I'd always kind of liked my name. I always thought it was pretty. Tack saying it made me freaking *love* it.

"So who are you, Gwen?" he asked me directly.

"I'm, um . . . a friend of Dog's," I told him.

"We established that, darlin'," he informed me. "How do you know my boy here?"

"She's Ginger's sister," Dog said quickly. Tack's entire, powerfully built frame went wired instantly and it was so damned scary, I forgot how to breathe.

"Tell me she's here to drop the money, brother," Tack whispered in a voice that was as scary as the way he was holding his body, if not more.

"She and Ginger aren't tight," Dog explained. "Like I said, she's cool. She's good people."

"She's blood of the enemy, Dog," Tack whispered.

Uh-oh-uh-oh-uh-oh.

I didn't want to be blood of the enemy, not anyone's enemy, but especially not *this guy's* enemy. He was hot but he was also freaking *scary*.

Time to sort things out pronto.

I pulled my purse off my shoulder and tugged it open, muttering, "Ginger. A pain in my ass. A pain in my ass since the day she cut off all the hair on my Barbies. She was three. I was too old for Barbies but they were *mine*. She couldn't leave them alone? What's with cutting their hair?" I looked up at Dog and said, "I think that's what psychos do. We should have known then. She's three, wielding scissors and causing mayhem and heartbreak." I kept blabbing as I dug in my purse, found my checkbook and then kept scrounging for a pen declaring, "She was always, *always* a bad seed."

I yanked out my checkbook, flipped it open, clicked my pen smartly, put the point to the check and looked at Tack.

"All right, how much does she owe you?" I asked irately, not happy to be bailing Ginger out *again,* especially when money and angry bikers were involved.

It was at this point I noted that Tack was staring down at me and he wasn't being scary anymore. He was looking like he wanted to laugh. It was a good look.

I didn't want to see his good looks, not his expressions or the rest of it all over his face (and hair and tats and body). I wanted to go home, whip up a batch of cookie dough, and eat it. All.

"Well?" I snapped.

"Two million, three hundred and fifty-seven thousand, one hundred and seven dollars," Tack answered. I felt my jaw go slack and his white flash of a smile surrounded by his dark goatee dazedly hit some recess of my brain. He finished with, "And twelve cents."

"Oh my God," I whispered.

Tack was still smiling when he dipped his head to my checkbook. "Think you can get that on one line, Peaches?"

"Oh my God," I repeated.

"You need mouth-to-mouth?" Tack asked, leaning in. I took a step back, clamped my mouth shut and shook my head. "Shame," he muttered, leaning back.

"My sister owes you over two million dollars?" I whispered.

"Yep," Tack replied.

"Over two million dollars?" I repeated, just to confirm.

"Yep," Tack confirmed.

"You haven't made an accountancy error?" I asked hopefully.

Tack's smile got wider and whiter. Then he crossed his

big, tattooed arms on his wide, ripped chest and shook his head.

"Perhaps this is foreign currency and you forgot. Pesos, maybe?" I suggested.

"Nope," Tack returned.

"I don't have that kind of money." I told him something I was guessing he already knew.

"Sweet jacket, Peaches, but I was guessin' that," he replied.

Well, the good news was, the tufts of fur didn't turn him off. The bad news was, my sister owed him over two million dollars.

"I think it'll take me a while to raise that kind of cash," I explained then finished, "maybe eternity."

"Don't got eternity to wait, darlin'," he responded, still grinning so huge, if he burst out laughing it would not surprise me.

"I figured," I muttered, clicked my pen, snapped shut my checkbook, shoved both in my purse and lost my mind.

I mean, I had reason to lose my mind and that reason had a name.

Ginger Penelope Kidd.

I looked up at Dog and demanded to know, "Why me? Why? Just innocently being born and seven years later, *zap!* God curses me with the sister from hell. Is it too much to ask for a sister who giggles with you and trades makeup secrets? Is it too much to ask for a sister who finds a great sale, calls you immediately but peruses the racks to stash great deals she knows would look *hot* on you, so you'll get a shot at them before anyone nabs them? Is it too much to ask for a sister who'll come over and watch the new *Hawaii Five-0* with you so you can both perv on Steve McGarrett and wish you had a Camaro? Is it? *Is it?*" I ended on a shout.

"Gwen, babe, think you should calm down," Dog muttered, and I could swear I could read on his face that he was wondering if he should knock me out for my own good.

"Calm?" I yelled. "Calm?" I yelled again. "She owes you guys over two million dollars. She cut the hair off my Barbies. She stole the lavalier my grandmother gave me on her deathbed and pawned it to buy pot. She got drunk and stuck her hand down my boyfriend's pants at Thanksgiving dinner. He was straightlaced, went to church and, after Ginger's antics...the hand down the pants was only the culmination, he caught her snorting coke in the bathroom too...he thought my family was insane, possibly *criminally* insane, and he broke up with me a week later. He might have been straightlaced and, looking back, probably boring but at the time *I liked him!*" Now I was shrieking. "*He was my boyfriend!*"

"Peaches," Tack called, and my body swung to him to see he'd moved into my space.

I tipped my head back and snapped, "What?"

His hand came up, fingers curling around my neck, then he dipped his face into mine and whispered, "Baby, calm down."

I stared close up into his blue eyes and instantly calmed down.

"Okey dokey," I whispered back.

His eyes smiled.

My body shivered.

With his hand at my neck, I knew he felt it and I knew it more when his fingers curled deeper into my flesh. Something flashed in his eyes that made me shiver someplace he couldn't see but I could feel. A lot.

Time to go.

"I could probably sell plasma and a kidney but I don't

even think that will get me enough money, so, um, can I just leave my sister to deal with this?" I asked politely, wanting to move from the strength of his hand but scared to do it.

"No one takes a blade to you for Ginger," he said quietly.

"Okay," I replied.

"Or at all," he kept going.

"Um…" I mumbled. "Okay." I said this because I didn't want anyone to take a blade to me for Ginger or at all and I didn't want that in a big way.

His fingers curved deeper into my neck and he pulled me up a bit so I was almost on my toes and his face was closer. Way closer. Too close. *Shiver* close.

"I don't think you get what I'm sayin' to you." He was still talking quietly. "This Ginger shit heats up, you get on radar, you mention my name, yeah?"

Oh no. This didn't sound good. This sounded worse than owing a biker gang two million dollars. And I suspected there weren't a lot of things worse than that but, if there were, Ginger would find them.

"Um…if you're asking 'yeah?' as in 'Yeah, I get you,' then no, I don't get you," I told him honestly because I was thinking with Tack honesty was the best policy.

"All right, Peaches, what I'm sayin' is, you get in a situation, you mention my name. That means protection. *Now* do you get me?"

"Um…kind of," I answered. "But why would I get in a situation?"

"Your sister has shit where she lived, she's shit where she didn't live, she's shit everywhere. You walked in here and had no clue. Don't bumble into another situation because others…" he paused, "…they might not find you cute like I do."

"Okay," I whispered, liking that he found me cute at the

same time regretting my decision not to call my father or, say, get on a plane and fly to France. "If I um...have to use your name...um, what does that mean?"

"It means you owe me."

Oh boy.

"Owe you what?"

He grinned but didn't answer.

Oh boy!

"Owe you what?" I repeated.

"I gotta get on my bike and get you out of a situation, we'll talk about it then."

"I'm sure I'll be fine," I assured him and said a short prayer in hopes of making that true.

His grin got bigger.

Then he let me go but slid my purse off my arm and before I could make a peep, he dug into it. I decided to let him have at it. He'd already touched me and I wasn't certain I wanted that to happen again. I wasn't certain what my response would be but I *was* certain that jumping his bones was high up on the list of possibles. I also figured he could best me in a fight for my purse so I was going to let him take what he wanted. My best lip gloss was in that purse but at that point, if he wanted it to give to one of his bitches, I was willing to let it go.

He came out with my cell, flipped it open, his thumb hit buttons, he flipped it closed, dropped it into my purse, then slid it back on my arm.

"You got my number, darlin'. You need it, use it. You don't need it, you still wanna use it, don't hesitate. Now, do you get that?"

I hitched my purse further up on my shoulder and nodded. I got that. He thought I was cute.

I fought back another shiver.

"Nice t'meet ya, Gwen," he said softly.

"Yeah," I whispered, "later." Then I turned to see Dog grinning down at me and I said, "Later."

"Later, babe," Dog replied in a way that made it sound like he'd actually see me later, which made me have to fight back another shiver.

I turned to the silent biker boys behind me, saw them all smiling, found this scarier than them being scary, lifted a hand and called, "Later."

I got a bunch of chin lifts and one "Later, darlin'."

Then I got the hell out of there.

CHAPTER TWO

I Keep Tabs

I DROVE HOME with a lot on my mind.

First and foremost, my sister and why I didn't disown her like my father and Meredith had. She wasn't even my full sister. She was my half sister. I'd never found her in my living room giving an unconscious man a blowjob, but she'd done worse to me. Way worse, so, seriously, I should just give it up and let it *go*.

In a cruel twist of fate, my father married my mother, who was a wild child, then he got married to an angel and they'd created a hell child.

Mom had left when I was three but she came back occasionally, and when she did we had fun. I didn't remember much but I remembered she was a blast. She wasn't about rules or discipline; she was about sticky food that made a lot of mess, fun places and good times.

That was until one visit, while she had me for the weekend, she met a guy she liked and she liked him a lot. She took him back to her hotel, gave me a bunch of candy and sent me outside to sit and wait for her to call me back in.

The manager of the hotel saw me sitting out on a bench, swinging my legs, eating candy, daydreaming and doing it for ages, so he called the police. By the time they came I'd wandered off because I was bored, and the police found me. I told the policeman my phone number that Dad made me memorize and they called. Then Dad came to get me. He had a rip-roarin' with Mom at the hotel while her one-day stand kept shouting at them to keep it down, he was trying to sleep, and I never saw Mom again. Ever.

I missed her for a while but I didn't know her very well and, anyway, at that time Meredith was already in our lives.

Meredith was awesome. She was the coolest stepmom ever. She was sweet and funny and she loved my dad like *loads*. She also kept homemade cookies in the cookie jar all the time and for a kid, a girl who was being raised by a man who was all man, that meant she was practically perfect.

She and Dad got married and I was the flower girl but not like normal flower girls. She walked down the aisle with one hand through the crook of her father's arm, one hand clutching mine. She made her special day *our* special day. She was making a public statement that she was walking down the aisle not only to take a man in marriage but to build a family. I was six and I never forgot how special she made me feel, never, not to this day.

But that was Meredith. It wasn't the first time she'd done it and it wouldn't be the last.

Then she and Dad had Ginger who was my mom times about five million.

This was the cruel twist of fate. For Dad, Meredith *and* me.

The second thing I was thinking about was all things Tack. What he said, the way he looked and how he made me feel.

I was already regularly sleeping with a man whose name I didn't know. A man I met at a restaurant just under a year and a half ago, took him to my home, slept with him and had the best sex in the history of womanhood. Fortunately or unfortunately, depending on when I looked at it, he kept coming back for more, proving again and again that that first time wasn't a fluke but a sneak preview of better things to come.

I didn't even give him a key. How he got in was as much a mystery as his name. But he did. He didn't come every night. Sometimes it was once a week. Sometimes twice. Sometimes he'd skip a week. Once he'd been gone for three, which freaked me out and then it freaked me out that it freaked me out.

But he always came back. Always.

With Mystery Man in my life I didn't need the trouble that Tack had written on him. Okay, so he thought I was cute and another bonus was that I knew his name *and* he knew mine (which, Mystery Man, by the way, did not know). But my sister owed him over two million dollars and he was scary.

He also said I could get onto "others'" radar and get into "situations." I didn't want to be on anyone's radar, and I made enough situations for myself, being half my mother's daughter. I didn't need Ginger dragging me into her situations.

And lastly, I was thinking about my Mystery Man. The days after he visited I always did. I always wondered what was with me that I didn't tell him to go. Now I was wondering, when I had what could possibly be the world's greatest lover visiting me in the dead of night, how I'd move on to someone else. I'd had three dates and no lovers since I met the Great MM. None of them came close to what little I had with MM and therefore none of them got to the second date or second base. Yes, the Great MM was that good of a kisser.

He was totally screwing up my life.

No. No, that wasn't true. *I* was screwing up my life.

This was what I was thinking after I parked my car in my drive, walked up to my house studying my boots, slid the key into the lock and opened my door.

However, even if I'd been paying attention, I wouldn't have been prepared for what happened next.

Once I cleared it, the door slammed, hard and loud. Then a hand in my chest slammed me into the door, again hard and loud. Then a man was in my space, his body deep in mine, pressing me into the door. I looked up into a pair of somewhat familiar black eyes.

I'd only seen those eyes once in light. He didn't turn on the lights when he visited me at night.

God, I forgot how beautiful he was. Even in my day-dreams he wasn't that beautiful.

"What are you doing here?" I whispered.

"Are you fuckin' *insane?*" he barked in my face.

I blinked at his surprising tone and angry question. Then I asked, "What?"

"Struttin' into Ride like you did. Jesus, are you insane?"

I blinked again. Firstly, because I was confused. How did he know I went to Ride?

Secondly, I was more confused. What was he doing here during the day?

Thirdly, I was even *more* confused because his unbelievably handsome face showed clearly he was extremely pissed off.

"Um…"

"Answer me, babe," he demanded.

Yikes. He was scarier than Tack, Dog and the entire biker gang all rolled into one.

"Gwen, I said answer me." His deep voice was beginning to rumble.

But I blinked again.

"You know my name?"

He stared down at me.

Then he stepped back and ran his hand over his short-cropped black hair at the same time he shook his head but not even for a second did he unpin me from his ferocious scowl.

"Jesus, babe, you're a piece of work."

"What?" I whispered.

He planted his hands on his hips and leaned back into my face. "Yeah, Gwen, I know your name. Gwendolyn Piper Kidd. Thirty-three years old. Self-employed, freelance editor. You pay your taxes on time, your mortgage on time and your bills on time. Married once for two years to a man who couldn't keep his dick in his pants and who has since married three other women and is currently engaged in his fourth divorce. Your father is Baxter Kidd, ex-Army, current construction foreman, married to Meredith Kidd, executive secretary to a hotshot divorce attorney who, incidentally, pulled your shit outta that mess you got into with that asshole. You hang with Camille Antoine who works dispatch for Denver PD and Tracy Richmond who works everywhere, mostly retail. You string along Troy Loughlin, who'd kill to get in your pants but you have no clue and he has no balls. Your sister is the definition of loser. You spend too much on clothes. When you go out, you show too much skin. And the only man you've fucked for a year and a half is me."

For the second time that day, my jaw was slack.

Then I closed my mouth only for it to fall open again.

Then I closed it only to open it to speak. "How do you know so much about me?"

"Sweet Pea, *I* know who *I* fuck," he shot back, and I felt my body move like he'd struck me. That's exactly what his words felt like, a blow. He didn't see it, or, more accurately, he disregarded it and went on. "Now tell me, what the fuck were you thinkin' walkin' into Ride like that?"

"I needed to talk to Dog," I explained because I couldn't get out any of the other ten thousand and fifty things I wanted to say.

"You needed to talk to Dog," he repeated.

"Yes," I replied.

"Babe, you were coasting under radar, now you're lit up like a fuckin' beacon."

"What does that mean?" I asked.

"It means you're fucked," he answered.

Belatedly, I was getting angry.

"Okay"—I moved an inch from the door, straightening my shoulders—"now what does *that* mean?"

"I think you get that your sister is a piece of trash," he informed me.

It was safe to say Ginger was a piece of trash. It was also safe to say my dad, Meredith or I could call her that. Even Tack and Dog, who she owed over two million dollars, could get away with calling her that.

The person who could not was the man standing in front of me, a man I knew intimately but this was the first time I'd seen his face by the light of day. And one I was discovering was a big, fat *jerk!*

"Do not call Ginger a piece of trash," I warned.

His eyebrows flew up and it sucked because he was so goddamned handsome, all that brown skin, those black eyes, that strong jaw, that thick, short black hair, his beautifully chiseled features and equally beautifully chiseled physique. All of it hinted at Hispanic or maybe Italian and all of it freaking, unbelievably *amazing*. But the worst for me, right then, was that he could be even more drop-dead beautiful with his eyebrows raised in disbelief like he thought I was an idiot.

"You're sayin' you don't know your sister's trash?" he asked.

"No, I'm saying *you* can't call her trash. *I* can call her trash but *you* can't."

He scowled at me some more and then muttered, "Fuck me."

"I think we're done here," I announced, and started to move to open the door. But I suddenly found myself pinned against it again by his big, hard, sculpted, exceptionally warm body with both his hands at either side of my neck. His thumbs were at my jaw forcing me to look up at him.

"Oh no, Sweet Pea, we're not done," he whispered in a scary voice. I fought my mouth dropping open again because he was back to freaking me out more than a half dozen members of a biker gang. I succeeded in this endeavor mainly because his thumbs were there.

"Step back," I demanded, and was pretty pleased my voice didn't tremble.

He ignored me and didn't move. Instead, he said, "Your sister has bought herself a load of shit, then she bought herself more. She's pissed off some serious people. The best end to this scenario is she turns up dead. I know there's no love lost between you two and I know it still sucks for you to hear that, but that doesn't make it any less true."

"Step back," I repeated.

He continued to ignore me. "The best thing you could have done when Darla showed on your doorstep was close the door, close your mind to that shit and go back to work. You didn't. You strutted your ass into Ride, got Tack's attention and, trust me, babe, you do *not* want Tack's attention. And doin' that, you made yourself visible to a lot of people you do not want to know you exist. That's done. Now, your sister's problems do not exist for you. Your sister does not exist for you. You keep your head down, be smart and keep yourself out of trouble. Which means you stick to what you know, who you know and where you know. You do not move out of regularly scheduled programming. You get me?"

"How do you know Darla was here?"

His brows shot together, making him now look scary *and* scarily impatient.

"Clue in, Sweet Pea, I keep tabs."

"You keep tabs?"

"You're mine so I keep tabs."

I felt my own eyebrows shoot together. "I'm yours?"

"Babe, I'm fuckin' you, aren't I?"

This was without question. I didn't see his face but that didn't mean he didn't talk. He was seriously bossy in bed and I'd know that deep voice anywhere.

"Okay," I started, "perhaps at this juncture we should discuss our relationship."

"Clue in again, Gwen, the reason our relationship is the way it is, is so I don't ever have to waste my fuckin' time doin' stupid-ass shit like discussing it."

Oh boy. Now I was getting really angry.

"I think you should step back and then I think you should go," I told him.

"And I think you should confirm you get me *then* I'll go."

"Fine, I get you, now . . . *go*," I snapped back.

He didn't move and his black eyes didn't unlock from mine.

Therefore, I called, "Hello? I get you. Now go."

Suddenly, his eyes warmed and his thumbs moved from under my jaw to slide over its edges.

Then he noted softly, "You're pissed."

Was he for real?

"Uh...*yeah*," I verified.

"Don't be pissed," he ordered.

No, seriously, he couldn't be for real.

"You can't tell me not to be pissed."

"Babe, you think I don't have better things to do than be here?" he asked.

Oh my God.

Did people's heads actually explode? Because at that moment I was pretty certain mine was about to.

"Then maybe you should be on your way," I invited, my voice sharp.

"The point is, I'm here."

"Well, I hate to break this to you, but you've made other visits I've enjoyed a *whole lot more*."

That was when he grinned and when he did, that was when my heart stopped beating.

Never, not once, not even that first night, did I see him smile. If he was beautiful normally, his face smiling knocked my freaking socks off.

Lordy be, the man had two dimples.

Two.

"Do you not get why *I'm* pissed?" he asked gently through his smile.

"No, I don't, and there's never a good excuse for being a jerk so, again, please, if you're so busy, allow me to stop wasting your time and just *go*."

"You fucked up today, Gwen," he told me.

"I think you've made that clear, baby," I shot back.

For some reason the warmth in his eyes deepened at the same time he whispered his warning. "Don't call me baby when you're pissed, Sweet Pea."

"Don't call me Sweet Pea at all, baby," I retorted.

"You call me baby when I'm fucking you," he stated, and I didn't know if this was a demand or a recall. It was probably both.

"Well, don't hold your breath for that to happen again."

The warmth in his eyes got deeper, hotter and his thumbs stroked my jaw again. I tried to pull my face away but his hands tightened and I stopped.

"You shouldn't make a threat you can't carry out," he advised, still talking gently.

"How many times do I have to tell you to go?" I asked.

He ignored me and declared, "*I* end things."

Seriously, he was *not for real*.

"It's good to experience change in life, refreshing, keeps your senses sharp," I informed him.

"Don't push that shit, Gwendolyn," he warned. "You won't like the consequences."

"What's your name?" I asked on a dare.

He called my dare and raised me. "You call me baby."

"What's your name?" I repeated.

"Sometimes honey," he continued.

"What...is...*your name?*" I demanded.

"But I prefer baby."

I rolled my eyes to the ceiling and snapped, "*God!*" at the same time I stomped my foot, realized my hands were at his waist and I pushed back.

He didn't budge.

My eyes rolled back to him. I instantly noted my mistake when I found one of his hands had disappeared and his mouth was at my neck. His lips at the skin behind my ear and then I felt his tongue there.

Without my permission, my body did a top-to-toe tremble.

His face came out of my neck, it got in mine, his hand returned to my jaw and he whispered, "Yeah."

Then he pulled me away from the door and like a freak of nature, one second he was there, the next he was gone.

I stared at the closed door then moved to the window and checked. I was right. He was gone.

Then I turned my back to the door and stared into my messy living room.

And I was thinking I was pretty sure he felt the tremble.

CHAPTER THREE

The Day of Epiphany

MY HOUSE WAS an old farmhouse that once graced fields but now was situated in a neighborhood of much newer houses. That was to say built in the last fifty years, on the close outskirts of Denver.

Once you made it through the narrow walls with kickass stained glass in the entryway, my house had a living room that ran the length of the front. To the right behind sliding inset glass doors was a dining room or den, but it was nothing now. Empty space. To the left, a swinging doorway into a big kitchen. Upstairs were three bedrooms, one somewhat small so I made that into my office, and a mammoth bathroom.

My father had not let me move in until he and his buddy Rick had installed a new bathroom. He said this was because the bathtub was imminently going to fall through the floor. I thought he was being dramatic because he hated my house and still does. Even so, why I thought this I really did not know because my father was not a dramatic person. Therefore, I shouldn't have been surprised when they started working on the bathroom and the tub proceeded to crash through the floor.

So Dad redid my bathroom, after, of course, he rebuilt

the floor. Now it was gorgeous with a claw-footed tub, pedestal sink, heated towel racks, the lot. He also redid the wood plank floors in my bedroom and the office and re-skimmed the walls in both rooms. Meredith and I painted my bedroom, and she made me killer roman blinds to go in the windows of my bedroom and office. My friend Tracy and I painted my office. I proceeded to the fun phase of renovation—decoration—while Dad moved onto the kitchen, which he worked on with Troy. The completion of this took five months because they both got sidetracked with other things like their own lives and the faucet in my half-bath downstairs not turning off and the roof leaking and the light switch in my bedroom not working and the furnace going out. Stuff like that.

But now the kitchen was fantastic, cabinets painted a buttery cream. A big, battered, rectangular farm table in the middle with six chairs. Butcher block countertops. Fabulous appliances that Dad sourced for me on the cheap through his construction network and because they were damaged but in places you couldn't see. I'd decorated it in countrified charm with a whimsical twist. I wasn't country, not by a long shot, but the kitchen was an old farmhouse kitchen so it demanded country and there were times I could be whimsical.

So after MM left, I went to my kitchen, made chocolate chip cookie batter, took the bowl, a spoon and a cup of coffee to the table and grabbed my phone.

Then I sat with one foot on the floor, one heel to the chair, and stared at it.

I should call Camille. Camille was a straight talker. She was smart. She was worldly and she had her head together. Camille was living with Leo, who was a cop, and they'd been together for five years. It was a good relationship, loving but challenging, because both Leo and Camille had attitude. But if they ever broke up it would be like Goldie Hawn and Kurt Russell breaking up—that was to say proof that the world would soon be coming to an end.

Camille, however, knew all about MM and she thought I was part nuts, part crazy letting him come to me in the middle of the night and not knowing his name. She had advised repeatedly that during the very next visit I should firstly kick him in the gonads and secondly call the cops.

Hmm.

I could also call Tracy. Tracy was a romantic. Tracy was not a straight talker. Tracy would rather endure torture than say anything that would make you uncomfortable or hurt your feelings. Tracy had three boyfriends and they were all jerks but she kept them around because she didn't have it in her to break up with them even though they were jerks. Before getting bored and moving on, which Tracy did frequently, she put up with a lot of shit because my sweet Tracy didn't have a backbone.

Tracy also loved the idea of MM. She was convinced one day he was going to reach out, turn on the light, frame my face with his hands, and tell me the sun rose and set for him through me. Then promptly marry me in a fairy-tale wedding and thereafter treat me like a princess to the end of my days. Even after all this time she was totally convinced this was going to happen and she never faltered in that belief. MM's most recent visit would probably make her dance in delight. She would never see it for what it was: jerky, intrusive and supremely annoying.

I couldn't call Troy because after what MM said about him, I was freaked out about Troy. Troy had always been just Troy. Troy had been around before Camille and Tracy. Troy had been around before I met Scott Leighton, when I met Scott Leighton, when I married Scott Leighton and when

Scott Leighton broke my heart. Troy was a friend, and the thought that he wanted to get in my pants freaked me out almost more than everything else that happened that day.

I stared at my phone and spooned up some dough.

Then I shoved the dough in my mouth, dropped the spoon, picked up the phone and made the first smart decision I'd made since MM's hand hit the small of my back the night before.

I dialed, swallowed and put the phone to my ear.

"What's up, girl?" Camille answered.

"The Great MM visited last night."

Silence. No, *total* silence.

Then, "Girl..."

Then nothing.

"He also came back today. He was here when I got back from doing something and he left just about twenty minutes ago."

More silence, this even more total like all the noise in the world was being sucked into a vacuum.

"Cam?" I called into the void.

"He left just twenty minutes ago?" she asked.

"Yep," I answered.

"He was there in the light of day?" she asked.

"Yep," I answered.

"And his skin didn't catch fire or anything?" she asked.

"Nope," I answered through a smile.

"What happened?"

It was then I broke the whole thing down for her from last night through Darla. Through Dog and Tack. Through the Great MM's surprise visit, loving chat and gentle explanation of the boundaries of our relationship.

When I finished, she muttered, "Shit."

"Shit what?" I asked.

"Girl, I know about Kane Allen, aka Tack, head honcho of the Chaos MC. And I know you *do not* wanna go there. Rumor is he's spent his term tryin' to clean up the club, with some success, but clean for those boys does not have the same definition as it does for the rest of the population. They call themselves Chaos for a reason, and these boys are not like other boys. These boys do not have the civilized filter other people do. They do not only not exist in a world of law and order, they exist in a world of survival where there is only instinct. They're animals, Gwen. No freakin' joke."

Oh boy.

"Well, I didn't exactly make a date with him," I reminded her.

"And don't, *ever*. You enter that world, there is no comin' home. You get me?"

Yikes.

"He was scary, Cam, I'm not going there," I assured her.

"God, I hope not," she said in a way that meant she didn't believe me. Then again, I'd met her in the middle of my divorce mess so she knew all about Scott, who was hot but who was a complete dick. And she also knew about MM, who was also hot, way hotter than Scott, and was proving to be of the Scott bent, namely a jerk.

"I'll talk to Leo, see what I can get about your sister," Cam went on. "The one thing I can say about MM is that he gave you good advice. You need to lay low. Ginger is Ginger, and she's been headin' down a path that's leadin' her to big trouble and seems she found it."

I listened to her take a big breath and I knew what that big breath meant. She had something to say she knew I wouldn't like. Camille was a straight talker but that didn't mean she didn't have a kind soul. She did. The kindest there was. Therefore when she continued, she did it gently.

"I know she's your sister, girl, but Ginger Kidd, she doesn't care who she brings down with her and she'll throw up anyone as a shield to protect her skinny white ass. She's in trouble and she gets a hint that she can use you, however she could use you, she's gonna do it, babe. No hesitation."

This was definitely true.

"I am, as of this moment, officially disowning her," I declared.

"Finally," Cam muttered.

"Call me after you talk to Leo," I told her.

"Gwen?" she called.

"Yeah, babe," I replied.

"I'm also gonna talk to him about MM."

Oh no. *Hell* no. Dad and Meredith didn't know about MM. Troy didn't know about MM. And Leonard "Leo" Freeman didn't know about MM. The only people who knew about MM were Camille and Tracy, and I'd sworn them to secrecy.

This said a lot about me and how I felt about MM, namely that I was ashamed of what I was doing and also why I was doing it. It more than hinted at desperate and slut, two things no girl should be. Ever. I loved Dad, Meredith, Troy and Leo. I did not want these people to think I was a desperate slut.

"Gwen—" Cam started.

"No, Cam, no. Do *not* talk to Leo about the Great MM," I stated firmly.

"Okay, girl, listen to me," she stated firmly back. "This guy can walk through doors. This guy has the means to investigate you and keep tabs. I know that now so now I know this guy has *got* to be on the grid and if he's on the grid, Leo can get a lock on him."

"Maybe so but I don't want Leo to get a lock on him."

"Why?" she asked, beginning to sound impatient. "He investigated you."

"That may be so too but as of today I am officially disowning my sister and officially ending my screwed-up non-relationship with the Great Mystery Man. It's over. Totally over."

Again, silence.

Then, "Seriously?"

"Seriously, Cam!" I cried. "I told you how he spoke to me. I told you what he said about our relationship. He *investigated* me. He knows *everything about me*. He says only *he* gets to end things. *He wouldn't tell me his name.* That situation was totally whacked before in a way I didn't think it could *get* more whacked and now that it has, wake-up call. It's over."

Again silence, then, "I hope so, girl. I said it before and I'll say it again. There are hot guys out there who are not motherfucking assholes. They do not use you to get off. There are men out there who know how to treat a woman right and you're gonna find one, babe, but the only way you can do that is to scrape off the one who doesn't treat you right."

There it was, Camille Antoine, straight talker. And Camille Antoine, smart girl who had her head screwed on right.

"Well, today has been the day of epiphany. Ginger and the Great MM are history," I declared grandly.

"Hallelujah," Cam replied.

Ten minutes later, we hung up. After that, I sat at my table, spooned up dough, ate it and stared at my phone, hoping that I could follow through with my grand statement.

Then I picked up the phone and called Tracy.

CHAPTER FOUR

Baseball Bat or Crowbar

I HEARD THE crash and jerked awake. Instant adrenaline pumping through my body making my skin and fingers tingle.

Someone was in my house.

I listened and heard not a sound but I knew. I knew.

The Great MM didn't make noise. Even if I moved something or work was being done on the house, he avoided it and moved silently like he could see any obstacles in the dark.

He did not make a crash. He'd *never* make a crash.

I turned to reach to the phone and wished I had a weapon. Even a baseball bat. Something that would make me feel less powerless. Less alone. I was happy for the company of an inanimate object if it could inflict injury.

I grabbed the phone and dialed 911.

"Nine-one-one, what's your emergency?"

"My name is Gwendolyn Kidd," I whispered. "I live at 332 Vine and someone has broken into my house. They're here, in the house. Send someone. I'm hanging up now and don't call back. This is not a prank."

I beeped off the phone, dropped it on the bed and rolled the other way, in the direction of my snow globe. I loved that snow globe. It was a Rosina Wachtmeister snow globe with a happy kitty in it, little flowers dancing around the base. If you turned it over and shook it, glitter danced around the kitty.

And, if I used it to clock someone on the head, they might not be able to rape me.

I snatched it up and ran on tiptoes to the opposite wall where I pressed my shoulder against it and stared at the door.

My heart was beating so fast I could hear it in my ears, my entire body was alive and I could feel every inch of it. I was terrified out of my ever-lovin' mind.

Someone was out there. I couldn't hear them but I could sense them.

Then I heard them, footfalls in the hall.

Ohmigod, ohmigod, ohmigod.

I tried to remember what the response time was supposed to be for cops. Seven minutes popped into my head even though I didn't know if that was the right number or the wrong number.

I didn't have seven minutes. He was close.

I silently inched up the wall toward my door staring at it. It was mostly closed. I'd started doing this in an effort to hear when the Great MM arrived. I didn't close it all the way. I left it open an inch. It wasn't a noisy door but it did have a creak.

The Great MM never made it creak.

The first thing I saw was the flashlight, not bright, an LED. Then I saw a shadowed hand, a man's hand, fingers out, fingertips touching my door. Slowly the hand pushed it open.

I stopped breathing. I didn't want him to hear me breathing. If I damaged my Wachtmeister snow globe bonking him on the head with it I wanted to make it count.

I lifted the snow globe and the door kept opening.

Then I heard sirens.

Thank you, God.

The hand stilled then it disappeared. The footfalls were faster and I heard them hit the stairs, thudding down.

Then I heard nothing.

Then I turned my back to the wall, slid down and cradled my happy kitty snow globe.

*　　*　　*

I was sitting in my kitchen staring into my living room.

I had both heels to the seat of my chair, my cheek pressed to one of my knees, my arms tight around my calves and my nightgown wrapped around my legs.

I was pretty pleased I'd worn my kickass, mocha-colored, soft-knit, short bat-sleeved caftan to bed. Caftans weren't known to be hot but this one was, mainly because it was uber-clingy in all the right places. This caftan *rocked* and it was the chosen nightwear for when you suddenly found your home filled with macho cops.

This was what I was staring at. The fact that my home was filled with macho cops. They were moving around in my living room looking at stuff while dipping spoons into the bowl of chocolate chip cookie dough that I unearthed from the fridge for them.

My window by the door was smashed, something I didn't hear, a lamp in the living room that was under a dust cover was also smashed. That's what I heard.

Other than that, no damage, and the officer who took me through the house was told by me, an authority on the subject, that nothing was missing.

But they didn't take my statement. Two officers became four, four became six and now there were eight. They told me I had to wait until the detective arrived.

I was not hip on police procedure and I couldn't say I wasn't grateful (considering the fact that I was super, double, extra, *way* freaked out) that they seemed to be taking this seriously by sending a large cadre of officers to stand guard in my living room eating cookie batter *and* a full-blown detective to talk to me. However, nothing was stolen and although my caller headed straight to the bedroom, and I doubted he was after my Wachtmeister snow globe, it seemed a garden-variety break-in that the uniformed officers could cover.

So I figured something was up and I figured that something was named Ginger Kidd.

Suddenly there seemed something interesting happening in the living room, someone had arrived, and five seconds later, there he was.

I stared at him.

Seriously, was this a cosmic joke?

In my doorway stood a man, a tall man, and there was nothing "ish" about how tall he was. He was just plain *tall*. He also had dark brown hair, dark brown eyes and a square jaw. His hair was thick. It curled a little around his neck and the collar of his leather jacket. His eyes were soulful. His jaw was strong. He was wearing a chocolate brown turtleneck under his dark brown leather jacket, jeans, a great belt and boots. A badge hung on that great belt. I had no doubt he was on the cover of the Men of the Denver Police Department calendar and I was going out first thing tomorrow to buy one.

Why was this happening? Why? What did I do? Not even a day and I'd been in the presence of three hot guys, all three I couldn't have. One was scary and was the head honcho of a possibly felonious but definitely antisocial motorcycle club, so he was out. One was scary and mysterious and a jerk, so he was out. And this one was not scary, he was gorgeous. He was also the detective assigned to my case, which meant he was probably not allowed to fraternize with a victim, namely me, and therefore he was out.

I didn't lift my cheek from my knee and he didn't tear his eyes from me as he walked into the kitchen. He grabbed a chair, twisted it around to face me, not too close, not too far away, and sat down. With his eyes still on me, he leaned forward, elbows to knees.

"Gwendolyn Kidd?" he asked in a nice, smooth, deep voice.

I nodded against my knee.

"I'm Detective Mitch Lawson."

Detective Mitch Lawson. Yowza. Great name.

I kept my cheek to my knee when I told him quietly, "That's the perfect name for a cop."

His brows went up slightly. This was not what he was expecting. He was probably expecting a "Hi," or a "Thank you for coming" or a "God, you're hot."

"It is?" he asked.

"Mitch," I whispered. "Strong, the last three consonants, that is, but not in a harsh way, in a soft way. And when you're with someone you care about and you're close and they say something you can't hear, you don't say, 'What?' you say, 'Mm?' real soft. Put that and the last together, soft and strong, things a cop needs to be...Mitch."

He stared at me.

I kept babbling. "And Lawson, goes without saying, *Law*...son. Son of the law." I pulled in a breath through my nose and then whispered, "Perfect."

He stared at me some more.

Then he said, "Gwendolyn sounds like a song."

Uh...nice.

I so totally loved my name.

"A short one," I replied.

"But a pretty one," he returned.

Uh...*nice.*

I smiled at him and Detective Mitch Lawson smiled back at me.

Yowza!

Then suddenly his neck twisted so he could look over his shoulder, his torso went straight and he stood, still looking behind him.

My eyes went there and I kept my cheek to my knee even as my heart skipped a beat.

The Great MM was standing there.

He wasn't in a fabulous chocolate brown turtleneck, leather jacket and jeans. He was wearing what he was wearing earlier, a skin-tight, navy, long-sleeved t-shirt that delineated every carved muscle in his chest, shoulders and arms, Army green cargo pants and boots. He was also wearing an unhappy expression and his eyes were locked on Detective Mitch Lawson.

Then his eyes moved to me and about a nanosecond later *he* moved to me, all masculine grace, a big cat on the prowl, fascinating.

My eyes moved with him but my cheek didn't leave my knee as he got close then bent over me, lifting his hand. I didn't know what to expect so I braced until I felt his fingers at my temple. They trailed lightly along my hairline, down behind my ear. I closed my eyes as he slid the hair off my neck. Then his warm hand curled there.

I heard him ask softly, "You okay, baby?"

Baby?

My eyes opened and slid to see him bent close to my face.

"Fine," I told him.

"You don't look fine," he noted.

"Well, I am," I returned.

"Then why are you curled into a protective ball?" he asked.

This was a good question.

I shrugged.

"Heard she was yours," Lawson noted.

MM straightened and turned to him. I was so surprised at this comment, for a variety of reasons, that my head came up so I could put my chin to the space between my knees.

"She's mine," MM confirmed decisively.

"I'm not his," I denied, probably not decisively.

Lawson was looking at MM but when I spoke his eyes cut to me. He stared at me what seemed intently for a few beats then one side of his mouth twitched and he looked to the floor a second before he looked back at me.

"I need to ask you a few questions," he said quietly. "You up for that?"

MM moved to my side, *right* to my side, in a way where his lower side pressed down my upper side and his hand slid around to the back of my neck.

"Ask," he ordered shortly, answering for me. Lawson looked at him then sat again.

I lifted my chin from my knees but MM's hand on my neck didn't move. His position seemed to be possessive, an indication to Lawson he was claiming me. But that hand... that hand seemed to be supportive, an indication he was worried about my state of mind and, furthermore, he cared.

Now, what did I do with that?

I focused on Lawson, not MM, and saw he was leaning forward on his knees again.

"Tell me what happened," he said gently.

I sucked in breath. Then I said, "I heard a crash, it woke

me up and I knew. I knew like you know when you have a bad dream and you jerk awake and your body is all tingly and you just know. You *know* someone is in the room to hack you up and you can't get rid of that feeling, you know what I mean?" I paused and he nodded. "I knew like that someone was in my house but I knew it was *for real*."

He nodded again and I kept talking.

"So, I called 911 but not before I thought I needed a baseball bat. But, while I was waiting for you, I decided I didn't want a baseball bat, I want a crowbar. A baseball bat has more surface area so the force of the blow would be disbursed. A crowbar would work better. What do you think?"

MM's fingers tightened on my neck but Lawson, clearly not following my ramblings, asked, "What do I think?"

"Baseball bat or crowbar? Which one would you want if you were in a scary situation?"

He paused a second, his eyes holding mine, before he answered softly, "Gwendolyn, I own a gun."

Jeez. Of course. He owned a gun. He could shoot a bad guy. He didn't need a baseball bat.

A gun would be handy but I wasn't sure I was ready for a gun.

"Oh yeah," I whispered, "right."

He smiled a small smile and prompted, "So you called 911..."

"Yes, then I grabbed my snow globe because that was all I had," I told him, and his brows drew together.

"The one in the living room?"

I had carried my happy kitty down when I went to greet the police. The officer who took me on a tour of my house eventually had to pry it from my hands and set it aside.

"The one in the living room," I answered.

"It's normally on Gwen's nightstand," MM added. Lawson's eyes lifted to him even though he didn't move his head but I twisted my neck to look up at him.

There it was. Proof. He could *totally* see in the dark.

"You noticed that?" I asked, and MM's black eyes tipped down to me as his fingers gave my neck another squeeze.

"Don't miss much, babe."

Hmm. I suspected as much but, even so, I didn't think this was good news.

"Unh-hunh," I muttered.

"Gwendolyn," Lawson called, and I looked back at him. "What happened after you grabbed the snow globe?"

"I walked to the wall and pressed against it, stared at the door and waited. I saw the flashlight first then I saw the hand pushing open my door really slowly." I stopped because MM's fingers tightened. This wasn't a squeeze. This was something else, and his fingers didn't loosen. I had to admit even though I didn't want to that the strong pressure felt good. "He got it open a foot, maybe more, and then there were sirens and he took off. I heard him running down the stairs."

"Him?" Lawson asked.

"It was a man's hand," I told him. "White, um...Caucasian." I used television show cop speak.

"A man's hand," Lawson repeated.

"Um...yeah," I confirmed.

"You're sure it was a man's hand?" Lawson asked, and I locked eyes with him.

Then I said softly, "It wasn't Ginger."

Another squeeze of the fingers from MM but this time they relaxed.

Lawson sat back and studied me.

"Your sister?" he asked.

"I know she's in trouble. Bad trouble. And I know that's why you're here and eight uniform cops are here for what is normally not likely a priority, all-hands-on-deck call."

I heard a noise come from MM that sounded like a manly, amused, deep but short chuckle. I looked up at him to see he was grinning. No teeth but he was grinning enough that both dimples had popped out.

When I looked back at Lawson, he had a small, one-sided smile thing going.

"We try to do our best," he muttered.

"Well, I appreciate it." I smiled back. "And I hate to disappoint you, but Ginger Kidd was not in the vicinity tonight or, if she was, she heard the sirens and took off. Even when she was a kid, she didn't like cops. I always loved cops, went right up and talked to them, made friends. She ran a mile. We should have known."

"She did that?" Lawson asked, looking amused.

"Often, first time she was six."

His face changed as realization dawned and he stated, "You're not joking."

I shook my head. "Nope."

"That was likely a good sign of future trouble," Lawson remarked.

"Don't get her started on her Barbies," MM put in. My body jerked and my head shot back to look at him.

Uh...what? What, what, *what?* How did he know about the Barbies?

My eyes narrowed on him.

"Do you know about your sister's troubles?" Lawson asked, and I tore my eyes away from MM and looked at him.

"No, except I know she owes the Chaos Motorcycle Club a lot of money and that would be *a lot,* a lot, but they already know I can't help them out with that because I'm not tight with my sister. They also know I also don't have that kind of money to give to them in order to get her fat out of the fryer."

"They do?"

"I had a chat with Tack today. He's aware that the Kidd cupboards are bare or at least I don't have two plus million stashed somewhere."

"You had a chat with Tack today," Lawson repeated, and something about him had changed and not in a good way. He looked pissed.

"Um … yeah," I answered.

Lawson's eyes flicked to MM then back to me. "You don't know anything else about what's happening with your sister?"

"No, except that there's more but I don't know what it is. And I don't *want* to know. I officially disowned her today. Therefore, officially, she is no longer my sister."

This garnered another squeeze from MM, but Lawson was watching me.

"So you wouldn't have any idea who might come visit you tonight?" Lawson went on.

I shook my head. "No idea. All I know is, they didn't take anything and they came right to my bedroom. Make of that what you will."

Lawson stared at me. Then he did it some more. Then his jaw got tight. Then a muscle jumped in his cheek, his gaze lifted to MM, he took in a breath and shook his head. Then his eyes locked with mine.

He leaned deeper toward me and said softly, "I'm gonna tell you what I make of this. What I make of it, Gwendolyn, is if my woman had a sister who I knew was in some serious shit, she would *not* be havin' a chat with Kane Allen, she would *not* be sleepin' alone, and therefore she would not *ever* have to worry about whether she needs a baseball bat or crowbar because she'd be in bed beside me."

Oh.

Wow.

MM's hand left my neck.

Uh-oh.

"Did I just hear you?" MM asked in his scary voice.

Uh-oh!

Lawson's eyes lifted again and again he did it without moving his head. "You just heard me."

Uh-oh!

"Um..." I started to take my heels off the chair when MM spoke.

"My boys clocked him on his second drive round to case Gwen's house. No one was close enough to get to her fast so we called it in to you boys three minutes before he even hit her sidewalk. You had units in the vicinity so he was in the house for less than two minutes before they arrived. Gwen was never in any danger."

What?

"It's luck we had units in the vicinity," Lawson returned as he stood.

"Bullshit, Lawson. Your boys have been cruisin' the neighborhood for two weeks, hopin' Ginger would make a visit," MM fired back.

"This area is hot but we don't sit on her house, Hawk," Lawson retorted.

Hawk?

I looked up at MM.

"Hawk?" I asked.

He ignored me as he was too busy scowling at Lawson. "Your boys were five minutes out, my boys eight. One way or another, she was covered."

His boys?

"She had to arm herself with a snow globe," Lawson reminded him.

I stood and looked up again at MM.

"Hawk?" I repeated.

"She was covered," MM repeated.

"Yeah, but *she* didn't know that," Lawson returned.

"*Hawk?*" I shouted, and MM's eyes dropped to me.

"Babe. What?" he clipped.

Oh my God. His name was Hawk.

Who had a name like Hawk?

I opened my mouth to confirm that his name was indeed Hawk then instantly remembered Lawson was there. I didn't want him to know I didn't know MM's (or *Hawk's*) name so I snapped my mouth closed right when I heard my father's voice.

"Where's my daughter?"

Yay! Saved by my dad.

I leaned in front of my no longer so mysterious Mystery Man *Hawk* and looked around Lawson to see my dad and Meredith coming through the opened kitchen door.

I'd called them when I'd seen my window busted out. I didn't want to but I did for two reasons. One, they'd find out eventually and sooner was always better than later when it came to Dad and Meredith. I'd learned that the hard way. And two, I needed a place to sleep because I sure as heck wasn't sleeping here and I knew I was too freaked out to drive myself but further, Dad would lecture me if he knew I drove freaked out. I'd also learned the hard way to avoid giving Dad (too many) opportunities to lecture me. He was good at it because with two daughters, and those daughters being Ginger and me, he had lots of practice.

"Gwen," Dad murmured when he hit the room. I

squeezed between the two angry hot guys that were pinning me in, half walked, half ran to my dad and threw myself in his arms.

Whether I threw myself in them, walked into them, or leaned into them, my dad's arms always did the same thing. They closed around me tight.

Suddenly I didn't feel so freaked out anymore.

I wrapped my arms around him just as tight, felt his familiar solidness, and I was even less freaked out.

"Gwen," he whispered into the top of my hair.

Back in the day, my dad was hot. He was almost as hot as the two men standing in my kitchen. I suspected the "almost" part of that had a lot to do with the fact that he was my dad. He was big and broad, had dark hair (now with a lot of silver in it) with hazel eyes, and he was lean and fit and strong. He'd always be lean and fit and strong because he was always doing something that involved carrying something, hammering something, dragging something, lifting something or sawing something.

That was, when he wasn't watching the Broncos.

And I had to admit, most of the time he was doing all of that he was in my house.

"I'm okay, Dad, just a little freaked," I said into his chest.

"Honey," Dad said into my hair.

Then I felt his lips leave my hair. I looked up at him to see he was looking over my head at Hawk and Lawson. He moved me to his side, his arm clamped around my shoulders, and Meredith got close. She took my hand. I squeezed hers and she squeezed back as I looked to see her give me one of her small, sweet, everything-is-gonna-be-okay smiles.

Then I heard Dad say, "Are you the police?"

He was asking this into the room, his question aimed at both Hawk and Lawson.

"Yes sir, Detective Mitch Lawson," Lawson replied, stepping forward.

Dad let me go to shake his hand then let it go and clamped his arm around me again, tugging me into his side in a way that my body jolted and then collided with his body.

Hmm. Seemed I wasn't the only one who was freaked.

"And you?" Dad asked and his eyes were on Hawk.

I looked at Hawk as Lawson took a step away, his face studiously blank, his eyes alert, taking in everything, namely the fact it was clear my family had no idea who Hawk was.

"Hawk," Hawk said, his hand extended, Dad let me go again, took it and Hawk went on, "Gwen's man."

I felt and saw Dad's body jerk in surprise as Meredith whispered, "Gwen's man?"

I had no reaction. I was too busy staring at Hawk with my mouth hanging open.

"Honey, you have a man?" Meredith asked, and I knew this question was directed at me but I was *still* too busy standing, staring at Hawk with my mouth hanging open to respond.

"Hawk?" Dad asked, his gaze never leaving Hawk.

"Flew Black Hawks when I was in the Army," Hawk stated, giving me the third piece of information about him. The first being he was great in bed, something I'd known for a year and a half, and the second being what was apparently his nickname, something I'd known for approximately three minutes.

But this was not what I was focused on. I was focused on the very small piece of information he'd relayed and what it meant for me. And that was that I was fucked.

I knew this was true when my father stated in a surprised yet clearly elated voice, "You're an Army man?"

Shit!

Dad was an Army man. He served four years in the Army before he got out and went into construction. There was a reason why Dad married Mom; he was a wild child like her. He credited the Army with sorting his shit out and saving his life. Problem for my mom was, she didn't sort her shit out when she was a soldier's wife. Dad would have stayed in the Army but being in the Army often meant being away. Mom had me and Dad knew Mom couldn't be trusted alone with me, so he got out to make sure I was raised right.

But Dad still loved the Army. Dad bought olive-drab t-shirts with the word "ARMY" on the front of them and wore them all the time. And Dad formed instant, unshakable bonds with any of his Army brethren. He did it all the time, when we were on vacation, when he was at the hardware store, when he was standing in line to buy a bucket of chicken. He had a sixth Army sense and if he got a whiff of Army, bonding ensued.

Like right now with Hawk.

"Yeah," Hawk replied, and Dad still had hold of his hand so he shook it fervently, a relieved, elated smile on his face.

All thoughts of his daughter's break-in had flown out of his head. I had a man. That man was an Army man. Not a man like Scott Leighton, who Dad told me after I divorced him he always thought was a pussy. He'd used the p-word right to my face. Then again, Dad pretty much hated Scott. All was suddenly right in Baxter Kidd's world and what was making it right was the man standing in front of him.

Yes, I was definitely fucked.

Dad let go of Hawk's hand and clamped me to his side again, looking down at me. "Honey, why didn't you tell us you were seeing someone?" he asked, giving me a shake and beaming at me like a lunatic.

"Um..." I mumbled.

"This is lovely, we'll have to have you over for dinner," Meredith put in. My head swung to her to see she was smiling brightly at Hawk.

That was Meredith. If it was a-okay with Baxter, it was hunky dory with her.

Shit!

"Um…" I mumbled, louder and more hysterical this time.

"Make your lasagna." Dad put in his order then turned to Hawk. "The lasagna is good, son, but it's her garlic bread that takes the cake. It's homemade, from scratch, all the way down to the bread."

Oh my God! Did my father just call my mystery lover "son" after only knowing him for five seconds? He'd never called Scott "son." The only thing he ever called Scott was "Scott" and "a pussy."

"*Um…!*" It came out like a strangled cry.

"Gwendolyn," Lawson called, and my frantic eyes few to him.

"Yeah?" I answered.

He took a step in to join our huddle, his hand in his jacket pocket, and he pulled out a wallet while speaking. "I'm done here but you need anything, hear anything you think I need to know or remember anything," he was pulling a business card out of his wallet and he handed it to me, his soulful brown eyes locked with mine, "call me, day or night. My cell is on that card."

"Uh…okay," I replied, taking the card, and his eyes released me and moved to Hawk.

"You got footage?" he asked.

"Yep," Hawk answered.

"You know this guy?" Lawson went on.

"Haven't seen the tape," Hawk replied, "but my boys

couldn't ID him. I'll have a look at it when I get back to base."

"The car?" Lawson kept at it.

"Ran the plates, it's stolen," Hawk answered.

"Is it too much to ask you to share that footage with us?" Lawson continued.

"It's already been e-mailed to the station," Hawk returned.

"Footage?" my father butted in, and Hawk's eyes went to him.

"Got a business, part of what I do is security. Gwen and I hooked up; I put cameras on her house. It's monitored 24/7. Couple weeks back, we installed more cameras to monitor the street. We got tape of the guy who broke in."

Dad's arm squeezed me and his face, which had been slightly bemused when Hawk and Lawson were talking, had started beaming again at the thought of my Army man monitoring my house in an effort to keep me safe.

What he didn't know was that it was an effort to keep tabs on me.

My eyes moved from Dad to narrow on Hawk.

"Bax, do you think this has to do with Ginger?" Meredith whispered to my dad, and I unnarrowed my eyes and looked at my stepmom.

She had a mass of somewhat curly, strawberry blonde hair that was streaked now with attractive white. She had a pixie-pretty face, upturned nose and cornflower blue eyes. She was petite, at least three inches shorter than me and eight inches shorter than Dad, standing at five foot five. This meant she could wear high heels, which she did almost all the time. Even now in the middle of the night, out to respond to the call of her stepdaughter who had a break-in, she was wearing stylish high-heeled boots. She'd taught me how to wear high heels and she taught me about style—in other words, how to embrace mine, however that came about—and with her encouragement, I did.

The skin around Dad's eyes got tight, he looked at the men and declared, "I have another daughter and she—"

Hawk broke in to announce, "We know about Ginger and it's likely Gwen's break-in has to do with Ginger's recent activities."

Dad's whole body got tight at my side and Meredith emitted a small gasp.

But me? I lost my temper.

I stepped out from under Dad's arm, grabbed Hawk's hand and snapped, "Can I talk to you?"

Then I didn't wait for him to answer. I turned and dragged him out of the kitchen, through the living room, up the stairs, down the hall and into my bedroom. I closed the door and it creaked then I turned, released his hand and stepped right into his space, getting up on my toes to get in his face.

"Why'd you do that?" I hissed under my breath.

He was looking down at me. "Do what?"

"Tell them about Ginger!" I was snapping now but still under my breath.

"Babe," he replied then said no more.

"Babe? That's your answer?" I asked sharply. "You can't tell them about Ginger."

His brows shot up. "Why not?"

"Because it will upset them and worry them and, I'll repeat, *upset them,*" I retorted.

His hands went to his hips and he replied, "Sweet Pea, I was a man with two daughters in trouble, I'd wanna know and I would not be happy that knowledge was kept from me."

"Maybe so but I'm a daughter with a sister in trouble who

knows a lot more about my family dynamic than you do. You might think you'd want to know but, trust me, Dad does *not* want to know and what's more, Meredith *shouldn't* know."

"You need to explain shit to them," he informed me, and I felt my temper spike so I got closer to his face.

"Don't tell me how to deal with my family," I snapped.

"I can keep you safe, Gwen, and I will but I'm not expending energy to sort out your sister's shit. She doesn't pull off a miracle, things are gonna go bad for her. They gotta know that's a strong eventuality."

There was a lot of ground I needed to cover so I started multitasking.

"I'm glad you brought that up," I told him. "*You* are not doing anything, not only for Ginger but also for me. You can take down your cameras and stop keeping tabs. You and I, we're over."

He grinned then he said, "We had this conversation earlier, babe."

"Yes, you told me *you* end things, but you live in Badass World. I live in the Real World and in the Real World, when a woman says it's over, it carries the same weight as when a man says it."

Hawk's eyes drifted over my face.

Then he murmured, "See my mistake."

"What?" I snapped.

His eyes moved to mine. "Shoulda given you time not fuckin' you, missed out."

"What?" I repeated on another snap.

His hands lifted and came to my jaw so I instantly jerked my head free of his hands and took a step back.

Then, so suddenly my breath flew out of me, I couldn't say for certain how it actually happened, I was pinned to the wall by his big, hard body, his hands were at my jaw in a way I couldn't jerk my face free, and his face was right in my face.

"About five seconds after I left you today, things between you and me, they changed," he informed me in a quiet voice.

I felt my brows draw together as my mind processed the fact that this was not good.

"Changed?" I asked. "How?"

"You got attitude, the kind I like. So I decided I'm gonna ride that attitude wave of yours, see how things work out."

I blinked. Then I did it again.

"You're going to ride my attitude wave?" I asked even though, firstly, I didn't really know what that meant so even if he affirmed I couldn't be sure how that would affect me. Secondly, I didn't like talking about him riding anything that had to do with me.

"Yeah," he answered, and I was right, I didn't know what that meant. I did know what it meant for him was that we weren't over.

"You're right," I told him. "Earlier today, things between you and me changed, but it happened about five minutes *before* you walked out and the way they changed means you and I are *over*."

His eyes never left me and he didn't speak but he shook his head.

"Listen to me," I demanded. "I just learned your name, not your real name, your nickname. I just learned you have a business, you have 'boys' and you watch my house. I've known you for over a year and you didn't tell me any of that shit directly. This isn't working for me anymore. This has been not right for a long time. Finding out you've intruded into my life, investigated me, kept watch on me without my knowledge makes it not only just not right but very, *very* wrong. Therefore, we are *over*."

He studied me for a while then his thumb swept my jaw before he remarked, "See you've decided not to make the right play."

"And *I* see that you think it's not the right play because it's not the play *you* want me to make."

He smiled and informed me, "You don't get it, babe. That heat in your eyes, that mouth of yours...." His thumb did another sweep as his face got even closer and when he spoke again, his voice dipped lower. "...used to be, I thought about visiting you, could let myself start to get hard. Now I just think about you, I start to get hard. You wanna play this with that attitude, Sweet Pea, I'm tellin' you, that is not the right play because that attitude of yours is *not* a turnoff."

"Stop calling me Sweet Pea," I snapped because I was again freaking out and I was trying to hide it.

His smile got bigger. "There it is," he whispered, "and I like it."

"Step away," I demanded, pushing at his waist where my hands were, but he didn't move.

"There it is again."

I clamped my mouth shut and glared at him.

He emitted another short, amused, deep, manly chuckle.

Then his lips hit mine and he murmured, "Hot."

And me being me, in other words my mother's daughter and a screaming loser, felt that one word murmured against my lips give me a tickle, a sweet one in a very private place.

Shit!

I pulled my head back the half inch his face and the wall afforded me and I called, "Hello? Break-in? Sister in serious shit? Parents downstairs? The middle of the night? I've got deadlines, loads of work to do, a house that's unsafe and I need to go to sleep so I can wake up tomorrow with the energy to get my life under control. Now can you please *step away?*"

He didn't step away but his hands slid from my jaw to curl around my neck and his face moved back an inch.

"Sure, babe, but you need to know you're not stayin' here tonight. Got boys on the way to board up that window and you're comin' with me."

I stared up at him, shocked at this news and, because I was a loser, titillated at the prospect of going with him wherever that would be. A major component of my daydreams the last year and a half centered around where he lived and spent his time. The idea of finally discovering the truth behind that, damn and blast, I had to admit was a discovery I really wanted to make.

Then I got smart and stated, "Dad will take care of my window tomorrow and I'm staying with him and Meredith tonight. That's why they're here."

He completely ignored me.

"You're comin' with me."

Seriously! This guy!

"No, I'm not."

"Yeah, Gwen, you are."

"I don't *know* you other than *knowing* you and what I'm learning I do *not* like. I had a break-in tonight and it freaked me out in a serious way. It scared the hell out of me. I know my dad and Meredith. I want to be with them tonight. I want to be someplace I know with people I know where I feel safe. I want to go home."

He studied me again then his thumb did another sweep, this time against my neck and, being a loser, it felt nice.

"I can see you need that so I'll let you do it," he said softly.

"Well, thanks," I replied not softly.

He grinned.

I glared.

He kept grinning as I kept glaring then he murmured, "Yeah, totally fuckin' missed out."

Then his head dropped and since I had no place to go, I couldn't avoid his lips brushing mine lightly in a way that made them tingle.

His head came up and he whispered, "Be smart, baby. My boys'll secure your house and you can come home tomorrow. Yeah?"

Then his thumb swept my neck again. I liked it again but before I could answer, he let me go and he was gone.

I stood with my back against the wall, staring in the space he'd been in, wondering how he could vanish into thin air right before my eyes. Then I realized I was breathing heavily.

Then I shook it off, telling myself I didn't actually care it was fascinating he could evaporate. Telling myself the fact that he had "boys," he flew Black Hawks, he had a "base," part of what he did was security and his nickname was Hawk was not fascinating either.

And also telling myself he could do what he wanted, I was going to do what I wanted, and he couldn't *make* me do what he wanted.

Ef that!

Then I set about packing a bag to go home with Dad and Meredith.

When I was in my bathroom getting my stuff, I grabbed my lotion and bath gel and stopped dead.

It hadn't registered with me until then, when I stood in my bathroom and stared at the plastic bottles in my hands.

My scent, the one I always used, was sweet pea.

CHAPTER FIVE

Hot-o-Meter

THERE WAS ONE good thing about having to spend the night with your parents after your house got broken into in the middle of the night because your sister was an idiot: when they had to get up early to go to work and you didn't so you could avoid the talk the next morning where they would want to know all about your idiot sister; how she put you in danger; how you put yourself in danger; why you didn't tell them right off the bat; and why you've been keeping your perfect Army man boyfriend to yourself.

So, sleeping in, I avoided talking to Dad and Meredith.

However, when I went to the kitchen for coffee, on the counter I found a note from Dad which said:

> *G—*
> *Tonight, dinner. 6:00 sharp. Be there.*
> *Your window probably won't be fixed for a week so pack a bag.*
> *Don't disappear or I'm calling Cam and sending Leo after you.*
> *Love you, Dad.*

They say men are attracted to women who are like their mothers and women are attracted to men who are like their fathers. This must be true considering I'm attracted to hot, uber-macho, bossy guys.

I also had a note from Meredith which said:

Morning honey,
There are fresh bagels in the fridge, Einstein's.
Whipped cream cheese, your favorite.
   See you tonight!

                            Hugs, Meredith

PS: I cannot tell you how happy I am for you after meeting Hawk! He's so cute! And he's sweet! And he's smitten! YAY!

Cute? Sweet? Smitten? With underlines? And...*yay?*

Obviously my dad wasn't attracted to women like me. Good to know.

After coffee, a bagel and note reading, I had taken more than my usual going-to-sit-at-a-computer-all-day care with my appearance because I kept running into hot guys. Usually I worked in yoga pants, camisoles or babydoll tees and lightweight hoodies. If it was summer, I might switch it up with shorts.

That morning I'd used Meredith's makeup and curling iron. Why she needed a curling iron with curly hair, I did not know, but she had everything that had anything to do with being a girl, one of the many reasons why I loved her.

I curled my long hair into a mass of curls and waves with a heavy fall of hair at the front. I also put on makeup, something I never did unless I was going out. The rest I couldn't help. I'd packed in the middle of the night after a break-in, meeting a new hot guy and another bizarre and annoying but, unfortunately, hot confrontation with Hawk. So it was just jeans and a light blue tee from Thrifty Stick, a cool boarder shop on Broadway. I didn't board but, like I mentioned, I could shop anywhere. It had a black skull and crossbones above my breasts that had a red "T" and "S" and red bands around the neckline and sleeves. To this I added a black belt, boots and a thin, hooded, cardie sweater.

And I was glad I'd curled my hair and done my makeup. I was also glad I had on my killer, wire-rimmed cop shades with the gray semi-mirrored lenses when I drove up to my house and saw it had a bunch of motorcycles and a big, black van parked in front of it.

Holy, freaking, *crap!*

I drove into my driveway trying to steer my little blue Hyundai in while still keeping my eyes on what appeared to be an army of bikers hanging out on my lawn and going in and out of my house.

Clearly my house wasn't hard to break into, as had been proved last night. It had been made easier by the fact there was only a board where the window should be but now the door was wide open and the board was gone. In fact, the entire window was gone.

And Tack was standing on my lawn with Dog. He was wearing cool mirrored shades too and they were pointed toward my car.

I barely pulled up the parking brake when Tack moved away from Dog and started in my direction. Therefore, when I got out, he was there, pinning me between my car and the door.

I looked up at him instantly comparing. Shorter than both Hawk and Lawson but he could seriously work facial hair. And I wasn't having a flight of fancy the day before. On the hot-o-meter he rang the top bell and he rang it *loud*.

"Hey," I said but it came out kind of breathy.

"Hey, Peaches," he replied, not breathy at all but deep and gravelly.

"Um…what are you doing here?" I asked, taking that opportunity to glance toward my house to see a biker had a tape measure and was measuring my window.

"Heard word you had a visitor last night," Tack said, and I looked back at him.

"Kind of, he was…uh, interrupted before I could, um…offer him some chocolate chip cookie dough," I told him.

This garnered me a white teeth surrounded by salt-and-pepper goateed smile. I made a mental note to stop being a smartass because, apparently, badasses liked smartass women.

Then Tack stated, "You didn't call."

"Um…no, I didn't call," I agreed.

"Told you, you get in a situation, you call," he went on.

I stared through my shades at his shades. He didn't sound biker-angry. He wasn't being scary. I would know because when he was you could see it, hear it and *feel* it.

I decided not to answer.

Tack continued, "So, I heard word you had a situation, you didn't call, I figure you're the kind of woman who wants the call. So, I'm callin'."

I looked at the bikers on my lawn and at my door. Then I looked at Tack.

"Sorry, I must have missed it. Maybe my phone ran out of juice."

"No, babe." He dipped his head to the side to indicate the bikers. "That's me callin'."

I looked back at the bikers then at Tack. Then it hit me that was how Tack made his call to announce that he was interested and he intended to do something about it.

Uh. Wow.

"Oh," I whispered.

I was thinking this was *not* good at the same time feeling warm and fuzzy all over.

I heard the purr of an engine. I leaned to the side to see a metallic dark gray, new-model, kick-freaking-ass Chevrolet Camaro rolling to a stop behind the black van. Gliding up behind that was another black van, this one newer, nicer, more expensive and very shiny.

The door of the Camaro opened up and Hawk folded out, also wearing shades. His were aviator glasses that were even more kick-freaking-ass than the Camaro and the Camaro was *hot*. Out of the van jumped a bunch of heavily muscled, cargo-pants and tight, long-sleeved-tee-wearing commandos.

Hawk's shades sliced our way.

Uh-oh.

I was wrong. *This* was not good. I was no longer feeling warm and fuzzy at all.

I heard a car door slam across the street, I leaned the other way to peer around Tack and saw a police vehicle with red and blue lights in the dash, not on the top, and walking across the street wearing his own wire-rimmed, super-hot shades was Detective Mitch Lawson.

Super, double, extra *uh-oh!*

The hot-o-meter started ringing like crazy as hot guys descended on me, my car and Tack from two directions.

Boy, was I glad I curled my hair.

Tack turned but didn't unpin me as they got close.

What did I do now?

I decided to play it cool but there was one big problem with that. I wasn't cool.

Hawk got there first and his shades didn't leave me when he stopped a few feet away.

"Babe," he greeted, but his voice was kind of rumbly in a way that I didn't suspect meant he was in a good morning mood.

"Hey," I greeted back.

Lawson arrived, rounding Hawk so he could get a clear line of sight to me, but his shades swept Tack, his mouth tight, before they landed on me.

"Mornin', Gwendolyn," he greeted, ignoring Hawk and Tack.

"Uh, morning," I greeted back.

"You sleep okay?" Lawson asked.

"Not really," I answered honestly.

"Got a remedy for that," Tack put in. Two pairs of shades sliced to him so mine did too. I saw he had his arms crossed on his chest and he was grinning.

Shit.

At this point, Hawk was done.

I knew this because he pointed a finger at Tack and then at Lawson saying, "You...you...talk."

I figured he was probably the only person on the planet who could get away with doing something like that with those two guys.

He took a step back and both Lawson and Tack moved. So did I, to clear my door and throw it to. When my car door slammed, Hawk, who had turned to walk with Lawson and Tack across my lawn, turned back to me.

"Babe. Stay."

I blinked at him through my shades.

Then I lost my temper.

"I'm not a dog!" I snapped loudly.

One second he was five feet away from me, the next I was pinned against my car.

"You stay or I'll carry you to my car and handcuff you to the steering wheel. Your choice. Two seconds."

Obviously I was right. Someone was not in a good morning mood.

"There's a police officer here. I think he'll frown on you carrying me to your car and handcuffing me to your steering wheel," I informed him.

"Lawson knows me, so does Tack. I promise you, Sweet Pea, I have to do what I have to do to deal with my woman, not a man in your yard will lift a finger to help you."

I wasn't certain I believed this statement but with the way he said it I wasn't going to test it. Things were tense enough. I didn't need biker vs. commando war on my front lawn with Lawson calling in police intervention.

So I gave in but I didn't do it graciously.

"You just slipped down two levels on the hot-o-meter," I informed him snottily.

"I'll survive," he shot back and turned away.

As he walked toward where Lawson and Tack were standing and waiting while watching me and Hawk, I walked to the hood of my car, jumped up to sit on it and crossed my arms on my chest.

Bikers and commandos alike swung their heads from me to the macho man, badass huddle. Me, I just watched the three hot guys talk, faces tight, eyes not even close to avoiding contact. Shades were locked to shades. This conversation was tense but it lasted all of three minutes. I didn't time it but my guess was it could have been even less.

Then they broke away from each other. Lawson headed to his vehicle but he gave me a low wave. Tack whistled, flicked his fingers and the army of bikers was on the move, jumping on bikes and loading up in the van. Tack's eyes came to me and he put a finger to his forehead and flipped it out before he jumped on a bike. Lawson's car started and Harleys roared. Through them taking off, Hawk broke off from talking to a slim but lean and cut man who was about two inches shorter than him and he came to me while the rest of the commandos unloaded what looked like boxes of equipment.

I hopped off the car to stand in front of him.

"I've just added reason three hundred and seventy-two to my list of why we are so *over,*" I announced.

"Had this conversation twice, not havin' it again," Hawk returned, his shades now locked to mine. "Last night my boys measured your window. A new one is being cut and they'll install it when it arrives. Now they're workin' on your security system. That'll take a couple days. Until then, you stay with me."

"Too late, I already had a macho man inform me where I'm sleeping tonight."

I watched his entire body get tight. It seemed like the very air around him turned a warning shade of red, and it took a lot but I just managed not to step back.

"And that would be?" he asked in a scary, quiet voice.

"My dad," I answered in a snotty voice.

His body relaxed as did his face and his mouth grinned showing both dimples.

"That I'll allow," he allowed.

Serious to God, he could *not* be believed.

"All right, I know you have selective hearing and block out entire sections of what I say but really, pay attention. First, tell your boys to stop their work. Dad is fixing my window and I don't want a security system from you. Second, I don't know what went down in that huddle but clearly you won and that makes you think you can waltz over here and boss me around but you are *way* wrong. Not only because I'm *not* your woman but also because I do not like to be bossed around. At all. Ever. And last, honest to God, honest to *God*, we...are...*over*."

I barely got out the word "over" when he yanked off his shades, then he yanked off mine, then he tossed both of them on the hood of my car. I was so surprised by this maneuver I was frozen stiff so he was able to execute his next maneuver without resistance. Therefore, I found my body flat against his, one of his arms was tight around me, the other hand was cupping the back of my head, he tilted it and his mouth slammed down on mine.

This was a problem.

There was a reason I never kicked Hawk out of my bed and that was because, usually before I could speak, he was kissing me.

And he was an *excellent* kisser. He could do a lot of things with his hands, his mouth, and other parts of his anatomy that were mind-blowing but even if he only ever kissed me it was highly likely I would be ruined for any other man.

Yes, he was that good. Really.

Therefore, when he finally lifted his head (and as humiliating as it was, he took his time and I let him), I had one arm tight around his back and one hand curled on the side of his neck both in order just to hold on. When his tongue was working my mouth, that was all I could ever do, just hold on.

"We over, Sweet Pea?" he whispered to me.

"I do not like you," I whispered back, still holding on.

He did that deep, amused, manly chuckle again, his hand moved out of my hair and became an arm wrapped around my shoulders before both his arms tightened, bringing me even closer. "Got things to do now, the boys'll be workin' here but I'll come back, take you to lunch."

Take me to lunch? We'd never even had a date and now he was casually telling me he was going to take me to lunch?

"I can't go to lunch. I have three deadlines and I only worked for a few hours yesterday. I have to go flat out if I'm going to make them. I'm eating lunch at my desk."

"I'll bring something. What do you want?"

God! What was *with* this guy?

"I have food in my fridge."

"Tom yung goong and pad Thai, J's Noodles," he said and I stared.

Two of my favorites. I had many but tom yung goong soup and pad Thai noodles from J's were very high on the top of that long list. And I usually bought them takeout to eat at my desk when I had a marathon workday going.

Then I stopped staring and I felt my eyes get squinty.

"How do you know everything about me?"

He didn't answer my question but it was unnecessary for him to do so since evidence was suggesting he watched me like... well, *a hawk*.

Instead, he asked his own question. "You didn't sleep last night?"

"My house got broken into," I reminded him.

"Thought you went to your dad's to feel safe," he replied.

"I can feel safe and still toss and turn because I'm obsessing about watching a man's hand push open my bedroom door at the same time worrying if I'd break my happy kitty snow globe when I had to clock him."

His arms gave me a squeeze. "That was last night, babe, this is today. You're good. It's over. Get it out of your head."

Was he high? Did he seriously think I could do that? Did he seriously think *any woman* could do that? I had at least twenty-five years of obsessing about last night left before I could get it out of my head.

"It's not that easy," I informed him.

"It's just that easy," he informed me.

I glared up at him.

He smiled down at me, with dimples. Shit, I liked those dimples.

Time to get to work.

"I need coffee. And I need to fire up my computer and get to work."

"Yeah," he murmured, dropped his head and, before I could avoid it, he brushed his lips against mine. Then, murmuring again, he said, "Later," leaned into me to grab his shades before he let me go. Then he prowled to his Camaro, all badass cool, on his way tipping his chin to the commandos. Then he folded into his kickass car and purred off.

I stood by my car for a while watching the street where I'd last seen him thinking one word.

Shit.

Then I grabbed my shades, avoided busy commandos, made my way inside and set a big pot of coffee to brew. When it was done I poured out about five mugs for various hardworking commandos.

Then, finally, I went to my office to fire up my computer.

CHAPTER SIX

To the Rescue

I'D HIT MY zone and was able to focus even with a bunch of commandos banging around in my house when I suddenly felt my hair shifted off one shoulder, swept across my neck, and over my other shoulder.

Then I felt lips at the skin at the back of my ear.

A delicious tremble radiated from my ear going up, down and out, and my eyes on the computer screen unfocused as I came crashing headlong out of my zone and careened happily into an entirely different zone. The lips left my ear and, dazedly, I saw a brown paper bag accompanied by a white plastic bag hit the desk by my keyboard. I looked at the bottom right of my computer screen to see the time was twelve forty-seven.

Lunchtime.

I swiveled in my chair and looked up to see Hawk standing there, tearing open the folded-over and stapled top of the bag.

I didn't say anything because I was too busy freaking out because this was the subject matter of a daydream. When I said that I meant I had actually daydreamed this and now I was living it.

Okay, not the Thai food but, many a time, I'd drifted off and dreamed about what it would be like if my Mystery Man showed in the light of day, coming up to me silently while I did the dishes in the kitchen and he slid his arms around me. Or while I was in the shower and he joined me.

Or while I was working and he snuck up on me and kissed my neck.

Just like I liked in the spot that I liked.

Exactly like he'd just snuck up on me and kissed my neck.

Just like I liked in the spot that I liked.

And it was better than a daydream. Not only because J's Noodles were a welcome addition but because it was real.

Damn.

He started pulling food from the bag as I struggled to pull myself together. I saw him reveal a lidded cardboard cup of soup and another container of noodles, both of which I knew, from experience with J's takeout, were for me. Next came chopsticks in paper and then he took out another container for him. Then he picked up the bag, dropped it on the floor and rifled through the other bag that had familiar red, orange and green logo on it. He took out a bottled water which I knew was for him when he set a can of diet grape soda by my food.

I stared at the soda. Then I looked back up at him.

"What? Do you follow me?" I asked.

"Sometimes," he answered, and I felt my eyes get squinty. "Sometimes my boys do it."

He turned away from me and went to my couch, sat down, set his water on a side table and opened the top of his food container.

"So do you have a big fat file on me at your base?" I asked, tearing the paper off my chopsticks then picking up my soup and pulling the lid off.

"Nope," he replied, "verbal reports. 'She went to J's, got soup and noodles, then to 7-Eleven for a diet grape.' Shit like that."

Unreal.

"Why?" I asked.

"Why?" he repeated.

"Why did you and your boys follow me?"

"Babe," he replied, then he dug into his noodles with his chopsticks as if this was nothing, him and his boys following me, sharing reports about my food and beverage preferences, intruding into my life without my knowledge. Then my eyes dropped to his food and his noodles looked like nothing but noodles and veggies. No sauce. No cashews. No peanut bits. No succulent shrimp. None of the good stuff. Nothing. Just noodles and veg.

This reminded me of the first time I saw him when we were at a restaurant. He had a steak, baked potato and steamed vegetables. I remembered noting then, somewhat drunkenly, that he didn't have anything on his potato. Not sour cream. Not bacon bits. Not cheese. Not even butter.

"What are you eating?" I asked.

"Noodles and veg," he pointed out the obvious then shoved some into his mouth with his chopsticks.

"Just noodles and veg?"

He chewed, swallowed and said, "Yep," then shoved more noodles in his mouth.

"No sauce?" I pushed.

More chewing then swallowing then, "Babe, I ate like you, I'd get a gut. In my work, you can't have a gut."

I felt my blood pressure rise. "Are you saying I'm fat?"

The double-dimple threat popped out and, chopsticks loaded with noodles and veg halfway to his mouth, he replied, "Sweet Pea, the way you eat means you got tits and ass. This is good because I like tits and ass. This is bad because Tack and Lawson like 'em just as much as me." Then he shoved his noodles and veg into his mouth and said with his mouth full, "Tack maybe more."

Shit.

"I need to focus on work," I announced.

He stretched his long legs out in front of him, crossed his feet at the ankles, clearly planning to stay awhile, and replied, "Then focus."

I glared at him. This was bad since he looked good stretched out in my office like that. Tracy and I had painted the walls white but I'd had the guy at the hardware store squirt a hint of orange in the paint so the white had warmth to it. My desk was long, white, sleek, narrow and girlie. My shelves were white and likewise girlie. The narrow, square tables on each side of the couch were equally white and girlie. My couch was cushiony and salmon colored with chartreuse and peacock blue toss pillows. I'd decorated heavily in light wicker and had white ceramic, circular, lacy shaded lamps dotting the space. It wasn't over-the-top girlie, all pink and ruffled, but it was definitely feminine space.

Sitting on my couch like that, Hawk looked like an invading conqueror enjoying a meal, bulking up before expending the effort to rape and pillage. Except he wouldn't have to rape, all the townswomen would line up for their turn.

Shit.

I swiveled to face my desk and sniffed my soup. Lemongrass. Yum. I swirled it with my chopsticks then took a sip.

Then I asked Hawk, eyes on my computer, "What's your real name?"

"Cabe Delgado."

He answered without hesitation and my head turned to him in surprise.

"Cabe Delgado?"

He shoved more noodles into his mouth and didn't answer.

"What kind of name is Cabe?" I asked.

He swallowed and captured more noodles, muttering, "Who the fuck knows? Ma's a nut."

His ma was a nut.

Interesting.

"Is Delgado Mexican?" I pressed.

"Puerto Rican," he answered, again without hesitation.

"You're Puerto Rican?"

"Look at me, babe, not full-blooded Scandinavian."

Nope, he was definitely not that.

"Were you born in Puerto Rico?"

"Nope. Denver."

A rare Denver native. Surprising.

I, on the other hand, was not a native. Dad had moved Meredith, Ginger and me to Denver from South Dakota when I was ten but I didn't share this piece of information because Hawk probably already knew that.

"So your parents are Puerto Rican."

"Dad is. Ma's half Italian, half Cuban."

No wonder. Puerto Rican, Italian and Cuban—the perfect ingredients for a hot, bossy, badass cocktail.

His brows went up. "Is this focus?"

Guess someone was done sharing.

I turned back to the computer, fished in my soup with my chopsticks, secured a big prawn, pulled it out and ate it.

Fresh, spicy, brilliant.

I washed the prawn down with another sip of soup. Then I tried to focus on work with Cabe "Hawk" Delgado stretched out on my couch. Unsurprisingly, I was completely unable to do this but hopefully I was successful at pretending I could.

I'd finished my soup, leaving the mysterious bits uneaten in the bottom. I loved that soup but those mysterious bits freaked me out and I never ate them. I'd taken a sip of my grape in preparation for the next culinary delight and opened my noodles when Hawk approached my desk, bending as he moved to snatch up the discarded bag.

He shoved his container in the bag while I pretended to ignore him. He was reaching for my soup container when I heard, "Hawk."

I twisted to see who I suspected was Hawk's Numero Dos, the slim but cut man that Hawk was talking to outside earlier. He looked to be the same ethnic cocktail as Hawk and, even shorter and slighter, since he'd shared his name was "Smoke" and he had a scar that went from his temple into his dark hair, I figured he was probably not someone you messed with.

"Company," he said to Hawk, his eyes not coming to me even for an instant, then, like his name, *poof!* he vanished.

Hawk moved, dumping my soup container into the bag and the bag into my garbage bin as he went. I moved too. Putting my noodles on my desk, I followed him.

When I hit the hall, Hawk stopped suddenly and turned so I ran into his front.

I took a step back, looked up at him and before I could say anything, he asked, "Any chance I tell you to stay up here you won't give me lip?"

"No chance at all," I answered.

He stared at me a second then shook his head like *I* was intruding on *his* greeting company at *his* house rather than me walking down the stairs in my own damned house to greet *my* company. Then he turned and proceeded walking to the stairs.

I followed and heard him before I saw him.

Then I remembered it was Wednesday and Wednesday afternoons were Troy Days. We had a standing Wednesday afternoon appointment for coffee or beer or whatever since he had Wednesday afternoons off because he worked Saturday mornings.

Shit.

"Who are you guys?" Troy asked as I walked down the stairs. "And where's Gwen?"

He came into my line of sight but by the time he did, Hawk had come into *his* line of sight. Troy was staring at him as I would guess anyone would have a tendency to stare at Hawk, Hawk being all that was Hawk. Then he jerked like he was pulling himself out of a trance and his eyes came to me.

"Gwen, honey, what's going on? You didn't tell me you were having work done."

"Hey, Troy," I greeted as I came to stand several feet to the side of where Hawk was standing several feet from Troy.

Hawk, however, didn't like this distance and I knew this when he closed it and he didn't close it by moving to me. He closed it by leaning to me, grabbing my forearm and giving it a tug so I had no option but to teeter sideways. I slammed into him, his hand left my arm, and he caught me by clamping his arm around my shoulders.

"Wednesday," Hawk muttered when he'd accomplished this feat, his eyes on Troy. "Shit, I forgot."

Troy stared at Hawk and then he stared at me. Then he stared at Hawk and me and he did all of this with his eyes wide and his mouth hanging open much like, I suspected, I looked on more than one occasion recently.

However, I didn't struggle against Hawk's hold because I was catapulted back to yesterday when Hawk told me Troy wanted to get into my pants and therefore I was standing there, staring at Troy with his sandy blond hair and blue eyes, wearing his suit from the bank, and comparing. He was a loan manager. He wasn't tall but he wasn't short. He was, however, taller than me. He didn't have a bad body but he wasn't ripped by any stretch of the imagination. And he was so far from a commando it wasn't funny.

Troy finally settled his gaze on Hawk and asked, "Who are you?"

"He's—" I started but Hawk spoke over me.

"Hawk, Gwen's man."

Shit! I wished he'd quit saying that!

"Gwen's man?" Troy whispered, now his face had paled.

Shit again!

"Troy, it's not—" I began.

Troy's pale face moved to me.

"You have a man?"

"Well...um—"

"Gwennie!" we all heard shouted and through the front door flew Tracy.

Troy turned to the door and all the commandos stopped dead. That happened a lot when Tracy Richmond entered a room, and I was unsurprised that even commandos weren't immune to Tracy's charms.

This was because she looked like a model, no joke. She was tall, taller than me by two inches. She had natural blonde hair that was long, sleek and straight as a sheet. She had dancing green eyes. She had perfect bone structure. She had a symmetrical face. She was thin with long, long legs and long, graceful, thin arms. She was not tits and ass. She was a human mannequin of the beautiful variety. Fashion designers the world over would be in throes of ecstasy, they caught sight of her. That was why any retail store in Denver hired her even though she was flighty and got bored easily so her average length of employment was around eleven months. If she told you something looked good on you, you'd visualize that you were her because you wanted to be her with every fiber of your being, you'd believe it and then you'd buy it.

"Cam called and said that Leo said that you got broken—" Tracy skidded to a halt beside Troy when her eyes caught sight of Hawk. Those eyes widened, her jaw went slack, and she stared at him. Then, before I could do anything about it, she got the *way* wrong idea, her face lit with sheer delight and she screeched, "*Ohmigod!*"

Then she jumped up and down and clapped while the commandos took in the show and she tore her gaze from Hawk and grabbed my hand still jumping up and down.

"Gwennie! Hurray!" she cried.

Shit!

I took hold of her hand and squeezed firm, "Trace, it's not what you—"

Before I could finish, she dropped my hand and looked up at Hawk. "I know you! And I knew *it!* Cam called me and told me you'd come over yesterday and Gwennie got broken into last night and here you are! To the rescue! Hurray!"

Shit, shit, *shit!*

"Trace—"

She looked at me. "I *told* you! Didn't I tell you?" She looked at Hawk and informed him, "I told her, like, a bazillion times!"

"You got broken into?" This was Troy breaking into Tracy's glee. I stopped looking at Tracy and started looking at Troy.

"Um...yeah but it wasn't a big deal," I lied.

"You got broken into?" Troy repeated.

"Is that why all these guys are here?" Tracy asked, her head swiveling around on her neck to take in the commandos then she looked at me. "What are they doing? Are they building a fortress?"

"They're putting in a security system," Hawk answered, Tracy's face instantly fell at this news and her eyes came to me.

"Oh, honey, does that mean you won't be able to get those Jimmy Choos you've had your eye on for-freaking-ever? You know, I can't hold them very much longer. Someone will notice."

That was Tracy: fashion before *everything*, even safety.

"She's not payin' for it," Hawk replied, Tracy's face instantly lit up again and her eyes flew back to Hawk while Troy's eyes narrowed on him.

"Hurray!" Tracy exclaimed.

"Babe, stop saying 'hurray.' This isn't what it seems," I finally got out, and Hawk's arm squeezed my shoulders.

"What is it then?" Troy asked me but didn't wait for me to answer. "And who is this guy? And who broke in? Are you okay? Did you get hurt? Do the police know? Did they catch him?"

I opened my mouth to answer but Hawk answered before me and *for me*.

"Like I said, I'm Hawk, Gwen's man. We don't know who broke in. Gwen's fine, my boys and I are lookin' out for her, and the police have been informed."

"Hawk," Tracy breathed, gazing up at him with stars in her eyes. "*Cool name.* Way cool. Super cool. Super, double extra cool."

Good God.

"Honey, you need a brief but I don't have time, I have work," I told her, and looked at Troy. "And I'm sorry, Troy, I can see you're concerned but things are a little crazy and I have deadlines. I can't do my Troy Day today. But I'm fine, totally fine. I'll call you and explain everything tomorrow."

Then I looked at Hawk and snapped, "And you. Will you *quit* speaking for me?"

"That's cool," Tracy said immediately before Hawk could reply and went on, "And by the way, honey, your hair is *the bomb*."

Troy wasn't cool. He was staring at me. Then he asked, "Does this have to do with Ginger?"

When he asked that, Tracy's eyes swung to me and they were wide.

"Ohmigod," she breathed. "I didn't think of that."

Troy didn't wait for my answer; he jumped straight to the right conclusion. He'd known me a long time but my escapades, even at their worst, wouldn't lead to a team of commandos installing a security system.

"What'd she do?" Troy asked.

"I don't know and I don't care. I've disowned her," I answered.

"Finally," Tracy muttered.

"*I* want to know and *I* care if it means, in a day, you've found and hooked up with Rambo," Troy clipped, jerking his head at Hawk.

Hawk did that deep, manly, amused chuckle.

Tracy missed the chuckle because she was declaring, "It wasn't a day. They've been seeing each other for a year and a half."

Uh-oh.

Tracy saw the look on Troy's face, realized what she'd done and said my thought out loud: "Uh-oh."

"A year and a half," Troy whispered, and my stomach lurched. He looked like I'd kicked him and not in a good place.

Shit, Hawk was right. Troy definitely wanted to get in my pants.

"Troy—" I whispered back, and Hawk spoke.

"Friendly advice. Next time, get your head outta your ass and stake your claim."

My body went solid but it still turned woodenly toward Hawk and I snapped loudly, "Hawk!"

Hawk looked down at me. "Man to man, babe. He's a man. He can take it and he's gotta know he fucked up."

For the first time in my life I was wishing murder wasn't illegal.

"I can see you're not in the mood for an intervention," Tracy said softly to Troy, "but, um…he's kind of right, honey."

This time, *my* mouth dropped open as I stared at my sweet, wouldn't-do-or-say-a-thing-to-hurt-a-soul Tracy saying something that hurt a soul.

And Troy looked at her just like I'd figure someone would look whose soul was just wounded.

Then he jerked around and started to go.

I pulled away from Hawk, rushed forward and grabbed his hand, saying, "Troy—"

He stopped and shook his hand free, his eyes narrowed on me. "Don't," he whispered.

"Troy—" I started, *again*.

"You need a washer changed or you're freezing your ass off because your furnace doesn't work, Gwen, don't call my number. Call Rambo there," he jerked his head toward Hawk, "and hope he knows how to use a fucking wrench."

Then he walked out my front door.

When he did I swung to face Hawk and Tracy.

"What the hell?" I yelled.

"Babe," Hawk replied.

"I know," Tracy said softly. "It was harsh, honey, but Cam isn't here and someone had to say it. She and I have been talking about it for *ages*. He should have made his move or moved on. He didn't do either. Now that you have Hawk, maybe he'll forget about you and move on."

Cam and her had been talking about it for *ages*? Why hadn't they talked to *me?*

I didn't ask this. Instead I shouted, "He's already moved on! He's got a girlfriend."

Tracy waved her hand in front of her face. "Hardly. Every girl he picks he picks so they'd be someone he could drop like a rock if you gave him an in. I don't like her. Cam doesn't like her. *You* don't like her. She's a whiner. No one likes a whiner. Even Troy. Therefore, easy to drop like a rock."

I looked at Tracy. Then I looked at Hawk. Then I looked at my audience of commandos.

Then I went into denial.

"This isn't happening," I announced. "I can't do this right now. My pad Thai is already cold. I need to nuke it, eat it and get work done. No one exists. I live in a world all alone."

Then I stomped through Tracy and Hawk, up my stairs and to my food.

When I'd grabbed my noodles and turned around, Hawk was in the door.

"Babe," he said.

"I don't see you. You don't exist," I informed him.

"Gwen, someone had to tell him."

"No, they didn't and if they did, it didn't have to be *you*," I shot back.

"I did him a favor."

"Really? You did? Should I call Troy and ask him if he thought you did him a favor, telling him that shit in front of me, Trace and your bunch of badasses?"

"Next time, he'll get his finger outta his ass."

Definitely exploring the boundaries of head explosion.

"Go away. I don't want to see you for, I don't know… maybe a million years. A million years ought to do it. If I have a million years, I think I'll get over being," I leaned forward, "*insanely pissed at you*."

He grinned.

Then he repeated, "Babe."

"Thanks for the food," I snapped sounding about as grateful as I felt, which was to say, *not at all*. I walked toward him and finished, "See you in a million years."

As I tried to move around him, he caught me with an arm around my belly. I decided not to struggle because firstly, I might drop my pad Thai, and secondly, I'd lose.

"What?" I snapped when I'd twisted my neck to look up at him.

"We're havin' dinner tonight," he informed me.

"No, we're not," I informed him. "I'm enduring dinner with Dad and Meredith where I'll have to explain about Ginger and *you*. Then I'm working until I fall asleep at the keyboard."

His brows drew together. "Are you that far behind?"

"Yes!" I shouted. "I was that far behind yesterday when Darla came to visit and I stupid, stupid, *stupidly* decided to go to Ride. Now I'm even *more* far behind and all this shit, Hawk, it is *not* helping."

"I should let you get shit done," he muttered.

"You think?" I snapped.

His arm curled, moving me to his front and curving around me so I had to execute evasive maneuvers not to lose my pad Thai.

"Hawk…" I warned when his head dropped. I twisted my neck to try to avoid it, his arm tightened, his other one wrapping around me, and I failed to avoid his lips hitting my neck.

"You need to get caught up, baby, carve some time out

for me," he murmured against my neck. I was about to say something snotty but wasn't able to when his tongue touched the skin behind my ear. I instantly forgot I was insanely pissed at him and then he said, "We're due."

"Due?" I breathed because I could still feel his tongue behind my ear.

His head came up, he looked at me and he repeated, "Due."

"For what?"

His black eyes warmed, the dimples popped out and his arms got even tighter, plastering me to his long, hard body.

Oh.

Due.

Mm.

I momentarily forgot that we were over as I stared into his warm, black eyes in the light of day, felt his long, hard body against mine and mentally recalled what that body felt like naked.

Mm.

"Babe," he called, and I blinked.

"Hunh?"

He smiled, this time with white teeth against his beautiful brown skin. He dropped his head and kissed me lightly.

"Get to work," he ordered.

Then, suddenly, he was gone.

I stood there with my pad Thai staring at my empty hall thinking, *Shit.*

CHAPTER SEVEN

Certainty Borne of Nothing but Instinct

I'D MANAGED TO get rid of Tracy, nuke and eat my pad Thai and return to my computer, but after an hour of work, my mind wandered. My foot came up so I could rest my heel on the seat, I swiveled my chair and I put my chin to my knee so I could comfortably stare out the window without doing anything too taxing, like holding my own head up.

I wasn't daydreaming, I was thinking about where I'd gone wrong.

Two years ago, after Tracy had successfully passed an online course in bartending, she'd stepped out of her chosen career of hopscotching through every exclusive retail clothing store at Cherry Creek Mall and scored a job at Club.

Club was a trendy eatery that had really good food, stylish, sophisticated glasses in which they served their drinks, three open fires that made the space warm and welcoming, every table was a booth, and it had a huge circular bar in the middle where you could see and be seen.

At the time Club was Cam, Trace and my top spot for seeing and being seen while drinking cosmopolitans. Though, to be honest, we went there because of the glasses, which were flipping *fantastic*. It now was not since Tracy had broken so many of their fancy glasses, her boss had to let her go. He did this with tears in his eyes because he, like any man with a pulse, was half in love with her. I'd seen it, I was there, so was Cam and it wasn't pretty.

But I was there one night a year and a half ago, drinking cosmos and keeping Tracy company on her shift.

I was well into cosmo number three and already slightly hammered because I was on some crazy diet where I was detoxing (though I had altered the diet to allow cosmos, of course) and therefore had nearly three cosmos under my belt with zero food for the day.

This was stupid, I could see this now. At the time, it didn't seem stupid because Tracy was my ride. Troy had dropped me off and Tracy was taking me home. I could get as drunk as I wanted, flirt as much as I wanted and cackle with Tracy as much as I wanted.

Then *he* walked in. The Great Mystery Man, now known as Cabe "Hawk" Delgado.

I'd fallen in love with him at first sight. No joke. He was hot but it wasn't lust. It was love.

Okay, it was part lust but it was mostly love.

There was no explaining this, even now, looking back. There was just something about the way he was. Wearing faded jeans, a tailored black shirt and great black boots, clearly comfortable and confident in his style and in himself. The way he moved, graceful yet powerful, masculine. With his prowl, his confidence, his natural charisma and his looks, he owned the room. And then there was the way he could sit at a booth and eat all alone and seem totally cool with that. He fiddled with his phone, receiving and sending texts, taking calls; he glanced here and there and he seemed like he was naturally alert to every nuance of the room but was at ease in his own company. It was freaking *awesome*.

To my delight, they'd seated him at a booth on my side of the bar.

As usual when going out (Hawk did not lie, when I went out, I showed skin, but that was me and Meredith taught me to embrace my own style so I did), I'd worn a skimpy, clingy, stretchy dress that showed lots of leg due to it being uber-short, lots of arm due to it being sleeveless and lots of back due to a low vee. At the time I'd owned eleven little black dresses and that dress was number three in my ranking of how hot they were. Now I owned thirteen and it had slid down to position five. I had on spike-heeled, strappy sandals, my hair was out *to there* and my makeup was "Do you come here often?"

I wasn't on the prowl. I was there to have a nice night with my girlfriend who was fucking up at work and needed moral support, but that didn't mean I couldn't look hot.

Sitting on my barstool, drinking cosmos like they were diet grape soda, I did everything I could to get Hawk's attention, twisting and turning on my stool, crossing and uncrossing my legs, sucking and twirling a cocktail straw, flipping my hair unnecessarily.

And as he ate (and as I surreptitiously watched him eat, and sit, and fiddle with his phone, etc.), he didn't even look at me.

So when he paid his bill, slid out of the booth and it was clear he was about to leave, I was devastated.

Yes, the feeling was devastated.

I knew in my cosmo-drenched brain that that man walking out the door was the end of my life. It was the loss of my last chance at happiness. It was the death of a dream.

And I'd turned to the bar, downed the last sip of my cosmo and contemplated hara-kiri when, suddenly, I felt a warm hand on the skin of my lower back.

I twisted my neck, looked up and there he was.

I held my breath and he asked, "You comin' or what?"

That was it. That was his pickup line.

You comin' or what?

I went. I grabbed my purse, gave the high sign to a staring Tracy and walked out of that restaurant with him. He loaded me into a black SUV, asked my address, took me home and fucked my brains out.

I'd never done anything like that before in my life, not even close. It was an unbelievably insane thing to do.

And it was magnificent.

Until I woke up the next morning and he was gone.

I knew I'd fucked up. He was amazing. I was a drunken one-night stand, I didn't have his number and didn't know his name.

I'd instantly plummeted into the depths of despair and washed away my hangover that very night with more cosmopolitans at Club. This time with Tracy bartending and Cam at my side, where I explained the depths of my despair at length, and every time the door opened or there was movement in that direction, I craned my neck, hoping he was coming in looking for me.

He wasn't.

It wasn't until three days later when I felt my comforter slide back, waking me from a deep sleep, my mind and body frozen in terrified panic, then his weight hit the bed, his never-to-be-forgotten voice said, "Hey, babe," his arms wrapped around me and he kissed me. Then he did other things to me, really, *really* good things.

Thus it began, and even though at the start I was hopeful it would change—I'd manage to ask his name or he'd ask my number or he'd knock on the door during the day or he'd spend the night and take me out to breakfast—it didn't change.

And sitting there in my office, staring out the window

when I should have been working, I realized that I was right there with Tracy all this time. I was hopeful. I wanted that feeling back that I had when I first saw him and the feeling I got, but I foolishly denied, every time he came to call. The butterflies in my stomach. The certainty that was borne of nothing but instinct that he was *the one*.

But a year and a half slid by and I kept my hope while losing my dignity again and again and again.

Now things had changed.

And now I was learning that he might be hot, he might be confident, he might move with grace and there might be a multitude of things that were fascinating about him but he also could be an annoying, bossy jerk who told me what to do, didn't listen to me and could hurt Troy's feelings without batting an eye.

On this thought my phone rang and I jumped. It was the house phone, which never rang. Everyone called my cell. But I'd turned off my cell so I could get some work done, thus Tracy coming by for a surprise visit after she heard about my break-in and she couldn't get hold of me.

Automatically I reached out and took it off its base then wished I didn't as I beeped the button and put it to my ear thinking it was probably a marketer because on the rare occasion my phone rang it was always a marketer.

"Hello?" I asked hesitantly, ready to hang up the instant I heard a marketer.

I didn't hear a marketer.

"*Ohmigod!*" Cam shrieked.

I blinked and my chin came off my knee. Camille Antoine was not a girlie shrieker.

"Cam?" I called.

"*Ohmigod!*"

Oh boy. I knew what this was.

"Cam, the break-in . . . it's cool, it's—"

"You *will not* believe *what happened!*"

My back straightened.

Ohmigod! Leo proposed! Tracy, Cam and I had been waiting for-flipping-*ever* for Leo to propose (Cam obviously more than Trace and I but just barely). None of us could figure out, since they'd known each other for five years and been living together for four, what was taking so long.

Now it had happened.

Yay!

"Oh, Cam, I'm so—" I started to gush.

But she cut off my gushing with "Mitch asked to be taken off the case!"

I blinked again.

Then I asked, "What?"

"The case!" she cried. "The *case!* It's the kind of case that could make his career. He scores a bust on this we're talking awards, commendations, *book deals.* And he asked to be taken off the case *because of you.*"

Words were filtering into my brain like "Mitch" and "taken off the case" and "because of you."

So, I repeated, "What?" but I did it in a breathy whisper this time.

"Gwen, I don't know what you did but whatever you did, he . . . is . . . *into you.* Everyone is talking about it. I've been waiting all day to get a break so I could call, then you weren't picking up your cell, so I had to wait to get home to my address book because I didn't remember your stupid home phone number. I cannot believe this. He is fine. He is *fine.* And he's *nice.* And he's *fine.* Did I say he was fine?"

"Cam—"

"I mean, the captain wouldn't take him off the case but the fact that he asked. Shit, girl. Shit. *Shit!*" she shrieked.

"Cam—"

"I love this. I'm talking to Leo the minute his ass walks through the door. We're setting up a double date."

"Cam!" I shouted.

"What?" she asked.

"I was broken into last night," I told her.

"I know all about that, girl," Cam replied in a "so what?" voice. "Meredith called me this morning and it's the talk of the station. I know all about MM too. I know everything."

Shit, would I ever learn? I should never take my friends home because Meredith wriggled her way into their lives being a good, funny, generous person. Then I never could keep anything secret. I learned that early but did I stop my stupid behavior? No! Meredith still talked to my friend Chelsea from junior high. Chelsea lived on the Costa del Sol in Spain with some English gazillionaire and she and Meredith chatted several times a year and I hadn't spoken to her in fifteen of them. We didn't even exchange Christmas cards.

Repeat after me: family here, friends there and never the twain shall meet!

"Cam, things have become complicated," I told her.

There was silence and then, "No, Gwen, *you* complicate things. I heard that MM declared his intentions and you contradicted him. Mitch heard it too. Stick to your guns. I know Mitch Lawson; I've known him for years. He's a good cop, a good man and he wants a house with a white picket fence, two point five kids, a dog and a woman who can match his libido, which, rumor has it, runs in the red zone. He's just never been able to find the one, even though he's expended a fair amount of effort looking. Girl, you could be his one!"

"Yeesh, Cam, how do you know so much about him?"

"Did I not say he was fine?" she shot back. "I got Leo but that don't mean I can't study fine, and I do."

This was true. She did. She'd studied fine for so long and with such diligence, she was at a professorial level in fine.

"I can't think about this, I have to work," I told her. "I have commandos in my house installing a security system. Hawk crushed Troy like a bug in front of Tracy *and* the aforementioned commandos. My sister is in some serious shit that is leaking into my life. And Tack declared *his* intentions this morning and there was an Official Meeting of the Badasses in my yard, the culmination of which I am not privy to but I know that Lawson and Tack retreated and, from your news, I figure it's to regroup. I also know that I've seen Hawk three times by the light of day and one of those times he brought me J's Noodles for lunch so I'm guessing he thinks he's the front-runner."

"He brought you J's Noodles?"

"Yes."

"How does he know about you and J's?"

"Cam, I told you yesterday, he knows everything about me! And now, when I say that, I mean *he knows everything about me.* He told me himself he follows me, or his boys do and report in. It's insane!"

"Why would he do that?"

"I asked and his answer was 'Babe,' which is how he answers a lot of my questions or responds to a lot of my yelling at him."

"I don't know, Mitch can be broody, but I would suspect he wouldn't answer a direct question with 'babe.'"

Good God.

"I can't think about Mitch, I can't think about anything," I told her. "I seriously need to work and all this is messing with my head."

"Well, you need to think about MM because once I heard that a man named Hawk claimed you as his own last night, I asked some questions about him and found out a lot and the lot I found out means you need to cut him loose."

Oh boy. That didn't sound good.

"I don't want to know about him either. After a year and a half I'm learning fast and the more interaction I have with Hawk, the more the threat that I'll be the first victim of spontaneous head explosion becomes imminent."

"You don't like him?"

"I don't have time to explain the complexity of everything I feel about Hawk right now. I have three hours to do ten hours of work and then I have to be at my parents' house. They know Ginger's in trouble and they may have disowned her but she's their daughter and she's my sister and they're going to worry. I know that because it sucks and I want to wash it away, but I'm worried. I have to gear up for facing that. I'm taking this all one step at a time."

There was more silence, then, "You don't sound too good."

I closed my eyes, leaned forward and my head collided with my desk.

Why was no one paying attention to me?

"Was that your head hitting your desk?" Cam asked in my ear.

"Yes," I whispered into the phone, keeping my eyes closed.

"All right, babe, I'll leave you alone but we need cosmos, *soon*. I'll talk to Leo about a double date. Maybe since you aren't a major player in this case Mitch'll be able to do dinner. Or maybe we can just plan a get-together at our house and no one will be the wiser."

I opened my eyes and stared at my lap. "This isn't letting me go, Cam, this is planning my romantic future with a man I barely know while I'm freaking out about how I'm going to get the man I also barely know but have been sleeping with for months to agree we're over when his ideas on that subject violently clash with mine."

Silence, then, "Really? You told him it was over?"

I shot up in my chair and cried, "Cam!"

"All right! All right. I'll let you go."

"Call Tracy, brief her with the limited intel you have, it'll save me time," I ordered.

"Gotcha."

"No double dates."

"We'll just get something in the calendar."

"Cam!"

"Later, babe."

Then I was listening to dead air.

I hung up the phone and put it on its base. Then I got up and went downstairs because I was pretty certain I had frozen Twix bars and I was pretty certain about this because I always had frozen Twix bars but it wasn't unheard of for me accidentally to eat my way through my stash while, say, watching a movie or just getting the munchies. Through copious experimentation I'd discovered that frozen Twix bars were proven to intensify focus. I needed my focus intensified so I was going to pull out the big guns.

I found I had frozen Twix bars.

Upon offering them to the boys, I also found that commandos didn't eat frozen Twix bars.

This was good. More for me.

I grabbed a twin pack, straightened my shoulders, with effort cleared my head and determinedly walked back up the stairs to my office.

CHAPTER EIGHT

How We Met

As I HEADED to Dad and Meredith's house I was feeling pretty good. I'd managed to make some headway on work and load up my files on my laptop before leaving my house.

I had a plan: eat dinner, explain shit to Dad and Meredith, do both of these things very fast then hole myself in Dad's den and work until my vision got blurry.

The only flaw in this plan was that I was tired. I'd only had about four good hours of sleep last night so I was running on empty. In my business, attention to detail was key and getting fuzzy was not good. But I figured I had enough mojo left to squeeze in two or three good hours of concentration and, if I got a decent night's sleep, tomorrow I could hit it fully loaded and kick some book-editing ass.

With my plan of attack all sorted out and my excuse of having to get work done a good one so Dad would cut his lecture short, I was feeling good, totally psyched up for dinner at my parents'.

That was until their house became visible and I saw a dark, metallic gray kickass Camaro parked out front.

I was beginning to understand why people were moved to acts of extreme violence when I parked behind the Camaro.

Even so, as I turned off my car and set the parking brake, I did take a moment to reflect on the fact that it was too bad Hawk and I were *so over*. I would love to ride in that Camaro.

I got out, rounded the car and grabbed my bag and laptop. Then I walked to the house.

If I were a different kind of woman, in other words if I didn't have my mother's blood in my veins, I would have walked to the house slowly, considering my options, calming myself, building a plan of attack.

I did not do this. I stomped up to the house, opened the door, encountered a wave of strong garlic smells and stormed in.

My parents lived in a big house on a slight rise. Stairs dead ahead leading to a landing with a big window. Huge living room to the left that had a small den off of it at the front of the house, another small conservatory-like space behind the den also off the living room. Enormous kitchen to the right with a big area for the dining room table. Half bath and utility to the back of the kitchen that led to a garage. Wall-to-wall wool carpet throughout except the kitchen, which was tiled. Three bedrooms and two baths upstairs, one shared, one off the master suite.

The garden level was an apartment that they'd rented out since I could remember to a woman named Mrs. Mayhew who had three cats. In her tenure in the apartment the cats had rotated due to kitty death and, once, kitty desertion though Mrs. Mayhew contended it was kitty theft and I was prone to believe her since she treated those cats better than most people treated their children. But Mrs. Mayhew never rotated. She had been old as the hills for as long as I could remember. She was also a silent neighbor. No loud music, no loud parties, no stream of constant visitors. And best of all, she put up with Ginger because she admired Dad, adored Meredith and cared a lot about me.

Before Ginger and I moved out (I never moved home after graduating U of C—Ginger took longer to move out and graduated high school by what we all considered a minor miracle), there were four bedrooms upstairs. After I moved out Dad had turned one of the smaller bedrooms into a master bath. And Dad, being Dad, and Meredith, being Meredith, meant the whole pad was well maintained, well decorated, homey, warm and comfortable.

Like it was right then with a fire burning in the grate of the living room fireplace and candles lit throughout.

But once I'd swept the house with a glance, seeing Dad was entertaining Hawk in the living room and the table was set for four, my gaze swung left again. I took in Dad in his armchair and Hawk on the couch, his back to me, his arm stretched across the back of the couch but his neck twisted to look over his shoulder at me.

I dropped my bags and opened my mouth to shout.

"Honey," Dad got there before me, straightening out of his chair, a bottle of beer in his hand, "why didn't you tell us Hawk was coming to dinner?"

"No bother! No bother!" Meredith's voice came at me from the right where I looked to see her rushing into the room carrying a dishtowel. "We have plenty. He's a big guy but I always make plenty. And Bax giving me the idea last night, I'd already planned for lasagna."

I was forced to delay my tirade when Meredith hit the entry area at the same time Dad did. Dad leaned in to kiss me and I automatically tipped my head back to accept it. Then I turned to Meredith and bent to give her a kiss and she lifted one arm to add a shoulder hug because this was her way.

I straightened and turned to Hawk who was standing at the side of the couch, arms crossed on his chest, exuding badass cool while watching my welcome home.

Then I opened my mouth to yell.

Dad again got there before me when he announced, "I'll just go whip up a cosmo."

I turned to my father. "Can't, Dad. After dinner, I have to work."

His brows shot up. "But we're having a family dinner."

"I'm behind," I explained.

Dad's expression changed and I knew it so well I could sketch a perfect rendition of it while blindfolded (that is, if I could sketch).

Lecture Face.

"Gwendolyn, how many times do I have to tell you, do not procrastinate."

"Your dad's right, honey, whenever you procrastinate you get all stressy and in a bad mood," Meredith put in.

"Don't put off for tomorrow what you can do today," Dad went on as if Meredith didn't speak.

"Then you eat food you shouldn't eat and go out and buy clothes you shouldn't buy and get even more grumpy," Meredith continued like Dad didn't speak.

"Peace of mind. That's what good time management skills bring you, peace of mind," Dad carried on.

"And you wouldn't have to take on so many clients if you didn't have to pay off your credit cards," Meredith kept going.

"I'm always telling you, you need to learn focus," Dad persisted.

"And I'm always telling you, *accessorize*. Accessories are the key. You just need to spend your hard-earned money on a few, fabulous core pieces in your wardrobe and you can make an entirely new outfit by just switching out a scarf!" Meredith declared then finished, "And scarves cost *way* less than owning ten little black dresses."

"I own *thirteen* little black dresses," I amended because, seriously, it was important to keep track.

"See!" Meredith cried.

It occurred to me then that Hawk was watching me, a thirty-three-year-old woman who had been taking care of herself for over a decade, get lectured like I was a teenager about the same time a buzzer went off in the kitchen.

"Bread's done!" Meredith exclaimed.

"Soup's up," Dad added on a smile aimed in Hawk's direction. "You can thank me later, son, for the joy you are about to experience."

"Everyone to the table," Meredith ordered, hurrying toward the kitchen.

"I need to talk to Hawk," I announced.

"Later, honey, Mer's garlic bread waits for no man… or woman." Dad grinned at me and moved toward the table.

My head turned toward Hawk to see him moving my way. Robbed of my opportunity to lay into him and maybe explain we were over in sign language or go into a trance and speak in tongues or possibly tap out my message in Morse code, hoping one or the other would penetrate his macho man anti-communication fortress, I decided to communicate my extreme unhappiness by glaring.

Hawk ignored my glare. I knew he was doing this when he got close, hooked me around the neck, yanked me to his side and propelled me to the table, head bent to my ear where he murmured, "See you're stressy and in a bad mood."

He lifted his head. I looked up at him to see he was grinning.

"Just curious, but do you know how much contract killers cost and, incidentally, would you have a recommendation?"

We had made it to the table when I uttered my comment and Hawk stopped us, turned me full frontal into his arms, threw his head back and burst out laughing.

I stared, completely forgetting my snit.

He had a great laugh. It was deep and resonant and I could tell it came straight from the gut.

Then, still laughing, he bent his head and kissed me. No tongue but it was a kiss, a definite *kiss*, hard and longish and right in front of my dad while standing at my family's dinner table.

When his mouth broke from mine and he lifted his head, I blinked then snapped, "You can't kiss me in my parents' house *in front of my dad!*"

"Just did, Sweet Pea," Hawk returned.

"Well, don't do it again." I was still snapping.

"Then don't be so hilarious," Hawk shot back. "You make me laugh, babe, I'm warnin' you now, when I'm done, I'm gonna kiss you."

"I didn't mean to be hilarious," I explained snottily.

"Well, you were."

"How can I control it if I don't know when you're going to find something funny?"

"Guess you better brace, babe, 'cause, the way you are, it could happen at any time."

I opened my mouth to retort when I realized we had an audience.

My head turned and I saw Dad smiling what I knew by sheer instinct (because I certainly hadn't seen it before) was a father's knowing, contented smile, warm with the knowledge his daughter had hooked Mr. Very, Very Right.

I also saw Meredith standing next to Dad wearing hot pads on her hands, carrying a tray of lasagna, sporting her own smile that stated plainly she'd married Mr. Very, Very

Right and she was pleased as punch her beloved stepdaughter had followed in her footsteps.

Totally...flipping...*screwed*.

I broke away from Hawk and declared, "I think I'll take that cosmo now."

Dad chuckled, moved toward the fridge and stated, "Don't think so, honey. You have to work later." He kept moving but looked over his shoulder at Hawk. "Another beer?"

Another? Beer?

How long had he been there and since when did muscular, body-like-a-temple hot guys drink beer?

"Yeah," Hawk replied, and I looked up at him.

"You drink beer?"

He looked down at me. "Yeah," he repeated.

"Won't that give you a gut?" I asked.

"Life's short, babe, you gotta live it every once in a while, and you don't drink water with homemade lasagna and garlic bread."

Well, his mother was half Italian; he would know.

I decided to ignore Hawk so I turned to the kitchen. "I'll help get the food."

"Thanks, sweetie," Meredith mumbled, placing the lasagna on a curly, wrought iron hot plate in the middle of the table.

Dad got me a diet grape, himself and Hawk a fresh beer and replenished Meredith's red wine. Meredith and I loaded up the table with fresh, hot garlic bread, a huge salad and every bottle of salad dressing known to man. Then everyone passed the food around and loaded up their plates while commenting on how good the food looked and smelled. At least Dad and I did this, Hawk just loaded up his plate.

I was mentally preparing for the Ginger discussion by

shoveling lasagna in my mouth when Meredith asked, "So, how did you two meet?"

I choked on hot lasagna and my eyes flew across the table to Hawk.

Hawk's dimples popped out.

I frantically chewed in hopes I could speak before Hawk said something that might make my head explode or worse, my parents', and as I did this Hawk's brows went up in a clear challenge.

Meredith spoke into the void. "Was it romantic? I bet it was romantic."

Meredith would bet that. Except for Ginger coloring her world gray every once in a while, Meredith's world was rose-hued. This had a lot to do with Meredith being Meredith, rarely having a bad day and always looking on the bright side of life.

This also had a lot to do with the fact that Meredith was and always would be head over heels in love with my father. She'd met the man of her dreams and she knew it the instant she saw him. That was why she fainted about two seconds later. And her fainting was why Dad caught her. She woke up cradled in his arms, her ass in his lap while he gently stroked her hair out of her face and looked down at her like a prince would gaze upon his newly revived princess.

I knew this because I was there when it happened, it made my toes curl then, and anytime I recalled it, it still made my toes curl. It was the most romantic thing I'd ever seen, and we were in a fast food burger joint.

Hawk and my meeting was *nothing* like that.

But Meredith would want it to be that way, not for her, for me. And I loved her more than life so, when I swallowed, as stupid and embarrassing as it was going to be, I gave her what she wanted.

And what I gave her, incidentally, was also the truth.

With my eyes glued to her, my heart racing and my mind trying to pretend Hawk wasn't there, I said, "When Tracy was working at Club, and screwing up the drinks all the time and breaking all the glasses, I was there one night because she needed moral support. I was drinking at the bar and suddenly I felt something strange, like I knew something big was about to happen. Then I looked at the door and I did it the minute Hawk walked in. I saw him and I knew what that big thing was because I thought right away, 'That's the man for me, that man is the perfect man for me. If I could choose any man in the world, it would be that man I would choose for me.' Then I drank at the bar while Hawk ate dinner. I tried to get his attention and failed. So when he got ready to leave, it hurt because I didn't want him to leave without him leaving with me. But he didn't leave without me. He came up, put his hand on my back and talked to me. And when I felt his hand at my back and turned to see him standing close, I felt like every wish I'd ever wished was granted." Meredith was staring at me, lips parted, eyes bright, and I finished, "So that's how we met."

Meredith's eyes were bright because they were filling with tears. She kept staring at me then she sucked in breath, looked down the table at Dad then back at me.

"That's sweet," she whispered.

Dad cleared his throat.

I looked down at my plate and forked into my salad. I tried, I really did, to keep my eyes to my plate, but even though I managed to keep my head bowed, my eyes lifted and I glanced at Hawk.

The minute I did, my eyes dropped back to my plate but my breath came out of me in a whoosh and the look on his face, even catching only a glimpse of it, was burned on my brain in a way I knew the scar of that burn would live there forever.

This was because, when I looked at him, Hawk didn't look like Hawk or not the man I was growing to learn was Hawk.

Hawk looked like the Hawk of my daydreams. His face was gentle but his eyes were intense, heated. Those black eyes were working, they were actually speaking, and I refused to allow what they were saying to penetrate. Still, I felt them burning into me even as I shoved salad into my mouth and looked anywhere but him.

"So...um...Hawk," Dad said into the silence, "did you see any action when you served?"

I heard Hawk's deep voice answer but I had decided to concentrate on shoveling food in my mouth, chewing and swallowing without getting tomato sauce on my tee, lettuce stuck in my teeth or strangling on an unchewed bite of garlic bread, so even though I wanted to know Hawk's answer, I didn't listen.

As if sensing my mood, Meredith quietly engaged me in conversation about the books I was editing while Dad and Hawk bonded over Army stories. Lucky for me, this took us to the end of dinner, which didn't last long and also didn't include me explaining things about Ginger.

Meredith was apologizing for not having made any dessert when we all stood and Hawk announced dinner tasted great but he had "shit to do."

Then his eyes cut to me. "Babe, walk me to my car."

I didn't know if this was an order or a request. I really, really wanted to run to a closet and barricade myself in it because after I told that story, I really, really didn't want to be alone with Hawk. But I couldn't do that with Dad and Meredith watching so I nodded.

Farewells, thank yous and come agains were called as Hawk and I moved to the door. Then we were through it. Then the door closed firmly behind us, the latch making a definitive noise. This was Dad's way of giving Hawk privacy, telling him he and Meredith were going to let Hawk and me walk to the car without spectators when I knew Dad and Meredith were *so* going to watch through the curtains (or at least Meredith was). But at this point I didn't care. At this point I felt so self-conscious it was a burn emanating from deep inside me as another burn, the one in my brain, the one that carried that look I saw on his face, made its presence felt.

Therefore, I had no reaction when Hawk took my hand and walked me down my parents' walk to his Camaro. I had no reaction when he used my hand to position me with my back to his car. I also had no reaction when he pinned me in with his big body and his hands settled on either side of my neck. I didn't even have a reaction when his thumbs put gentle pressure on the undersides of my jaw and forced me to look up at him.

In the cold, February dark of a Colorado evening, I saw his black eyes lit by streetlamps and finally had a reaction. And that reaction was to instigate avoidance tactics without delay. And the avoidance tactics I decided on were picking a fight.

"I didn't tell them about Ginger," I stated hurriedly. "I need to set up my laptop and get in a few hours of work but because I didn't do it at dinner, now I have to go in there and explain things about Ginger. That's gonna suck. I had it all planned out. I was all psyched up. Now I've totally lost my mojo because of you. You ruined my plan by showing up."

Clearly not feeling like fighting, Hawk took no umbrage and his thumb swept the curve of my jaw as he replied, "I briefed your dad before dinner. You can go in and get right to work."

I blinked up at him. "You briefed Dad?"

"Yeah."

"What did you say?"

Hawk answered an answer that was far from complete, "He knows more than you, you know more than your stepmom."

"What does that mean?"

"That means your stepmom doesn't need to know the shit swirling around your sister, or at least she's not gonna hear it from me. You already know too much and aren't gonna know any more. Your father needs to know it all so I told him and he agrees with me about you and your stepmom."

I didn't know where to start so I started in the middle.

"You told Dad everything?"

"He asked questions, I answered, so . . . yeah."

I wasn't sure how I felt about that. What I was sure about was that I couldn't turn back time so I had to let it go.

"How was he?"

His thumbs went away from my jaw as his hands slid down to rest where my neck met my shoulders.

"Not happy but not surprised," he answered.

I knew how Dad felt because I felt the same way.

"How did you keep this from Meredith?"

"She was cookin'. I asked for some time, your dad took me into his den and I closed the door. We got out and she didn't ask. Their conversation, if they have one, can be private. She's his woman, that's his call."

I had no verbal response to this but I felt gratitude. Hawk was right, Dad would want to know and he wouldn't be happy not knowing. Hawk was also right, Meredith shouldn't know unless Dad felt she could handle it and he should tell her himself.

Even though I felt gratitude, I didn't express it. Instead my eyes slid to the side.

"Babe," Hawk called when they did, and my eyes slid back. "What you said earlier—"

Oh no. We were *not* going to talk about earlier. I'd gladly walk barefoot on a bed of hot coals and at the end of that journey take a swan dive into the boiling lava at the mouth of a volcano before I talked about earlier.

Therefore, instantly I tried to jerk my neck away and move out from in front of him, but he moved faster, pushing in closer, pinning me to the car. His hands came up to cup my jaw, forcing my face to tip to him.

"Babe," he repeated when my eyes stared at his ear.

Guess I had to talk about it.

"I was making it up," I lied to his ear. "Meredith is a romantic. I couldn't tell her how we really are. Not then with Dad there, not privately, *not ever.*"

"Babe," he said yet again.

"It's not a big deal, or at least it isn't now. When you disappear, it will be then. Meredith will be sad, but I'll handle it."

"Sweet Pea, look at me," he ordered quietly.

My eyes slid to his.

"I asked to be seated in that booth," he informed me.

I sucked in breath at what he might be saying.

Then I breathed it out on a, "What?"

"Clocked you before you clocked me, Gwen."

I stared up at him, incapable of speech.

"Saw you through the windows as I was walkin' up. Your friend was with you and you were laughin'."

Oh my God.

His head dipped closer and I held my breath, feeling his eyes burning into mine.

"Still see you," he whispered.

Oh my God!

His thumb swept my cheekbone then his fingers went back into my hair as his other hand slid down my neck, over my shoulder and around my back, his head came down and he kissed me.

This kiss *was* with tongue, lots of it, his *and* mine. It was wet, it was deep and it lasted a really long time.

As usual I was holding on when he lifted his head and my body was quivering in places he could feel and in better places only I could feel and my private places were *way* better.

"Get to work, Sweet Pea," he murmured against my mouth, pulled me gently away from his car, bleeped the locks, opened the door, folded in, fired up the Camaro and purred away.

I'd long since lost sight of his taillights but I was still standing there, a residual quiver dying away, my mind stuck on one thought.

He could still see me laughing.

CHAPTER NINE

Squishiness

I FELT THE intense warmth of Hawk's hand at the small of my back and my eyes opened. I'd been dead asleep. I felt confusion with a hint of excitement before his weight hit the bed and he turned me to him.

Then his arms closed around me, pressed my body the length of his and my confusion cleared.

I was in my parents' house.

Before the shadow of his descending head hit its intended target, my hand shot up and covered his mouth.

"What are you doing?" I hissed through a whisper.

His hand came up, fingers wrapping around my wrist, and he pulled it away.

"What do I always do?" he asked back, also whispering.

"You broke in my parents' house!" I was still whispering and hissing.

"Yeah," he replied like this was perfectly okay.

"We can't have sex when my parents are practically right next door!"

He was silent, his body still, then he moved fast, his face disappearing in my neck as his arms got super tight and he rolled me to my back with his torso on mine. It was then I heard his muffled laughter.

"Hawk!" I snapped, my hands at his sleek-skin-over-hard-muscle bared shoulders, pushing back.

His head came up and his weight came off me as he rested both forearms into the bed on either side of me.

He looked at me through the shadows. "Babe, not gonna fuck you," he murmured.

"You just said, 'What do I always do?' And we always have sex," I returned.

"Yeah, babe, but it starts with a kiss."

Oh. This was true.

I stared at his shadowed head through the dark. "Then what are you doing here?"

"You're here."

"So?" I prompted.

One of his hands came to my face and I felt his fingers glide along my hairline before they moved into the hair at the side of my head.

"Last night someone targeted you and got close enough to you, he freaked you out. When that happened, my boys were eight minutes away and I was an hour away."

"You're telling me something I know, Hawk."

"That's not gonna happen again."

He had sounded amused, at first, then informative. His last sounded like a vow.

My stomach got squishy.

I resisted the squishiness and reminded him, "Dad's right next door."

"He's a man who can take care of himself and you, Sweet Pea, but there are people out there who don't know that. They see my ride sitting at the curb, they'll think twice before they fuck with anyone in this house."

Holy crap. He was protecting me. And Dad. And
Meredith.

Wow.

"So you're here just to, um...*be* here?" I asked.

"That and make sure you sleep."

Uh.

Wow.

It was getting harder and harder to battle the squishiness.

He went on, "And get some sleep with you. I'm fuckin'
wiped."

Uh.

Wow.

SuperHawk, World's Greatest Lover and Major Badass,
got wiped.

Interesting.

"Babe," he called.

My body jerked out of its amazement and I asked,
"What?"

"You gonna do that?"

"What?"

"Sleep."

No. No, I was never going to get back to sleep. I'd got my
second wind after standing in the cold when he left earlier
and I'd managed to blow through a huge amount of work,
staying awake and fresh until my concentration started wan-
ing around a quarter to midnight. I'd closed down and hit
the sack feeling an exhaustion I knew would mean I'd sleep
deep. The minute my head hit the pillow, I was out like a
light.

Now I was wide awake.

"Yes," I lied.

His head dropped and he did something new, something
he'd never done except in the lead up to something else. And

that was to lightly kiss the indention at the base of my throat in the middle of my collarbone.

Then he slid off me, turned me to my side, curved his body into mine, hitching one of my knees up with his so his heavy, warm thigh was resting on mine. His arm stayed tight around my belly, he leaned in and kissed the skin behind my ear, then his head settled on the pillow.

Guess Cabe Delgado didn't verbalize his goodnight, he acted it out.

Mm.

I lay there in the warm curve of his body under his arm, feeling his breath on my neck thinking, *Holy shit, MM is spooning me!*

Tracy would do cartwheels of pure joy for a mile if she knew this. Cam might have a heart attack.

I didn't know what to do except let the feeling my body was communicating to my brain penetrate and that feeling was *I really, really like this.*

My ex-husband Scott never spooned. I spooned his back but he never cuddled into me. Even after sex. He was a slam, bam, thank you ma'am type of guy. He took his orgasm, pulled out, rolled away, turned off the light and fell asleep.

And he snored.

He didn't cuddle. He didn't sweet-talk. He didn't do any of that. Not even in the hopes of priming me for round two. With Scott, there was never a round two. This was, I would discover later, because, by the time he had sex with me, he was too exhausted to do it again because he'd already had sex with someone else that day. Or two someone elses. Maybe even three. Who knew? That was how much of a horndog he was.

Hawk's weight settled into me, his arm relaxed, his breathing evened and I knew he was asleep. Asleep spooning me.

What did I do with this? How did I make us be over when I *liked* this? And what he said outside by his car. And the fact he didn't like the thought that I or my family might be targeted and he did something about it.

This was not a man who would crush Troy like a bug and boss me around. This was a man you'd make up in a daydream.

And this was what filled my head until it only was drifting through my head until my body started to relax into Hawk's and then I fell asleep.

I could have been in dream world for a while but it felt like seconds before I felt Hawk's arm get so tight it nearly hurt, cutting off my breathing. My eyes opened and in that instant the heat of him was gone.

I rolled, seeing his shadow by the bed. He was pulling on his cargos.

I got up on an elbow and opened my mouth to say something when he moved again, his knee hit the bed, his finger rested lightly on my lips and I watched as his shadowy head shook in the negative once.

Uh-oh.

Then he was gone.

About a nanosecond later I heard a scuffle, some exerted gasps, then a hard, loud thump as if someone's body hit the wall.

Then I heard my sister Ginger's unmistakable shriek, "*What the fuck!*"

I threw back the covers and leaped from the bed, seeing the lights going on in the hall.

"Ginger! Jesus!" I heard my dad yell before I hit the hall to see Ginger pinned against the wall with Hawk's hand in her chest. Hawk standing in cargoes with the top button undone, Dad in the hall wearing only pajama bottoms staring angrily at Ginger, and Meredith joining late, like me. Unlike me she was wearing one of her long, lacy, satin negligees, what she always wore, even when I was a kid, though some of them were short, and I always thought she was quite simply *it* because of her sexy nightwear.

"What are you doing here?" Dad asked Ginger, his eyes narrowed on her, apparently unsurprised and unconcerned that Hawk was standing in his hallway in the middle of the night, bare-chested and barefoot with the top button on his cargos undone.

For my part, I was unsurprised that Ginger was dressed like Darla had been yesterday except she was wearing a camisole laced up the front. It was at least one, maybe two sizes too small so the lacing gaped and it showed skin and a hint of boob. She also wasn't wearing fishnets but tights that had big holes and runs in them everywhere. And she also really needed a refresh on her makeup since her mascara and eyeliner were giving her raccoon eyes. Lastly, her curly strawberry blonde hair was the definition of a rat's nest.

My sister. Serious skankage.

"I grew up here," Ginger snapped back, and Hawk stepped back, dropping his arm and moving to me.

"Yeah, but the last time you were here I think I made myself clear you weren't welcome back," Dad returned. My eyes slid to Meredith to see she was standing there, both arms wrapped around her belly, her pixie-pretty face pale and her lip quivering.

Seeing that, my gaze moved back and I mentally speared my sister with imaginary giant African tribal lances.

"Fuck, I just need a fuckin' shower and somethin' to eat. I've got some shit goin' down. You can't even let me have a fuckin' shower?" Ginger shot back.

"Mouth, Ginger," I warned because Meredith hated it when we cursed. She said ladies didn't curse. Of course, I cursed in my head and sometimes they came out of my mouth but I *never* did it in front of Meredith.

Ginger leaned toward me and hissed, "Fuck you, *Gwennie*."

"It's the middle of the night," Dad butted in to inform her.

Her head jerked toward Dad. "So fuckin' what?" Ginger returned.

"Ginger, remember who you're speaking to," I snapped at her, and her eyes shot to me.

"Fuck you again." Her eyes swept me then she asked, "What're you even *doin'* here?"

"Escapin' your shit, which leaked to her house last night," Hawk replied.

Ginger's eyes sliced to him then to me then to Hawk then to Dad and Meredith.

"I see, I'm your daughter, I got shit goin' down and I can't even have any of your *precious* water to take a *fuckin'* shower. But Gwennie, sweet, wonderful, *perfect Gwennie*, she can crash here with her fuck buddy," Ginger said to them.

I sucked in breath as I felt Hawk's body get tight beside mine.

Meredith snapped, "Ginger!"

"What?" Ginger snapped back. "You're givin' me shit about bein' here in the middle of the night but Gwen, perfect Gwen, she can play with her fuck toy right next door and you don't give a shit?" she asked.

I sucked in another breath as fury radiated in a swell from Hawk, Dad's face got so red I feared he'd have a heart attack but Meredith, she moved. She walked right up to Ginger and slapped her hard across the face, snapping Ginger's head to the side.

Everyone moved then because Ginger lunged to attack Meredith. Dad pulled Meredith to safety and Hawk pinned Ginger against the wall again with his hand at the same time he held me back from getting in a hair-pulling, bitch-slapping fight with my sister, doing this with his other hand in my belly.

I stopped pushing against him when Ginger fought him, kicking out at his legs with her feet (and not connecting) and tearing at his forearm with her tatty, peeling black-painted nails, which I feared would inflict some damage. He held her against the wall with one hand, his face set and tight, his jaw so hard it looked like it would shatter.

"Get your hand off me!" she shrieked.

"Calm the fuck down," Hawk returned.

"I said *get your fuckin' hand off me!*" Ginger repeated on a screech.

Then we heard it. Glass shattering. Everyone went still and stayed still except Hawk who, after his preliminary freeze, sprinted to the stairs. That was when we heard two more noises, glass breaking much quieter, then two identical whooshes followed by two muted booms.

Then we saw the unmistakable dance of firelight from the stairs.

"*Hawk!*" I screamed, not thinking and dashing to the stairs.

Dad caught me around the belly with a strong arm and pulled me back. He tossed me behind him, lifted a finger in my face and ordered, "Stay here!"

Then he raced down the stairs.

"Bax!" Meredith cried but I moved.

I turned to her and yelled, "Go! Put on some shoes and a jacket. Get some for Dad." When Meredith didn't move, I screamed, "Go, go, *go!*"

Meredith turned and ran to her room and I turned to Ginger.

"Be smart," I snapped. "Stay here."

She glared at me and returned, "Bite me."

I didn't have time for Ginger so I didn't give her any. I ran to the guest bedroom, pulled on my boots and grabbed Hawk's boots and tee. I was turning to leave the bedroom when I collided with something and that something was Hawk. He had a blanket and he threw it around me, wrapping me up before I could twitch, then I was lifted into his arms and we were moving.

I smelled smoke and felt heat. Then I smelled fresh air and felt cold. I was put down on my feet and Hawk's arms left me. I struggled with the blanket, still carrying his tee and boots, and got my head clear just in time to see him race back into the house, barefoot and bare-chested. I shrugged off the blanket, dropped his boots and tee in the yard and rushed to the side of house, down the incline and jumped down the short wall to the walkway to Mrs. Mayhew's apartment. I banged on her door and shouted because sometimes she didn't hear too well. I kept doing it until the outside light went on and her door opened.

Peering up at me from her old-lady height, her blue hair looking like it normally looked, not like she'd been sleeping on it, she breathed, "Gwendolyn, what on—?"

I cut her off. "No time, Mrs. M, get a jacket, put on a pair of shoes. Quick, quick, quick! There's a fire upstairs."

I didn't wait for her to obey. I ran into her house, shooing cats out, and darted to her bedroom. I had her fleecy, old-lady robe in my hands by the time she got to me and I threw it at her then rushed to the closet. I pulled out a pair of fur-lined snow boots, hooked her arm with mine and scuttled her out the door.

When we were outside she stopped and held on to me to keep herself steady while she tugged on her boots. By the time we made it to the front of the house, Meredith was there, a cell to her ear, her body wrapped in a blanket. But I stopped and stared when I saw Dog, of all freaking people, with Dad's front garden hose going full throttle, aiming it at flames coming out of the front window of the house.

"Where's Dad and Hawk?" I shouted at Meredith. She took the phone from her ear and replied, "They're in there. Bax got the fire extinguishers."

Shit!

My father had been a volunteer firefighter for ten years. He had fire extinguishers everywhere. He *and* Hawk were *so totally* the kind of macho idiots who would try to battle a blaze with fucking *fire extinguishers*.

I sucked in breath, told myself panic wouldn't help anyone, nor would a screaming hissy fit, both of which I wanted very badly to do.

Then I pulled a quaking Mrs. Mayhew closer to my side and asked Meredith, "Ginger?"

Meredith shook her head and her eyes slid to the side of the house where the tree that Ginger used regularly to sneak out of the house was planted. Dad had threatened to cut that tree down a million times, but since there was another one on the other side of the house, Meredith refused to allow it, said the house would look wonky.

Now, even though my sister was a *complete and total bitch*, I was glad he didn't because I knew she escaped down that tree.

This clashed with my thoughts that she took off and left her mother and me up there and didn't say a word or think of another person in her family. Especially after my childhood home was firebombed because of her *fucking shit*.

I held Mrs. Mayhew closer and stared at the house, willing Dad and Hawk to come out as Dog kept the hose aimed in the window.

The sirens could be heard and the firemen came. It took them approximately a millisecond to get their shit sorted and start battling the blaze. Dad came out wearing a coat and boots but Hawk emerged from the dancing flames still bare-chested and barefoot.

I rushed to his boots and tee and met him with them in my hands.

He threw an arm around me and guided me to the sidewalk where my parents and Mrs. Mayhew were standing, now with Dog.

Hawk yanked his tee over his head but spoke as he tugged it down his abs.

"Wanna tell me why the fuck you're here?" he clipped at Dog.

"Orders," Dog replied.

"Gwen or Ginger?" Hawk asked.

"Gwen," Dog answered.

Hawk's face got tight but I was too busy freaking out because it was also covered in soot.

Therefore I got close and put my hands on his abs.

"Baby," I whispered, leaning carefully into him and looking up, "you okay?"

He looked down at me. "Yeah," he grunted.

"You sure? You're not burned anywhere?"

He had looked down at me but it took him a minute to focus on me.

His arm slid around my shoulders and he pulled me closer.

"I'm good, Gwen," he muttered to me, then his eyes went to the flaming house.

My eyes went to the house too. Then my arms slid around his middle, I pressed in close and I rested my cheek on his pectoral. That was when his other arm closed around me.

Neighbors came out, Dad, Meredith and Mrs. Mayhew moved close, and we watched the firefighters battle the blaze.

CHAPTER TEN

Pros and Cons

I WOKE UP but kept my eyes closed as I lay in my bed feeling bright, Denver sunlight against my eyelids.

Then I reached out a hand and slid it across my bed.

I was alone, Hawk was gone.

I slid my hand back, tucked both under my cheek and curled my legs into my belly as I opened my eyes.

There were people in my house, the kitchen. I knew that because my bedroom was over the kitchen and I heard low murmurs drifting up from there.

This was likely Meredith and the commandos. She was probably making them homemade donuts they would refuse to eat and regaling them with stories of my former boyfriends, none of whom, except Hawk, she actually liked but she never told me that until I'd dumped them or they'd dumped me.

Dad was probably at work. His house had been fire-bombed, he'd battled the blaze then he'd watched firefighters battle the blaze then he'd talked to the police then one of Hawk's boys came in an SUV. Hawk loaded Meredith, Dad, Mrs. Mayhew and me in it and Hawk's boy (this one, who looked half wrestler, half giant, was named Mo) whisked

Mrs. Mayhew to her friend Erma's place and Dad, Meredith and me to my house. Dad had taken a shower while Meredith and I pulled out the couch in my office and made the bed. Dad and Meredith hit the sack, I hit the sack and sometime later, likely right before the break of dawn, I felt Hawk hit the sack next to me. He'd rolled into me, curled deep, but I fell back to sleep before I knew whether or not he was in dreamland.

Even with all of this I suspected Dad was still at work. The entire eastern seaboard could fall into the sea and Dad would go to work then get on the phone, call all his men and ask why they were still at home, grieving over loved ones and the loss of national monuments as the country came to grips with a colossal tragedy. Then he'd tell them they should be on the site, there was work to be done.

Of course, he only had his pajama bottoms and coat, but that wouldn't stop him.

I closed my eyes and sighed.

Detective Mitch Lawson had showed last night. He'd talked to Hawk first, then Dad and Hawk, then Meredith and me. When he got to Meredith and me he mostly wanted to know if we were all right and didn't ask probing questions. Then he'd given my arm a reassuring squeeze as he gazed into my eyes, his eyes intense (but still soulful), then he took off.

Dog had disappeared prior to the cops and Lawson showing up. This was why Hawk didn't come with us to my house. Hawk went to find Dog. I didn't know why but I didn't ask questions. I was in an extremely rare Do As I'm Told Mood so when Hawk got bossy, I didn't give him lip. I did exactly what he ordered me to do. I got in his boy's SUV, got my family to warmth and safety, got them settled and went to bed.

On that thought, my eyes tipped down the bed and I saw Hawk walk into the room. This surprised me. I thought he'd be out doing Hawk things, covertly gathering intel for top-secret assignments, interrogating suspects in windowless rooms made of cement, beating infidels into submission, stuff like that.

It also surprised me he had on a fresh pair of Army green cargo pants and a skin-tight, but clean, long-sleeved burgundy tee. Guess his boys delivered changes of clothes. I wondered if they took orders and had credit at Nordstrom. If they did, this would be on the pro side of my Should I Explore Things with Cabe "Hawk" Delgado List.

Hawk's eyes didn't leave me as he walked to the bed, sat on his side and leaned deep, his torso across the bed, his forearm in it, his face ending up close to mine.

"How you doin', Sweet Pea?" he asked quietly.

"Can you do me a favor?" I asked quietly back.

"Depends," he answered.

Figured.

"Next time you're in a house that's firebombed, can you pause to put on a shirt and shoes before you sally forth into the inferno?"

I watched from close as he grinned and his dimples popped out.

Then his eyebrows went up. "Sally forth?"

"Okay, you didn't sally, you raced. You know what I mean."

Something about his face changed and I couldn't put my finger on it because his eyes moved to my hair. Then he fell to his front, bracing his weight on his opposite forearm as he lifted his other hand. He ran his fingers along my hairline, down around my ear and he shifted the hair off my neck. Then his eyes came to mine.

I held my breath because they were heated and intense like at dinner last night.

"Yeah, I know what you mean," he whispered. I wanted to tear my eyes from his, I really did. I just couldn't. "You were worried about me."

"You were fighting a fire in a pair of cargo pants," I explained, trying to sound casual and probably failing.

His heated, black eyes held mine for a long time. So long I felt my lungs start to burn.

Then he said, "All right, next time I'm in a house that's firebombed, I'll put on a shirt and boots before I tackle the inferno."

"Thanks," I whispered.

His eyes moved over my face then he asked, "Now that we got that outta the way, you wanna answer my question?"

"What question?"

"How you doin'?"

"I'm fine."

His eyes held mine again for several long seconds before he whispered, "Liar."

"I am," I decreed.

"Gwen, baby, you're curled in a protective ball again."

Shit. I was.

I uncurled and pushed up, taking pillows with me so I could rest against my headboard. Hawk moved too, pulling himself up and in so his hip was beside mine and his weight was leaning into his hand on the other side of me.

"Is Meredith downstairs?" I asked.

"Yeah," he answered.

"Is she making homemade donuts?" I asked.

"Is that a hopeful question or a serious one?" he asked in return.

I had to admit, it was hopeful, but I would only admit that to myself.

Therefore, I didn't speak.

He grinned again and answered, "No, she's makin' eggs and bacon."

Meredith made good eggs and bacon but her donuts were better.

"Do I have eggs and bacon to make?"

"Apparently, since she's doin' it in her nightgown and your robe and she doesn't have a car and neither do you so it's doubtful she went out and hit a store."

I probably did have bacon and eggs. At least eggs, they were a standard ingredient in all kinds of cookie dough.

"Where's Dad?" I asked.

"Some guy named Rick came an hour ago with a change of clothes then took your Dad to work."

See!

"My dad's a nut," I muttered.

He lifted a hand and nabbed a lock of my hair, tugging it, then his hand fell.

I thought that was a sweet thing to do.

Hawk could be sweet. Hawk was a cuddler. Hawk saved my life or, at least, delivered me safely out of a burning building.

All three for the pro side of the Should I Explore Things with Cabe "Hawk" Delgado List.

Shit.

That was what I was thinking before he asked a question that would explain why he was being sweet.

"You want the good news or the bad news?"

Great. There was bad news.

"Can I have the good news and you tell me the bad news in the next millennium?"

"Sure," he agreed, and I didn't think that was good.

"The bad news," I mumbled.

His face got serious. "Ginger got away."

My face, I was sure, got confused. "What?"

"She got away."

"From what? The fire?"

"That and the guys who firebombed your house to smoke her out."

Oh shit.

"They didn't firebomb my house to kill her?"

"Babe, my car was at your curb."

"So?"

"You think they'd think I'd let anyone in that house die?"

I crossed my arms on my chest and stared at him. "I know you're a step down from superhero, Hawk, but seriously?"

He grinned. "You think I'm a step down from super-hero?"

Oh *shit!* Time to cover.

"I was being facetious," I informed him.

His grin got bigger. "No, you think I'm a step down from superhero."

"Don't you have good news to tell me?" I prompted in order to change the subject.

"Probably it was that night I gave you the triple orgasm." He stayed on the current subject and my mouth dropped open.

Then I snapped it shut to ask, "What?"

"That night when I did that thing with my mouth and fin-gers and you—"

"I didn't have a triple orgasm, Hawk," I snapped, but the truth was, I did.

"Babe, you did, I counted."

"No, it was just really long," I lied.

"Gwen, don't you think I know when you stop comin' and start again?"

"No, I don't think you know," I retorted.

"It happens enough," he observed, and he was right.

There was one for the con side of the Should I Explore Things with Cabe "Hawk" Delgado List. Hawk was arrogant.

"Hello?" I called. "Good news? Or, maybe you can tell me why Ginger getting away is bad news."

He grinned at me then finally changed the subject.

"Ginger getting away is bad news because, I had Ginger under my thumb, I could have handed her to Lawson. Instead, I tackled the inferno in your dad's livin' room and the bitch got away."

I felt my brows draw together. "Hand her to Lawson?"

"Only safe place for her to be is with the police. She cuts a deal, they cut her jail time, or, if she's got half the shit they think she's got, they hand her to the Feds who give her a new identity. Ginger Kidd testifies then she disappears but she does it breathin'."

"The Feds?" I whispered.

At my whisper and possibly the terrified look on my face, Hawk's face gentled. "Babe, you know she's in serious shit."

"Yes," I confirmed. "But *the Feds?*"

"Her shit is *serious*," he repeated with variation.

I looked at my lap and whispered, "Damn."

Hawk lifted my head with his thumb and finger at my chin until my eyes met his, then he dropped his hand and went on. "I had her under my thumb, they wouldn't have made a play for her. They wanted to smoke her out and get me occupied. They succeeded in that."

"She was only there a few minutes. Did they have enough time to conceive and execute this dire plan?"

"They're resourceful."

That wasn't good news.

"But she got away," I finished.

"She got away," Hawk affirmed.

"And Dog?" I asked.

"Found him. He's allergic to the police so he took off. He arrived after the fire started, doin' a drive-by, keepin' an eye on you for Tack. He didn't see anything, not even Ginger, or she'd be at the Chaos compound right about now."

"Keeping an eye on me for Tack?"

His look shifted to unhappy. "Told you, babe, you do not want Tack's attention, but you got it."

"I got it, I know, but I don't *get* it. Why was Dog doing a drive-by?"

"Tack's orders, keepin' you safe."

I stared at him.

Then I breathed, "Keeping me safe?"

He stared back at me.

Then he asked, "Babe, seriously?"

"I met him once," I reminded Hawk.

"Twice," Hawk reminded me.

"Okay, twice," I amended.

"Yeah," Hawk agreed.

"So, I don't get it. I barely know him. Why would he send Dog out to keep an eye on me?"

Hawk stared at me again then he repeated, "Babe, seriously?"

I threw up my hands and straightened in the bed, crossing my legs under me. "Yes, Hawk, seriously. What is *up* with *that?*"

His eyes narrowed before he asked, "Do you remember our conversation last night?"

Uh-oh.

"Which one?" I asked hesitantly.

"The one where I told you I clocked you before I even walked into the restaurant where you were sittin', entertaining every man in the room."

"I wasn't entertaining every man in the room!" I snapped.

"Babe, you were."

"Was not."

"You were."

I leaned in a bit. "Was *not*."

"Sweet Pea, you were flippin' your hair, fidgeting on your stool, suckin' straws, but just your laugh is enough to make a man's dick get hard."

Another con. Sort of. I mean, all that stuff I was doing for *him* and I was certainly glad to know, after all this time, he noticed, but I wasn't going to tell him that.

And it was nice he liked my laugh.

Moving on.

"And this has to do with Tack...?" I prompted.

"Are you not seein' the pattern here?"

"Uh...no."

"Were you *not* in your yard yesterday with Lawson, Tack and me?"

Uh-oh.

"I was there," I snapped.

"And were you *not* in your livin' room when your boy Troy showed?"

Hmm. I was seeing his point.

"That doesn't count. I've known Troy—"

Hawk cut me off. "Counts for him."

He was probably right.

Hawk continued. "Counts for me."

I crossed my arms on my chest. "Can you get to the point?"

"The point is, you're the kind of woman whose furnace breaks down, she calls you, you haul your ass over to her house to fix it, even if you're in the middle of a game."

Oh shit. That had happened. I'd called Troy right in the middle of a Broncos game.

God, I *hated* it that Hawk knew everything about me.

Another con!

"And you're also the kind of woman who a man sees curled in a protective ball, he's moved to do what he can to make certain that doesn't happen again."

I felt my eyes get squinty. "Is that why you're here?"

He shook his head. "I'm here 'cause when you come, you come hard, you don't hold back but you do hold on and you do it tight. I'm here because, when you call me baby in this bed, I feel it in my dick. And I'm here because you don't hesitate throwing attitude when every other woman I know doesn't have the guts to say boo to me. Seein' you scared and wantin' to do something about it was just an extra reason that made me want to be here."

I had no response to that so I didn't make one.

Instead, I said, "And Tack?"

"The attitude, babe. You threw a hissy fit in Ride, and not a lotta women surrounded by members of the Chaos MC would rant about her sister, Barbies and a fuckin' TV show."

My eyes got squintier. "How do you know this shit?"

"I got eyes on Ride, Sweet Pea. I watched the whole show, and you leak that to Tack I will *not* be happy."

This surprised me. "You have eyes on Ride?"

"Yeah."

"Why do you have eyes on Ride?"

"You don't need to know that."

This was true. Not only did I not need to know, I didn't *want* to know.

"Okay, you made your point," I told him. "Can we get on to the good news?"

"Yeah," he replied. "The good news is, the fire was contained to the living room. My brother works for the DFD. He's been to the scene this morning and reports your laptop is all right."

He had a brother? He had a mother who was a nut who named him a somewhat unusual but definitely cool name and a brother who was a firefighter?

I was finding it difficult to process all this information coming at me. A year and a half and nothing but nocturnal visits and multiple orgasms and now all of this.

"You have a brother?" I asked.

"Yeah," he answered.

"Do you have any other siblings?" I asked.

"Yeah," he answered.

"What? A sister? Brother? Two? Twelve?" I pressed.

"Another brother," he answered.

Good God. There were three Italian–Cuban–Puerto Rican male Delgados roaming the earth. How did I not know this? As a woman, I should have instinctually felt their presence.

"Where are you?" I continued my interrogation.

"What?" he asked.

"In the lineup, where are you? Firstborn, middle, last?"

"First."

Shit, no wonder he was bossy. The firstborn of three boys.

"Babe, did you hear what I said about your laptop?" Hawk called.

I blinked and looked at him.

Then I asked, "What are their names? Falcon and Eagle?"

His dimples popped out then he shared, "My name is Falcone."

"Your name is Hawk."

"No, babe, my middle name. Falcone."

I blinked again. "Your middle name is Falcone?"

"I told you my mother was a nut."

"What is that? Italian?"

"Yep."

"So what are your brother's names?"

"Von and Jury."

Jeez. His mother *was* a nut.

"Did your dad have no input into the naming of his children?"

The dimples deepened. "He strapped her with three boys, Sweet Pea. She wanted girls. She married my dad, three boys from his seed, she knew she was in for a lifetime of fights, blood, drunkenness, puke and pregnancy scares. That's what she got. Layin' that shit on her, he wasn't gonna fight her on names."

He needed to stop. He was freaking me out. This was TMI. Major TMI.

"TMI," I muttered, staring at him.

"What?" he asked.

"Too much information, Hawk."

"Babe, we're all in our thirties. Von is married. We grew up, learned control and to be smart. The drunkenness, puke and pregnancy scares are history."

He'd left out the fights and blood.

Then something came to me. "You don't use protection with me."

"I did the first few times."

This was true, he did.

"But—"

"Rifled through your shit, saw your birth control pills. Put you on radar, saw you shared that body with no one but me, decided it was unnecessary."

My eyes got squinty again. "You rifled through my shit?"

"Gwen, baby, clue in. I was makin' you mine. When I make a woman mine, I do my homework."

I stared at him, uncertain what this meant and deciding for sanity's sake not to ask.

Then I mumbled, "I need a homemade donut," because I did. I needed three. Then I needed to get my ass to the mall. I felt another little black dress coming on.

I was interrupted in my plan of attack on the mall when Hawk plucked me out of bed, twisted me, I landed on my back and was pressed into the mattress by his weight.

"See you're gettin' stressy," he muttered, his eyes scanning my face, his hands skimming my body.

Mm.

"My childhood home was firebombed last night and I don't know what to do about you. Of course I'm getting stressy."

His face disappeared in my neck and he murmured in my ear, "I can teach you better ways to deal with stress than downin' donuts."

I knew this to be true since he'd already expended a fair amount of effort on those lessons. Except for stressing out about why I was letting him visit me, after a night with him my body felt like I'd received a one-and-a-half-hour full-body massage at the hands of a master while in a steam room.

I put my hands to his shoulders and exerted pressure, saying, "My stepmom and your commandos are in the kitchen."

His head came up and he looked down at me, his eyes warm and my belly got squishy. "We'll be quick and quiet," he whispered.

He could be quick? He'd never been quick before. He was a man who took his time and he did this in a *good* way.

"I can't have sex in a house that Meredith is in. And I can't have sex with you because I haven't decided what to do about you."

I wasn't paying attention so when his hands met the hem of my nightshirt then went in and up, the warmth of them light on my skin made me shiver.

"How about I help you decide," he offered, then his head dipped and his lips slid across my jaw and that felt nice. Coupled with his hands still moving on me, I did another shiver.

I pulled myself together. "No, I need to make the decision on my own. I'm compiling a mental pros and cons list of whether I should explore things with you."

His head came up, his lips in a minor grin, but the dimples were there. One of his hands stilled but the other one came out of my nightshirt, lifted and ran along my hairline.

"What you got?" he whispered.

"You're bossy, arrogant, intrusive, annoying and you crushed Troy like a bug without thought or remorse. Those are cons," I shared honestly.

His minor grin amplified.

See! Totally unrepentant.

"Oh, and you don't listen to me," I added.

More grinning then, "Do I have anything going for me?"

"On the very rare occasion you can be sweet, you're a cuddler and you carried me out of a burning building. Those are the pros."

"I'm a cuddler?"

"You spoon."

His brows went up. "That's important enough to put on your list?"

"Uh . . . yeah."

He stared at me, grinning nearly at a smile, then he noted, "Fuckin' ridiculous what women think is important."

My eyes got squinty and I snapped, "Con!"

The grin became a smile when he whispered, "You forgot a pro, baby."

"No," I corrected. "So far, that list is exhaustive."

His hand in my nightshirt moved up and the warmth of it cupped my breast. I sucked in air and stilled. Then I melted and let out the air on a quiet gasp when the skin of his palm slid across my nipple.

"Definitely a pro," he muttered while watching my face, then his head dropped and he kissed me. This was a triple threat because his tongue in my mouth, his hand at my breast (now with thumb action that was *nice*) and his hard, heavy body pinning mine to the bed was irresistible.

He was right, definitely a pro.

His mouth released mine, his thumb stopped its brilliant torture and his fingers cupped my breast. I found my fingers curled around the back of his head, my other arm tight around his back, and one of my calves had moved to hook around the back of his thigh.

I was gazing up at him firm in the knowledge that I wanted to discover quick when he grinned and his warm hand gave my breast a firm squeeze.

"See what I mean, baby?" he whispered. "Definitely pro."

I blinked. Then I stiffened.

Then I stated, "And see what *I* mean, baby? Definitely arrogant."

He did that manly, deep, amused chuckle, dipped his head, kissed the indentation at the base of my throat, his hand disappeared from my breast and he rolled off me, taking me with him. We were on our feet beside the bed, his arms around me, before I could blink.

"You need to work, get shit done," he declared. "Tonight I need you focused."

"On what?" I asked.

His face got closer and his arms got tighter. "On *me*."

Oh boy.

"My parents are staying here," I reminded him.

"I got a place," he reminded me.

His lair. Hmm. Another shiver, which he felt and I knew it because it caused him to grin another grin.

His arms gave me a squeeze. "Work, then tonight I add to the right side of your list."

I opened my mouth to tell him I should make my decision without my mind muddled by his superhuman sexual powers, but I didn't get a word out. His head bent, his mouth touched mine and then, *poof!* he was gone.

I swayed a second without his strong arms around me and his solid body to rest against. Then I turned to stare at the bedroom door.

Then I muttered, "I hate it when he does that."

But I didn't. If I was honest, I thought it was cool.

CHAPTER ELEVEN

Dress. Heels. Focus.

I WAS SCORING through work again after getting eggs, bacon and coffee from Meredith; sharing in her delight that it was "only the living room, honey, and I've been after your dad for months for a new couch" and "I really needed a few days off, so now I get to put my feet up" (told you she always looks on the bright side); saying hello to the commandos; having a shower; accepting delivery of my laptop, bag, purse and jacket direct from the "scene" from another of Hawk's commandos; and holing myself in my office.

Cam and Tracy had called. Cam because she heard talk at the station about the firebombing. Tracy because she heard about the firebombing from Cam.

Troy didn't call and this was either because he was nursing his wounds or because Cam and Tracy had kept this news from him because they thought he was probably nursing his wounds.

I gave some time to considering calling him but ended up deciding to give him time to nurse his wounds. Or at least this was what I told myself I was doing. Really, I was chicken.

Everyone knew that I was no-go zone for chitchats outside of initial briefings about my childhood home getting firebombed, all of which were done. They knew I was about work and focus. So when my cell phone rang, I was surprised.

Then I figured it was Troy.

I picked it up, looked at the display and it said "Hawk Calling."

I stared at it. I didn't have his number programmed in my phone mainly because I didn't have his number.

I flipped it open and put it to my ear wondering if Tracy was playing a practical joke and, if so, how did she pull it off and, more importantly, *why?*

"Hello?"

"Babe," Hawk replied.

Nope, not Tracy playing a practical joke.

"Hawk?"

"Little black dress, high heels, seven thirty," he stated.

I blinked. Then I asked, "What?"

"Tonight."

"Tonight what?"

"Tonight, you in a little black dress and high heels. I'll be there at seven thirty."

Ohmigod! Hawk was asking me out on a date!

My belly got squishy.

"Are you asking me out on a date?" I asked just to confirm.

"Sweet Pea, I've been fuckin' you for a year and a half."

My belly stopped being squishy.

"I know."

"So no, I'm not askin'. I'm tellin' you, dress, heels, I'll be there at seven thirty."

Uh . . . what?

"So, you're not asking me out on a date, you're telling me we're going out on a date," I guessed though I knew it was accurately.

"That's about it," he replied.

"You can't *tell* me we're going on a date!" I snapped.

"Just did, babe."

"Con," I muttered because that was a serious *con*.

He chuckled his deep, manly, amused chuckle, then he ordered, "Get work done. I want your focus on me, not work."

"I don't think I'll have time for a date. I'm buried." This was a lie. With the work I got done last night and today, I was catching up. I totally had time for a date and I had a life creed that stated that any opportunity to wear a little black dress was to be taken up, no ifs, ands or buts. However, I was making an exception.

"Was made pretty clear last night even before I fought a fire side by side with your old man that I had their blessing, Gwen. Don't think they'd step in if I dressed you myself and carried you kicking and screaming to my car."

This was, unfortunately, true.

I shifted focus to something else annoying.

"Did you program yourself into my phone?" I demanded to know.

"Yeah," he answered.

"When?"

"Before I handed it off to Fang."

"Fang?"

"My boy who brought you your shit."

Jeez. That guy's name was Fang? I could see it. I'd noticed his eyeeteeth were somewhat prominent. But I couldn't imagine he'd be okay with that nickname considering it seemed to be making fun of this unfortunate dental anomaly and he looked like he could hammer a human body through cement with his fist if he thought someone was making fun of him.

"Why?" I continued.

"Why what?" Hawk asked.

"Why did you program yourself into my phone?"

Silence then, "Babe."

As usual, there was no more.

"Babe what? We've had a non-relationship for months, now we've shifted and I've explained I'm uncertain about this shift *and* our future."

"You can be as uncertain as you want, Sweet Pea, I'm certain enough for both of us. Dress. Heels. Focus. Seven thirty."

I opened my mouth to say something but I had dead air.

I flipped my phone shut. Then I stared at it.

Then I tossed it on my desk and snapped, "God, he's *so infuriating.*"

But even as I said it, I knew deep down that first, I was happy I had the opportunity to don one of my little black dresses and, second, I was just a *wee bit* excited that I finally, *finally* had a date with Cabe "Hawk" Delgado.

I went back to work pretending that I wasn't thinking that I hoped I got to ride in his Camaro.

*   *   *

It was nearly seven thirty, Dad was home and in my office watching television while Meredith was pottering around, likely rearranging all the stuff in my drawers and cupboards in the kitchen. I was in the bathroom freaking out about my date with Hawk.

This freaking-out business was partly due to the fact that I was getting ready for my date with Hawk and not sticking to my guns about *not* going on a date with Hawk and the fact that, again, I was likely making stupid choices about all things Hawk.

It was also partly due to the fact that I really, *really* hoped he liked my dress.

The commandos were done with my security system and I knew this because Smoke had given Meredith and me a rather long lesson on how to use it.

It seemed complicated. I'd never had an alarm system but I figured usually you punched in some numbers and presto! Security. But mine included panic buttons in my office, my bedroom, kitchen, living room and, overkill, the bathroom. It also included different codes for different types of alarms, say, windows and doors only or to activate the sensors in the house. There was also a different code that sent the message to "base" that there might be an unknown situation and they should come in "soft," whatever the hell that meant.

Neither Meredith nor I were good with remembering numbers and when Meredith ran to get a piece of paper to write them down, Smoke looked at his feet and a muscle clenched in his jaw. Then he herded Meredith and me into the kitchen. There he sat us at my big, battered farm table and quizzed us on the three different codes until we memorized them.

He wasn't really patient with this endeavor, especially when Meredith leaned in to me and whispered, "I don't understand what the big deal is, sweetie. I mean, I don't want to embarrass you but your dad and I, we *do* know you and Hawk are..." her voice dropped, "*intimate*." I avoided Smoke's eyes as Meredith went on. "I mean, it isn't like he isn't here looking out for you."

I bit my lip and shrugged. I didn't know what else to do. She thought Hawk and I were an item because Hawk was making her think we were an item and I wasn't helping matters by playing his game. Clearly, she thought I was safe under his care. I didn't want to mess with that. Especially not the day after her home had been firebombed because of her other daughter's shit.

I also didn't want to talk with my stepmom about being intimate with *anyone*. Meredith was cool, she'd always been cool, but she was also the only mom I knew and she was definitely a *mom* and she had been from the very beginning. You didn't discuss sex with hot guys with your *mom,* especially not super-multiple-orgasm sex.

Dad, by the way, learned the codes in about two seconds. He'd always been good with numbers. It was his way.

The doorbell chimed then clunked as I was staring into the mirror lining my lips and suddenly I felt butterflies in my stomach. The kind I felt when I first saw Hawk and the kind I'd denied feeling every time since when he visited me.

"I'll get it!" Meredith yelled from downstairs. I sucked in breath and finished with my liner, filling in with lipstick.

Trust Hawk to press my doorbell for the first time *now*. I probably wouldn't get butterflies in my stomach if he suddenly materialized in the bathroom. I'd probably get annoyed.

I ran to my room, grabbed my clutch and wrap then ran to the door and closed it a bit so I could look in the full-length mirror on the back.

Little black dress, check. In fact, it was my numero uno little black dress. The best of the lot. Sleeveless and it had a deep vee in front that showed cleavage, a way deeper one in the back, and it had a blousy drape around the middle but clung like a second skin to my hips and the tops of my thighs were it stopped. It was *way* short. So short, it was almost Darla-slash-Ginger mini-jean-skirt short except without the skank component. And it was made of an awesome material that even on the blousy parts it caught at flesh and revealed things it was pretending it conceal. It was fabulous.

High heels, check. In fact, they were strappy sandals, black, sexy spiked heel. They made my legs look brilliant. Killer.

Hair out to there. Smoky makeup.

The whole thing, the be-all-you-could-be of date apparel. I hoped.

I rushed out of my room shouting "See you later, Dad!"

"Have a good time, honey!" Dad shouted back. "Tell Hawk not to worry about the doorbell, I'll fix it this weekend!"

Bonus to Dad being evacuated to my house due to smoke and fire damage. Resident handyman.

"Will do!" I yelled, though I seriously doubted Hawk was losing sleep about my clunking doorbell.

Then I rushed down the stairs to see the living room dark but a light and voices were coming from the kitchen. Meredith was probably offering Hawk a beer. When Meredith was in my house, I gave up the position of Head Hostess. I'd learned it was the best way to go. She could probably go to the White House for a state dinner and the First Lady would step aside and let Meredith take over.

I hustled to the kitchen and stopped dead in the doorway when I saw Meredith chatting with Detective Mitch Lawson.

I was freaked out last night, what with the fire and Dad and Hawk battling the flames with fire extinguishers, I hadn't taken the time to admire yet again how hot he was. Now that he was in my kitchen and I was in a little black dress with hair out to there, when his eyes turned to me and he froze, I had the opportunity to process yet again how hot he was.

So I took it.

He recovered first.

"Gwendolyn."

God, I liked it that he always said my full name.

"Hey, Detective Lawson."

He did his small smile then he invited, "You can call me Mitch."

"Um...okay."

Lawson's eyes swept me then he looked at Meredith.

"I'm sorry, Mrs. Kidd, but could you give Gwendolyn and me a moment?"

"Oh!" Meredith cried at the same time she jumped. She'd been processing how hot he was too. "Sure. Of course. I'll just..." she rushed to the fridge and grabbed two beers "...get Bax and me a drink." She closed the fridge then rushed to the door of the kitchen saying, "Nice to see you again, Detective Lawson."

"Mitch," he corrected.

"Mitch," Meredith called as she continued escaping.

Oh boy. Alone in my kitchen with *Mitch*. No eight cops in the living room. No Hawk...yet. He was late.

I walked a bit into the kitchen. "Uh...is everything okay?"

His head tipped to the side. "Yeah, why?"

"Uh...you're here and, uh...you're an officer of the law and there's the small fact my sister is in some serious trouble so..." I trailed off.

"I'm here because of your sister but not because anything is wrong."

"Oh. Okay," I replied.

"Or, anything *else* is wrong," he amended.

"Oh. Okay," I said again.

"I just wanted to ask a favor of you."

I took a breath and then repeated, "Oh. Okay."

And, by the way, I felt like an idiot repeating those two words but what could I say? I was in a little black dress waiting for Hawk. Lawson was hot, I knew he was into me and he was there to ask a favor. I didn't know what to do. The situation seemed uncertain, not in a good way or a bad way, just in an unpredictable way.

He studied me a second then, his voice dipping quiet, he ordered, "Gwendolyn, come here."

Without delay my feet moved me closer to him because I was a woman and when a hot guy told you in a quiet, deep, attractive voice to come to him, you just did it.

I forced my feet to stop when I was a foot away from him.

When I stopped, he said softly, "You look pretty."

He told me I looked pretty.

Nice.

"Thanks," I whispered.

"Goin' out with Hawk?"

I pressed my lips together. Then I nodded.

He smiled.

Then he straightened and moved into me so the foot that separated us became more like six inches.

Or less.

His hand came up and he rested it on my waist, and before I could say anything or move, he started talking.

"I don't want to offend you when I say this but after last night, I need to say it."

Uh-oh.

I'd tipped my head to look up in his soulful eyes and they seemed more soulful than ever.

"What?" I asked before I could get lost in his soulful eyes.

He hesitated then stated, "Your sister, Ginger, she's not too smart."

Oh. Well, I'd expected something else. I didn't know what but, seeing as his hand was on my waist and he was in my space, it wasn't Ginger.

"I kind of know that," I replied.

"You probably know this too and if you didn't before the

last coupla nights, then you do now, but she doesn't think about who she's draggin' into this."

"Yes, the last couple of nights I've learned that."

He nodded. Then he said, "So, the favor I'm askin', if you see her again, I want you to call me."

My body got tight, but it was only automatic. Nevertheless, he felt it and got closer, his hand gripping my waist, his other hand lifting to do the same on the other side.

"I can't say what's gonna happen to her. If she plays it smart, if we can cut a deal, if we can protect her. There are no promises here, Gwendolyn. What I can say is, whatever happens, she's safer with us than she is on the street, and *you* are definitely safer if she's with us and not on the street."

I could see this.

He kept going. "And, for you, we get her in custody, I'll do what I can for her."

Oh. Wow.

"Thanks," I whispered.

His fingers dug in, giving me a squeeze as his mouth gave me a smile.

"Just want to be clear, I don't want you to try to detain her. But if you see her, she shows, she gets in contact with you, you won't be helpin' her out, even if she tells you you are, by keepin' it from us. Just call me, tell me what she said, where you saw her and if you know where she intends to go."

"You want me to inform on my sister," I surmised.

"Yeah," he replied, no hesitation, no bullshit.

"Okay," I agreed, no hesitation either.

He smiled again.

Then his fingers gave me another squeeze and he asked, "How're you handlin' this?"

God, he was nice.

"Well, there are life lessons I'd prefer to learn, say, how

to make the perfect soufflé, not that I can keep my head in a crisis that involves fiery destruction, but I'm doing okay."

His brows went up. "You want to learn to make the perfect soufflé?"

"Um…" I was uncertain where to put my hands. There wasn't enough space and I was carrying my clutch and wrap. But when his fingers gripped me again and pulled me an inch closer I had no choice but to lift them and rest them on his chest.

Hmm. That was better.

"Not really," I went on. "More like, I'd like to learn to make chocolate chip cookie dough in thirty seconds or less."

He smiled yet again.

"But I wouldn't be averse to learning to make the perfect soufflé," I continued, "if it was chocolate."

His smile deepened.

Yowza!

Then his smile faded and his face got soft, as did his voice. "Lotsa shit happenin', Gwendolyn. Scary shit. You sure you're okay?"

Totally nice.

"Yeah," I whispered then, do *not* ask me why, I went on to share, "but I'm a little worried about Meredith. She's using the fire as an excuse to buy a new couch and have a few days of rest and relaxation but I can tell she's upset. She's just not talking about it. And *I* don't want to bring it up if she doesn't want to talk about it. But, Ginger, she's Meredith's daughter and I think—"

"She loves you," he cut me off.

"What?"

"I could see it last night, the night before, she cares about you. Ginger is her daughter and her daughter is bringing you trouble, your dad too. She feels responsible for that and she doesn't know what to do with it."

He was probably right.

Lawson continued, "You need to talk to her about it. Assure her you don't hold her responsible. Take that load off her because she's gonna be focusing on other shit too, like the trouble Ginger has made for herself. She doesn't need to worry about how you feel about the trouble Ginger is bringing on you."

"You're right," I said quietly.

He lifted a hand and tucked hair behind my ear while his soulful, dark brown eyes watched then he rested his hand curled around my neck, his warm palm at my throat.

This was nice too. Too nice.

His eyes came back to mine. "Yeah, I'm right."

"We're not like this, Meredith, Dad and me," I assured him quickly, not certain why I was doing it, just feeling the need to do it. "Ginger is..." I shook my head "...she's different than the rest of us. I don't know why. She just always has been. She's—"

"I know, Gwendolyn," he said gently in a way that made me know he knew.

I nodded, feeling relief, and his fingers gave my neck a squeeze.

Right then the back door opened. Lawson and my head turned and Hawk was there.

He was wearing much what he was wearing the first time I laid eyes on him. The tailored shirt was midnight blue this time but no less fantastic. Jeans. Boots. Great belt. Black leather jacket that was an awesome style and hung great on his broad shoulders. And a Nordstrom bag dangling from his hand. No, a Nordstrom *shoe* bag dangling from his hand.

My body stiffened and Lawson's hands gripped me tighter.

Hawk closed the door behind him but didn't tear his eyes from Lawson and me.

Then he put his hands on his hips, the bag banging against his thigh.

"Am I interrupting something?"

"No," I said hurriedly.

"Yeah," Lawson replied at the same time.

I took a careful step back and Lawson's hands fell away.

This was when Lawson and Hawk went into a macho man, death match staredown.

I stepped into the non-verbal, motionless fray before it became verbal and full of motion.

"He just came by to ask me to call if I see or hear from Ginger," I explained to Hawk.

Hawk's eyes had cut to me when I spoke but the second I finished, they cut back to Lawson.

"Thought I made myself clear," he growled.

"You did," Lawson returned. "But you'll remember, I didn't agree."

"You do not use my woman to make your career," Hawk went on like Lawson didn't speak.

I pressed my lips together and got tense mainly because I felt anger, a lot of it, rolling off Lawson then I heard it in the rumble of his quiet voice.

"Careful," Lawson warned.

"She is not in this," Hawk continued. "Ginger doesn't exist for her. That's what's in here and that's what's communicated on the street."

"Last two nights proved that wrong, Hawk. Ginger's unpredictable and you know it."

"Right, but any of that shit goes down, it gets communicated through me, not Gwen."

"She gets desperate," Lawson started, "and by the way,

Ginger Kidd passed desperate about a week ago, she's gonna make extreme choices. Gwendolyn is in that line of fire. You and your boys are good, Hawk, but you can't cover her 24/7 and keep your other shit in line."

"Let me worry about that," Hawk returned.

"She needs to know what to do," Lawson replied.

"Yeah, and I'll tell her," Hawk shot back.

Another macho man, death match staredown ensued, but luckily before it could advance to hand-to-hand combat, Lawson broke the staredown and looked at me.

"You have my card," he said, and I nodded because I did have his card, I just didn't know what happened to it. He nodded back and finished, "I'll let myself out."

Then he leaned into me, right in front of Hawk, bent and kissed the hinge of my jaw, his lips causing goose bumps to rise on my skin.

Oh boy.

He lifted his head, looked in my eyes and whispered, "Stay safe. You need anything, even if it's just to talk, call me."

I nodded.

His gaze sliced through Hawk then he walked out of the kitchen and into the living room.

I watched while practicing deep breathing. Then, slowly, I turned to Hawk to see he hadn't moved. He was still standing there with his hands to his hips, the Nordstrom bag hanging from his fingers, his eyes on me with a look in them that could only be described as un...hap...pee.

Uh-oh.

CHAPTER TWELVE

The Us You Wanted Us to Be

I STARED AT Hawk. Hawk stared at me. When his unhappy look didn't shift, I decided to speak.

"Hey," I said.

He kept staring at me. Then he moved to the table lifting the Nordstrom bag and pulling out a familiar box with the words "Jimmy Choo" on the top. It wasn't familiar because I *owned* a box like that, just that I'd *seen* them the multiple times I'd tried on a pair of Jimmy Choos. He dumped the bag on the table and then put the box on the table. Then he sent it sliding down the table toward me.

As it was shoes, and Jimmy Choo shoes, reflexively I moved fast. My hand darting out to catch it before something tragic happened, like a pair of Jimmy Choo shoes falling to the floor.

With my hand resting on the box, I looked at Hawk, my heart beating fast.

"What's this?" I asked.

He dipped his head to the box and growled, "Open it."

Hmm. Still unhappy.

I dropped my clutch and wrap to the table, picked up the box and opened it.

Then my heart seized.

In it was a pair of silver watersnake platform sandals—slim slingback strap, peep toe, four-and-a-half-inch spiked heel. Elegant. Gorgeous. Scary expensive.

The shoes Tracy had been hiding in the shoe storeroom at Nordstrom for me for the last six weeks. Shoes I wanted so badly I could taste it. Shoes I told myself I would save to afford. Shoes I was never going to buy because I could never afford them, even with Tracy's discount.

But my mission was to own a pair of Jimmy Choo shoes before I died. Some women had career goals. Some women wanted to be good mothers. Some women wanted to do their bit to save the world. My life goal was owning really beautiful, really expensive shoes.

My eyes lifted to Hawk.

"I don't understand," I whispered.

"Those the shoes you wanted?" Hawk asked.

I blinked.

"Yes," I answered.

"You got 'em."

It took some effort but I succeeded in not hyperventilating.

"You bought them for me?" I asked as it hit me. Security system. Panic buttons. Window repair. Shoes that cost over seven hundred dollars.

What was going on?

"You wanted them," he answered like it was as simple as that.

I felt my head get light. "How? Why?"

"Babe, you gonna put them on or what?"

"How? Why?" I repeated.

He sighed then, "Your friend said you had them on hold. I know where your friend works. I sent my girl to find them.

She found your girl, your girl got 'em off hold, I bought 'em, now they're here."

His girl?

I was too freaked, and the subject was Jimmy Choos, so I didn't ask about that.

He stopped speaking and I prompted, "That's the how, what's the why?"

"Gwen, you wanted them."

"That's it?" I asked.

"That's it," he confirmed.

"I also want my own personal tropical island paradise," I told him. "Are you going to get that for me too?"

The unhappy look shifted from his face and his mouth twitched. "That might take a while."

I stared at him and my belly felt squishy, my heart felt like it had grown a couple sizes and was threatening to burst out of my chest, plus something tingly was happening in my throat.

Then I forced out, "I don't know what to say."

"Don't say anything," he returned. "Just put on the fuckin' shoes so we can go eat. I'm hungry."

"Okay," I whispered, pulled out a chair, sat, unstrapped my strappy black sandals and slid on my new silver watersnake, kickass Jimmy Choo platforms.

Just like when I tried them on at Nordstrom. Utter perfection.

I sat with one calf outstretched, staring at my foot and thinking I might have just found heaven on earth, shoe-style, when Hawk spoke.

"You gonna sit there and stare at those shoes for the next decade or you gonna get your ass in my car?"

My head tipped back and my feet were encased in Jimmy Choo shoes, so Hawk being annoying deflected right off me.

"I'm going to stare at them for a decade," I replied, smiling at him.

His eyes got that heated and intense look, my heart swelled even further, and he said, "Babe, quit fuckin' around and let's go."

I was still smiling when I stood, grabbed my wrap and clutch off the table and walked to him on my new Jimmy Choos while Hawk watched.

Then I stopped close to him, put the hand that was clutching my wrap to his chest and I leaned in.

"Thanks, Hawk," I whispered because I didn't know what else to say. Those words were far from enough but I had to say something. And not because he bought me a beautiful pair of shoes that I wanted but because he heard Tracy mention it in passing and he sent "his girl" out to get them for me. And because I had a break-in and in two days my window was fixed and I had a security system installed. And he was sticking around to protect me, and because he was, likely due to his, Dad's and Dog's efforts, the fire that started in my parents' living room didn't engulf the house, *and* my laptop had been saved.

And since "thanks" wasn't enough, I leaned in, lifted up and touched my mouth to his.

The second I did this, his head slanted and his arms closed around me, tight, yanking me deep into his body as his tongue invaded my mouth. My touch of lips turned into a full-blown, super-hot, leading-to-sex-on-my-battered-farm-table *kiss*.

My clutch and wrap had fallen to the floor because both my arms were around his neck, my body was plastered to his, one of his arms was tight around my back, the other hand had slid in my dress then down and was cupping the cheek of my ass, skin to skin (I was wearing a thong, which was a smart move on my part not only to avoid panty lines but because his warm, strong hand cupping my ass felt freaking *great*), when I heard my father clear his throat.

My body jerked, Hawk's head came up and turned to the door as his hand slid out of my dress and up to the small of my back but his arms didn't move even as my hands went to his shoulders and I pressed.

Slowly, my head turned and I saw my dad walk in, a small smile playing at his lips, his eyes to the floor.

Oh my God. My father just saw me in a clinch with Hawk. A clinch that included Hawk's hand *in* my dress *cupping* my ass.

Kill me. Someone. Kill me.

"Meredith forgot the bottle opener," Dad mumbled as he walked to the utensils drawer.

"We might be late," Hawk replied, still not letting me go, "or not home at all."

Oh my *God*.

My eyes flew to his face and got squinty but he missed this because he was looking over my shoulder at Dad.

"Right," Dad muttered, turning back to the door as Hawk let me go, then stepped back and bent to retrieve my bag and wrap. "Have a good time," Dad called as he walked out of the kitchen.

"Later, Dad," I called back, my voice sounding strangled.

Then Hawk's hands were on me, he turned me so my back was to him and I felt my wrap settle on my shoulders.

He turned me to face him and handed me my clutch.

"Did that just happen?" I whispered.

"Yep," Hawk replied, grabbed my hand and tugged me to the door.

"My dad just saw us making out with your hand on my ass," I added detail, just to confirm.

Hawk opened the door and pulled me through, repeating, "Yep."

"Well, at least I got my Jimmy Choos before I died. Now you can take me to the nearest railway crossing and I'll throw myself in front of a train."

Hawk kept his hand firm in mine as he led me down the steps of the back stoop, toward the gate of my backyard, and he did this while chuckling.

"I'm not finding this funny," I told him as he lifted the latch on the gate, pulled it open and tugged me through.

"Babe, you've been married. He knows you aren't a virgin."

"Uh...yeah but—"

"And he knows what type of guy I am because he's the same type of guy so he pretty much knows I'm not gonna have a hot piece like his daughter and not kiss her with my hand on her ass, not to mention do other things to her."

"You can quit talking now," I told him.

He beeped the locks on the Camaro, opened the door and ignored me. "You think he waited until he put his band on her finger to get your stepmom in his bed, babe, you're very wrong."

He shoved me in the car while I put my hands over my ears and chanted, "La la la," over and over again.

Even though I was chanting, I could still hear him chuckling.

Hawk slammed the door and I buckled in thinking *Time to move on*.

Hawk got in beside me, fired up the Camaro and we purred from the curb.

Nice.

Hawk drove and he did this silently and he did this for a while so I filled the conversational void.

"The security system is done."

"I know."

"Smoke taught us how to use it," I went on.

Silence, then, "Smoke?"

"Your Numero Dos."

"My Numero Dos?"

I turned to look at him. "Yeah. The Hispanic guy that supervised the work."

Another beat of silence, then Hawk burst out laughing.

"What's funny?" I asked into his laughter.

"Smoke," he said through his laughter.

"Uh . . . yeah. Smoke. That's how he introduced himself."

He stopped laughing but was still grinning when he stated, "Babe, he was fuckin' with you. His name isn't Smoke. It's Jorge."

I stared at him. Then I said, "He's not known as Smoke?"

"Nope."

"That's not, like, his street name or something?"

A brief chuckle then, "No."

"Why would he tell me his name was Smoke?" I asked.

"Because he's like that and because you'd believe him and because you believed him, he probably found that hilarious."

I crossed my arms on my chest. "Well, you have another guy named Fang. You're called Hawk. Why wouldn't I believe a name like Smoke?"

"Fang is definitely a Fang and Hawk is who I am."

Fang was, unfortunately for him, definitely a Fang.

"No," I stated, turning my head to look at him again, "you're Cabe Delgado."

"I used to be Cabe Delgado, Gwen, but shit happens in life and that man is still in me but now I'm not that man."

Interesting.

"What does that mean?" I asked.

"You still addin' to your list of pros and cons?" he asked back.

"Yes," I replied.

"The pros win out, Sweet Pea, and uncertainty becomes certainty, then I'll tell you what that means."

Now I wanted to know what *that* meant.

I decided my best bet for the moment was to pass on that.

So I looked back out the windscreen and changed the subject. "You have a girl?"

Something weird and tense filled the car and it was coming from Hawk when he asked back, "I have a girl?"

"The girl who got me my shoes," I explained, freakishly scared to look at him due to the strange tenseness.

Then the tenseness evaporated, *poof!* like it was never there when he answered easily, "Yeah, I have a girl."

Um…*weird!*

I hesitantly pressed forward. "What kind of girl?"

Hawk unhesitantly shared, "A secretary, receptionist kind of girl."

Interesting.

"What's her name?"

"Elvira."

I turned to look at him again. "Elvira?"

"Yeah."

"Is she mistress of the darkness?"

"She gets in a bad mood, definitely."

Hmm.

"Does she have bad moods often?" I asked.

"She works with thirteen guys who naturally produce high levels of testosterone and feed on extreme situations, which means she has to have attitude. A woman with attitude comes with bad moods so, yeah, she has bad moods often."

There was a lot there so I broke it down.

"You have thirteen guys?"

"Yep."

"Like, you *employ* thirteen guys?"

"Thirteen guys and a girl, yeah."

Hmm.

"And these guys produce high levels of testosterone and feed on extreme situations?" I went on.

"Yep."

Oh boy.

"What kind of extreme situations?" I asked, but I wasn't sure I wanted to know.

His hand came out and wrapped around my thigh before he said in a gentle voice, "Babe, trust me. With my work, ignorance is bliss. Yeah?"

Oh boy. I was right. I didn't want to know.

Time to switch subjects.

I looked back out the windscreen. "So, attitude comes with bad moods?"

"Definitely."

"You think I have attitude."

"Definitely."

"Are you saying I have bad moods?"

His hand at my thigh gave me a squeeze as he said an amused, "Babe."

Hmm!

He went on, "Though, discovered today I can alleviate Elvira's bad mood by sending her to Nordstrom to buy a pair of shoes that cost as much as a used car and I can make you kiss me for the first time by givin' 'em to you."

I turned to look at him. "I've kissed you."

"No, you've kissed me *back*. *I* kiss *you*."

This was true.

"Plan on more shoes in the future, Sweet Pea," he

muttered. My belly got squishy again, my heart swelled again and that tingly feeling in my throat came back.

Therefore, I announced, "This is freaking me out."

He glanced at me then looked back at the road. "What?"

"You, being sweet. Generous and sweet. Generous, forthcoming about your life...*ish,* and sweet. It's freaking me out."

"Why?" he asked.

"This isn't us," I answered.

"This is the us you wanted us to be, Gwen," he returned.

"I'm not sure about that," I lied.

"Bullshit, babe," he called me on it. "I know you wanna pretend I wasn't there but I was at your parents' dinner table last night."

Oh shit. We were back on this.

"I told you I was making stuff up," I lied again. "Meredith is romantic. She fainted when she met Dad because she knew he was the man of her dreams, *with one look,* she knew. She loves me. She wants that for me, she always has so I gave it to her."

His hand left my thigh so he could shift as he stated quietly, "Gwen, baby, you meant every word you said."

"Did not," I returned.

He stopped the car and I saw we were parked outside Tamayo on Larimer Square in lower downtown Denver, otherwise known as LoDo. Tamayo had brilliant Mexican food. Tamayo had unusual, delicious cocktails and guacamole that proved there was a God. Tamayo had a gorgeous mural behind the bar and a sun terrace. Tamayo was awesome.

My eyes went to him as I felt Hawk turn to me.

"Don't," he ordered softly.

"Don't what?" I asked.

His hand lifted, fingers curling around the back of my

neck and he pulled me to him. "Don't pollute what came out of your mouth last night."

Suddenly I realized this was important to him, not a little, a lot. And not a lot, but *a whole lot.* And I didn't know what to do with that but something about it scared the freaking *shit* out of me.

"Hawk—" I whispered, and his hand slid from my neck to my jaw but his thumb moved up to press against my lips.

"Don't," he repeated.

"Okay," I whispered against his thumb.

He dropped his hand and unbuckled my belt then he folded out of the car. He was at my door before I could rest one Jimmy Choo–clad foot to the pavement. He took my hand, pulled me out of the car, kept hold of my hand and Hawk, me and my Jimmy Choos walked into Tamayo.

CHAPTER THIRTEEN

Totally Missed Out

I WOKE UP and heard Hawk's murmur from what seemed like far away.

He was on the phone.

I opened my eyes.

I was in Hawk's bed.

I tucked my hands under my cheek, closed my eyes and the night before came sliding into my brain.

All of it. And there was *lots*.

First up, Tamayo had cocktails called Tamayopolitans. Pineapple-infused tequila, cranberry and guava. Delicious. Refreshing. *Dangerous*.

I was not averse to drinking outside a cosmo if the cocktail had "opolitan" somewhere in its name so Tamayopolitans it was.

And lots of them. And lots of food. And lots of me *talking*.

Hawk's sharing component of the evening was clearly used up during our car ride. The dinner conversation consisted of Hawk asking questions and me answering them. He might have known everything about me but it was clear he wanted to know how I felt about everything about me.

So he asked me about my mom and I told him that, as great as Meredith was, Mom taking off sucked, the fact that she could do it and *did*. He also asked me about my dad and I told him all about my dad, all the reasons why I loved him and all the reasons he was a great dad (kind of one in the same but I still went into detail about both topics). Ditto with Meredith. The opposite with Ginger, though I did share that regardless of the fact that Ginger was Ginger and there wasn't a lot to love, she was still my sister and I'd never given up hope that she'd pull her shit together eventually. Until now.

He asked about Cam, Leo and Tracy, but it was me, me on my fourth Tamayopolitan, who shared about Troy. About how I was worried now that his crush was outed he'd disappear from my life and I'd miss him if he went away.

Hawk also laughed with me when I told a joke or a funny story and I laughed with him when he made some comment that was amusing.

And lastly, he was into everything I said. He was concentrating only on me. It was like every word that poured forth out of my mouth was a piece to the puzzle that was the meaning of life and he had some of the pieces but he wanted to make sure he got them all. His relaxed and comfortable yet intent concentration, the fact that not one woman who walked by caught his attention, in fact, nothing but me caught his attention—there was something about it that felt good. As in *really* good.

It was easy, it was fun, the food great, the drinks plentiful, my company amusing and hot as all get-out and I had fabulous shoes.

It was the best date I'd ever had.

It was after Tamayopolitan number six that we left and the second part of the night started.

We were in the Camaro and purring through the streets of Denver, me wondering where the night would take us next and getting a quiver in a private place at where my wonderings were taking me when Hawk's phone rang. He took the call, said a few words, flipped his phone shut and swung a uey.

"Gotta go to base, babe. There's a situation I need a brief on. Urgent. Can you hang in my office?"

At his question, I thought, *Oh my God! I get to see his base!*

And since I was slightly inebriated, I was pretty certain I didn't hide my excitement even though the word I chose to use was, "Sure," it came out peppy and eager. I knew this because, when I chanced a glance at him, he was grinning.

He drove into the basement garage of a high-rise office building in upper downtown, guided me to the elevator, taking me up to the fourteenth floor. The elevator opened and there was a vestibule at either side of which there were two hallways. Hawk went right then right again and down the hall where he chose door number two and used a keycard to access it.

I walked in with him and stopped dead.

Instant cool.

Commando Central!

The windows to the view at the back were darkened even against the evening skyline. In front of me in theater style with elevated platforms were three levels, four workstations at each level, all sorts of knobs and buttons and telephones on the consoles of the workstations. Behind me, rows of screens set into the wall, machinery under them with numerical displays, every one of them filled with some action, people, places and things. There were three offices off the theater area to the left; all but the last one on the top level had floor-to-ceiling windows that clearly showed what the occupant was doing at all times. To the right, more doors, only two: one was a big conference room with more floor-to-ceiling windows, one a door but no windows.

The room was filled with commandos, some I'd seen, some I hadn't, some sitting at workstations, some obviously waiting for Hawk to arrive.

One was "Smoke."

"Hey, Smoke," I called, waving at him.

Commandos looked to their boots and shuffled their feet.

"Hey, Gwen," Smoke replied.

I tipped my head to the side and asked loudly, "Next time you need to make up a nickname to fake someone out, can I pick it?"

There was more shuffling of feet, Smoke grinned at me and I heard Hawk chuckle, then he handed me a keycard and put his hand in the small of my back.

"Babe, top office, hang there. I'll come get you as soon as I'm done," he ordered, and I looked up at him to see him jerk his head to the dark office at the top.

I nodded and, not thinking, my body and brain having absorbed six Tamayopolitans, my feet encased in Jimmy Choos he'd given me, my belly filled with yummy food he'd bought for me, my night having been spent sitting across the table from him, I put a hand lightly on his abs, lifted up on my toes and touched my mouth to his.

Then I clipped across the shiny black floors, up the side aisle steps and used the keycard to get into his office, not realizing I had a bunch of commando eyes following me, some admiring, all curious.

Upon entering and turning on the light I found Hawk's office was uber-modern and totally clinical. No photos on the desk or credenza. No medals on the walls. No trophies on shelves or plaques displayed. No personal paraphernalia. There weren't any files on the desk, pencil holders, notepads, not even a computer, just a phone. The whole thing was decorated in black, light gray, black leather and chrome and so clean a doctor could perform surgery there. There were four television monitors on the wall, blank screens. There was a long black couch. There were two black chairs in front of his desk and a big, high-backed swivel one behind it. That was it.

I considered my options for time spent in Hawk's office and I decided to text Cam and Tracy about the date instead of trying to rifle through drawers. First, if I rifled through drawers that would be intrusive and very wrong—he might have intruded in my life but that didn't mean I needed to return the favor. Second, and more important, I figured he maybe had cameras in there and would find out I did it, which he probably would frown on and Hawk pissed was a scary thing.

So I sat on the couch and texted Cam and Tracy about the date and received ecstatic texts back from Trace and cautionary texts back from Cam which mostly consisted of her begging me not to imbibe even a drop more alcohol.

Hawk said it wouldn't take very long but he was wrong. So since it took a long time, I had six Tamayopolitans, my belly was full and I'd had two interrupted nights of sleep during which there were intervals of high emotion including break-ins and firebombs, I eventually passed out on his couch.

I woke up to Hawk lifting me in his arms.

"I can walk," I mumbled.

"Yeah?" he asked, then suggested, "How 'bout you do that on level ground when you're in those heels."

He wanted to carry me? Okay, I was all right with that.

I shoved my forehead in his neck and wrapped one arm

around his shoulder, the other around his neck and muttered, "'Kay."

He walked me down the steps by the console workstations, but even when we got to level ground, he didn't put me down until we were outside the elevator. When he did, I leaned heavily into him.

"Tired?" he asked.

"Six Tamayopolitans," I explained but I kind of slurred the word "Tamayopolitans" mainly because I was sleepy and because I was still a little drunk.

He chuckled and pulled me closer.

When we were inside the elevator and I was again pressed into him, I noted, "Your briefing lasted a long time."

"Reports from the field, things changed, we needed to abort mission, regroup and reengage."

This was all scary language my mind refused to process so I lifted my face from his pectoral and tipped my head back to look at him. "Let me guess, I don't want to know?"

He grinned down at me. "No, you don't want to know."

"You're grinning," I observed. "Does that mean there were no casualties?"

"Not the good guys," he replied.

Again, scary. Again, mind refused to process. Though, good news.

I planted my cheek in his pectoral again and mumbled, "Good to know."

He gave me a squeeze. Then he guided me out of the elevator and into the Camaro. Then I fell asleep again.

The last part of the evening was when I woke up because the Camaro had quit purring. He had parked. He helped me out of the car, through a door and I knew one thing. I wasn't home. I knew something else. I didn't care. I just wanted to sleep.

So I muttered, "Bed."

"Gotcha, Sweet Pea."

Hawk helped me stumble up some stairs that made a lot of noise and I was curious to look around, I just didn't have the energy. I spied a bed, groped my way to it, divested myself of little black dress and awesome shoes and face-planted in it.

Now it was morning.

Shit.

I pushed up on a hand and shoved my hair out of my face. Then I stared.

I was in humungous bed in a cavernous building and when I say cavernous, I mean *cavernous*. It had to be a warehouse at one point. I could see daylight pouring in from enormous windows that went from floor to at least three stories up. I could also see there was a dusting of snow sometime in the night. And I could see that the warehouse was in the middle of nowhere, frosted scrub all around, a large creek or small river running close to the building. Further, I could see I was on a platform that had an iron railing that was not decorative in the slightest but industrial.

I looked down the foot of the bed and saw a wide expanse of plank floors and at the end, a big cube made of glass block, the door to it open, a bathroom.

My first stop.

My eyes moved to the floor and I saw my dress and Jimmy Choos tangled with Hawk's jeans, shirt and boots. Something about that I liked, something about that made my belly squishy.

Oh boy, I was in trouble.

I held the covers up to my breasts, shifted to the side of the bed and dropped my torso down, reaching out. I decided against my dress and grabbed his shirt. Then I lifted up and shrugged it on while in bed. I threw the covers back and held Hawk's shirt closed with my hand as I got out and wandered to the bathroom. I was half dazed from still being sleepy and having a good, relaxing night and half dazed because I was in Hawk's lair.

The bathroom was nice, clean, tidy, if utilitarian. No personal touches there either like there weren't any in the bed area. Just thick, soft midnight blue and dark gray towels on the railings and folded and stacked on shelves over the toilet. The midnight blue and dark gray was a theme, the sheets and comforter were the same colors.

I used the facilities and then washed my hands. Then I looked in the medicine cabinet because you pretty much were thrown out of the Girl Club if you didn't snoop at least in the medicine cabinet. I'd given his desk a pass; I had to look in the medicine cabinet.

Toothpaste. Deodorant. Floss. Shave cream. Razors. Two extra toothbrushes. That was it.

I opened a toothbrush and went to town on my teeth. If he was upset I used a toothbrush I'd buy him a new one. I couldn't afford Jimmy Choos or workmen who would make my living room habitable but I could afford a toothbrush.

I rinsed, flossed and wiped my hands. I did a few buttons up on his shirt and folded back the long sleeves. Then I walked out.

When I did, I was feeling nervous. This was different. This wasn't what we had. This wasn't fuck buddies or us fighting all the time. We'd had a date. He'd given me shoes. He'd carried me from a burning building. My father didn't mind walking in to see us in a carnal clinch. Meredith thought he was the bomb. I knew where he worked. I'd met some of his men. What I said at dinner with my parents was important to him.

Now I was in his lair.

My mind rifled through this information and then some as I walked to the stairs and walked down them slowly, spotting him in the kitchen but not looking at him. I was taking in the cavernous space.

A seating area in the middle with a big, wide couch, two recliners on either side, a big flat-screen TV all on a thick rug. Weight and exercise equipment down the opposite wall, a lot of it: weight bench, bars of weights, treadmill, stationary bike, rowing machine, elliptical machine. A desk in the far corner at a diagonal, facing the room, this showing personality, papers and files and a laptop on it. He used that desk and it showed, not like the rest of his place. A kitchen that had a big horseshoe bar with stools around it, another countertop against a column of brick wall between gigantic windows, top-of-the-line appliances. In between all of this there were some big rugs on the cement floor but mostly it was just open. Wide open.

Jeez, how on earth did he heat it?

My head turned left and I bit my lip when I saw under the bed platform an area that was definitely Hawk's space. Floor-to-platform shelves stuffed full with books and CDs. A very nice stereo. A battered old chair and ottoman that wasn't like the other furniture or equipment, not new, not stylish. There was a table next it, equally battered. A floor lamp behind the chair, its base going up and the shaded bulb drooping over the chair to provide light to read. A tatty, frayed old rug on the floor, so big, it filled the area. At the end, another cube, this paneled in a warm, worn wood, the door to it closed. That space was like it was from a different world, it didn't fit, it seemed snug and cozy, inviting.

Interesting.

I hit the bottom of the stairs and could delay no longer.

My eyes turned to him.

He was in the kitchen, bare-chested, coffee mug held aloft, eyes on me.

And in that instant, it hit me.

The pros outweighed the cons. I wasn't uncertain anymore. I was certain... *very* certain.

He could be bossy and a lot of what he did freaked me out or pissed me off but when he was sweet, generous, sexy and open it was better than my best daydream.

By far.

And I was good at daydreams. I'd spent a lot of time daydreaming. I made up the best daydreams ever.

So for reality to surpass that certainty slotted in and, when it did, it held firm.

I rounded the horseshoe and saw he was wearing track pants, black with dark gray stripes down the sides, bare feet.

Hot.

I went to him, right to him and didn't stop until my body hit his, my arms slid around his waist and I pressed my face in the skin of his chest.

There I mumbled, "Mornin', baby."

One of his arms glided around me, pulled me closer and he said into the top of my hair, "Mornin', Sweet Pea. You sleep okay?"

I turned my head to press my cheek to his chest as I nodded.

"Good," he murmured, giving me a squeeze.

I squeezed him back.

"Coffee?" he asked, and I nodded against his chest again. "How do you take it?"

I slid my cheek against his warm skin as I tilted my head back to look at him, my brows going up when my eyes hit his black ones. "You don't know?"

His mouth twitched. "No."

"Cream, half a sugar."

His brows went up this time. "Half a sugar?"

"I save my sugar for when I eat it in cookie dough."

He chuckled, his arm tightening for a second as he did then he kept looking down at me. I watched his eyes get lazy. I'd never seen that, his eyes getting lazy. It was sensational.

Then he bent his head, touched his lips to mine and let me go.

He moved to the coffeepot at the counter by the wall. I moved to the horseshoe bar and leaned against it.

"I used a toothbrush," I informed him.

"Good," he replied, grabbing a mug from some shelves that were fixed to the brick where there was a bunch of shiny, midnight blue stoneware, stainless steel utensils hanging from hooks off the bottom shelves, gleaming pots and pans on the top.

Guess he didn't need me to buy him a new toothbrush. And it also appeared from the near-new look of his eating and cooking supplies, he didn't cook or eat much at his lair.

"Do you move the furniture back and have football matches on Saturdays with your commandos?" I asked the brown skin over defined muscle of his back as he poured my coffee.

"No," he answered, but I could hear the smile in his voice.

"Rugby?" I went on.

He twisted to the fridge and opened it, repeating, "No."

"Paintball?"

He took out the milk, closed the fridge and looked over his shoulder at me, grinning. "No."

"Hmm," I mumbled.

He finished my coffee and brought it to me then rested

a hip against the counter, his body facing mine, our bodies touching.

I took a sip from my coffee as he did the same with his.

He made good coffee.

"You make good coffee," I shared.

He had no response.

I tilted my head back to look at him. "And you're tidy."

His brows drew together. "I'm tidy?"

"Your bathroom is clean, there isn't a tangle of cargos and skin-tight shirts all over the floor, and your stockpiles of guns and ammo have obviously been cleared away."

The dimples popped out.

Then he replied, "Disordered house, disordered mind, disordered life, babe."

This was true. I knew it because Dad had taught me that and it was also a principle I lived by, which was why my living room drove me batty.

"I can't picture you cleaning," I shared.

"I don't. Janine does it."

"Janine?"

"Takes care of this place, takes care of base. Janine's in charge of order so I can focus on other shit."

"Hmm," I mumbled.

He employed a lot of people. He drove a top-of-the-line Camaro. He installed elaborate security systems. He could afford expensive designer shoes. He could heat a cavernous warehouse to the point he could walk around barefoot and bare-chested and I was comfortable in only his shirt and a thong.

"You live in an old warehouse," I pointed out the obvious.

"Yeah," he agreed to the obvious.

"This is a lot of space, Hawk."

"Yeah," he agreed.

"*A lot* of space," I went on.

He grinned then took a sip of coffee. I did the same.

When his mug came away from his lips, he stated, "Don't like close. Need room."

Interesting.

"Well, you've got it."

He grinned again, put down his coffee mug, took mine from my hand, put that down too, and then moved into me at the front, his hands sliding around at my waist to my back, wrapping around and pulling me to him.

I rested my hands on his chest and looked up.

"You're cute in the morning," he told me.

"I am?" I asked.

"Cute and sweet."

"Mm," I mumbled, glad he thought that, but I'd always been a morning person. I was a night person too. I was an anytime person when I wasn't stressy and in a bad mood.

One of his hands left my back. I watched his eyes get heated and intense as they studied my face.

Then he did something beautiful, something amazing, something that, if I'd had any doubts as to my certainty, they would have disintegrated.

He tenderly slid the backs of his knuckles against the skin of my cheek while he muttered, "A year and a half. Totally fuckin' missed out."

My belly went squishy.

Yep, definitely certain.

"Hawk," I whispered, and his hand cupped my jaw.

"How much work did you get done?"

"What?"

"You were relaxed last night, not stressed, you good with work?"

"Um…" I mumbled, not wanting to think about work

or life or anything, wanting instead to just live this real daydream.

Hawk continued, "I gotta go do something this morning, boys'll be here in a few minutes and I want you here when I come back."

I stared into his eyes.

Oh my God.

Yay! He wanted me at his lair when he came back!

My mind shifted to work.

Oh shit.

Boo! I needed to get home and hit it.

I melted into him and my hands slid up his chest to his neck.

"One of my deadlines is today. I'm close to finished but I still need to get some work done." His arm squeezed me. I continued and I did it in a quiet, slightly scared, slightly hopeful voice, but my decision was made and my decision was about him so I figured he should know it even though it scared the freaking shit out of me. "I want to be here when you get back, baby, but I always make my deadlines. It's a promise I give my clients and—"

"Babe," he cut me off, "it's cool."

"I do want to be here," I restated to make sure he got it, but I did it on a whisper.

His hand at my jaw tilted my head back further as his dipped closer to mine. "I'm gettin' that, Sweet Pea," he whispered back, "and I like it."

He got it. And he liked it.

I licked my lips and nodded.

He touched his lips to mine then lifted his head an inch and said, "I gotta go with the boys. I'll call Fang. You take your time, get dressed, shower, get some food, whatever you wanna do. He'll be here in thirty minutes, take you home.

I'll leave a key for you, take it. The security code is three-three-six-four. When you're done, come back."

"Okay," I agreed readily.

His arm around me pulled me closer and his hand at my jaw slid back into my hair as I watched his eyes grow hot.

"We're past due, babe. Definitely. Even more since I had to watch you last night in that dress and those shoes and then you passed out practically naked in my bed before we got to play. Plan for an energetic evening."

Wow.

"Okay." I breathed it this time and again I did it readily.

He smiled a smile that, with his eyes hot on me and his body close, I saw was hungry.

Yum.

My fingers glided over his hair and put on pressure as I lifted up on my toes and my eyes dropped to his lips.

Therefore I watched them form the words in a mutter, "Totally missed out."

Then he kissed me, hot, hard, with tongues, and his hand at my ass pulled my hips into his as I held on and my legs and insides turned liquid.

He broke the kiss on what sounded like a frustrated growl and I liked that so much, it made me press closer. When I did, his mouth touched mine then came back then again and then his teeth nipped my lower lip.

Um...*nice*.

"Hawk," I whispered, still holding on.

"Baby, let go. You don't, I lose a client and no more fancy shoes."

I considered this, weighing shoes against sex with Hawk in his cavernous lair.

Then I kept holding on.

He smiled, his arm giving me a squeeze, his mouth

touching mine again then he let me go and stepped back. I moved to lean against the bar in an effort to hold myself up and he lifted a hand and ran the side of his index finger along the skin under my chin.

Um…*nice!*

"Later," he promised.

"'Kay," I replied.

His hand moved to my neck and gave it a squeeze. He moved away, dug in a drawer, pulled out a key which he dropped to the counter and then he strode to the stairs. I watched until he made it to the top. I grabbed my coffee, sipped at it and watched some more as he opened and shut drawers on his dresser and the wardrobe, then got dressed.

I heard the vehicles outside as he was sitting on the bed putting on his boots, and me and my coffee mug wandered to the stairs as he came down them. He hooked me with an arm at my shoulders, guided me to the door under the bed platform, through it to another cavernous space that held his Camaro, a black SUV, a motorcycle under a cover and still there was enough space to park my car, my dad's car and a motor home.

He grabbed a box that hung from a cable and had two big round red buttons on it. He pressed one, the colossal door slid up, cold from the outside assaulted me, but I only minutely felt it as he walked me to the end of the building and turned me to him. I succeeded in evasive maneuvering with my coffee mug right before he laid another hot, wet one on me.

He lifted his head and muttered, "Energetic."

"Gotcha," I replied. He grinned then I watched him prowl to one of three SUVs, seeing one of his commandos had jumped from the driver's seat and was rounding the vehicle to get in on the other side as Hawk took the wheel.

I stood there in the cold, in his shirt, carrying a shiny,

midnight blue coffee mug, completely unembarrassed because I was completely happy in my real-life daydream and I waved the commandos off as they drove away.

None of them waved back though I got a couple grins and one amused head shake.

Then I grabbed the box, hit the button, the big door groaned down and I reentered Hawk's lair.

*   *   *

I was on the bed platform making Hawk's bed when it happened.

The phone rang and, obviously, I ignored it.

Then the answering machine on one of the heavy, dark wood nightstands clicked on. An electronic voice asked the caller to leave a message then the caller left a message.

The minute I heard her voice, I froze mid pillow fluffing.

"Hawk?" Hesitant. Probing but unsure. "Honey, I hope everything's okay. You didn't show last night. I'm Thursday." Pause. "I hope you don't mind me calling." Still hesitant. "But I'm worried. Um…" Pause. "Call me, okay?" Another pause, then hurriedly, "Just so I know you're all right." Pause again then, "Um…okay, um…bye."

There was a buzz because she'd hung up and then silence.

I stood there, pillow in hand, staring at the answering machine, something unpleasant sifting through my stomach.

She was Thursday?

Thursday?

What the hell did that mean?

She was Thursday. Yesterday was Thursday. She was expecting a visit from Hawk.

She was Thursday.

That something in my stomach slid up my gullet, filled my mouth and it tasted of acid.

CHAPTER FOURTEEN

Filler

FANG IDLED AT the curb while I did my walk of shame up to my house. It really wasn't a walk of shame, but no one seeing me in the daylight hours in a little black dress and fabulous shoes would know that.

Fang, I found to my fortune, was not a master communicator. This was good and bad because this meant I could slide into my head and stay there the whole way from Hawk's lair. This was good because I needed to be in my head to sort my shit out and this was bad because I didn't want to be in my head and because I couldn't figure out how to sort my shit.

I opened the door and saw Meredith, Camille, Tracy and Mrs. Mayhew all sitting on my furniture and drinking coffee at the left side of my living room. The furniture had been uncovered, the floors had been swept, the mist of dust on all surfaces had disappeared. The renovation equipment had vanished. The right side of the living room was just as tidy but it was empty. A peek through the glass doors to my once-empty den showing it was now storage for tools, tubes, cans and equipment. The walls still needed to be re-skimmed, the floors refinished, the fireplace mantels stripped and redone and the light fixtures replaced but at least it looked like a living room

Jeez. It was ten o'clock. Meredith had been busy.

I stared at them and I loved them. I loved them all. And I loved that Meredith made my living room look like a living room.

But I wanted cookie dough. Aloneness and cookie dough.

No, I *needed* aloneness and cookie dough.

Like, *a lot*.

"Hey," I called.

"Have a good night?" Meredith beamed.

"Um..." I mumbled.

"That's a pretty dress," Mrs. Mayhew complimented.

"Thanks, Mrs. M," I replied, walking in thinking she was being so Mrs. M, saying I was wearing a pretty dress when I'd walked into my house in the clothes I'd worn the night before which everyone knew screamed *slut!*

"Heard you got a hot one on your hook," she remarked, smiling at me huge.

Well, I thought so, but I was worried I was on *his* hook.

"Um..." I mumbled again.

"You okay?" Cam asked, looking at me closely.

"Um..." I mumbled yet again.

All female eyes focused intently on me as it appeared I was incapable of speech.

Then Cam moved.

"Right," she said smartly, jumping up from the couch. "Shower, yoga pants, let's go!" she ordered and clapped her hands, coming to me, bustling me to the stairs and up them, right to my bathroom.

I turned at the bathroom door and looked at her.

Cam was my height, all legs and booty, minor cleavage that wasn't much to write home about but it didn't matter because she was flat-out, heart-stopping gorgeous. Big almond eyes, full lips, fabulous cheekbones, elegant jaw, perfectly arched brows. She was the exotic, African American yin to Tracy's girl-next-door yang. This used to give me a complex, seeing as my two best friends were akin to catwalk models let loose on society. I learned to control my feelings of inferiority through copious imbibing of cosmos and shopping for fantastic clothes I could don that would build my confidence whenever I went out with them.

"Cam," I said.

"You're freaked," she replied, reading me, as usual, like a book.

Not, of course, that I was being mysterious.

"Something happened," I told her. "Well, a lot of some-things happened but—"

"Shower, babe, I'll make a fresh pot and meet you in your office with Tracy. You got fifteen minutes." Then she turned and walked to the stairs.

There were a lot of things about Cam I loved. Being me, and allowing my life to career out of control occasionally, one of the best of them was her ability to control a situation and be decisive.

I did as I was told, and in yoga pants, camisole and zip-up hoodie with wet hair, I met Cam and Tracy in my office.

Tracy handed me a mug of joe.

I took it and my eyes slid to Cam. "How'd you ditch Meredith and Mrs. M?"

This I knew was a feat. Meredith was the only mom I knew, and she worried about me even though I was thirty-three and even when there wasn't anything to worry about. Mrs. M was Grandma to me and every kid on the block, be they thirty-three, three or sixty-three. If you were younger than her, she was your grandma, and nearly everyone I knew was younger than her except her friend Erma who evidence was suggesting was dating Father Time.

"I didn't have to," Cam answered. "Mrs. M is going with Meredith to her house to meet the insurance guy. But I did have to promise a full briefing."

"You aren't giving a full briefing," I declared, sitting in my office chair and taking a sip of coffee.

"Of course not," she muttered.

"What's with the face?" Tracy asked and I looked at her.

"What face?"

"*Your* face," she replied. "You look…I don't know how you look. I thought the date went great. Last night I got twelve texts about how great the date went. Now you don't look like the date went great."

My eyes slid to the window. "It did."

"So?" Cam prompted and my eyes slid to her.

"Thursday called," I answered, Cam's eyes closed slowly but Tracy's expression shifted to confused.

I stared at Cam. Cam knew something.

"Thursday called?" Tracy asked.

I ignored her.

"Cam?" I called, her eyes opened and a light shone in them, a sad light, an unhappy light. "Cam," I whispered.

"You told me you two were over," she said softly.

This was true.

"Thursday called?" Tracy repeated, sounding impatient, and I looked at her.

"Great date, the best, better than my wildest dreams. He was into me, he was interested in everything I said, he was funny, he bought me Jimmy Choos," I told her, and her eyes lit up.

"I know, his lady, Elvira, who's hilarious by the way, she swore me to secrecy but I thought that was *so cool!* Totally generous. I offered my discount but she said no. Just handed over a company credit card. Awesome!" Tracy ended on a cry and a bounce on the couch.

"Yeah, awesome, until Thursday called," I replied, and Tracy looked confused again.

"What's up with Thursday?" she asked.

"I don't know," I answered then looked at Cam. "But you do, don't you?"

Camille's eyes held mine. Then she sighed.

Then she spoke. "Cabe 'Hawk' Delgado is on the grid," she stated. "In fact, he's so on the grid, he's all over the grid. There's some mystery and a lot of speculation about his activities but he's Mr. Grid. If it's happening in Denver, he knows about it, and speculation says that sometimes he's in on it, though no one knows how. Also, no one knows exactly what he does, or *all* that he does, they just know he's a busy guy."

I already guessed this and, at that point, I didn't care about this.

So I prompted, "And?"

She pulled in breath, that breath that said she was preparing me for something not so fun.

Then she started to give me the not so fun. "One thing that doesn't have any mystery when it comes to Delgado is His Days."

"His Days?" Tracy repeated.

Cam nodded at her. "Otherwise known as His Women."

"Shit," Tracy muttered, her eyes cutting to me, but my eyes stayed glued to Cam as I struggled to breathe.

Then I choked out, "Talk to me."

Cam pressed her lips together then she said, "Girl, I'm so sorry."

I felt a tingly sensation in my throat and it wasn't the same happy one as last night.

"Talk to me, Cam," I whispered.

Another breath then Cam stated, "Okay, Delgado is known to claim women. He does this and slots them into a schedule. They come and go but while they're there, they're claimed. He investigates them and it's made clear no one goes near them. When he's done with them, he's done. One moves out, he moves another one in."

"This can't be," I told her. "I don't have a day."

Cam swallowed. Not a good sign.

"What?" I asked.

"Girl—" she started.

I leaned forward and repeated. "*What?*"

"You're known as Filler."

Oh my God.

"I'm known as *Filler?*" I whispered.

She nodded. "He's feeling like a switch-up, or one of his women is out of town or he's got a slot open he hasn't filled yet, he comes to you."

"I'm known as Filler," I repeated.

"Honey—" Tracy whispered.

"Who knows me as Filler?" I asked Cam.

"Um…" She hesitated then said, "Everyone now."

"Everyone now," I repeated.

She nodded.

"Lawson?"

She bit her lip and nodded again.

Oh my *God!*

"Tack?" I asked.

"Probably," Cam answered.

I looked to the floor. Then it hit me and I looked back at Cam.

"She knew," I stated.

"What, babe?" Cam asked.

"Thursday, she knew. She knew what she was, who she was, her day. She knew his *name*. She knew his *number*."

"Well, um—" Cam started.

I cut her off. "I guess, if you get a guaranteed slot, you get his contact details. But Filler, now Filler is just *filler*."

"Gwennie, sweetie," Tracy whispered.

I shot out of my chair and shouted, "I don't *believe* this!"

Camille and Tracy shot up too.

"Gwen, babe, listen to me. The talk now is he's off routine. This shit with His Days, it is for them what it was for you, night visits, stringent boundaries. He doesn't date them, he just sleeps with them."

"*So?*" I yelled, crashing my mug to my desk, coffee sloshing over.

"So, this is good, you've broken through," Tracy put in quickly and, as ever with my dear, sweet Trace, hopefully.

"No, Trace, this isn't *good*," I returned. "This is *humiliating*."

And it was. It was humiliating. Deep down to the core humiliating. And the worst part of that feeling was that I did it to my damned self.

Again!

I lifted my hands, slid my fingers in my hair and held on. "I can't believe this. I don't know what to do with this," I told the floor.

"Maybe you should talk to him about it," Cam, of all people, advised, and my head lifted so my eyes could narrow on her.

"Are you *high?*" I yelled, and her face flinched. "I'm *filler*, everyone *on the grid* knows it. God!" I pulled my hands through my hair and threw them out to my sides repeating, "*God!*"

"Babe," Cam said softly, "calm down."

I lifted my hands again to press my palms to my forehead and through my arms I looked at her.

"I want him," I whispered my secret.

"Then talk to him," Cam whispered back.

"I wanted him to be special," I kept whispering.

"Girl," she kept whispering too and got closer, wrapping her fingers around my arm, "talk to him."

"For him to be special, he has to make me feel special. Not like Scott made me feel." I heard Tracy make a soft whimper. She knew how Scott made me feel, they both did. "And definitely not *worse* than Scott made me feel."

Cam's other hand came up and wrapped around my arm, pulling them down, she stepped in close, her hands sliding up to grip mine as Tracy moved into our little huddle.

"I did this to myself," I whispered.

"Baby," Cam whispered back as Tracy slid her arm around my waist and she whispered, "Honey."

"I wanted to believe I could break through," I went on.

"Maybe you have," Cam replied.

"I think you have," Tracy put in.

"I held on, hoping to break through." I kept talking like they didn't speak.

"Gwen, take a breath and clear your head," Camille advised.

I dropped my head and looked at my toes. Dark berry polish, a winter color. I needed summer. I needed sun. It was time to take a vacation.

"I'll always be filler," I told my toes.

"Oh honey," Tracy whispered.

Suddenly I pulled away, lifted my head and announced, "I need to finish on my deadline." I looked at Cam. "Can I stay with you and Leo tonight?"

"I don't think that's a good idea," Tracy stated.

"Yeah, babe, you can," Cam replied.

"Cam!" Tracy snapped and Cam looked at her.

"She needs space," Cam returned.

Tracy looked at me. "He's coming to you tonight, isn't he?"

"No," I told her. "He wants me to go to him."

Her eyes lit and she moved in close. "Then *go*."

"No," I replied.

She put her hands on my shoulders. "Gwennie, this is shit. I get it. This sucks but I can't help but think that—"

I stepped back and her hands dropped. "I can. I can think it. And I'm not even mad at him, Trace. I'm not. This is me. I did this to me. I allowed this to happen. And if I'm ever going to have any self-respect after this fucking, *fucking* mess, I'm the one who has to stop it."

"That's a bad decision," Tracy said firmly.

"Maybe so, but it's the one I've made," I replied and straightened my shoulders. "Scott fucked me over and I loved him. That killed me. I even knew it was happening and I allowed it until I couldn't put up with allowing it anymore. With Scott, I waited too long to look after myself, hoping he'd sort his shit out, and I waited too long with Hawk. Even if things have changed for him, I'll always know what I allowed myself to be, what other people think of me. No wonder both Lawson and Tack thought they could make a play. They want to get in there, and who can blame them? A sure thing who opens her bed and her legs, no questions asked, no expectations, just an opportunity to get off and go your own way until you're done. Shit!"

"That isn't who you are," Cam declared.

"No? Seems like it to me," I shot back.

"Then, girl, you're *wrong*," Cam retorted.

I shook my head. "I can't think about this now. I have

to work. I'll come over as soon as I send my files," I told Cam.

She studied me then she said quietly, "All right, girl. I'm off today. I'll get ice cream."

"Cookie dough," I corrected.

"Cookie dough," she whispered.

"Gwennie—" Trace started, and my eyes moved to her.

"I love you, babe, you know I do, but not now. I can't take your hope now. Please."

"Okay," she whispered.

"I need to work," I repeated.

"Right," Cam replied.

I nodded my head once and twisted to turn on my computer. I snatched a Kleenex out of the box on my desk to mop up the coffee spill as I heard them move out of the room.

"Gwen?" Cam called, and I turned back, coffee-wet Kleenex in my hand, she was in my door. "Scott was an ass and Delgado controls his life to within an inch of it. He got one dose of you in the light of day and he's shifted his entire way of doing things. You are not who you think you are," she told me.

No, she was wrong. I was *exactly* who I thought I was and the worst of it was, Cabe "Hawk" Delgado knew it.

"I have to work," I told her.

"You're not who you think you are," she repeated.

I stared at her.

"Cookie dough," she whispered, then disappeared from my door.

* * *

"Ready, ready," I said to the courier who was standing inside my door. He was waiting, visibly impatiently, for me to finish writing out the check from the amount I'd jotted down when I called Nordstrom to find out exactly how much a pair of fabulous silver watersnake platform peep-toed slingbacks cost.

I signed the check, ripped it off and shoved it in the envelope with the note I'd dashed out while I still had the courage.

> Hawk,
> For the shoes. You need to find a replacement for my shifts.
>
> Gwen

I licked the envelope, closed it and handed it to the courier.

"You don't have a name of the company?" he asked me.

I shook my head. "No, I just know the building, four-teenth floor, turn right off the elevators, right again down the hall and second door down on the left. Tell whoever you hand it to to give it to Hawk."

His brows shot up. "Hawk?"

"Hawk."

He eyed me like he thought I had a screw loose.

Then he muttered, "Whatever," and took his leave.

I shut the door behind him.

Then I walked upstairs and sent my work to my author with my notes. I packed a bag. I wrote a note for Dad and Meredith and left it in the kitchen. Then I got in my car, which Meredith and I had gone to get from her house the day before.

Then I went to Cam and Leo's.

CHAPTER FIFTEEN

Ferret Rescue

I SAT AT Cam and Leo's kitchen table with Leo. I was in my nightshirt. Leo was in a gray t-shirt and plaid pajama bottoms. Cam had an early shift. Leo had a late one.

Leonard Freeman was all bulky, compacted muscle on an average-height frame, kind black eyes and midnight skin. He was man from head to toe, which made him perfect for Camille because, except for her lack of cleavage (which was camouflaged by her ample booty and beautiful face), she was all woman.

Leo took a sip of coffee and so did I.

Then he started, "Gwen—"

Nope. No. Where Camille Antoine was a straight talker, Leo was a sage. If he lived back in ancient Greece, Leo would kick Plato's ass. He had life figured out and in a flash he could read people and situations and know exactly what was going on. This made him a good cop but a dangerous friend.

Desperate, I shifted focus, and because I was desperate, I opened my mouth and inserted my foot.

"Why haven't you asked Cam to marry you?"

His eyes widened and he stared at me.

Shit. Shit, shit, *shit!* Did I actually say that?

"Um…" I started to backtrack but couldn't figure out how.

"She wants to get married?" Leo asked, and it was my turn to stare. Apparently, Leo being able to read everybody didn't extend to his live-in girlfriend.

"Well…" I hesitated, "yeah."

"Seriously?"

I blinked.

"Uh…" I hesitated again, "*yeah.*"

"I thought she was happy with the way things were," he told me.

"She is," I told him.

He stared.

Well, I brought us to this dire pass, I had to lead us through it.

Shit!

"Are you happy with the way things are?" I probed cautiously.

"Fuck yeah," he replied.

Well, at least that was firm.

"So…um, your hesitation with making it official has to do with…" I trailed off and lifted my eyebrows.

"It's fine like it is. Why change it?" he asked.

Okay, I was careening down the highway to the danger zone so I might as well shift up and engage the rocket launchers. The problem was, this meant explaining women to him, and men never really were able to process that.

"All right, this is the gig," I said and straightened in my chair, shifting my booty in it to indicate what I was saying needed his close attention. "Women like clothes, they like shoes, they like flowers and they like people to look at them and think, 'God, she's gorgeous.' The more people who think that, the better it is. The one day in your life where you get all that rolled up into one is your wedding day. And it comes with *jewelry* and *presents* and ends with a *vacation* where it's practically law that you have to wear fabulous underwear and have lots of sex."

Leo flashed me a white smile showing that, likely, most of what I said was lost on him, but I got through with the fabulous underwear and lots of sex so relief flooded through me.

Therefore, I reached out a hand and wrapped it on his forearm. "So, you give her that then you come home and it's the same as it was before except you have towels and china in your house you didn't have to buy."

His arm twisted and he caught my hand then he gave it a squeeze.

Then he muttered, "This sounds good."

"Well, lucky for you, you got it for free. I'm considering going on the road, holding classes for men, explaining things. I just need to hook up my commissions with wedding planners and really bad cover bands."

This got me another white flash of smile even as he noted, "Engagement rings don't exactly come cheap."

"This is true, but I'm Cam's best friend and I'm not going to mess with any of that kitchen and bathroom bridal shower stuff. It's all about lingerie." I let his hand go and crossed my heart then lifted my hand, palm out. "Swear."

"You break that promise, darlin', and I gotta sort through garlic presses and other shit to find the bottle opener, you know I'll make you pay," he threatened.

"Camille doesn't have a garlic press?" I asked, fake aghast.

This got me another white flash.

The white faded and his eyes grew intent. "She worried about this?"

"Cam?"

"Yeah."

"Yeah," I answered honestly and quietly.

"Shit," he muttered.

"She wants to be yours, Leo," I told him.

"She is mine, Gwen," he told me.

"Then let her show the world every day by giving her a ring."

He held my eyes. Then he nodded once.

Then he said, "I gotta get to the gym."

I nodded back, saying, "I gotta get home."

He stood and I took a sip of coffee. I thought he'd go to the sink but he came to me. I tipped my head back to look at him just as his hand cupped the back of my head and his face got close.

"This," he whispered, "this right here is why Cabe Delgado finally woke the fuck up."

My heart seized but I wheezed, "Leo."

"No more to be said, darlin', think about that," he declared, pulled my head forward an inch, kissed my hair and then let me go and walked his mug to the sink.

God, I loved Leo. He was the shit.

I looked out the window. The snow was long gone. February was leaking into March. In Denver this meant anything goes weather-wise. Blizzards, lying out in the sun in your bikini or both within an hour.

My phone hadn't rung and Hawk hadn't attempted to penetrate the Antoine/Freeman fortress. Even if he didn't get my check and note yet, he went back to his lair to find I wasn't there.

He was no call and no show.

This said it all, and I told myself I was relieved, but I wasn't.

*   *   *

As I drove up to my house I noted that the good news was, Dad and Meredith's cars weren't there.

Dad called the night before to say that he and Meredith were going to spend the day at their house cleaning and sorting through stuff. I told him I wanted to get a few hours of work done to stay on target and then I'd come and help.

The bad news was, there was a Harley in my drive and on that Harley sat Tack.

Shit.

I pulled up to the curb so I wouldn't block him in and he threw his leg off his bike. He started to the front door, so I headed there.

"Hey, Peaches," he greeted when I got close.

I had not bothered with makeup or hair. I'd taken a shower and put on another pair of yoga pants, a camisole and a zip-up hoodie. I hoped I looked like hell but the way he was watching my hips move as I walked, I was guessing I didn't. Or at least my hips didn't.

"Hey," I replied.

His eyes lifted from my hips to mine. "Got a minute?"

"Depends," I answered. "Are you here to tell me Ginger owes you three million dollars now?"

"Nope."

"Are you here about Ginger at all?"

"Nope."

"Are you here to freak me out in any other way?"

"Nope."

"This would include asking me for a date," I warned.

"Babe, don't date," he replied.

This was a surprise so I tipped my head to the side. "You don't?"

"Do tequila shots followed by five hours of sex count as a date?" he asked.

"Um...no," I answered.

"Then I don't date."

I smiled at him.

Then, stupidly, I asked, "You can have sex for five hours?"

He smiled at me.

Yikes.

Moving on.

"Okay, you can have a minute."

"Obliged," he muttered.

I opened the door and the alarm started beeping. I panicked because I forgot the code. Then I deep breathed and remembered the code. I punched it in and the beeping stopped.

Shoo.

I turned to see Tack followed me in and closed the door.

"See you domesticated," he noted, glancing around.

"No, my stepmom has been in residence due to fire damage to her living room. She domesticated."

His eyes came to me. "She in residence now?"

"She's at her house cleaning up fire damage."

"That sucked, babe," he said softly.

"Tell me about it," I agreed and walked into my house, dumping my bag and purse on my couch. Turning, I found he followed me and he did it close.

I tipped my head back to look at him.

"I don't have any tequila," I remarked, and he threw his head back and laughed. His laugh was just as gravelly and rumbly as his voice and I had to admit, I liked it.

Shit.

Time to lay ground rules.

"You should know, yesterday, I made a new life decision. I've sworn off men."

His brows went up. "You have?"

"Yep."

"Hawk know this?"

"I haven't shared directly, but I sent a message."

His eyes grew intense. "Why?" he asked.

"It's a long story and I don't mean to be rude or anything but I have to get some work done. Then I have to gather up all my little black dresses and high-heeled shoes and take them to Goodwill. Then I have to go help clean up fire damage. Then I have to come home and make cookie dough. So maybe we can have your talk."

He ignored my suggestion. "Sounds like you got a full day."

"I have a full life."

"Seems to me your fixin' to punch some holes into that, no Hawk, no high-heeled shoes."

"I've decided to take up hiking."

He grinned.

"And ferret rescue," I added.

His grin turned to a smile.

"Um... you wanted to talk?" I prompted.

"Yeah—" he started, but didn't continue, because right then, the room exploded.

That's right, *exploded.*

One second we were standing there bantering and the next the windows blew inward, glass shattering and plaster bursting from the walls *everywhere.* Then, of course, there was the loud noise of multiple automatic weapons all around.

I stupidly froze but luckily Tack didn't. He picked me up at the waist, bent low but somehow managed to carry me through the living room to the kitchen, where he put me on my feet and threw the door closed.

"What's happening?" I shouted, forgetting to pause and, say, check for bleeding gunshot wounds on him *or* me.

"Fuck," he muttered, yanked his phone out of his jeans and flipped it open all the while crowding me across the kitchen until I hit the wall at the back at the same time the noise came into my living room.

I put my hands on him as he pressed in, shielding me with his body. "Tack!"

The noise stopped.

He had his phone to his ear and he had obviously engaged. "Drive-by, Gwen's house. Sounds like three, four weapons. I'm cut off from my bike and Gwen's car. I need immediate recon and I need to know why the fuck they targeted her house." He paused. "Right." Then he flipped his phone shut.

I was staring up at him, my throat feeling clogged, adrenaline surging through my system, every centimeter of skin on my body tingling, a feeling that was becoming all too familiar.

"Tack," I whispered.

He looked down at me. "Stay here, hang tight. I'll be back."

He'd be back?

What did he mean, he'd be back?

Then he was gone.

Oh God. Shit. What did I do? Someone shot up my living room!

My purse was in the living room. My phone was in my purse. Shit.

Why hadn't I put a phone in the kitchen? Why? Why, why, *why?* First thing whatever morning it would be when it was *safe* again to be in my fucking *house*, I was putting a phone in *every room*.

The kitchen door opened and Tack was there, his arm extended to me. "Gwen."

I was still pressed against the back wall and my panicked eyes went to him.

"What?" I snapped.

"Come here," he said.

Was he crazy? *Here* was the living room! And ten seconds ago that room *exploded!*

"What?" I snapped again.

"Now!" he clipped back, and I moved.

Rushing to him, he grabbed my hand, dragged me through the nightmare that was my living room, out the front door and straight to his bike. He threw a leg over then I climbed up behind him, wrapping my arms around him and holding on tight. The engine roared, he backed it out, turning into the street and then we shot away.

*   *   *

Tack drove behind Ride where the garages were. I'd never been there but saw that there was a rectangular, one-story building. He rode right up to the door and stopped. I hopped off, he followed, grabbed my hand and a biker had the door held open for us as Tack took us into the building. It looked like a bar and bikers were all hanging around though they were hanging around alert and their eyes all came to Tack and me.

"Callouts, brothers," Tack growled, but that was all he said. He kept dragging me through the bar and around it to a back hall as men moved toward the front door.

Tack pulled me down the hall. It was filled with doors and he took me to the last one. He pushed it open and pulled me in. It was a bedroom and it needed to be cleaned, *badly*.

A biker followed us in and Tack looked at him and then he looked at me.

"You done with Hawk?" he asked what I thought was insanely.

"What?" I asked back.

"Babe, gotta know, you done with Hawk?"

"Um . . . yes," I answered.

He stared at me and then asked, "You sure about that?"

"Yes! What are you—?"

I didn't finish my question. The minute he got my answer he turned to the biker.

"Hawk shows, any of his boys, you aim to maim and you get her outta here. Yeah?"

Oh my God!

"Tack!" I shouted, and he swung to me.

Then both his hands came to either side of my head and he pulled me up to his face.

"You may be done with Hawk but Hawk doesn't finish with a woman until he finishes with that woman. Not to mention, you just bought yourself a situation. I don't know why but I'm *gonna* know. And since I was there and nearly got filled with bullets right alongside you, peaches, now this is *our* situation. Do you get me?"

I was really, *really* afraid I did and by getting him that meant, for me, I'd jumped out of the frying pan smack into the freaking fire.

"Tack," was all I could say.

"You get me," he muttered, let me go and walked out of the room, slamming the door, and I heard it lock.

I stared at the door.

Oh boy.

CHAPTER SIXTEEN

Not on My Watch

MY BODY JOLTED and my eyes opened.

I was asleep on the unmade bed in what I was assuming was the Chaos Compound.

Night had fallen. I had been locked in a while but luckily my biker rations included a delicious pastrami on rye with melted Swiss cheese, curly fries and a thick chocolate shake chased by a diet pop.

I was worried about my dad and Meredith who would be worried about me and I was freaked way the hell out at the same time I was bored out of my skull. However, I never guessed when I chanced lying down on the unmade bed that I'd fall asleep.

Guess I fell asleep.

I tried to sense what made me wake and I couldn't. I listened and looked into the dark room that was lit pretty well by lights coming in through the window.

I stared at the door and listened harder.

That's when I heard it. A muted thump like a body falling to the floor. A *big* body hitting the floor. Maybe a big *biker* body falling to the floor.

Holy *crap*.

I scurried off the bed and blindly searched the room for weapons. There I was in another situation where I needed a crowbar.

I didn't have time to find a weapon. There was a gunshot blast and I saw it because it blew off the lock on the door.

Shit!

I made a run for it, jumping on the bed and dashing over it toward the window (which I'd earlier noted was barred but it was my only hope). I was caught jumping off the other side of the bed with an arm around my belly. I made an "oomph" noise then I was turned and tossed over a shoulder.

This was when I decided to struggle and scream. I kicked and twisted and shouted my head off and in the hall my abductor bent fast. I landed hard on my feet then found myself shoved harder into the wall.

"Shut it, Gwen, and cool it or I'll bind you and gag you. I'm not kidding."

As I listened to the familiar deep voice, I stared into the shadowed face of Hawk.

I shut it and cooled it. Then I found myself back over his shoulder.

Once we made it to the bar, shadowy commandos flanked him. I also saw shadowy biker bodies littering the floor. The lights were out, no power at all, not even on the beer signs.

We made it out the door and Hawk and his troop jogged to SUVs.

Yes, even with me over his shoulder, Hawk jogged to an SUV.

Okay, maybe he wasn't one step down from a superhero. Maybe he *was* a superhero.

Hawk opened the door of the passenger side of one and I was tossed in. Hawk rounded the hood as he holstered his weapon and I watched his other hand do hand motions as the commandos dispersed. He folded in beside me, started up the SUV, reversed like a speed demon so I quickly belted in and then we shot out of Ride's premises and onto Broadway.

I took a deep breath and then started, "Hawk—"

"Do not speak," he growled, and I felt my breath catch.

He didn't sound pissed. He sounded *pissed*.

He dug into a pocket of his cargos and pulled his cell out. He flipped it open, hit some buttons and put it to his ear.

A couple of beats and then, "Bax?"

Oh shit. Dad.

"She's fine. I've got her."

Shit!

Hawk stopped at a light. "Don't know but she was in a safe place. Probably just freaked."

"Can I talk to him?" I asked, my hand extended for the phone.

His head turned to me and I saw his face in the streetlights.

I pressed my lips together and dropped my hand.

Okay, so, I couldn't talk to my dad.

And also, I was in trouble.

Good to know . . . or *not!*

"Yeah, let me talk with her, see if she's had food, get her shit together. Yeah?" Pause. "Right. Later."

He flipped his phone shut and threw it on the console with just enough strength to make it clatter angrily.

I sucked in breath. Then I gave him a few moments to calm down. Then I tried again.

"Hawk—"

"Swear to God, Gwen," he replied on another growl, and didn't finish, but that was enough. I clamped my mouth shut. He clearly needed a few more moments.

He drove and I knew where he was driving. To his lair.

I stayed silent the entire way. I also stayed silent when he stopped outside the big rolling door to his big garage. I also stayed silent and stayed put when he got out, went in a door to the side of the big rolling door and then the big rolling door slid up. Further, I stayed silent when he climbed back in and drove into the garage, parked, grabbed his phone and got out.

I got out too.

He went to the box on the cable and closed the door. I waited. Then he went to the inside door, pushed it open and strode in. I sucked in a calming breath while I heard him beep in the numbers on the security panel and then followed.

I moved and stopped under the platform. He moved around and turned on lights. The one by the chair in the corner. Two standing lamps in the seating area. He hit a switch and lights I hadn't noticed that hung on long cables from the ceiling lit the kitchen.

I leaned against an iron column that held up the platform.

"Can you explain to me why you're so angry?" I asked quietly.

I thought it was a good question. I mean *I* didn't lock myself in the Chaos Compound. *I* didn't do a drive-by on my house. *I* just happened to be in the wrong place at the wrong time and unfortunately that place was my own house.

"First," he replied, walking slowly to me and I knew it was not a good sign that he started by counting, "you just forced war."

I blinked. Then I asked, "War?"

"War, me and my boys against the Chaos MC."

"What?" I asked. "Why?"

"Babe," he stated, and stopped a few feet away from me. "You were locked in Tack's room at the Compound. That's a declaration. My boys and I had to infiltrate it to get you out. This will not go over well."

"Um...I think you may be misinterpreting things. See, Tack was there when someone shot up my living room and I think he was trying to protect me."

It must be said, though not to Hawk, that I *thought* this and I did it hopefully so I wouldn't have a nervous breakdown. I thought other things too, things akin to what Hawk was saying but I didn't let them have too much of my headspace considering they'd give me a nervous breakdown. I'd never had one but I was pretty sure nervous breakdowns were things to be avoided.

"Even Kane Allen, he decides to play a good Samaritan, is gonna drop the victim of a drive-by at the police station. Not claim her as his and ride out to hunt down the perpetrators unless he's," he leaned forward, "*claiming her as his.*"

Uh-oh.

"Okay, I can see that as bad, but *he's* doing it. I made no such declaration."

"Then you wanna tell me why Tack was there during the drive-by?"

"He was at my house when I got home this morning."

"So?"

"He wanted to talk."

"So?"

"So, he promised not to say anything to freak me out, so I agreed to talk."

"All right, Sweet Pea, let's go back to why you weren't somewhere else this morning, for instance," he took a threatening step forward, "*here.*"

Uh-oh.

"Hawk—"

I stopped talking when he took another threatening step

forward and seeing as his legs were so long, this meant he was close. Too close. Really scary close.

"Yesterday," he said in a terrifying, quiet voice and got closer so I slid away from the column and took a step back. "I left here," he kept coming at me so I kept stepping back, "and when I left here," I kept moving, he kept coming, "you were sweet and cute."

I hit bookshelves and was forced to stop. Hawk didn't stop. He pinned me in, his head tipping down to look at me but he didn't touch me. He pinned me in with the sheer force of his badassness.

"Then," he went on, "yesterday afternoon, I get this fuckin' note with a fuckin' check. The note, I don't get. The check, babe, the check is a smack in the fuckin' face."

Hmm. Maybe I didn't think that out very well.

"So I check the device on your car and see you've holed up with a cop," he continued.

"You have a device on my car?" I whispered, and his scary, angry face turned scarier and angrier so I shut my mouth.

"I come home," he stayed with his subject, "and I got a message from Gayle. So I get the note because I get that you heard her message and then you listened to some bullshit that your friend fed you and you didn't pick up the phone or get your ass to my place so you could talk to me. You went off half cocked and doin' it pissed me way the fuck off."

All right. Since we were on this subject then we had to talk about this subject.

"I know about Your Days," I whispered.

"Yeah? You do?"

"Yeah," I kept whispering, "I do. And I know I'm filler."

"No," he returned. "You know a bunch of cops with shit for brains and nothin' better to do with their time called you that. And somethin' else, babe, that shit is totally made up. It's complete bullshit. Gayle calls herself Thursday because she's got another man who doesn't do it for her and he goes out and gets shitfaced on Thursdays and doesn't come home until the bars close so I feel like her, I visit her. I don't have a schedule. The only woman I've investigated with any thoroughness and the only one I watch is you."

"But you said when you make a woman yours, you do your—"

"No, Gwen, forget about what you thought you read into what I said. I'm tellin' you now, straight out, how it is. And I'm not gonna feed you shit about there not bein' others. There are others. And I think you get that I'm not a man inclined to waste my time doin' precisely what I'm doin' right fuckin' now, explaining myself."

Oh shit. Now I was getting mad.

"I see," I stated quietly. "We're right back where we started."

"No, if we were back where we started, somewhere in the last couple of days I'd have had a piece of your sweet ass."

My mouth dropped open.

He could not be believed!

"I don't believe you!" I yelled.

"It's not true?" he asked.

"No, see, the last couple of days my sister's *shit* has leaked into my life. Did I do anything wrong? No! I don't live in your world. I knew Dog. I knew he was good for Ginger. I figured he'd sort her out. I didn't know what would happen when I went to Ride! How the hell would I know? I didn't open the door to the guy who broke in! I didn't guide the fire bombers to my parents' house and hurl a flaming bottle through the window! I went home today, that's it. I just went home and got *caught* in a *hail* of *gunfire!* But after that was over, I just did what I was told. I'd never been shot at before. Tack seemed to know what he was doing so I figured it would be good to be with someone who knew what they were doing. I didn't know he was going to lock me in his Compound and start a war! I've just been doing the best I can do in a seriously bad situation. No! In *multiple seriously bad situations!*"

"Gwen—"

"And I don't need you to be a jerk on top of it."

"Gwen—"

I threw my hands out to the sides. "My living room was shot up today. With me *in* it!" I screeched.

His hands came to my jaws. "Baby, calm down."

"*You* calm down! You can walk through walls and silently down bikers. I don't have those abilities, Hawk. I was in another situation where I needed a crowbar! That *sucks!* And after that, I need cookie dough. Or at the very least really good Chinese food from Twin Dragon or, better yet, Imperial."

His thumbs swept my jaw and he said quietly, "All right, baby, I'll get you Imperial."

I shook my head but unfortunately didn't shake his hands free. "No, the other night, I liked you. Tonight, I don't," I announced. "I mean, thank you for saving me from biker prison but now I want to go home…" It was then I realized I didn't have a home, my parents' didn't have a home, and therefore I was fucked, so I finished lamely, "Or… wherever."

"You are where you're gonna be until whatever the fuck is happening is over, babe," Hawk declared.

"Hello?" I called. "Let me remind you that you live in Badass World and *I do not.* You can't *tell* me where to be."

"I sure as fuck can, Gwen," he replied.

"No, you can't," I returned. His hands slid to my neck and his fingers curled deep.

"Listen to me, Gwendolyn," he growled, and I missed that somewhere he got un-pissed but I wasn't missing that he was now re-pissed and him saying my full name only underlined it. "As far as intel we got goes, Ginger was nowhere in the vicinity today when you had your drive-by. So that means one of two things. Those shots were meant to take out Tack or they were meant to take you out."

"No one wants me dead," I returned.

"No, but they want Ginger to suffer, and she's your sister and they might not know you're not tight and, last, they're gettin' desperate, so, like I said, they could have meant to take you out."

Holy fucking *shit!*

I closed my eyes and muttered, "Why does this keep getting worse?"

I opened my eyes when Hawk answered, "Because your sister is a piece of trash." I was going to let him have that this time, but I didn't get the chance to tell him that because he went on. "Now, we don't know but we need to assume you're a target, which means your parents may be targets, which means protection. You're safe here so you're gonna stay here. I'll do what I can for them. And I'll do what I can to bring peace with Tack because I need him as an ally with this shit and I don't need more to deal with and that includes you giving me lip."

"You're going to do what you can for my parents?" I asked and he stared down at me, his fingers flexing into my neck.

"Sweet Pea, look at me."

"I am looking at you." And I was!

"No, really, look at me."

I was really looking at him!

He kept talking. "Gayle's never been here, she's never gonna be here, and her place got shot up in a drive-by, she asked my advice, I'd tell her to talk to the police. Now, do you get where I'm comin' from here?"

"Not really," I told him, and his fingers flexed again so I asked, "You said you investigated me and watched me and not them, why?"

He looked over my head and muttered, "Jesus."

"Now you aren't looking at me," I observed, and his eyes cut back down to me.

"I'm good, babe, and I know you like it. I know you like what I can do to you, but that isn't it for you with me and now I know it never was. And for me, you're you. That meant I needed to engage."

My heart skipped a beat.

"What?" I whispered.

He kept going. "I did the normal shit, looked into you and I found out Ginger was your sister. I found out you showed too much skin when you went out. I found out you talk to strangers like they're your best friends. I found out you don't live in the real world, you live in a dream world where you don't pay a fuckuva lot of attention to what's happening around you and you make questionable life decisions. I found out you gave what you have to give only to me. Because of that, it became clear you needed looking after. So I did."

"I can look after myself, Hawk," I partially lied. This was true in normal circumstances, it wasn't when I was getting shot at.

"Bullshit," he replied.

I wasn't going to fight that, not now, not with bullets flying, so I decided to fight something else.

"You didn't complain about too much skin the other night," I reminded him.

"Yeah, babe, that's because your ass was in my ride and on my arm the other night and your focus was entirely on me."

Hmm. That was a good answer.

I kept at it. "I don't live in a dream world."

"Gwen, you took one look at me, decided I was the one, I said four words to you and you took me to your goddamned house *and* your goddamned bed and didn't say word fuckin' one when I kept comin'."

He had a point there.

Time to retreat.

"I'm hungry and I need to go to the bathroom," I announced.

His fingers flexed on my neck again when he declared, "Christ, you're a pain in my ass."

"Okay, then let me use your bathroom and then your phone to call a taxi so I can go to a hotel."

He glared down at me and flexed his fingers at my neck again but this time he used them to pull me in and up.

"You say I don't listen to you but you haven't been listenin' to me. We're gonna ride this wave, you and me, what we got, what we had the night before last, even, fuck me, what we have right now. Don't think for a second you can give me the sweet taste you gave me yesterday morning and then freak out and think you can cut ties. And while we're doin' it you're not getting filled with holes, kidnapped, tortured and mutilated for your fuckin' sister. Not on my watch."

I had to admit, that last part gave me some relief and made my belly get squishy. Though I didn't admit this verbally, I just stared.

He held my stare then he sighed, his hands relaxed on my neck and I was able to move away two inches but that was all I got.

"I'm callin' one of my boys to get Imperial and then you're callin' your father and then I'm callin' Lawson so he can come here and talk to you about what happened at your house today. What do you want from Imperial?"

I was hungry so I wasn't going to bicker. And anyway, Imperial was the best Chinese food in Denver. It would be a crime against nature to bicker when Imperial was on offer.

"Sesame chicken and hot and sour soup," I told him then added, "oh, and crab cheese wontons."

He stared at me then he asked, "Anything else?"

"No."

"You sure?"

"I'm usually too full to try their desserts so I don't know if they're good, so if you don't have a roll of cookie dough in your fridge, it wouldn't be unwelcome if one of the commandos swung by King Soopers and got some. Chocolate chip or sugar cookie."

"I don't have cookie dough in my fridge."

I knew this. The morning before I'd checked in his fridge and he had yogurt, cottage cheese, fresh fruit, slices of smoked salmon and veggies. It was a wasteland in there. He didn't even have condiments.

He studied my face while I thought this, then remarked, "Babe, it isn't a punishable offense not to have cookie dough."

"Maybe not but you don't have condiments."

"Ketchup and cottage cheese don't go real good together."

I felt my lip curl in disgust then I watched his lips twitch in amusement as his hands at my neck gentled entirely and one thumb stroked the skin under my ear.

"You good?" he asked softly.

"About what? You and me? My living room being a disaster? Or war with Tack which, by the way, I should note, is *not* my fault."

"Any of that," he answered.

"No," I told him truthfully.

His lips twitched again and he advised, "You need to quit bein' such a smartass."

"Why?"

He went on like I didn't speak. "At the same time bein' so cute."

"That I'll agree with, cute is becoming a problem."

The lip twitch turned into a grin. "You gave Lawson sweet and cute and you gave Tack smartass and cute." His fingers flexed again and pulled up as his head came down while he muttered, "Lucky for me, I'm the only one who's got it all."

"Hawk," I said when his lips were against mine.

"What?" he asked.

"I need you to feed me."

"Right," he murmured, then brushed his mouth against mine, but when he pulled away he didn't go very far and his eyes locked to mine.

"Don't try dodgin' me again, Gwen," he warned, and I tensed at his tone. "Your friend's man is a cop or not, I'll come and get you. You almost got dead today. That's twice in a week. That shit's gonna stop and it isn't Tack who's gonna make it stop for you. Got me?"

"I'll quit being a smartass if you quit being so bossy."

"I see you didn't take me seriously."

"I'm being perfectly serious."

"It's impossible for you not to be a smartass."

"Likewise for you and bossy."

He stared into my eyes.

Stalemate.

Then he let go, took half a step back and dug in his cargos for his phone.

He handed it to me and ordered, "Call your dad."

I took it and muttered, "Bossy."

Hawk sighed.

I flipped the phone open and called my dad.

CHAPTER SEVENTEEN

Protect Gwendolyn Kidd Duties

I WOKE UP and I knew I was in Hawk's bed.

I stretched out an arm and found the bed empty so I opened my eyes and listened. I could hear nothing.

I rolled and looked across the wide expanse of his warehouse to see the sun shining in everywhere. I tucked my hands under my cheek, and as I let sleep drift from me, I let thoughts drift in about the night before.

Dad was freaked and Meredith more so. Firebombs were bad enough; automatic weapons ratcheted it up to a new level of bad. Especially when reports came in that my car was at the front of the house and my purse and bag were on the couch "at the scene." My disappearance wasn't handled very well, and though it wasn't my fault, I felt badly about it.

What was more than a little frightening about this was that when Cam got the call at dispatch and she couldn't contact me, she contacted Dad and Dad immediately got hold of Hawk. Somewhere along the line they'd shared phone numbers and Dad had become "Bax" to Hawk and Hawk had become Protector and Knower of or Go-to-Guy to Find Out All Things Gwen to Dad.

I wasn't sure this was good.

I handed over Hawk's phone after I spoke with Dad and Meredith and he made a call and gave his orders. These were carried out to the letter and they included more than an order for Chinese. I knew this when commandos arrived and there were three of them. They brought Imperial but they also brought King Soopers bags. When I unpacked them I found they had diet cola, diet grape, two percent milk (Hawk only had skim and, seriously, what was the point of skim?—this a thought I relayed to him prior to his call to the commandos), eggs, bacon, lunchmeat, bread, a variety of chips, two rolls of chocolate chip cookie dough, two of sugar cookie dough and a plethora of condiments.

Hmm.

They also brought my desk and when I say that I mean they brought *my desk*—my chair, my desk, everything on it and in it, my computer all the way down to my box of Kleenex. They boxed it all up and delivered it, putting the desk in the opposite corner to Hawk's, setting the boxes around it but hooking up the computer.

They also brought my purse and, scarily, my two big suitcases. Yes, *two* of them. Upon inspection I found the suitcases packed carefully and full. Clothes, underwear, nightgowns, shoes, face products, my sweet pea lotion and bath gel and a good selection of makeup. This would have stunned me, the ability of commandos to pack, but I was told by Hawk that Elvira had been activated to do my packing. I wasn't certain how I felt about an unknown woman going through my stuff, but it couldn't be denied the results were excellent.

Lawson showed and I ate my food while I gave my statement. Lawson didn't look happy and this had to do with the fact that I'd endured a drive-by, the fact that Tack essentially abducted and detained me afterward, and the fact that he was taking my statement while I was sitting cross-legged in one of Hawk's recliners in his seating area while spooning up hot and sour soup. How I knew this, I didn't know. I just knew it.

When Lawson was done, he came to me and bent over me, getting close right in front of a stony-faced Hawk.

"Head up, sweetheart, eyes open, stay safe," he whispered.

"Okay," I whispered back because I figured that was good advice and because he called me "sweetheart."

He tucked my hair behind my ear and gave me a smile. Then he straightened and gave Hawk an unhappy look. Then he left.

I spent the rest of the night sorting out my cell and suitcases while Hawk talked on his phone. I didn't unpack clothes but I did unpack toiletries and I populated Hawk's shower, shelves and medicine cabinet with girlie shit.

I didn't ask if I could do this. He wanted me there, I was going to be there.

Though he also didn't complain, comment or even give me a look and he knew I'd done it because I had a lot of girlie shit, it was everywhere, and he'd visited the bathroom.

I didn't know what to make of that, so I decided to ignore it and then let it freak me out at random, which was when stuff I buried that I should deal with usually freaked me out.

I had twenty-seven missed calls and fourteen texts, all from a freaked-out Dad, Meredith, Cam, Tracy, Leo and even Troy. Word had got round about the drive-by. I returned Cam and Tracy's calls, but I shied away from Troy. I hadn't had any cookie dough and Imperial was good but it didn't set me up to deal with Troy.

I crashed while Hawk was still on the phone. He was either busy or giving me space and since he had so much of it, that was easy to do.

I woke momentarily when he joined me in bed and curled into me. The instant his arm went tight around my belly and he settled, I fell back to sleep.

Now was now and I didn't know what to do now. There were too many things to contemplate and just the thought of them exhausted me and I'd just woken up.

I sighed and as I did, my cell rang.

Saved by the cell.

It was on the nightstand. I reached out, grabbed it and I turned the display to see I had a call from Tracy.

I flipped it open and put it to my ear. "Hey, babe."

"Hi, how are you doing, honey?"

She was tweaked and my conversation with her last night didn't assuage her tweakedness. Then again, most people lived their whole lives not having a friend who got caught in a drive-by then disappeared for hours because she was imprisoned in a motorcycle club's compound.

"I'm okay, I just woke up," I told her, shifted and lifted, leaning against the headboard, and I saw movement so I looked down the bed to see Hawk at the top of the stairs. Bare chest again. Bare feet again. Track pants again. Eyes on me.

Mm.

"Are you sleeping all right?" she asked.

"Yes," I answered as Hawk approached the bed.

"Are you sure?" she asked.

"Yeah, honey, I'm sure. Really, like I said last night, I'm okay," I replied as Hawk made it to the bed then, *whoosh*, the bedclothes were pulled down.

My body locked in surprise.

Oh boy.

"Are things okay with Hawk?" she asked.

"Um…" I answered as I watched Hawk bend then his

fingers curled around my ankles, he yanked me down the bed until my back was to it again then he spread my legs.

Oh boy!

"Gwennie?" Tracy called.

Before I could move a muscle, Hawk put a knee to the bed then he shifted his big frame between my legs.

Oh boy!

"Trace, I think…" I trailed off when Hawk's hands went to my hips, pushing up my nightshirt and then his head bent and he kissed the skin just above my panties.

My belly lurched in a good way.

"You think what?" Tracy asked, then went on quickly without waiting for me to answer. "Okay, I'm going to say it and I know you don't want to hear it, but I'm glad you're there. I know you're confused about things but I think this speaks volumes that he…"

She kept speaking but I wasn't listening because Hawk's hands kept pushing up my nightshirt and his body was going with it, raining kisses on the skin of my belly and midriff as he went.

"You know?" Tracy asked.

"Um…Trace, I gotta go." And I did because my nightshirt was under my breasts, Hawk's hands had spanned the undersides and my nipples had gone hard and tingly.

"Is everything all right?"

Oh yeah, everything was all right. Everything was *just fine*.

"I'll call you later," I told her, but it was breathy because Hawk was now kissing me between my breasts.

"You sound funny," Tracy noted.

"I'm fine, babe. I'll call you later."

"Okay, I'll let you go. Bye, babe."

"Bye," I gasped, because both Hawk's hands slid up and both Hawk's thumbs did a pass over my hard, tingly nipples.

I flipped the phone shut. "Hawk," I breathed and then he moved fast.

The nightshirt went all the way up, forcing my arms with it, then I was free of it. He tossed it aside, his hand slid up my arm, grabbed my phone, tossed it to the nightstand, then it came to my face, his fingers at my cheek, his thumb curving around my jaw, he positioned me and kissed me.

Oh...*boy*.

I was primed for the kiss, way primed, so I allowed it and kissed him back. It sucked he was such a great kisser, which meant I had zero control, but at that point I was not complaining. Not at all.

His hands went down to my hips, over my bottom, down the backs of my thighs, pulling and sliding up at the same time until they were behind my knees and then he yanked them high.

I held on, one arm around his back, one hand cupped on his head.

His mouth broke from mine and his lips slid to my ear as I lifted my head and kissed the sleek skin of his shoulder.

"Bet, just with that, you're ready for me," he muttered in my ear.

It was an unbelievably arrogant thing to say, but he would win that bet.

"Let's see how fast I can get you to come for me," he suggested. My body twitched because it was intrigued by this suggestion, then his hand slid down my belly and right in.

Oh yeah.

My back arched and a whimper slid out of my throat on the word "Baby."

His fingers slid through the wetness between my legs. "Ready for me," he growled.

Then his fingers moved. They did this in demanding,

delicious ways and Hawk proved he could get me to come for him really fast and really, *really* hard.

I was in the middle of a very sweet orgasm when his hand disappeared, his body disappeared, my panties were hauled down my legs and they disappeared then his mouth was there.

Oh yeah.

"Baby," I gasped, my fingers gliding over his cropped hair.

He was good at this because he liked doing it. This was not a chore for Hawk. This was not something to get out of the way or done to gain brownie points. This was something he got something out of, nearly as much as me.

Then he added fingers to the workings of his mouth and tongue.

Yes!

My hips surged up. "Hawk," I moaned.

God, this was good. It was so good orgasm two shifted in but he didn't stop. His mouth, tongue and fingers kept right on going so that meant right on the heels of orgasm two, I experienced orgasm three. It wasn't one long one, no way. It was one long, brilliant, awe-inspiring one followed by another long, brilliant awe-inspiring one.

Totally a superhero.

In the middle of it, Hawk's fingers and mouth vanished, his body vanished, then he was back, my knees were again hauled up and he was inside me.

Oh yeah!

God I loved this. He was strong and that meant he could drive deep, he could go fast and he could do it hard, all of which I liked a whole lot.

His face was in my neck and I wrapped him tight in my limbs.

"Honey," I breathed.

His hand went between us, finger back to my golden spot and my body jolted.

"Hawk, baby," I moaned when what his finger and cock were doing to my body rocked straight through that body.

"You gonna dodge me again?" he asked in my ear, driving in with his cock and pressing and rolling with his finger.

"No," I gasped.

"Promise, Gwen," he demanded.

"I promise," I gasped.

His head came up and he looked down at me, and when he did, I stared. I'd never seen his face like that in the light. I'd never seen it like that ever.

God...*God,* but he was beautiful, always but more so with him filling me, pounding into me, touching me, his heavy weight bearing me down, his face dark with hunger, his eyes heated and intense.

God.

It was building again, just looking at him (not to mention all the other stuff).

"You gonna ride this out with me?" he growled.

Oh yeah. Yeah, I was *definitely* going to ride this out with him.

"Yes," I whispered.

"You gonna give me sweet?" he went on, growling and pounding and pressing and rolling, relentless, amazing.

"Yes," I whimpered because I could feel it, *he* was about to give *me* sweet. Again.

His mouth touched mine. "I feel that," he whispered. "Fuck, Gwen, beautiful. Always so fuckin' beautiful. You're there, Sweet Pea."

"Yeah, baby," I breathed against his lips, my hips surged up, my limbs got tight, my back arched, I came yet again, it was brilliant and awe-inspiring yet again and he kissed me so my moans slid into his mouth.

I held on as I came then I came down and he kept surging into me, his lips slid down to my ear where I listened to him grunt as he went faster, harder. I fucking loved holding all that was Hawk, the immense power of him wrapped in my limbs.

His hands spanned my hips. He pulled up and thrust deep as his grunts turned to groans then finally he planted himself inside me and stopped.

Unbelievably magnificent.

I held on like I always held on because before, I didn't want him to go. But before, I eventually loosened my hold because I knew he'd eventually go.

Now it wasn't the middle of the night. Now he wasn't a shadowy lover whose name I did not know. Now neither of us had anywhere to go.

So now what did I do?

My limbs loosened and he pulled out. I closed my eyes as he slid off to my side.

This was familiar. Get off then retreat. Pull out and pull away. Close off.

I opened my eyes as the heat of him stayed glued to my side.

His torso was partially lifted, his head was bent, his eyes were watching his hand glide from my hip to my waist, in over my belly between my breasts and then up to my neck. I felt his finger slide down my hairline, pushing my hair off my neck, then his hand moved to my jaw. He gently twisted my neck then his hand went away as he bent in closer. I felt his tongue touch the skin behind my ear as his hand slid back down my body. Finally, his arm came to rest low on my belly and curved around my hip.

He'd never done this before. This was different. This was better. Seriously better.

Oh boy.

"Just two this time," he murmured into my ear. "Losin' my touch."

"What?" I whispered, and his head came up but he stayed close, pressed in, his face near mine.

"My mouth and fingers, babe, you only came twice."

"Um... well, I came once before and once after so I'm pretty sure I'm covered."

He grinned then he bent and touched his mouth to the base of my throat. His head moved away but he locked his eyes to mine.

They were heated and intense.

Shit.

"How do you heat this place?" I asked, directing post-coital pillow talk to the mundane for sanity's sake. I didn't want a play-by-play. My head was messed up enough, I didn't know where this was going, I didn't know what I was thinking and I was scared as hell of what I was feeling. Talking about how great sex was with Hawk only intensified all of that.

"What?" he asked back.

"You live in a warehouse with cement floors, Hawk, it's a minor miracle you can heat this place."

His response was to shift. Bending over my body, he grabbed the covers and pulled them up over us.

He thought I was saying I was cold. Then he instantly did something about it.

Okay, maybe I *did* want to talk about how great sex was with Hawk because experiencing him being sweet and thoughtful messed with my head a whole lot more than his ability to give me four really fucking fantastic orgasms in the span of thirty minutes.

His arm went low on my hip again and he turned me to my side facing him, his legs tangling with mine, his arm pulling me close.

For my part, I rested my hands to his chest because I liked touching him and because I liked this. This wasn't retreat. This wasn't slam, bam, thank you ma'am. This was nice.

"It's not as bad as it seems," he belatedly replied.

"Your heating bills must cost as much as my mortgage," I remarked.

He smiled at me. "No."

"You would know," I muttered, looking at his throat.

"Yeah, I do, Sweet Pea, and you need to refinance. The interest you're payin' is ridiculous. I'll sort a meeting with my financial advisor."

My eyes lifted to his as I felt my belly start to get squishy.

"You'll sort a meeting out with your financial advisor?" I asked.

"Yeah," he answered.

Uh-oh. He was being sweet and thoughtful again.

"Is that part of your Protect Gwendolyn Kidd Duties, to make sure I don't get gouged by mortgage lenders?" I asked.

He kept smiling and his arm got tighter. "There are many facets to my Protect Gwendolyn Kidd Duties."

"Care to expand on that?"

"Not really."

I held his eyes. Then I mumbled, "Unh-hunh."

His smile got bigger and I knew this because his dimples pressed deeper.

"Unh-hunh?" he prompted.

"Man of mystery," I replied.

His hand trailed up my back and his head dipped closer to mine. "I like surprising you, Sweet Pea. Whenever I do something you like, your face gentles." He touched his mouth to mine and moved back a smidge. "It's a good look," he finished on a whisper.

Wow.

"My face does that?"

"Oh yeah."

"Hmm," I mumbled.

"Saw it again just now and before, twice."

"Before? Twice?"

His lips brushed mine then slid down my cheek to my ear where he whispered, "Yeah, baby, both times my mouth wasn't between your legs, right before you came."

Definitely my belly was squishy.

"Hawk—"

"Lights on if it's dark when I fuck you, missed that look for a year and a half too. Not missin' it again."

Now my throat was tingly and I could feel my heart swelling.

I slid one of my arms around to his back, I pressed in closer as my neck twisted slightly so my lips were at the skin of his. "You didn't let me do anything to you," I whispered.

"You can do whatever you want to me in about two minutes," he whispered back, his hand drifting down to my ass then pushing in.

"Whatever I want?"

"Whatever you want, baby."

"Oh my," I breathed, and he chuckled in my ear.

Nice.

I pressed even closer.

His head suddenly came up. I looked up at him and saw it was tilted. He was listening.

Then he clipped, "Fuck."

"Fuck what?"

He didn't answer. He knifed out of bed taking me with him.

When I was on my feet by the bed, I repeated, "Fuck what, Hawk?"

He looked down at me but grabbed my hand and started pulling me to my suitcases.

"Get dressed, babe. We have company."

"We do?" I asked as he stopped me by my suitcases.

"Yeah," he answered.

Oh shit.

"Good company or bad company?" I asked, his hands went to my hips and he pulled my naked body into his.

"Right now, Sweet Pea," he growled, "any company is bad company."

I had to admit, with his warm, solid, naked body pressed to mine, I agreed.

There was a banging at the door and I jumped. Then I pulled from his hands and bent to my suitcases. Hawk prowled to his wardrobe.

I grabbed items and flew to the bathroom.

I'd used the facilities, brushed and flossed, washed my face, put on my underwear and was pulling my hair up in a high ponytail when the door to the bathroom opened without even a knock.

I jumped and whirled to see Hawk standing there wearing dark brown cargo pants and tight olive drab thermal.

A thought popped into my head and, stupidly, it popped out of my mouth.

"How many pairs of cargo pants do you own?"

His eyes went from my underwear to me.

Then he announced without preparing me in any way, shape or form, "My family's here. Surprise visit. They've heard about you. Jury's got a big mouth."

My breath rushed out of me with an audible *oof*.

Then I whispered, "What?"

"Ma's makin' breakfast."

His ma? His *ma* was making *breakfast*?

I felt my eyes get huge and I repeated, "What?"

"It'll take her a while so whenever you're ready to come down."

Again I asked, "What?"

But I did this to a closed door. He was gone.

I turned to face the mirror where my eyes were just as huge as I expected and my face was pale.

Then I whispered, "Shit."

CHAPTER EIGHTEEN

Cleaver

I STARED IN the mirror.

I'd grabbed my clothes in a tizzy, but even if I didn't, I was unprepared.

In normal circumstances, any meeting with the parents necessitated a carefully strategized trip to the mall, a manicure, pedicure, facial, hair trim and at least a week of psyching yourself up.

At least.

I didn't have that.

Instead I'd grabbed a pair of mocha, roll-top yoga pants, a cream, ultra-slim fit camisole and my lightweight, close-fit, zip-up hoodie with the super-awesome stitching and it was, what I thought at the time, the mega-awesome color of a pastel, neon orangy-peach.

Now I was thinking it looked ridiculous.

Seeing as it was Sunday morning and normal folk didn't dress to the nines with full-on makeup for a surprise family breakfast visit, I didn't do makeup. But I did spritz with perfume.

I sucked in breath. I couldn't be up there ages and I couldn't escape this.

Welp! What will be, will be.

I exited the bathroom and headed to the stairs, hearing children screaming over a low murmuring of adult voices.

I looked right as I walked down the stairs and I saw a gorgeous older woman at the stove, bacon in the skillet, its scent filling the air and her head was turned to me. Two Hawk-looking, also gorgeous, tall, lean men sitting identically at stools, long upper thighs splayed manly wide, feet to the rung and their heads turned to me. Another, older, Hawk-looking, handsome, tall, lean man standing at the opposite end of the counter, his eyes on me. Hawk, with his back to me, leaning his hip against the end of the horseshoe, his neck twisted so he could look at me. And lastly, two black-haired kids, both boys, ages indeterminate but I was guessing somewhere in the area of two and six, racing through the vast space and not knowing I existed.

"Hey," I called five steps from the bottom. Yes, I was counting. I had five steps to go without falling on my face.

"Hey," one of the men at the stool replied, grinning, no dimples, but his brother at the other stool was also grinning and he had dimples. So did the older man.

I walked across the space, which was a long way normally but an epic journey with Hawk's family's eyes following me.

I didn't know where to head so my feet took over and led me to Hawk. I stopped at his side and no one had looked away. Not one of them.

Yikes.

Hawk's arm slid along my shoulders, he curled me as he turned me so my front was pressed into his side, close, too close, and I looked up as I prepared to gain distance, only to see his eyes warm on me.

"You good?" he asked softly.

No. One could not say I was good. One could say I was freaking out.

I nodded my lie.

"You want coffee?"

"Coffee would be good," I whispered, and started to pull away but Hawk's arm tensed, his head lifted and turned toward his mother.

"Ma, could you get Gwen a coffee?"

My body jolted and my head whipped toward her. "I can get it."

Then I stilled.

Something was wrong. Not just wrong, *very* wrong. And it was the look on Hawk's mother's face that was wrong. There was sadness there and I didn't know her, I'd been in her presence less than a minute, but that sadness touched my soul.

"Maria, honey, Cabe's girl needs coffee," the older man prompted quietly. Hawk's mother's body jerked and then she swept that sadness clean away.

Um. What the fuck was that?

"Right, of course, Gwen?" she said, hurrying to me. "I'm Maria. Cabe's mother."

She extended her hand and I took it even though Hawk didn't let me go so I could do this. Her fingers curled around mine and she looked up at me from her petite height as I smiled down at her thinking, *No wonder Hawk was hot.* She wasn't a spring chicken but she was still a complete knockout.

Her hand squeezed, mine squeezed back, she smiled a small smile, let me go and moved away.

Hmm. Not sure how that went.

"I'm Von," one of the men at the stools put in, and my head turned to him. He was the dimpled one.

"Hi," I replied. "I'm Gwen."

He was already grinning and the grin got bigger when he muttered, "I know."

Okey dokey.

"Von's wife, Lucia, is a nurse, babe, she has a shift at Swedish this morning. The hellions who will eventually graduate to tearing up my place are his," Hawk put in, and I nodded up at him.

"Jury," the other man at a stool added, and my eyes went to him.

"Hey," I replied.

"Your laptop work okay?" he asked.

I suspected Jury was the firefighter and I also suspected he was on the cover of the Denver Firefighters calendar, picture used for the month of July, he was that hot. If the firefighters merged with the police officers and they did a group shot that included Lawson and Jury, the paper might spontaneously combust.

"Yes, thanks for getting that for me," I said to him.

"No problem," he muttered, staring at me. In fact, they were all still staring at me, except Maria, who was pouring coffee.

"Agustín," Hawk's Dad boomed, moving in my direction, a huge smile on his face, his looks so similar to Hawk's it was uncanny and boded well for Hawk's future. Hawk's Mom was a knockout, his dad, like my dad, had managed to age without losing but a modicum of hotness. He lifted his hand and I took it when he went on. "Gus."

"Gus," I shook his hand, "Gwen."

He let my hand go but kept smiling at me huge then his eyes swung to Hawk.

"Cabe, good taste. Nice eyes. Great hair. Fantastic ass," he remarked, and I froze in shock.

"Gus!" Maria shouted, swinging around as the male Delgado brood chuckled.

Gus turned to his wife. "It's true."

"*Madre de dios,*" she snapped. "That may be so but you don't *say* it in *front* of her!"

Gus rocked back on his heels and crossed his arms on his chest. "Why not?"

Her eyes sliced to me then back to her husband and she swung an arm out to me. "Because look at her. You've offended her."

"Um…" I put in hurriedly, "I'm not offended." And I wasn't, just surprised. I looked at Gus. "Cookie dough," I explained. "My booty is carefully crafted from copious intake of cookie dough."

"Whatever you're doin', sweetheart, it's workin'." He grinned, then advised, "So don't stop."

"Divorce. *D-i-v-o-r-c-e.* Tomorrow. I'm callin' my lawyers tomorrow," Maria threatened, and this seemed like a practiced speech.

"Woman, you don't have lawyers," Gus returned in a way that seemed practiced too.

Hmm. Maria and Gus bickered. This was somehow familiar.

"Well, I'm finding some!" Maria snapped, then looked at me. "How do you take your coffee?"

"Milk and half a sugar," I replied quickly.

"Half a sugar won't help that ass," Gus observed helpfully. Hawk's body started shaking and I knew he was silently laughing

But that was when Maria turned swiftly, reached up, grabbed a mug and threw it at Gus.

Yes, she *threw* a *mug* at *Gus*.

Gus, clearly experienced with evasive maneuvering,

ducked and the mug hit the counter and bounced off to fall to the floor, luckily unharmed because, seriously, Hawk's mugs were kickass.

I stood stock-still and stared.

"Woman!" Gus yelled when he straightened and planted his hands on his hips. "Are you crazy? Now *you've* freaked Gwen out!"

Frighteningly, Maria's eyes came to me. "Learn," she warned, pointing a finger at me and leaning in. "All of them, they're like this. Do not let them get away with it. Put your foot down right off the bat, Gwen, do you hear me?"

"I hear you," I whispered.

"I didn't put my foot down right off the bat," she told me. "Dazzled by his good looks, that was me. Don't get dazzled by Cabe's good looks, Gwen, learn from me. He's just a man. He might do things to make you think differently, but believe me, he's just a man."

"I'm not sure that's true," I shared. "I haven't seen it with my own eyes but I think he can walk through walls."

More male chuckles and more shaking of Hawk's body against mine, but Maria didn't think anything was funny. "He can't. I see now, you're dazzled. Shake that off, *querida*. The sooner, the better."

"Uh…okay," I agreed because she sounded serious.

Her finger jerked to Gus. "Behave!" she ordered, then turned back to my coffee.

Hawk's head dipped so his mouth was at my ear. "You dazzled, Sweet Pea?"

I twisted my neck to catch his eye. Then I whispered, "Behave."

He grinned at me and my body jolted, not from surprise but because a young human ran into it.

I looked down into the black eyes and beautiful face of

a Hawk-like little boy as he shifted to the front of me then slapped my thigh.

"Well, hello, little person," I said to him.

He slapped my thigh again as Von warned, "Javier."

"Orange!" the boy shouted, then slapped my thigh again and pointed at my hoodie.

"Yep, orange," I replied then pointed at my yoga pants. "What color is this?"

"Brown!" he yelled and clapped his hands.

I smiled down at him. "Excellent. Now, what color is this?" I lifted my hand and tugged at my ponytail.

"Pretty!" he hollered. I couldn't help it, I laughed and then crouched down so I was almost eye to eye with him.

"I'm Gwen, who are you?"

"Javier!" he yelled and clapped again.

"Santo," I heard from my side and I looked to see the older boy standing there, removed, watchful, eyes on me.

"Santo?" I asked and he nodded. "Hey, Santo."

He didn't reply, his body started swaying, but his eyes didn't leave me.

"You're handsome," I informed him.

He kept swaying and studying me.

"Do you like your uncle's big lair?" I asked.

His head tipped to the side. "Lair?" he repeated.

I swept an arm out to indicate the space. "His house."

"We can't run at home" was his response.

I smiled at him. "You like it."

He took a step toward me and stopped.

"Sunny," he replied.

I looked at the windows then back at Santo. "Yeah, baby, it's very sunny."

"We can run and climb," he continued.

"But you do it careful, right? So your grandma won't get worried?" I asked.

"Careful." He nodded.

I kept smiling. "How old are you?" I asked.

"Five," Santo answered, taking another step toward me and holding five fingers up in front of my face.

"Three!" Javier yelled. I looked at him to see he was having difficulty controlling his little hand to show me three so I reached out and gently tucked two fingers into his palm.

"Three," I said softly.

"Three!" Javier agreed, joyfully looking at his hand.

"Can you hold it?" I asked.

His gaze turned intent on his hand, his mouth twisted and he nodded.

Slowly I removed my hand and he held up his three fingers.

I touched my fingertips to his soft, still-chubby cheek before dropping my hand.

"Perfect," I told him.

His eyes came to me and he clapped again, then he hurtled himself at me. I braced at the last minute so I didn't go down on my ass, the kid was freaking strong. His arms went around me and he gave me a slobbery, three-year-old kiss on my neck then yanked my ponytail.

As fast as he did it, he let me go and raced away.

Totally Delgado.

Santo raced after him.

I stood and found eyes on me again, all around, no grins this time. Delgado intensity was coming at me from all sides.

Weird.

Hawk's arm came back to my shoulders and he curled me into his side again. I looked up and only had a second to prepare before his mouth hit mine for a very brief, very hard, very sweet kiss.

When his head lifted, I found my arms had wound themselves around his middle.

I stared into his eyes and couldn't read them and lost the ability to try when his hand came up, knuckles skimming my cheek, and down, where it curled around my neck.

I forgot we had an audience when I re-focused and the look he was giving me set something wrong inside me.

"Are you okay?" I whispered.

"No," he replied.

"Hawk—" I started, but I didn't know what I was going to say.

His hand squeezed my neck. "Totally missed out."

Something was happening here, something important. I just didn't get what.

"Hawk," I breathed.

"Fuck me, totally missed out."

"Baby," I replied softly.

"Coffee, *querida*." I heard, my neck twisted, and I was surprised to see Maria standing there, offering me coffee.

I took it with a, "Thanks."

"No problem," she muttered, her eyes shifting quickly to Hawk, then she turned back to the bacon on the stove.

"So, Gwen, what do you do?" Gus asked.

I looked at him, relieved at a normal question and how it shifted an atmosphere that had bizarrely grown heavy.

"I'm a book editor," I answered, then took a sip of coffee.

"Like it?" Gus asked.

"Yes," I answered.

"What's your dad do?" Gus went on.

"Construction, ex-Army and part-time handyman because his daughter bought a money pit," I told him.

Gus smiled. "Keeps us young, lookin' out for our kids, no matter how old they are."

"Well, I endeavor to give my father every opportunity to stay young."

Gus's smile widened. "Bet he loves every minute of it," Gus guessed wrongly.

"He lectured me for five hours not to buy that house. I bought it anyway. When the bathtub crashed through the floor into the living room, he had to take an hour-long time-out so he wouldn't strangle me and be known on online encyclopedias as a daughter killer, so I'm not sure he loves every minute of it."

"Trust me," Gus stated, still smiling, "he loves every minute of it."

"Okay," I decided to agree.

"And your mom?" Gus kept interrogating me.

"Meredith is a secretary for a divorce lawyer," I answered.

"Meredith?" he asked.

"My stepmom."

"What's your mom do?" Gus kept at me.

"Pop," Hawk said low, and Gus's eyes went to his son.

"She disappeared when I was little," I answered readily, and the Delgado intensity hit me again coming from all sides.

"Sorry, Gwen, I didn't know," Gus said.

"It's okay, Gus, it was a long time ago," I replied just as Hawk's neck twisted so he could look toward the door.

I looked up at him to see his brows knit and heard him mutter, "Who now?"

He let me go and moved to the door as I took another sip of coffee, smelled bacon, and my stomach informed me I was hungry.

Javier came running into the kitchen. He smacked his grandma on the leg and shouted, "Bacon!" and I grinned.

There was a commotion at the door. I twisted to look and saw Meredith leading, moving swiftly, her face panicked. Dad was coming behind her, his strides long, his face set in granite. And a woman was following them wearing jeans, boots, a blousy top shot with silver and a cool, beat-up leather jacket. She looked half hippie, half biker babe, a look she pulled off and one I liked so much I felt a new phase coming on. She also looked familiar, but I didn't know how.

I tensed and turned, putting my coffee cup to the counter. What now?

"Gwennie, sweetie, she wouldn't—" Meredith started, her eyes glued to me. She didn't even glance at the Delgados.

"Gwendolyn!" the woman I didn't know shouted then broke into a run toward me. "My God, my *God*. A drive-by!" She passed Meredith and threw her arms around me as I froze, my eyes on Meredith. "My baby, nearly shot to death!" the woman wailed, swaying me side to side.

"Uh," I started. "Do I know you?"

She jerked away, her fingers curving around my upper arms so hard I could feel her nails through the material of my hoodie.

"Do you know me?" she whispered.

"Gwen—" Dad began, but the woman let me go and she whirled on Dad.

"*Does she know me?*" she shrieked, and even Santo and Javier stopped scampering and stared.

"Libby," Dad clipped, but I felt the color slide from my face as I took a step back.

"Libby?" I whispered, and she swung back to me.

"Yes!" she snapped. "Libby! Your mother!"

Oh my God! Gus was a voodoo master. One mention and then, *poof!* there she was!

My eyes flew to Hawk to see he was closing in on me as I swayed. Luckily, he made it to me, his arm hooking around my chest as he positioned his tall frame behind me and he anchored me to him before I could teeter and fall.

"You don't have to protect her from me," my mother hissed at Hawk, her eyes slits.

"I'll take the boys outside," Von muttered, moving off his stool toward his sons.

But I didn't look to see this happen, I only sensed him move because I kept staring at my mom.

My *mom*.

"Well, this answers that." Mom was still hissing, and she turned to Meredith. "I take it *you* didn't share the letters and photos I sent," she accused. Hawk's arm tightened and my eyes shot to Meredith.

"I—" Meredith started.

"No, *I* didn't," Dad put in, moving in behind Meredith and sliding an arm around her waist.

Letters? Photos?

"I should have known when I didn't get anything back," Mom retorted, then her eyes focused on Meredith. "*My* baby wouldn't leave me hanging. *My* baby would reply to me!"

"It was my decision to keep you out of Gwen's life, not Mer's, so eyes to me, Libby," Dad ordered.

"Oh my God," I whispered.

Mom's eyes didn't swing to Dad, they swung to me. "You can say that again!" she shouted.

"You think you could take a second, calm down and see Gwen and Hawk have company and maybe we can discuss this in private?" Dad suggested.

"No! No I do not!" Mom shouted.

"Right, in other words, things haven't changed," Dad clipped.

"Fuck you!" Mom clipped back, and my body jolted.

Hawk entered the fray. "Bax asked you to calm down. Now, this is my place and I'm tellin' you to do it."

Mom swung to Hawk. "Do I care?"

Oh my God. My long-lost mom had a foul mouth *and* a death wish.

"Are you gettin' why I did what I could to keep this woman outta my daughter's life?" Dad asked Hawk angrily.

"I'm not getting it," I whispered.

"Of course you wouldn't, baby," Mom stated.

"Gwen honey, I kept the letters and I'll give 'em to you," Dad told me. "First letter she sent, with photos, was when your Aunt Mildred died and left you ten thousand dollars. In it she says she was working in Africa with starving children and needed money for food and medicine when she was really in Boulder workin' as a bartender in a Harley bar and needed money to keep herself in dope."

Boulder? *Boulder?* I thought my mother lived in Rapid City.

I stared at Dad.

Great. Just great. My mom was foul mouthed, had a death wish, lived thirty miles away from me and was just like Ginger.

Fantastic.

All this I thought in my head.

"Please tell me this isn't happening" was what I whispered out loud, and Hawk's other arm wrapped around my ribs.

"Second letter, and honey, there were only two, was when you graduated from high school and I turned your school fund over to you. It was flood victims that time," Dad went on, and my eyes went to my mom as Dad continued, "What's it now, Lib? You hear about the drive-by and think to get in on the insurance payout or you hear she hooked up with Hawk and think to get something from him?"

"It's me," Hawk stated, and I twisted my neck to look up at him. His gaze was steady and unhappy on my mother.

"I don't know who you are," Mom snapped at Hawk.

"Bullshit," Hawk replied, and my body jolted again.

"I've never seen you in my life," she returned.

"You were Pope Rountree's old lady, until he threw your ass out, and you were at his place three times when I took meetings with him there," Hawk replied.

Mom ducked her chin and turned her body slightly to the side.

What Hawk said was true.

Oh my *God*. My long-lost mother had a foul mouth, a death wish *and* she was a gold digger!

"That explains it, why you wouldn't get out of Rick's fuckin' livin' room until we took you to Gwen, the whole time, red-faced and shoutin'. Because you knew, we took you to Gwen, we took you to Hawk," Dad surmised.

My mother stared at my father and then shifted attention *and* blame.

"*My* daughter was the victim of a drive-by because *your* daughter," she jabbed an angry finger at Meredith, "is a piece of *shit*."

Meredith's face paled, Dad's got red and I lost my mind.

"Don't you dare," I whispered, and Mom swung to me and I watched, holy crap, I *watched* her carefully rearrange her face.

"Baby—" she whispered.

"Don't you 'baby' me, you lived *in Boulder?*" My voice went high on the last two words and Hawk's arms got tighter, but I leaned forward. "You lived in Boulder and you never came to see me?"

"Your father wouldn't let me!" she replied on a shout.

"Who cares!" I shouted back. "If you want to see your kid, you'll move heaven and earth to see your kid! You want to stay in contact, you don't send two letters! You send two thousand!"

"Gwendolyn—" she started.

"I can't believe you," I cut her off. "I can't believe I don't see you for nearly thirty years and when I do, it's because you know Hawk and you know he can afford Jimmy Choos!"

Direct hit, she winced before she rallied.

"Yesterday you nearly died," she told me.

"Uh...*yeah*, I *know*. I was *there*," I replied sarcastically.

"I'm your mother! I'm worried!"

"You weren't worried when Brian Takata broke my heart in tenth grade and I slid into the depths of despair. Meredith was! And it was then Meredith taught me the healing properties of cookie dough, and let me tell you, it was a good lesson to learn because cookie dough goes a long way to mend a broken heart. And, by the way," my tone was acid, "Meredith taught me a lot of good lessons you weren't around to teach."

"Gwen—" Mom tried to cut in, but I kept on going.

"And you weren't worried when Scott Leighton crushed me to the point I knew I'd never fall in love again. Meredith was. And I didn't have enough money to hire a good lawyer when Scott was jacking me around so Meredith got her boss to represent me and Scott quit jacking me around! You were in Boulder, or wherever, but wherever was close enough for you to be there and you never were. Meredith was!"

"Yeah, I'm around and I know people, I hear things, and I know you're in trouble because *Meredith's* bitch from hell of a daughter is *causing* you trouble." Mom returned.

I tore from Hawk's arms, taking two swift strides forward so fast Mom reared back.

"That's my sister you're talking about," I snapped in her face. "And those are family problems and you...are not... *family.*"

"Gwe—" she started.

"Get out!" I yelled.

"I don't believe—"

"You should. You initiated a play for *my man's* money," I bit out, thumping my chest with the flat of my palm. "You insulted *my sister.* You made *my dad* get red in the face. And you upset," I leaned in but pointed at Meredith, "*my mom!*"

She reared back again and I watched her face get pale but she didn't move.

"I told you, get out. You don't, I'm siccing Hawk on you!" I threatened.

Her eyes slid to Hawk and I felt his badassness close at my back but I kept my eyes locked to my mother.

Then her gaze came to me. "You know," she whispered, "I don't see even a little of me in you."

She said this like was an insult.

"Thank God," I replied.

Her mouth got tight then she tossed her hair, which, unfortunately, was my hair except dyed to look that way now. Then she turned and, without looking at anyone, she marched to the door.

I marched to the fridge, pissed and sliding straight into full rant. "You know, I'd rather be firebombed again. No!" I corrected myself as I yanked open the fridge and reached for the cookie dough. "The drive-by. I'd rather endure another drive-by than go through that again."

I slammed the fridge door and walked to a butcher block of knives, yanking one out at random. I slid out a cutting board from the shelves then I went to the horseshoe counter by where Meredith was standing and slapped the cutting board down.

"And you should know, Meredith, that I do not blame you. Ginger is Ginger, we're all family, we all get that." I twirled my knife in the air. "It isn't like we didn't know this would eventually come to pass."

I slammed the cookie dough down on the cutting board and started to slice into it when strong fingers curled around my wrist and I felt a hard body pressed against my side.

I looked up at Hawk.

"Give it up with the cookie dough, baby," he whispered.

"No way, Hawk, it's cookie dough all around," I replied, tearing my wrist from his hand and again circling my knife in the air.

He pressed his lips together. Then he suggested, "All right, then maybe in your present state you shouldn't be wielding a cleaver."

"I'm not wielding a..." I trailed off when I brought the knife I was carrying up between us and saw it was a huge-ass cleaver. "Shit," I muttered.

His hand came back to my wrist and he took control of the cleaver. Then he stretched out an arm and handed the cleaver off to his hovering mother.

It was then I remembered we had an audience and it was then I remembered that life pretty much sucked for me, and so it was then I burst out crying.

Hawk folded me in his arms, I grabbed onto his thermal, my fingers fisting tight at the back, and I shoved my face in his chest.

His hand slid up and curled warm around the back of my neck.

There was silence which led into murmurings of

conversation and my parents introducing themselves to Hawk's family. I ignored this because the presence of other beings during a breakdown, well, it was pretty much mandatory to ignore them but when they're the family of the hot guy you're sleeping with, you just met them and they just witnessed an unpleasant family reunion that ended in you ranting and brandishing a cleaver, it was a moral imperative.

When my tears subsided, my eyes automatically searched for the face that would make everything better.

I turned my head and focused on Meredith.

"I know Maria's making breakfast but can you make me homemade donuts?" I whispered.

"I'll go get the biscuit dough and vegetable oil," Dad announced instantly, and I felt rather than saw him move because my eyes stuck to Meredith.

She had tears hovering in her eyes too, but still, she smiled at me.

Yep, everything felt better.

I smiled back as I pressed my cheek to Hawk's chest and his arms got tight.

Then I shouted to my dad, "Don't forget the chocolate fudge frosting!"

"Gotcha," Dad shouted back.

I felt something on my other side and I traded one cheek for the other in Hawk's chest as I turned my head and looked up to see Gus there.

His eyes were on Hawk. "Good to know, even after a family drama, Gwen's still hard at work on that great ass," he noted.

"Gus!" Maria shouted.

I laughed.

So did Hawk. I didn't hear it, but I felt it up against me.

It felt really nice.

Hawk's laughter faded.

I missed it when it was gone until Maria muttered, "She might be dazzled but she's not afraid of using a cleaver. I see good things," and I got Hawk's laughter back again.

*   *   *

Hawk was gone on an errand unexplained and night had fallen.

Earlier his family and my family ate eggs, toast, bacon and homemade donuts made from taking biscuit dough from a tube, punching a whole in the middle of it, deep frying it and then slathering it with frosting.

Homemade donuts were nearly as good as cookie dough for soothing trauma, not quite but they worked that morning mainly because Meredith made them.

Dad and Gus got on. Meredith and Maria got on. Von and Jury were both cool but attentive, very like their brother. But I spent most of my time after donut consumption playing hide-and-seek with Javier and Santo. There weren't a lot of places to hide but there was a lot of room to seek. I made one mistake and that was tickling them when I first found them, which they liked so they made me do all the seeking and then they made it easy to find them. In the end Javier tried to hide in plain sight. And he did this while giggling and calling "Nennie!" because he couldn't quite say Gwen.

Finally, after Maria and Meredith did the dishes, everyone said their farewells and went away, Hawk came to me and explained he had "shit to do." He didn't go into detail, and I didn't demand it, but he did kiss me before he left.

I unpacked my stuff and arranged it on my desk, booted up my computer and worked, making myself a sandwich when I got hungry, breaking the seal on the condiments to do so and trying not to think of Hawk out with his commandos, causing mayhem and maybe getting hurt.

Now I'd swiveled my chair to face the dark windows, the haze of lights of Denver not far away. The fact was we were in Denver, just a lost, abandoned part of it. Once the developers cottoned on, it would probably be made into lofts and trendy restaurants.

I had both my heels up on the seat of my chair, both my arms wrapped around my calves and I'd dropped my chin to my knees.

I stared out the windows realizing I had a foul-mouthed, gold-digger mom who didn't care one bit about me. I had a shot-up living room and a sister in serious trouble. I had a reputation as a sexual plaything. I was living with the man whose sexual plaything I had the reputation of being. I had a biker out there somewhere who had the way wrong idea about me. And, even with all that going down, it seemed I was living a daydream.

How the fuck did all that happen?

I heard a noise and turned my head to the door to see Hawk striding in, all masculine grace, body at his command.

Mm. Yum.

He walked, I watched and did a full body scan.

Well, today's good news, Hawk was home and he wasn't riddled with bullets, bleeding from stab wounds, scored by shrapnel or missing a limb due to an explosion.

"Hey," he said when he made it to the kitchen and kept coming at me.

"Hey," I replied, watching him coming at me, my chin to my knees, my brain processing that I was enjoying the show.

He rounded the desk and approached me from behind and he did this so he could bend in and touch his lips, then tongue, to the skin behind my ear.

Mm. *Yum*.

His mouth stayed there to say, "Baby, there a reason you're in a protective ball again?"

"I sit like this a lot," I told him.

"Yeah?" His lips went away and he swiveled my chair to face him as he crouched in front of me. "Why?"

"It's comfortable."

He studied me a second, his eyes scanning my face.

Then he asked, "So this doesn't have to do with your mom showin' up outta the blue and causin' a scene?"

Hmm. Maybe it partly had to do with that.

I decided not to reply.

Suddenly he stood, plucked me straight out of the chair and turned on his boot to walk through the warehouse while carrying me.

"What are you doing?" I asked, sliding my arms around his shoulders.

"Showing you comfortable," he answered.

Oh boy, I had a feeling I knew where this was going.

"I need to save my work," I told him.

"You can save it later," he told me, and kept walking.

"Hawk, seriously, what if there's a power outage?"

"Then you should have saved it before you curled up, Sweet Pea," he replied.

He made it to the seating area, sat in a recliner, reached down to the lever and then we were jerked back flat with me on top of him.

Okay, maybe I *didn't* know where this was going.

His arms came around me as my head lifted up.

When my eyes hit his, he stated, "Now, babe, *this* is comfortable."

He was not wrong.

I stretched out fully, my hip in the seat, one of my legs

hitched over his thighs, and I rolled my torso onto his, all the while looking down at him.

Then it was my turn to study him.

Face relaxed and, as ever, handsome. Eyes warm but alert. No dimples. Pure male beauty from hair to chin and parts beyond.

When his hand came up and pulled my hair away from my face, holding it scrunched at my neck, I spoke.

"I'm glad to see you're home and not riddled with bullets."

He grinned then muttered, "Smartass."

"And also not scored by burning shrapnel."

More grin, more dimples, more handsome.

Total daydream.

"Do I want to know where you've been?" I asked a question that threatened to blow my daydream to smithereens.

"I've been paying visits," he answered readily, which I suspected indicated that this discussion would not freak me out, set off a new bout of tears or send me straight to the fridge.

"To?" I prompted.

"To people who have big mouths and who'll share that I'm not real thrilled about my woman being the target of a drive-by, or present during one, and if that shit happens again, those responsible will feel pretty fuckin' uncomfortable and they'll be feelin' that sooner not later at the same time my boys and me are lookin' for the ones who did it in the first place."

"Oh," I whispered for I had no other response.

"We still don't know who was behind it," Hawk shared. "Tack's made enemies. It could be them. And Tack's made it clear you're somethin' he wants, so it could even be his shit that's leaked to you."

This was news and not good news. I already had enough shit leaking into my life. I didn't need more.

"Really?" I asked.

"Really," Hawk answered, looking as happy about this news as I felt. "Tack's position as president of the Chaos MC was a hostile takeover. Chaos started as a brotherhood of hell-raisers. They didn't make trouble but that didn't mean they didn't seek it out and embrace it when they found it. They always had the garage and auto supply, but it was just a front and not very big. Their crimes were relatively victimless, knife fights with other bikers who were looking for trouble, shit like that. They grew and sold pot, good shit, made a fortune, built up the garage and the store. Things degenerated, didn't help that internally there were two factions in the club always fighting, butting heads. Good and bad. Bad won out and the brotherhood is a brotherhood so even with bad leadin' the club, the others followed. Stopped growin' pot, started transporting. Not dealin', just moving product from point A to point B. Lucrative, far more than the pot. The garage and store got built up more. But you start doin' bad shit, more bad shit follows, and it did. Made deals, made alliances, built the business, and not just the legitimate ones, broke deals, broke alliances, fought wars, fuckin' insane. This world, their world, is a different world set right here in Denver. There are no rules, no laws, but they got instinct on their side."

I was pretty shocked Hawk was explaining this but even more shocked that he shared so many words.

"Instinct?" I asked when he stopped talking, fascinated at the same time mildly freaked out.

"You can be pretty smart when you're actin' on instinct in order to survive. These guys, they are far from dumb. These guys have been doin' this so long, they're masterminds. And I'm not jokin'."

"Oh," I whispered.

"Through this shit, the last twenty years, Kane has been growin' the custom bike and car business. Quiet, at first, and patient, it turns out. He's had a plan, all this time, twenty fuckin' years. Slowly building the reputation, slowly getting attention for it, now everyone knows about it. Hard to keep doin' seriously bad shit when journalists and photographers are writin' stories and takin' photos and Hollywood movie stars are visiting your garage. He talked the club into feedin' the money into Ride, branched out, built stores in C Springs, Boulder. Now it's nearly as lucrative as the illegal shit and he made it that way so, when he made his move to take over, standard of living for his boys wouldn't take that big of a hit, they cut ties with that other shit. So, that's what he did."

"The Chaos MC is clean?" I asked.

"Wouldn't say that, babe, but they don't peddle flesh or transport drugs anymore."

"That's good," I noted.

"Yeah, in the sense that Kane and his boys don't face a future where it might be that their only wardrobe choice is an orange jumpsuit. Problem is, they were good at safe transportation and now that they don't offer that service, sometimes demand gets cut off from supply. This has made some very dangerous people not very happy. And Kane is the man behind their unhappiness. He's got boys in his ranks would be happy to go back to what they were doin'. There's unrest, he's dealin' with that, and there's outside pressure, and he's dealin' with that. He's a marked man and until he figures out who's behind the rebellion in his club and the outside factions sort out their shit and move on, he's got problems."

"How is, um…" I took in a breath and then asked, "Ginger involved with that? Is it the drugs?"

"Nope," Hawk replied.

Oh shit.

"Did she let them peddle her flesh?"

"No, babe," his arm gave me a squeeze, "she was the inside man on the theft of three custom cars and a custom bike, a shitload of gear and the contents of a safe."

"The inside man?" I asked.

Hawk paused to study me then his fingers sifted through my hair and I realized he did this for the same reasons Cam took in breath. He did it to prepare me.

"Her chosen profession, Sweet Pea. She's got one thing goin' for her and that is that no one takes her seriously. She was smart enough to listen and learn in a lot of places. She sold information, she provided distraction for a price and, for a price, she provided access. She wasn't smart enough not to keep her shit quiet, not to be invisible and not to fuck over the wrong people. She wasn't choosy, she's equal opportunity. She fucked everyone and now she's fucked."

"How many people has she fucked over?" I asked.

"Too many," Hawk answered.

"And their danger zone levels?"

"Off the charts," Hawk replied. "Kane and Chaos are the least of her troubles, and, Gwen, they may have cleaned up but that doesn't mean they play by the rules. They caught her, they'd deal with her their own way. They would not hand her over to the cops. They'd find a way to take back what she owed them and they'd be creative about it."

My body gave a tremble as my hand clenched against his thermal. When it did, his hand left my hair and he slid his knuckles down my jaw.

"Yeah, baby, it is not lookin' good for Ginger," he whispered.

"Will you find her for me?" I blurted, and then I tensed.

I couldn't ask that. I couldn't ask Hawk and his boys to wade in—

"Already tryin', Sweet Pea." I stared and he talked. "Not for her, for you, your dad and your stepmom."

Uh...*wow*.

"I...I don't know what...you are?" I stammered.

"Gwen, I carried you through fire. That shit's gotta stop."

"Right," I whispered, my belly squishy, my heart swelling, my throat tingling, my eyes looking into his.

His eyes smiled. "You can pay me back, you make dinner."

"Making dinner would be payback?"

"Nope, not all of it, but it'll carve a bit off what you owe me."

I felt my lips tip up as my head tipped to the side. "Does that mean I have to steam vegetables?"

"Is that a problem for you?"

"No, but the only things you have in your fridge are fruit, cottage cheese and vegetables. Your mom used all the eggs and bacon and I had lunchmeat for lunch so that leaves veggies for dinner. I'm not sure my system will accept nothing but veggies for dinner. It might react and my guess would be that reaction would be violent."

He grinned at me then remarked, "There are stores in Denver. Some of them even carry groceries."

"Now who's the smartass?" I mumbled.

"All right, babe, get your shoes and get your ass to the Camaro. We're goin' to the grocery store."

"And still bossy," I went on mumbling.

"Are you hungry?" he asked.

"Yes," I answered.

"Do you want vegetables for dinner?"

"Heck no."

"Then get your ass up, get your shoes and get in the Camaro."

"B-o-s-s-y." I spelled it out like his mom did earlier, moving to exit the recliner, but his arms suddenly closed around me. I found myself plastered to his chest, his hand slid up to cup my head, tilt it then pull my lips down to his.

Then he kissed the smartass right out of me.

After that, I got up and did what I was ordered.

* * *

"Baby," I breathed.

"You're there," Hawk growled in my ear, hand cupping my breast, fingers rolling my nipple, his other hand over mine, his finger manipulating mine at the golden spot while his cock drove inside me.

He was right, I was there. My head flew back, collided with his shoulder and I came. Hard.

His hand between my legs took mine and he wrapped both our arms around my middle, his other hand still cupping my breast as he drove me down and he thrust up. His face was in my neck, his deep grunts shivering through me.

Then he ground me down as he pounded up, kept the connection and he growled into my neck.

"Baby," I whispered, my neck twisting, his head came up, his mouth took mine and his tongue slid inside.

God, I loved the taste of him.

He held me close and connected as he kissed me then his mouth released mine. He pulled me off his cock, twisted me around, put me on my back in bed and followed me down. His body covered mine, his hips between mine. I wrapped my calves around his thighs and my arms around his back.

His face went into my neck and my fingers trailed the skin of his back.

"Hawk?" I called.

"No, baby, to answer your question, I'm not a superhero," he said into my neck, my body stilled and I realized he was joking.

"Arrogant," I remarked but I did it laughing.

His head came up, he smiled down at me and my hand automatically slid down, around, up his chest to his neck to cup his cheek, my thumb touching his dimple.

"Gwen?" I heard and I jerked my eyes from their contemplation of his dimple to his.

"Yeah?"

"You called me, babe."

"I did?"

His smile got deeper; I saw it and felt it as his dimple moved under my thumb.

"Yeah, you did," he answered.

"Sorry, I got mesmerized by your dimple."

He went still then his face dipped close and he murmured, "Christ, like it when you're sweet."

I felt my body melt under his and my hand slid back across his hair.

"I remember what I wanted to say," I told him softly.

"So say it, Sweet Pea," he said softly back.

"Thank you for telling me about Ginger and Tack and being so nice about Mom."

His hand came up and his fingers trailed my hairline before he whispered, "You're welcome, baby."

"And thank you for making me safe," I went on.

"Gwen," he whispered.

"And for trying to find Ginger."

"You can stop now."

I ignored him. "And for saving me from biker prison."

"You already thanked me for that, even though you did it during a rant."

"Well, thank you again because it was kind of filthy in there and I wasn't a big fan of touching anything or, um… sitting on anything so that made it more uncomfortable than just being locked in a room for your own protection but against your will."

"I'll make sure Janine doesn't fall down on the job keepin' this place clean," he remarked.

"I'm being serious," I said quietly.

His hand cupped the side of my head and his thumb circled at my temple.

"I know you are," he quietly replied.

"My life is a mess." I shared something he already knew.

"This will pass, Gwen."

I pulled breath in through my nose and then said on the exhale, "I hope so."

His hand slid down and his thumb glided across my lips. "One positive thing you learned today. It's lookin' good for you. Your mom's a mess, babe, but she's still a babe."

I felt my brows draw together. "Did you just call my mom a babe?"

"You look like her," he replied.

Well, that wasn't so bad. My mom was a mess, Hawk was right, but she had pretty kickass style.

"You act like Meredith," Hawk cut into my thoughts.

I focused on him. "I do?"

"When you're bein' sweet and not ranting or hacking at cookie dough with cleavers."

I smiled. "I didn't hack at cookie dough with a cleaver."

He grinned down at me. "It was close."

He was right and I felt my body start to shake with laughter.

He watched me laugh until I was just smiling at him then he dipped his head and kissed the base of my throat. He rolled off me, pulled the covers over us, reached out to turn off the light on his nightstand and turned me so my back was tucked into his front. Then he pressed into me and reached across me to turn off the light on my nightstand. He pulled the hair off my neck and kissed the skin at the back of my ear. After that, he wrapped his arm around me, pulled me deep, hitched my leg with his and settled into the pillows.

Hawk's goodnight.

No slam, bam, thank you ma'am. Instead, talking, laughing then cuddling.

I guess I could deal with firebombs and drive-bys and learning my mom was still a mess after all these years if this was how I ended my day.

I lay in the dark of Hawk's cavernous warehouse, in his big bed, his big, warm body close, the memory of his goodnight sweet and fresh.

Yeah, I could deal with all that if this was how I ended my day.

But now I was wondering if Hawk felt the same.

CHAPTER NINETEEN

One Hand Up

MY EYES OPENED and I saw it was dawn. There were lights on in the warehouse and I knew they were over the kitchen. I heard Hawk's murmur, he was far away, on the phone.

I scooted to the edge of the bed, dropped my torso down and felt for my nightshirt. I found it, searched for my underwear, found that and lifted up. I pulled my nightshirt over my head, shoved my arms through and then shimmied my undies up while in the bed. I got out, wandered to the bathroom, did my thing, wandered out and down the stairs.

Hawk was still on the phone, dressed in uniform of skintight, long-sleeved tee and cargo pants. His hair was slightly wet and he already had his boots on.

He was leaning one hand into the back counter, he didn't move and his eyes didn't leave me as I walked his way. I lost sight of him when my body collided with is, my cheek pressed to his chest and my arms went around him. He took his hand off the counter and wrapped his arm around me.

"Yeah, report it to Lawson, set up the meet with Tack," Hawk said into his phone.

I sighed into his chest. He wasn't going about his own business, he was going about mine.

"Copy that," he went on, "be there in twenty."

He flipped his phone shut and shoved it into his cargos. I tipped my head back and looked up at him as his other arm closed around my shoulders.

"Sleep okay?" he asked, his chin dipped to look at me.

"Mm hmm," I answered.

He dipped his chin further and his mouth touched mine. His arm around my back also dipped, scrunched up my nightshirt then he held it up with his arm as his hand cupped my ass, skin to panties.

Nice.

When his mouth went away I asked back, "Did you?"

"Yeah," he replied.

I took in a breath and asked, "Is something going on?"

His arm at my shoulders squeezed as did his hand at my ass. "We have news."

"Good news or bad news?"

"Both."

"Uh-oh," I mumbled.

"I don't have a lot of time but do you need coffee before you hear it?"

"Is that your way of asking me if I need Valium before I hear it?"

He smiled and I got more squeezes.

Then he spoke. "Drive-by was about Ginger. Not Tack."

"Is that the good news or the bad news?"

"The good, means we know who we're lookin' for and why they did what they did. Since Tack's thrown down for you and I made things clear yesterday, they also know they bought themselves two sets of enemies they do not want. Ginger knows a lot, pissed off a lot of people and she can cause a lot of trouble, the police and Feds get to her, but she isn't worth the heat my boys *and* the Chaos MC are gonna bring down on them. They bought that, pullin' that shit, and they don't want it and won't want that heat to get hotter. It's a guess but this means you and your parents are likely safe."

"That *is* good news," I noted.

"Yeah, but that doesn't mean we don't play it smart. You with me?"

I wasn't sure I was but I nodded anyway.

"What's the bad news?" I asked.

He hesitated then explained, "Jorge took a meet with Dog yesterday. Apparently, you told Tack you were through with me and he took this as tacit permission to make his play. Seein' as he's Tack and not the kind of man who asks your sign, tells you he likes your smile, buys you a drink and hopes to get him some, but instead locks you in a room and thinks when he returns from causing havoc and exacting retribution, you're gonna be waitin' for him to do whatever he does to make his claim, he's not feelin' like backin' down from war. It didn't help that my boys bested his and captured the prize. Now there's face to be saved. We sent in lieutenants and they weren't able to make a deal. Now the captains have to meet."

Oh boy.

"Do you want to go into more detail about war?" I asked but I wasn't sure I wanted more detail.

"Did you tell him you were through with me?"

"Um…" I mumbled, trying to pull back a bit but his arm and hand got tighter so I stopped trying. "I was in a bad mood," I explained.

"Shit, Gwen," he muttered.

"I also told him I'd sworn off men, was going to take up hiking and set up a ferret rescue."

He stared down at me. Then he said, "Babe, let me tell you something about men."

Uh-oh.

"Um…" I began in an effort not to learn anything about men. Hawk wasn't the only man who was a mystery to me. Men on the whole were a mystery to me. I had no clue why they did half the shit they did and I'd long since decided I didn't want to know. You could spend decades trying to figure that shit out and never succeed. Ignorance, I decided, was bliss when it came to men. I'd learned to go with the flow and hope I didn't get chewed up too much in the process.

Hawk kept talking. "Sayin' shit like that to men like Tack is like a dare."

"What?"

"He's the president of an MC. He's got money. He's got balls. He's got brains. He's got charisma. He's got power. Men like that, women are easy. Men like that don't want women who are easy. They want women who are smart-asses and they're cute. A woman like that tells you they want nothin' to do with men and are gonna set up a ferret rescue, men like Tack take that as a challenge and challenges are what they feed on. They live and breathe for challenge. You sayin' what you said to Tack is the same as a man comin' up to him and shovin' him in a bar. He's gonna react to that, strongly, and best the situation no matter what he has to do to do it."

"That's crazy," I told him, because it was.

"That's Tack."

I stared at him. Then it hit me.

"It's also you."

His hand squeezed my ass. "You're learnin'."

Then something else hit me.

"What happens when you best the situation?"

"What?"

"What happens when it isn't a challenge anymore?"

His hand left my ass so his arm could curve around my waist and he pulled me closer, muttering, "Sweet Pea."

I pulled my torso back as best I could and kept my eyes glued to him.

"Is that an answer?" I asked.

He kept his eyes locked to me and asked back, "You gonna give me you?"

It was my turn to say, "What?"

"Babe, yesterday, you said your fuckwad ex crushed you. And I know this to be true because, for days, I watched you approach every situation between us with one hand up as if you're wardin' off a threat. When I do something you like, your face gentles because I've surprised you, you haven't had shit like that from a man. You just walked up to me and slid your arms around me sweet. I've made you come for me and I've been inside you. You've shared gratitude. But, Gwen, that hand's still up, wardin' me off. You haven't given me you, not even close. There is no way I've bested this situation."

That was an answer. It just wasn't *the* answer.

"Okay, so say you best the situation."

"I haven't."

"Say you do."

"Gwen, I haven't."

"But say you do."

"I do, then we'll see how that plays out."

Not a good answer. I *knew* how it played out. Scott Leighton taught me that.

I looked at his chest and muttered, "I need coffee now."

"Gwen," he called.

My arms slid from around his back so my hands could press against his chest.

His arms got tight. "Gwen."

I pressed harder on his chest.

He shook me gently and ordered, "Gwen, give me your eyes." I looked up at him and he asked, "You want false promises?" I didn't answer so his face dipped closer. "Baby, I can't tell the future."

"I can," I whispered and pushed hard on his chest.

I succeeded in gaining a few inches until he hauled me right back, his arms locking around me.

"There it is, Gwen, this is that hand you got up," he said quietly.

"I need coffee, Hawk."

I tilted my head down and pushed again at his chest but his hand came up, twisted in my hair and tugged back gently so I was looking at him.

"All right, babe," he said, "there's two ways this plays out. I best this situation and you give me all of you, honestly, I could find that's not what I want and we both move on."

I yanked my head back but he held firm and kept talking.

"Or," he went on, "I find treasure and a man who finds treasure does everything he can to protect it and keep it close. I don't know which way this is gonna go but I'm willin' to ride it out and see. That's not a risk I've taken in a long time, Gwen, that's a risk I've avoided. But I'm takin' that risk with you. You step away now, that tells me I'm not worth it to you to take that risk with me."

I stilled my struggles and stared at him.

"You gonna step away?" he dared.

"I need to think," I whispered.

He shook his head. "No. No, you don't. You live in your head too much, you curl up and shut shit out and spend so much time doin' it, you forget to live your life. You can't live your life in your head. That isn't livin'. Trust me, babe, I know. I've been doin' near the same thing for a while now.

So long I forgot what it feels like to be alive. You got in my face that day you got back from Ride and reminded me what it feels like to be alive. Feels good, Sweet Pea, so I'm not goin' back now."

Something was clogging my throat but I still managed to ask, "What are you talking about?"

"You drop that hand and quit fendin' me off, I'll tell you."

"You tell me now, maybe I'll drop that hand," I returned.

"Doesn't work that way, Gwen."

I started to get mad and said, "Of course not."

"Babe, you don't get it."

"I do," I told him. "It's your way or no way."

"There's that hand again."

God! How could I forget how annoying he was?

He wanted it? He was going to get it.

"I loved him," I announced, Hawk's body got still and I went on, "A lot. Looking back, I have no freaking idea why but at the time, I was sure. Completely sure. I *knew*. I was absolutely certain. No doubts. None at all. Does that sound familiar?"

"Babe—"

"Ginger fucked him on our wedding day."

On that, Hawk's body locked and I nodded.

"No joke. No one knows. Not even Cam and Tracy. Then, later, Ginger was in some trouble, less than she has now, but she needed to crash at our place, so I let her. I was out, don't remember what I was doing, came home and found them at it again. It all came out then, Ginger told me and Scott didn't deny it. Ginger, I got it. Ginger did that kind of shit all the time. But Scott, even though I knew, I locked myself in my head and went into denial and pretended. Hoped he'd grow up and grow out of it. But you wake up real fast when you walk into your home and find your husband fucking your sister."

Hawk stared at me and I kept talking.

"You know, the funny thing is, I think Ginger did it to warn me off. I think Ginger knew exactly what kind of asshole he was and that was her fucked-up way of protecting me. She wasn't gleeful when it happened, she didn't throw it in my face. She seemed relieved. But me, I loved him. I was so sure and I didn't want to admit I got it that wrong. And when you're that sure and end up getting it that wrong, you lose faith in yourself, your ability to make the right decisions about your life. So, Hawk, there's a reason that hand's up. Because I was sure about you too and for a year and a half you gave me nothing but really great sex. Now you want more but there is no way, no way in hell I'm not going to proceed with extreme caution."

His hand cupped my head and his arm pulled me close while he whispered, "Baby."

No. No. He couldn't be sweet and get to me. He needed to give me something a whole lot different than sweet.

"You told your man you'd be there in twenty and I need coffee," I reminded him. "And I need to think. You might not want that, but tough. It's what I do. So let me go."

He didn't let me go. He held me tight and stared into my eyes.

"Hawk—"

"All right, babe, I'll let you go, but I'll give you this to think about when you crawl into your head. For eight years I've been dead. I had people loyal to me that I trusted and I didn't let anyone, not one fuckin' person, into those ranks. Then I see this woman at a restaurant who laughs in public like she's giggling with her girls over coffee at her kitchen table. The only thing I had to give that woman, I gave her. I know everything about you, Gwen, because my boys had orders to report to me *daily*. Where you went, what you did, who you were with, how you spent your money, who you met, who you talked to on the phone, when the lights went out in your bedroom and they knew you were asleep. I told myself it was because you needed lookin' after but it wasn't that, Gwen, it was never that. I didn't know it then. I didn't know it until Jorge phoned me and told me to get my ass to base because you were on screen in Ride. I didn't go to base, I demanded a report, got it and went to your house because I knew your shit just got hot and I knew I was not gonna let anyone harm you. Then I saw the tapes and I knew the next day that both Lawson and Tack were throwin' down and that's when I knew no one was gonna have you, not anyone but me. I haven't let anyone in in eight years, Sweet Pea, except you. Now you still got all I've got to give but I'm not gonna trust you with the rest until you trust me. So when you crawl into your head, think about that."

And with that, he let me go and then he was gone. He didn't vanish, his place was too big to pull that off, but I was immobile with shock, fear and something else. Something a whole lot different. Something warm and beautiful and that was even scarier.

So I didn't turn around to watch him leave.

CHAPTER TWENTY

Unoccupied

I sat in Hawk's battered old chair and stared across his cavernous lair.

I'd just finished my voyage of discovery. I didn't go so far as to look through his desk and bedroom drawers, but after he left, I'd poured a mug of coffee and searched the only space I knew that was really his.

I went under the bedroom platform and checked out his shelves.

He had a lot of CDs; he liked music, plain to see. His tastes were all over the place. Rock 'n' roll, the old stuff, seventies mainly. Heavy metal, all good, no hair bands. Jazz, the sweet kind, from days gone by, not the saxophone-heavy new kind. Blues, Billie Holiday and Robert Johnson, nice. R&B, some rap and, rounding out this selection, even some classical.

In other words, nothing there to get a lock on anything—there was too much of everything.

I went to the books, and although there were a lot of them, they didn't tell me anything more. He didn't relax with an exciting thriller or an intriguing mystery. Most of the books were about things I didn't even know they wrote books about and I was a book editor. Manuals on strategy of war, hand-to-hand combat, martial arts philosophy. Biographies of war generals. History books of battles. Nothing else. Not even a slim volume of poetry to give me some insight.

So I curled up in his chair and looked across his space as my mind filtered through what I knew of the bed platform and his office. This also gave me nothing. What you saw with Hawk was what you got. His life was narrow, organized and controlled. There was no personality to it. He had a family, brothers, nephews—family that was close and they cared about him but there were no photos. No scrapbooks. No frames of ribbons earned for feats executed in the Army. No DVDs that showed what kind of films entertained him. No art on the walls that reflected his taste. His furniture and fittings were stylish and expensive, definitely, but they were also heavy, masculine and durable. Even if they were attractive, they were utilitarian.

Except this nook. This chair. This table. This lamp. It didn't fit but it also didn't tell me anything yet somehow I knew it said it all.

All I sort of knew was, if what he said before he left and even what he said about when he first saw me was what I thought he meant, I meant something to him before I walked into Ride.

Daily reports.

You didn't demand daily reports on someone you didn't care about in some way, even if it was a distant, freakishly stringent, emotionally controlled way.

I sighed. Then I made a decision. I untucked my feet from under me and walked up the steps to get my phone. Then I walked to the kitchen, got myself a fresh mug of joe, and I walked back to Hawk's chair, took a sip of coffee, put it to the table and tucked myself into Hawk's chair.

I flipped open my phone and scrolled down. Then I stared.

My belly got squishy and my heart swelled right before I smiled softly at my phone.

Hawk had programmed four listings in my phone. One that just was "Hawk," which I assumed was his cell. Under that was "Hawk Base," under that "Hawk Base Private" which I assumed was his private, direct line at the office and under that "Hawk Home."

Apparently, Hawk wanted me to be able to contact him if I needed to contact him.

For shits and giggles, I scrolled down to "Hawk Home" and hit go. A couple seconds later the phone upstairs, the one on one of the end tables by the seating area, the one in the kitchen and the one on his desk all rang.

I smiled again and hit the red button. Then I scrolled up to Hawk and hit go.

It rang twice before it was answered with an industrious but definitely sassy, "Hawk's phone, you got Elvira. Talk to me."

I didn't talk to her due to my surprise that she answered the phone.

"Don't got all day," she prompted.

"Um . . . sorry, I was calling Hawk," I said stupidly.

This was met with silence.

Then a high-pitched, "*Gwen?*"

"Uh . . . yeah. Um . . . is Hawk—"

"Girl!" she cut me off. "How you doin'?" she asked conversationally, like we'd not only met but given each other manicures. Then again she'd packed my bags for me so she probably thought she knew me.

"Uh . . . fine," I answered.

"Good to hear," she replied. "The shit's gone down with you happened to me, basket case. No doubt. Then again, I had Hawk gathering the boys to launch an all-out rescue operation on a biker compound to save my ass, maybe not."

"Yes, that does make me feel a modicum of safety," I agreed.

"Modicum!" she hooted like that was hilarious. Then again, it was. Hawk and his commandos provided much more than a modicum of safety.

"Um...thanks for packing my bags," I offered.

"Girl, thank *you!* Sortin' through your shit was like a trip to female Candy Land. You got thirteen little black dresses," she informed me.

"I know," I replied.

"Each one red hot, scorchin'. Seen you on camera loads, girl, thought it was about your ass, maybe your hair, but now I know it's about those little black dresses," she said.

"Unh-hunh," I mumbled.

"Anyway, what you need?" she asked.

"Is Hawk there?" I asked back.

"Negatory," she answered. "He's in the middle of somethin', can't take calls, forwarded them to me."

Hmm. This didn't sound good.

"Can you give him a message to call me?"

"Sure, but you can tell me what you want and I got authority to take care of it. Boys are busy but I know you're quarantined at the Hawk Hangout so you need somethin', let me know and I'll find someone who can sort you out."

"That's nice but I just wanted to know if it's okay if I asked my girlfriends to come over."

"When you want us to be there?"

Us?

"Um..."

"I get off at five o'clock, could be there at five twenty," she went on.

"Well…the thing is, I'm um…" I stopped because she'd gone out to buy shoes for me and then gone to my house to pack for me. The latter she did well, making sure I had everything I needed. It was a nice thing to do, even if she was getting paid to do it. Clearly she wanted to befriend me and I didn't want to hurt her feelings.

"The thing is what?" she prompted.

Oh hell. Nothing for it.

"The thing is I want my girlfriends over to talk about Hawk."

"I know Hawk," she offered.

"Yes, but he's your boss."

"Sho' 'nuff, girl, so you need me there."

"I do?"

"Hon, Janine may be in charge of doin' the grunt work to organize his life but who you think gives her her grocery orders and sends her out to buy cargo pants? *Me.* You want the lowdown on Hawk, ain't no one better equipped for that action."

"Wouldn't that be inappropriate?" I asked and I heard her hoot (again).

"Fuck yeah, but who cares?" she asked back then went on, "Listen to me, Gwen. I been working for Cabe Delgado for seven years. When I walked my ass into this place to interview for the job, I thought I'd died and gone to heaven. Hot guys everywhere. So much fine ass, shit! I woulda worked here for nothin'. First day, thirty minutes in, these boys, they became a pain in my ass. Sortin' their shit out is like herdin' cats. Luckily, eye candy provides job satisfaction, if it didn't, I'd have gone to the supply cabinet and got myself a baton and wailed on some commando ass long before now. Then, coupla days ago, Hawk walks in and tells me to go to Nordstrom. Nordstrom! I didn't ask, I just grabbed the company card and hauled my ass outta here. I was all over that shit. You think I won't do all I can do to see that my duties include occasional trips to the mall, you...are...*wrong*."

Oh boy.

"Perhaps you aren't going to be able to be very objective during the discussion," I suggested.

"You bet yo' ass I won't be objective," she agreed then continued, "I'll see you at five twenty, what do you drink?"

"Um...cosmos."

"I'm all over that," she declared, then ordered, "Call your girls and see you later."

Then she gave me dead air.

Hmm. I was uncertain how that went. What I was certain about was that Elvira was going to be there at five twenty.

I called Cam and Tracy, found that they both could make a five twenty come to a meeting of the minds about Cabe "Hawk" Delgado. I gave them directions to the lair and a heads up about the Elvira addition and I sipped more coffee.

Then, because I could be a girlie idiot, I flipped my phone open just to see Hawk's numbers on my contact list. As I was scrolling down, the bar highlighted "Ginger."

I stared at my sister's name. As I did it, I thought about the fact that the best-case scenario was my sister going into the witness protection program and I avoided any thoughts of the worst-case scenario because they threatened to give me hives.

Then I got a wild hair, hit go and put it to my ear.

"What?" she answered.

Holy crap. She answered!

"Ginger? It's Gwen."

"I know, bitch."

Okay, maybe I didn't care that my sister might disappear into the witness protection program.

The problem was, I cared about the possible worst-case scenarios.

"Are you okay?" I asked.

"What do you care?"

"Ginger—"

"Listen, got shit to do. Don't waste my time callin' and pretended you give a shit, okay?"

"I *do* give a shit," I replied.

"Right."

Sarcasm.

Welp, guess that meant that Ginger's serious trouble didn't make Ginger reflect on her way of life and familial relationships. Why was I not surprised?

"Yes, right, Ginger. Listen to me, I know we're never going to be tight, you don't drink cosmos and I don't do acid trips, but you're my sister. I've been living a taste of your problems and I'm worried. You might not believe me, but that's the real deal. I'm worried, Dad's worried and Meredith is worried."

"None of you were worried the other night when I needed a fuckin' shower," she retorted.

"That was before the firebombs and drive-bys."

Silence.

"Maybe I can do something for you," I offered softly into the silence.

"Oh yeah, right, now you're willin' to do somethin' for me. All these years, you treat me like a piece of shit. Your livin' room gets blown to shit, you wake up. Is that it?"

"All these years I didn't treat you like a piece of shit," I denied, and I did this because it was damn well *true*.

"Unh-hunh." More sarcasm.

Now I was getting mad.

"Unh-hunh," I repeated. "I don't know what it is with you but if you have time to process this, we will. See, *I* didn't cut the hair off *your* Barbies. *I* didn't steal *your* shit to buy drugs. *I* didn't put my hand down *your* boyfriends' pants. And *I* didn't fuck *your husband.*"

"I knew you'd eventually throw that in my face," she returned.

Was she for real?

"You fucked my husband!" I yelled.

"Yeah, Gwen, and then you got shot of his ass. You never shoulda hooked up with that dickface in the first place. Now you're shacked up with Hawk fuckin' Delgado, of all fuckin' people, you should be kissin' my fuckin' feet."

This point had merit.

"I knew you did that for me," I said quietly.

"Someone had to wake your shit up."

Oh. My. God.

Was that sisterly love I was feeling for Ginger? I couldn't quite tell since I hadn't felt it for what seemed like centuries.

"Ginger, honey, please listen to me—"

"No. I don't know what Conan told you but you have no idea what's goin' down with me. What I know is perfect, sweet Gwennie doesn't have the tools to help me sort this shit out. No one does. Not even Conan. I'm in this alone and I don't give a fuck. I've always been in it alone."

"Maybe if you'd accept a little help—"

"Fuck you, Gwen. You don't want to help me. You want the drive-bys to stop."

"Yes, I do. Definitely," I agreed. "But I also don't want my sister to be out there on her own against multiple bad guys when maybe I can help."

"There *is* no help for this."

"Ginger—"

"Don't fuckin' call back, Gwen. Ever. Yeah?"

More dead air.

I flipped my phone shut on a hissed, "*Shit!*"

It rang instantly and I flipped it back open, thinking it was Ginger, and put it to my ear.

"Ginger?"

"No," I heard, "Troy."

Oh shit.

"Troy," I said quietly.

"Yeah, remember me?"

Uh-oh.

"Troy, I—"

"Got your house shot up. I called four times, no call back. Heard you were okay from Tracy. You call when your bathroom faucet doesn't shut off but you don't call when I'm worried out of my mind, I hear your living room's been shot to shit?"

"Things have been a little crazy."

"Gwen, you got your *house* shot up in a *drive-by,*" he returned. "I know things are crazy but too crazy to call your fucking *friend* and let him know you're all right?"

"Mom came by yesterday," I informed him. "I was a little out of sorts."

"I can see Meredith would be freaked about—"

"No, Troy, not Meredith. *Mom.*"

Silence.

I took in a deep breath. "Hawk hurt you and I'm sorry about that. He's ... um ... well ... whatever. That's the way he is. I didn't know what to say to you so—"

"You didn't know what to say to me because you've been hiding a relationship from me for a year and a half. And, like a chump, you're on the town with Rambo and I'm working in your kitchen and on your house all that time."

"It wasn't like that," I declared, and it wasn't. I just had no intention of telling him what it *was* like.

"Bullshit. It was just like that. So I figure I deserve an explanation of why you'd play me for a chump, Gwen."

All right, I was getting mad again.

"Actually, Troy, what it was like is none of your business. I didn't play you for a chump. You're my friend. When you need something, you call on your friends."

"Yeah, you have no problem doing that."

"And you don't either," I shot back. "Wasn't it me you called when you got that terrible flu and I took you to the doctor and I took you home and I made sure you had your medicine and enough Kleenex and cleaned out your vomit bowl? News flash, Troy, I do not like vomit *at all*. I avoid vomit like I avoid orange-hued lipstick, in other words, at all costs. But I'll deal with it for a friend."

"Gwen—"

"And wasn't it me, when you wanted to impress that girl, that came over and made a three-course meal for you to claim as your own when you had her over to your house?"

"I—"

I cut him off and pulled out the big guns.

"And wasn't it me who dropped everything and flew down to Tucson with you so you could help your mom arrange to bring your father back up to Denver for his funeral?"

"Honey—"

"This wasn't a one-way street and you know it," I cut him off again. "I gave as good as I took and it upsets me that you'd say differently. Now, my living room is a disaster, I can't go home, my parents can't go home, my sister is in trouble and my mother showed up out of the blue because she heard I hooked myself a man who could afford Jimmy Choos so she wanted to get in there and get...whatever. I haven't seen her for decades and there she was. I found out she'd always been close but didn't give a shit to get closer until she thought she could get something out of it. I'm sorry Hawk hurt your feelings, and on top of all this, I've been worried that I'd lose you because of it. But I don't need this shit now, Troy. I need my friends around me and if you aren't that, I don't know what to say except it would kill to find that out now after all we've been to each other."

"I'm in love with you, Gwen," he whispered, no hesitation, he socked it right to me. I sucked in breath and didn't respond, just stared at my lap experiencing the pain that shot through my heart. "Honey?" he called when I didn't speak.

"I wish you would have told me," I whispered back. "I can't say what would have happened if you did but now . . . now I can't deal with this, Troy. I love you, I think the world of you, but I have a man in my life. I don't know where it's heading, all I know is that what he makes me feel scares the fucking hell out of me and I need to focus on that."

"I know why he scares you, honey," Troy replied gently.

"Why's that?"

"Because he's got Scott Leighton written all over him."

I sucked in an audible breath.

"Troy—"

"You do that. You've always done that. The good-looking guys that think their shit doesn't stink and walk all over you."

Oh God.

Troy went on, "It hurt enough when Scott wore loafers. How's it going to feel like when the guy wears combat boots?"

"I'm not sure he's like that."

"I met him once, didn't know him at all and he didn't hesitate with what he said to me in front of you, Trace, and whoever the fuck those guys were. He didn't give a shit about me. What makes you think, he's got something to say you don't like, or he plans to do something that'll hurt you, he'll give a shit about you?"

"I think I know him better than you do, Troy, and he's not like other people. He actually thought he was doing you a favor."

"Well, Gwen, he thought wrong. You and I, we've always been close and now we're having this conversation. That's what *he* did. He might have told you he was doing me a favor, but that guy is the kind of guy who pisses in corners. You're territory and he saw me infringing on that so he drove in that wedge. Don't think it was anything else."

"I don't want to hurt you any more, babe, but I don't think he thinks of you as competition," I said gently.

A beat of silence then quietly, "Right."

"Troy, don't do this to us."

"I didn't, Gwen. Rambo did."

I opened my mouth to speak but got more dead air.

I flipped the phone shut, stared at it and then, again, hissed, "*Shit!*"

And again it rang in my hand.

I flipped it open immediately and put it to my ear.

"It's not nice to hang up on—"

"Babe," Hawk cut me off.

"Hawk?"

I was surprised. I thought he was incommunicado.

"Give me a good reason why you're callin' Ginger."

I sat frozen then realized he knew everything about me, which must include monitoring my calls.

"Hawk—"

"You don't know her."

"Hawk—"

"You don't know someone, you sure as fuck don't talk to them."

"Hawk—"

"You talk to her and someone's monitoring her communication, they hear you, they find you or they make assumptions."

Okay, something new to add to my list of why Hawk could be annoying, and that was when he was right.

"I saw her name on my contact list and got a wild hair," I admitted.

"No, you saw her name on your contact list, it reminded you you're worried about your sister and you phoned her," Hawk laid it out.

"Well, kind of the same thing."

A sigh, then, "Babe."

"I thought you were occupied," I changed the subject.

"I was but base got the ping on your phone, Mo called Jorge, Jorge is at my back and he's not occupied like me. He gave me the message you're contacting your fuckin' sister and I got unoccupied."

"Oh," I muttered.

"Gwen, baby, do me a favor. Trust me enough to do what I can for your sister. And trust me enough that I can deal with the emotional fallout we find there's nothin' I can do for your sister. Yeah?"

I looked from my lap to his books, to his CDs, to his lair.

"Gwen, you there?" Hawk called.

He got unoccupied. For me.

He wanted me to trust him with emotional fallout.

I stared at his lair. It still gave me nothing.

Even so, I knew Troy was wrong.

"I'm here," I said quietly, "and I'll do you that favor."

"Thanks, Sweet Pea," he said quietly back.

"My girlfriends are coming over later, is that cool with you?" I asked.

"Yeah, babe."

"Elvira has decided she's my girlfriend," I shared.

"No surprise," he replied.

"Do you need to get reoccupied?" I asked even though he wasn't giving me an impatient or preoccupied vibe but I was guessing, if he was forwarding his calls, he did it because he was in the middle of something important that required his full attention.

Attention he shifted for me.

Shit.

"Yeah," he answered.

"Okay, I'll let you go."

"Later, babe."

"Later, Hawk."

Dead air.

I flipped my phone shut and gazed unfocused into his lair.

Then I flipped my phone open again and called information to get the number for my insurance agent because I needed to report my drive-by.

CHAPTER TWENTY-ONE

Queen of Crash and Burn

"OHMIGOD! THIS PLACE is so *cool!*" This was Tracy, who was sashaying into the warehouse looking around like she just hit the candy garden with chocolate stream at Willy Wonka's. Her eyes caught sight of Elvira who was in the kitchen. "Hey girl! What's up?"

"Job satisfaction, beanpole, what's up with you," Elvira replied on a huge smile thus taking the sting out of her nickname for Tracy (I hoped).

If Cam was yin to Tracy's yang, Elvira was yang to *all* of our yins. She had to be no more than five foot four. She was round. Her skin was smooth, perfect mocha. Her hair was cropped at the back and sides but there was a thick, heavy bang at the front with blonde streaks in it. And she was so far from wearing commando gear it wasn't funny. If Hawk's dress code allowed Elvira's outfit, I wanted a job there. Short, mustard yellow sweater dress, off-the-shoulder neckline and thigh-high, spike-heeled, fire engine red suede boots.

Elvira was in the kitchen creating what she declared were "boards" except she was creating them on Hawk's big, square, midnight blue plates. She was doing this because she came into the warehouse laden with bags from Crate and Barrel and Fresh and Wild, places, she informed me, she took off work early so she could pay a visit. These bags contained brand-new martini glasses (a set of four, long stemmed, ultra sleek), a martini shaker, a mammoth wedge of brie, a French baton, grapes, apples, assorted olives, gherkins, red onion marmalade, assorted crackers, assorted chocolates and an enormous chunk of pâté.

Oh, and she brought the ingredients for cosmopolitans.

She had me at the martini glasses. The rest of it made me declare my undying love for her and I told her she'd officially been accepted into my girl posse.

No joke.

When I did this, Elvira just laughed and I figured she just laughed because she already thought she was in my girl posse or intended to be.

"Good God, this is where he lives?" Cam asked, wandering in behind Tracy, also looking around with surprise and a small but unguarded hint of wonder.

"He likes space," I answered.

"He'd have to," Cam replied.

"Who're you?" Elvira demanded to know, eyeing up Cam and Cam looked at her.

"Gwen's best friend," Cam answered.

Tracy had made it to the bar and she leaned both forearms into it, saying to Elvira, "We share that title."

Elvira looked over her shoulder at me where I was positioning myself at the back counter.

"If that's true, girl, you better make up your mind 'cause you can't have two maids of honor. I got a friend, she tried that shit, did her head in. Those two competed for everything. Sure, first it seems all good, two bridal showers, two bachelorette parties, two women bent on givin' you your every whim. But that shit turns nasty. They all ended up fightin' and by the big day, no one was talkin' to anyone else. It was a disaster. I had to step in and the dress didn't fit. They had to lace the fucker together with a shoestring at the back. You can't walk down an aisle and hide a shoestring. So I scooted in from the side. Looked funny. I don't like lookin' funny. Now I don't talk to her either but it ain't because of the shoestring. It's because she works my *last* nerve. She always did but I guess I'm just too nice, that is, until I don't feel like bein' nice no more."

I was stuck back on "you can't have two maids of honor" and therefore fighting back hyperventilation at the same time flashing pictures filled my head of a commando-style wedding. Hawk in black cargos, me in a white flak jacket festooned with lace. The picture of me carrying a bouquet of flowers and Hawk carrying an automatic weapon. The picture of me admiring Hawk's huge-ass hunting knife. The picture of Hawk carrying me out of the reception in a fireman's hold while bullets flew and flames caused by Molotov cocktails danced on the dance floor.

Tracy was stuck on it too, her flashing pictures way, *way* different than mine, and therefore she clapped and shrieked, "There it is! Elvira's the insider and *she* says this is going somewhere!"

"Oh God, I don't even have my ass on a stool and I already seriously need a cosmo," Cam muttered.

"Well, get yo' ass back here and man the shaker, girl," Elvira said to Cam and then looked at Tracy. "As for goin' somewhere, I don't know if Hawk's the marryin' kind and, you asked me a week ago, I would have said *hell* no, but a week ago he also wasn't the shoe-buyin' kind so right now my guess is anything goes."

"Cam, hurry, cosmo," I whispered.

"I gotcha covered, babe," Cam muttered.

"Well, I see good things but I always saw good things," Tracy declared, hitching her ass up on a stool and leaning forward to grab an olive off Elvira's board.

The bread knife Elvira was using clattered to the counter and Tracy bought her hand a quick, sharp slap.

"I'm not done," Elvira declared when Tracy snatched her hand back and held it with her other one, staring at Elvira in shock. "It's about presentation. Don't *mess* with my presentation."

"Okay," Tracy whispered, her eyes sliding to me. I pressed my lips together and Elvira went back to work and, scarily, she also went back to talking.

"Boys at the base, not big on gossip, it's frowned on, doin' anything too girlie or sissy, and I say frowned on in the sense that, you do that shit, you court bein' water boarded."

Holy crap!

Elvira went on. "They might share whose ass they've tagged but that's pretty much it. Worst part of the job. Who ever heard of a job where there's no gossip? But I can tell you this," she turned to me and jabbed the bread knife in my direction, "*you* been an object of fascination for a *good* long while."

Oh shit.

Elvira went back to her bread. "No talk. No whispers. Hawk would freakin' go psycho badass on their asses and Hawk's badass enough, goin' psycho, no one wants to go there. But that don't mean looks weren't exchanged and a look sometimes says it all."

In order to steady my breathing, I looked to Cam, who was the steadiest person I knew. Cam was coming back to the counter with a shaker full of ice and she was biting her lip.

Oh *shit*.

"Cam?" I called.

She stopped biting her lip but kept her eyes to the martini shaker when she replied, "Yeah, babe?"

"Do you have something to say?" I asked.

"Sho' she does," Elvira put in. "I heard the reports. I know the names of your girls. Camille. She works dispatch. Dispatch is at the station. Cops, they don't mind gossipin' so she knows the shit went down today."

I was leaning against the back counter but at this, I moved to the horseshoe, positioning myself beside Elvira to get a closer look at Cam.

"What shit went down today?" I asked.

"You didn't tell me about any shit in the car," Tracy put in, her eyes on Cam.

Camille poured vodka but Camille did not speak.

"Cam," I prompted.

Cam put down the bottle of vodka and looked at me.

Then she declared, "I don't want to like him."

I felt a flutter in my belly.

Elvira reared back, her eyebrows shooting up. "Why not?"

"He's…" She trailed off and reached for the cranberry juice.

"Cam," I repeated.

She put down the cranberry juice and looked at me. "Okay, well, Leo called, told me what happened. He told me what happened right after it happened because he was there. In fact, he couldn't *wait* to call."

"What happened?" Tracy asked.

"Hawk Delgado went psycho badass, that's what happened," Elvira answered.

"He what?" I whispered.

Cam nodded. "On Jerry Travers."

"Who's Jerry Travers?" Tracy asked.

Cam looked at her. "As far as Cabe Delgado could trace it, he's the guy who started the shit about Gwen being filler."

Oh boy, I said in my head but in my belly there was another flutter.

"Oh boy," Tracy whispered out loud.

"Oh boy is right," Elvira confirmed.

"What happened?" I asked Camille.

"Well, Leo says Delgado isn't stupid enough to walk into a police station and assault a police officer. That doesn't mean he couldn't make his displeasure clear and he did, crystal, and he did this *public*."

"I love this," Tracy breathed. "How did it go down?"

"Leo says he got in Jerry's space, got in his face and tore him a new one right in front of everyone," Cam answered. My belly graduated from flutter and started getting squishy. "And that new one he tore him is wide and gaping. Everyone's talking about it."

"Really?" Tracy whispered.

Cam nodded then looked at me and her expression was embattled. She didn't know what to make of this. "Leo was overjoyed. He even used that word, overjoyed. That man has *never* used the word overjoyed. Firstly, he's not a big fan of Jerry Travers because Jerry Travers talks trash about you and because he's an ass. I know Jerry. This is true. He *is* an ass, and he didn't say that shit to me because he knows we're tight. Secondly, Leo thinks you're the shit, you know that, girl, and Delgado walkin' in there to lay down the law about trash-talkin' you, well, he thought that was a little bit of all right."

I thought it was a little bit of all right too.

I looked down at the boards.

"Hurry, Elvira, if you don't, I'm breaking out the cookie dough," I told her.

"Cookie dough is for heartbreak and sister trouble, why would you break out the cookie dough?" Tracy asked.

"Cookie dough has many functions. It isn't just for

heartbreak and sister trouble. It's also for when you're freaking out about your love life," I replied.

"I'll tell you this," Elvira announced, fanning out little slices of French baton on the plate next to fanned-out little slices of apple all surrounding a gleaming, clean bunch of succulent grapes in the middle, "Hawk put me on radar, watched my every move for a year and a half and activated the troops when I caught trouble, there'd be no cookie dough *in sight.* I'd be on my knees next to the bed prayin' to the good Lord, thankin' him 'cause he heard my words. Then I'd put on my little teddy, the purple one, looks good against my skin, and I'd get in bed and count down the minutes until he got home."

"I wear nightshirts to bed," I informed her. "Though I do have a sexy caftan."

Elvira twisted her neck to look at me. "Saw that caftan, hon, in your laundry. It was pretty nice. But Hawk strikes me as a satin-and-lace man."

Hmm. It appeared Elvira was thorough when she went through my stuff to pack my bags.

"Is he a satin-and-lace man?" Tracy asked.

"No, he's a take-it-as-it-comes man," I answered. Or, more accurately, take-it-off-because-it's-in-the-way man.

Elvira grinned huge. "Mm hmm."

I looked at Cam. "Camille. Cosmo."

Cam lifted the stainless steel pitcher and started shaking.

"All right, I'm just gonna say things might have started out a bit slow," Trace began with a screaming understatement, "but sometimes it takes men a little while, you know, to understand they want commitment."

"Tell me about it," Camille muttered, yanked off the top of the martini shaker and started pouring.

I bit the side of my lip and slid my eyes to Tracy.

Then I said, "Leo's committed to you."

"Unh-hunh," Cam kept pouring.

"He totally loves you," Tracy put in.

"Mm," Cam mumbled, putting down the shaker and starting to hand glasses around.

"You got a man with commitment troubles, girl?" Elvira asked, plopping the wedge of pâté in the middle of some fanned-out crackers.

"Five years together, four in the same house," Camille answered.

"Oh boy," Elvira muttered, using the bread knife to attack the wrap on the brie.

"I see good things, I see them soon, I feel it in my bones," I quickly announced, taking my cosmo. "He's close, Cam, I know it."

"I know it too!" Trace added, but Elvira was looking at me.

Then she looked at Cam. "I read people," she stated, lifting the bread knife to her face and circling the blade an inch away from her skin as I held my breath. "Faces. They tell no lies. Like that TV show. I got the gift. And your girl here, she tells no lies. I ain't one to blow sunshine, seein' as I've known my share of commitment-phobes, so many I could write the Denver Directory of Commitment-Phobes, but she sees good things, she feels it in her bones, she's your girl, she's tellin' no lies, which means," she stuck the bread knife in Cam's face, "you give this boy some time."

After Elvira laid down the law and Cam was staring at the knifepoint two inches from her face, I reached out, wrapped my hand around Elvira's wrist and pulled her hand and the knife down. When I did, her eyes swung to me.

"Hawk has a rule about proper usage of knives in his house," I muttered.

"I bet he does," Elvira replied. "He got a rule about the proper usage of ninja stars?"

"Probably," I muttered because this was actually probably true.

"Can I have a cosmo?" Trace asked, and Cam finished handing them out.

"Boards're done," Elvira announced, plonking the brie next to the grapes. "Let's retire to the sittin' room."

The girls grabbed the big plates of food and I went to the shelves to get little plates and we all moseyed over to the seating area. Cam and Tracy took recliners. Elvira and I sat at opposite ends of the couch. The food sat on the coffee table in front of us and we all stared at it partially because no one wanted to touch anything without Elvira's consent and partially because she was right, it was about presentation and she definitely had flair. The food looked great. Good enough to be photographed for a magazine.

"Well?" Elvira asked. "What you all waitin' for? Dig in."

We all fell on the food like vultures.

I was shoving a slice of French baton smothered in red onion marmalade, pâté and topped with gherkin slices into my mouth when Elvira observed, "I shoulda bought some of those little spreaders. With the fancy handles. Crate and Barrel had some good ones. You got brie and pâté and kickass stoneware, you need fancy-handled spreaders."

Hawk's cement, iron and brick warehouse lair could handle slim-stemmed, sleek martini glasses but I figured it would expel fancy-handled spreaders.

I didn't tell Elvira this.

Instead, I asked the room (which meant Tracy and Camille since Elvira didn't really know me), "Do you think I live in my head?"

Tracy and Cam instantly looked across the coffee table at each other.

"That means yes," Elvira translated through a mouth full of brie and apple wedge.

I looked at Trace then I looked at Cam. "You do?"

"Girl—" Cam started.

"It's okay," Tracy said quickly. "We all do what we need to do to protect ourselves and you need to live in your dream world."

"I don't live in a dream world," I said, but this wasn't true. A lot of the time I did. It just wasn't *all* of the time. "I live my life. I go out. I have fun. I put myself out there."

"Leo calls you Queen Crash and Burn," Cam announced and my eyes went to her.

"What?"

"Queen Crash and Burn. You get all dressed up, go out, smile, chat, flirt…then it's all, 'Hey! Great talking to you! Later!' No number. No nothin'. They think you're into them and they're gonna get them some and off you trot and you don't look back. Queen Crash and Burn."

Uh…wow.

"I do that?" I asked, but I knew I did. I didn't *know* I did until just then, having it pointed out to me, but when it was, I knew I did it.

"Totally," Tracy confirmed on a whisper.

"Did Delgado say you lived in your head?" Cam asked and I nodded. "Why?"

"We were having a…discussion. I told him I needed to think about what he'd said and then he said I didn't need to think, I live in my head, I shut things out. He says I haven't given him me. He says I have a hand held up, fending him off," I answered.

Tracy and Camille's eyes went back to each other.

"See you do that too," Elvira noted.

"I'm open and friendly!" I declared.

Cam sighed, sat back and took a sip of cosmo.

Preparing me.

Oh shit.

Then she stated, "Babe, I know you've had a lot goin' on the last week but have you had a chance to think about what's gone down with you and Delgado?"

"Yes," I replied instantly. "I think about it all the time."

"And what you come up with, hon?" Elvira asked.

"I don't know, I have to think about it more," I answered, Elvira rolled her big eyes and she did this at Tracy. Tracy giggled.

Crap! I was living in my head again.

"Okay," I asked Cam, knowing I was living dangerously, "tell me what *you* think about it."

"I will," Cam replied.

Great.

Welp! I'd asked for it and in pure Cam style, she was going to give it to me.

"Has it occurred to you that, after all that time doin' nothin' but the nasty, you spoke to this guy once, *once*, and he was all up in your business?" Cam asked.

No. No, that hadn't occurred to me.

"No," I whispered.

"So, say you opened your mouth for more than just to do a little somethin'-somethin' when he visited you at night, where do you think you'd be right about now?" Cam continued.

Oh my God.

I didn't reply but Camille answered for me. "I'd say right where you are, babe."

Oh. My. *God.*

"I—" I started.

"You've had that hand held up for a year and a half, Gwennie," Trace said quietly.

"Mm hmm," Elvira mumbled into her cosmo.

God! I hated it when Hawk was right!

"Do you...do you..." I stammered, "think I should take down that hand?"

"Yes," Tracy said instantly.

"Absolutely," Elvira added her vote.

"Jury's still out on that one," Cam replied, got up and declared the discussion was over, it was time for me to sort myself out and she did this by announcing, "I'm making more cosmos." Then she glided into the kitchen on her four-inch heels.

I leaned forward and grabbed a bunch of grapes and a bigger bunch of assorted chocolates. I needed to think about all this.

Or, maybe, I didn't.

Shit.

Cam made cosmos, we drank, we ate and I really wanted to bring up some of the other stuff that Hawk said, mostly because Elvira was there, she said she'd worked for him for seven years and she might provide insight. However, Elvira also needed to keep herself in killer sweater dresses and fire engine red suede boots so I didn't want to get her into trouble or alternately water boarded should she gossip about her boss. Therefore I kept my questions to myself.

I also did this because, bottom line, I should ask Hawk.

I heard the earsplitting creak of the garage door going up and the room went wired. This was coming from Tracy because she was excited for me that Hawk was home. This was also coming from Elvira because she was excited to see me interact with Hawk. This was further coming from Cam because she wanted to dissect him with her awesome mental powers and decide how she would cast judgment. And last, this was coming from me because I was like Tracy; I was excited Hawk was home.

Another creak came meaning the garage door was going down then the inner door opened and in he prowled under four sets of female eyes. I was looking over my shoulder at him and noting he was not self-conscious with four sets of female eyes watching him. He was Hawk, confident, assured, graceful, powerful, all of it exactly the reason he first caught my eye.

Oh boy.

He walked right to the back of the couch behind me and I tipped my head back to watch him do it.

"Hey," I said quietly.

He bent at the same time his hand swept my hair off my shoulder, across my neck to my other shoulder, his head dipped in and I felt his lips at the skin behind my ear.

Lips still there he whispered, "Hey babe."

"Mm hmm," I heard Elvira mumble, and I processed this but only minutely mainly because I was processing my belly flutter coupled with a quiver in a private place.

He straightened, his hand curled around my neck and he took in the girl posse with his black eyes.

"Ladies," he muttered.

"Hey," Tracy breathed.

"Yo, Hawk," Elvira greeted.

Camille just looked at him.

He let go of my neck, rounded the couch and I scrambled to scoot away as he sat between me and the armrest. One of his arms moved to wrap around my shoulders, pulling me to him as his other hand came out and nabbed my cosmo. I turned my head and watched him sip from the martini glass.

As I did my mind warred, one faction making my belly feel squishy that he was drinking from my glass, the other faction wanting to reclaim my cosmo before he drank any more.

It was no surprise which one won out.

"Do you want your own?" I asked pointedly.

"Yours'll do." He ignored my point, handed the glass back to me and leaned forward to grab some leftover apple slices. Then he leaned back, casually tossing one in his mouth.

I turned to the girl posse and explained, "Hawk's body is his temple. In about a minute, he'll go into anaphylactic shock when the vodka processes through his system. No need for alarm, I have the adrenaline injection handy."

Tracy giggled again. Elvira laughed right out. Hawk did his manly, deep, amused chuckle and even Cam grinned.

"Mo says you left at three thirty," Hawk remarked when the laughter died and I looked at him to see his eyes were on Elvira.

I looked at Elvira and she was nodding. "Sho' did."

I bit my lip and looked at Tracy.

"Is this gonna be a creatively concealed line item?" Hawk asked as he leaned forward and grabbed some stranded grapes, his head tipping to the decimated food boards.

"I've set up Gwen as her own cost center," Elvira replied, unruffled.

My eyes got big.

"Probably a good idea," Hawk muttered, leaning back.

I gulped but Tracy put her drink aside so she could sit on her hands in order not to clap them in glee.

I looked at Hawk. "Would you like a proper meal?"

"Will you display symptoms of posttraumatic stress after you're forced to steam vegetables and spoon out cottage cheese?" he asked back.

I felt my eyebrows go up. "Is that what you want for dinner?"

"Yeah," he answered.

"Then yeah, probably. Will my cost center include visits to the psychologist?"

He grinned just as his arm curved fast and tight, pulling me into him. My cosmo arm shot out to avoid collision as my chest hit his chest, his hand slid up into my hair to cup my head, he tilted it and my mouth hit his.

The kiss was short but any kiss from Hawk was sweet.

Though some were sweeter.

When he let me back an inch, he said, "Babe," through a smile.

"I thought you told me you were going to kiss me if I made you laugh."

"I did."

"I didn't make you laugh," I pointed out.

"No, but I'm gonna kiss you when you make me wanna laugh too."

"So, I don't even get any verbal warning?"

His hand slid down to my neck. "Those are the breaks, Sweet Pea."

"Sweet Pea," Tracy breathed, and suddenly I remembered I had an audience.

I pulled away and sat back, scanning the posse. Tracy was smiling flat out, in twilight, la-la land of happiness, firm in the knowledge she'd always been right. Elvira was grinning into her martini glass but still likely lamenting the fact that the commandos wouldn't be receptive to the hot gossip she had to share. Cam was swirling the dregs of her cosmo in the bottom of her glass, eyes openly assessing on Hawk, not wanting to let go of a year and a half of thinking Hawk was a motherfucking asshole, but I could tell, she was getting swayed.

"I need to steam vegetables," I declared. "Does anyone want steamed vegetables?"

"Not for me," Tracy answered.

"I gotta be gettin' home," Elvira said, sucking back the last of her cosmo.

"Me too, early shift," Cam put in.

Hawk reached out and confiscated my glass again when Tracy added, "If Cam's going, I'm going. She's my ride."

Hawk took a sip then aimed his eyes at Tracy. "You wanna hang with Gwen, I'll take you home."

"You will?" Tracy asked, eyes big, an offer of a ride home further endorsement that she was right never to give up hope.

"Sure," Hawk answered.

Her eyes darted back and forth between Hawk and me before she said, "I'd like to stay."

"Then stay," Hawk returned, handed me my drink and leaned forward again to nab the last of the apple slices.

The girl posse mobilized. Tracy and I said good-bye to Cam and Elvira at the door, me assuring them I had clean up covered. When they called their adieus, Hawk's farewell was a jerk of the chin from his position standing in the opened fridge. After they left, Tracy and I went to the kitchen, Hawk went to his desk, flipped up his laptop and I saw the screen illuminate his face before he turned on the desk lamp. Tracy tidied while I steamed veggies and spooned out cottage cheese. Hawk approached when I was dumping veggies on the plate and Tracy was shaking another batch of cosmos. We retired to the seating area, Tracy back to her recliner, Hawk in his corner, me pressed to his side while he ate.

With Tracy, Hawk wasn't like he was with me during our date. He conversed. He was at ease, sometimes funny, not exactly open but not deliberately closed and, if it could believed, often charming.

Hmm.

By the time Hawk excused himself to put his plate in the dishwasher and go back to his laptop, Tracy was practically shimmering with joy and this only had a little to do with the fact she'd drunk three cosmos.

She and I chatted and giggled (mostly giggled) and finally Hawk took her home. When they were gone, I finished tidying up, got ready for bed, climbed in and was about to nod off when I heard the garage door open. It wasn't long after when the lights went out one by one through Hawk's lair, I heard him moving around the bed platform, I felt his warm hand on the small of my back then his weight hit the bed.

I rolled into him before he could curl into my back.

His arm wrapped around me. "So, what's the verdict?" he asked into the dark, totally knowing why the girls were there that night.

"Apparently, I'm Queen Crash and Burn," I answered.

"Come again?"

"Leo calls me Queen Crash and Burn. I flirt then I leave them hanging."

"Babe," was his reply.

"It didn't occur to me but I guess I do this."

"My boys call you Mistress Blueballs."

My body got tight and his hand slid into my nightshirt, pushing it up.

"They do?" I asked.

"Yep," he answered, the nightshirt still going up.

"Elvira said they don't gossip."

The nightshirt went way up, my arms were forced to go up with it then it was gone.

Totally a take-it-off-because-it-gets-in-the-way man.

His hand slid down my back and right into my panties to cup my ass.

Mm. Nice.

"They don't talk around Elvira," he went on. "They learned. She's pathologically friendly, in your business and adopts every woman who drifts in and out of their lives. Hard to scrape someone off when you're workin' with their new best friend."

Hmm. This said a lot, since she'd done this with me and Hawk apparently didn't give a shit.

I decided maybe for now I should let that one go.

"Mistress Blueballs?" I prompted.

"You know I've watched you. They saw it happen. You give all the right signals, the promise of you so hot they'd sell an organ to get in there, then you close down."

Hmm.

His hand at my ass pulled me deeper into his body as his knee forced its way between my legs so I had no choice but to hitch my leg around his hip and his head came up before his face disappeared in my neck.

"What else was decided tonight?" he whispered against my skin. I shivered and my arms slid around him, the one at the bottom forcing its way under his weight so I could get to the sleek skin and muscled contours of his back.

"They gave me food for thought," I replied also in a whisper and felt his smile against my neck.

"Right," he returned quietly then I felt his tongue.

Mm.

My hands started moving on his back as I pressed my hips into his and his thigh moved higher.

Mm.

"Troy says you're gonna walk all over me," I announced for reasons unknown even to me and I said it. "In combat boots," I finished.

His head went back to the pillows. "You talked with Troy?"

I nodded against the pillows, wishing I hadn't said anything because saying something lost me his mouth. "After Ginger."

"Babe, he doesn't know me enough to say shit like that."

"He said the same thing. You didn't know him enough to say what you said to him."

"I see he didn't take that opportunity to man up," Hawk muttered.

"It was harsh, Hawk," I whispered.

"It was real, Gwen," he returned. "I pissed around with you for a year and a half without makin' any real moves and any time in that time you could have moved on. How long's he been doin' it and what's the chance that, he doesn't wake the fuck up, he'll do it again with another woman?"

Well, he had a point there.

"He told me he's in love with me," I shared again on a whisper.

Hawk's body went still then his hand slid from my ass, up my ribs to cup my breast.

Then he did a nipple swipe.

Yowza.

"Then he'll appreciate it when you tell him, no matter what happens, I promised you I'd handle you with care," he whispered back

Um . . . *yowza!*

"Hawk," I breathed but he lifted my breast, bent his head and pulled my nipple into his mouth.

Yowzayowzayowza!

I moaned.

His mouth released my breast, it came to mine as his thumb circled my hard nipple and he ordered, "Touch yourself, baby, while I work your tits."

"'Kay," I agreed on a breath and did as ordered.

The instant my finger touched the golden spot, his head slanted, his mouth took mine in a kiss, his finger met his thumb for a nipple roll and that's when I forgot about Troy, cosmos with the girl posse and living in my head. I dropped my imaginary hand, stopped fending Hawk off and lived in the now.

CHAPTER TWENTY-TWO

All I Can Ask

HAWK FLIPPED ME to my back.

"Baby," I gasped. "I wasn't done."

He ground his cock into me. "You got a time limit up there, Sweet Pea," he grunted. "You can't bring it home, I take over."

This was true. Hawk allowed the top for a while. Then, if I couldn't "bring it home," he stopped allowing it.

Like now. Now he pulled up my leg, kept it high with his bicep behind my knee, arm wrapped around, hand warm on my inner thigh and lifted up with his other hand in the bed, arm straight.

Then I watched his head drop so he could study our connection, his eyes heated, his face hungry. He liked what he was seeing. Just watching him, I felt a strong pre-orgasm vibration.

Then he did that thing he does with his hips, I whimpered because I really, *really* liked that thing he does with his hips then he started driving into me again.

"Hawk," I breathed, my hand trailing down, my fingers separating around his pounding cock, feeling our connection, the power of him riding me. Beautiful. Wet. Hard. Hot.

His eyes came to mine and he did that thing with his hips again, my neck arched and I came.

Not long after, Hawk did the same.

He released my leg and his heat and weight came to me. I took it gladly, welcoming it by wrapping all four limbs around him.

His face was in my neck and I glided my nose down his shoulder.

God, he smelled good.

His mouth came to my ear. "Got shit to do, babe," he murmured.

It was morning. The morning after the girl posse meeting of the minds. The morning after he promised to handle me with care.

"Okay," I whispered.

Even though he had things to do, again this was no first thing in the morning nookie, slam, bam, thank you ma'am. His mouth came to mine and he kissed me lightly and again then again before he nipped my bottom lip.

Shit but I liked when he did that.

So much that when he started to roll off me, I rolled with him so I was on top, straddling him, my forearms in the bed, my breasts brushing his chest, my hair framing both our faces.

One of his hands spanned my hip, the other one gathered one side of my hair, holding it at my neck.

"Gwen," he said softly.

God, I really loved my name.

I lifted a hand and put it to his face, my thumb moving over his brow, his cheekbone, to where his dimple would be if he was smiling then across his lips and he let me do this, his eyes locked to mine.

"Do you promise to handle me with care?" I whispered, my heart racing.

His hand at my hip curved around my waist pulling me down to him and his hand at my neck did the same so our faces were a breath away.

"Promise," he whispered back.

"Swear?" I pushed.

"Swear, baby."

"You had a hand up too, Hawk," I told him.

"Dropped it a while ago, Gwen."

Shit. He had. He totally had.

I nodded then bent my head the quarter inch I needed to touch my lips to his. His arms got tight, he rolled me to my back and my lip touch became a long, hard, wet, delicious kiss.

His head came up and he asked, "You just give me you?"

"I'm gonna try," I answered.

"All I can ask, Sweet Pea," he muttered, did the triple touch with his lips again, denied me the nip then stated, "We're goin' out tonight."

Oh yeah. I liked that.

"Okay."

"Dress sweet for me, baby," he ordered.

"Okay," I repeated.

He smiled down at me, his dimples popping out then I got the belated nip on my lower lip.

Nice.

*   *   *

"Babe," Hawk answered his phone.

It was early afternoon and without the freezer full of frozen Twix bars calling my name, firebombs, drive-bys and commandos installing security systems, I'd had two days of uninterrupted, flat-out work. I was getting ahead of the game. I had another author send me her files but the deadline was far away, so work was steady, I was golden and my invoices that month were going to be awesome.

"My insurance guy called," I replied into the phone, wandering to the window, staring at the not-very-attractive scrub, hardscrabble and somewhat attractive, small-river-maybe-large-creek flowing by. "I need to meet him at my house."

"When?" Hawk asked.

"Three," I answered.

"I'll send one of my boys," Hawk replied.

"Thanks, baby," I whispered, he didn't respond so I went on, "Can I ask about tonight?"

"What about it?"

"Well, is it a little black dress and heels night? A glittery top with jeans night? Or a t-shirt and motorcycle boots night?"

"You own motorcycle boots?"

"No, but there are about a gazillion Harley Davidson stores in and around Denver. Maybe your boy can take me on a pit stop."

"A gazillion?" he asked, sounding like he was smiling.

"Maybe a bazillion, just down from a gazillion."

I heard a manly, deep chuckle.

Then, "Babe, not big on a woman in motorcycle boots."

"Okay, that's out," I muttered and got another chuckle.

"Somewhere between dress and heels and tee and boots. That work for you?" he finally answered.

"Yes," I replied then cried, "Oh! Meredith called. She wants to do dinner but she can't make dinner at their house because cleanup just started so she wanted to know if we want to meet them at Rock Bottom Brewery."

"Call Elvira, tell her to check the schedule and give you my parents' number," he said.

"Your parents' number?" I asked.

"They liked your folks, they'll want to come."

I lost sight of the scrub, hardscrabble and small-river-maybe-large-creek as my eyes went blurry. This was because it was one thing for our parents to be thrown together in an out-of-control family drama that involved cleavers and weeping but it was totally another to casually arrange a meeting of the parents like it was just any other dinner.

"Gwen?" he called.

"What?" I answered.

"Thought I lost you."

"I'm here."

"All right, so call Elvira."

"'Kay."

I got that out but I was incapable of further speech. It just hit me that my Mystery Man knew my parents, I knew his, he wanted me to set up a meet-the-parents dinner even though we'd already met each other's parents, not to mention they'd met each other, and we were practically living together.

Therefore it just hit me that I was freaking way the fuck out.

And this was because he said that if I gave him me, he could find out that I'm treasure.

But he could also find out I wasn't what he wanted.

But mostly I was freaking out because I just realized I really wanted to be what he wanted. I really wanted to be treasure. As in *really*.

"Gwen," he called again, sounding slightly impatient.

Oh no! I was making him impatient!

"What?" I answered.

"What's up?"

I couldn't tell him.

"Um..." I quit speaking.

Hawk was silent. Then he sighed, another indication of impatience.

Shit!

"Gwen, baby," he said softly. "What'd I promise you?"

I closed my eyes. He'd promised me that, no matter what, he'd handle me with care. And I was guessing that Cabe "Hawk" Delgado was the kind of man who kept his promises.

"Sorry," I whispered then admitted, "Don't mind me. Minor freak-out. It happens."

"Babe," he replied, now sounding slightly amused.

"Hawk?" I was still whispering.

"Yeah?"

I sucked in breath then shared, "It happens a lot."

"No shit?" he replied, definitely sounding amused now and not slightly.

I let out the breath.

Moving on!

"Don't you have stuff to do?" I asked. "Beating infidels into submission, shit like that?"

"Sweet Pea, what do you think I do for a living?"

"Well," I started. "You fly on your supersonic jet to hot, humid, tropical, war-torn nations, execute your duties as a soldier for hire which means doing things like blowing up bridges and beating infidels into submission."

"Hard to do that and get home to take you to dinner," he noted.

"Hawk, your jet is *supersonic,*" I reminded him.

He burst out laughing and I smiled a relieved smile into the phone and listened.

When he was done laughing, he said, "Babe, I had a supersonic jet, your ass would be in it, I'd take you to a hot, humid, tropical nation but only so you could spend the days in a bikini and I could fuck you on the beach."

Oh. Wow.

"Your daydreams are *way* better than mine," I breathed.

"This shit gets done, Gwen, that won't be a dream," he replied, I sucked in another breath and then got dead air.

Nice.

*   *   *

When Hawk's boy, Brett, parked in my drive, I saw the windows of my house boarded up, likely something Hawk or possibly Dad arranged.

I'd previously met Brett. He'd been one of the commandos who installed my security system. He was blond and blue-eyed and kind of had the boy-next-door-thing going for him, if the boy next door had more weight and exercise equipment than Hawk. In other words, Brett was ripped *and* he was bulky.

But Brett wasn't like Fang. Brett talked. I knew this because I knew Brett had worked for Hawk for three years. Brett also used to be in the Army. And Brett had a girlfriend named Betsy who was pregnant. They were getting married but not until after the baby came because Betsy didn't want to be fat in her wedding pictures. I told Brett I could see that, I wouldn't want to be fat in my wedding pictures either.

I let us in my house and Brett went to the security panel, punching in the code. This was a relief, considering I'd forgotten it.

Then I surveyed my living room.

"Boy," I whispered, looking around at the destruction, then my eyes went to Brett and I finished, "Bullets do a lot of damage."

Then for some reason, perhaps because I was there when that destruction happened, that destruction could have happened to *me* and it brought it all back or because now my living room was even further away from being habitable *and* my furniture was shot up, my face scrunched and I burst into tears.

Shockingly, Brett folded me in his beefy arms and this was such a nice thing to do, I took advantage, circled his waist with my arms and pressed in.

"This is all fixable, Gwen," he said to the top of my hair, and I nodded against his massive chest but didn't reply so he went on, "And none of this is important. The only thing that might not have been fixable but *is* important didn't take a bullet. Hold onto that." Then his arms gave me a squeeze.

I was thinking Betsy was pretty lucky and because this big guy holding me made the unknown Betsy lucky and was also being so nice to me, I squeezed him back.

Fortunately I had just enough time to get myself together and wipe my face before the insurance guy arrived. He was just as stunned as I was. It was clear he didn't often get called out to do estimations post-drive-by. Flood, yes. Fire, probably. Drive-by, no. He wasted no time in doing a tour, making notes, telling me the procedure, giving me some forms and he got out of there. I didn't blame him. Lightning might not strike twice in the same place but a drive-by was a crapshoot.

Brett hung out downstairs while I went upstairs to peruse my closet for my outfit for the night. I also unearthed the big canvas bag that I used to drag my clothes in to the Laundromat when I didn't have a washer and dryer. Hawk had a washer and dryer in the little paneled room in the space under the bed platform. This room also held a super-deep-bowled huge sink that had a super-powered hose-like spray attached and it was where I fancied he cleaned the blood off his weapons. I wanted to launder my caftan, wear it and assess Hawk's response. I also planned a trip to the mall immediately after the Ginger trouble was over. My underwear was sexy in an understated way (or, at least, I thought so) but it was bought mainly for comfort, not style. It wasn't out-and-out sexy and my sleepwear wasn't sexy in *any* way. I was going to buy satin and lace and study the response.

I packed a small bag with my outfit, some jewelry and bits and pieces that would be nice to have around. I was zipping up the top and considering raiding my freezer for my Twix stash and adding it to my bag when I heard it.

Gunfire in the living room.

I froze for half a second, that alert-alive feeling assaulting my system instantly, my skin tingling, my heart beating, then I dashed to the phone as I heard someone thundering up my stairs and I hoped it was Brett. I really, really hoped it was Brett.

I still went to the phone and had it out of the receiver but didn't manage to dial 911. An arm locked around my waist, wrenching me backward, a hand batted mine and the phone clattered away. I twisted my neck to ascertain if it was Brett but I knew it wasn't.

It wasn't.

Then I kicked, screamed, bucked, elbowed and scratched and the man who had me was having trouble holding onto me.

Someone else entered the room, I heard a weird popping and crackling noise, something was touched to my neck and I went out.

CHAPTER TWENTY-THREE

Patience

"You get the picture?"

Lying on a filthy bed in a filthy apartment, whereabouts unknown, with my mouth gagged and hands bound behind my back with hard, tight, plastic strips that hurt a lot and the same with my ankles but fortunately over my boots, I watched Darla, with a black eye, bruised cheekbone, busted lip and angry marks on her neck, talk into the phone. She'd taken a picture with her phone of me lying there and sent it to multiple someones, one of whom she was talking to on the phone.

"Yeah, that's from me, bitch," she hissed into the phone. "We got her and you can have her for two hundred large."

Well, the good news was, I was worth two hundred large, which was a lot. The bad news was everything else. Absolutely everything else. Including the fact I was gagged and bound, the plastic restraints biting into my wrists and I feared they broke skin, or at least it hurt that way. I was in a filthy apartment somewhere I didn't know. I'd been transported there lying in the back of a filthy van which was uncomfortable and, at times, like when the van turned and I was powerless to stop myself from rolling and slamming

into the walls, painful. I didn't know what had become of
Brett but I didn't think whatever it was was good for I figured Brett had orders to protect me, he'd follow those to the
letter and guns had been fired. Furthermore, he had a baby
on the way and he was nice. And, lastly, Darla wasn't working alone.

There were three men with her. One was, at that very
moment, bent over a mirror snorting cocaine into his nose.
Another was in the bathroom, the door open and I could
hear him relieving himself.

But the third was sitting on a chair pulled up to the bed,
his forearms, which I'd scratched and shredded, were resting
on his thighs. Dangling between them held in his hand was a
gun and his very unhappy eyes were on me.

Hysterically I noted he could have been hot if he wasn't
so rough, he wasn't so freaking scary and he so obviously
didn't want to shoot me.

"Oh yeah, you're right," Darla went on, and my eyes
went from scary, murderous kidnapper to Darla. "I *was* your
friend, until I got picked up and worked over because of your
shit. Now, not so fuckin' much."

Your friend?

Oh God. She was talking to Ginger.

Ginger didn't have two hundred large! And if she did, she
wouldn't give it up for me.

Shit, I was screwed.

"Bullshit," Darla snapped into the phone. "You got that
and you got more. I know it, you stupid bitch, so don't think
I'm a stupid bitch. Now you get it together and call me and I'll
tell you where the drop off is. And, 'cause we're friends, I'm
givin' you a discount and first dibs. You don't call me back in
an hour, I shop your sister out to people who'll pay a lot more
and be a lot less gentle than me and Skull."

Instinctively I knew Skull was the scary, murderous kidnapper. I knew this because Skull was the perfect name for him.

And scarily I grew even more concerned about what "a lot less gentle" meant considering Skull and his crew had not been gentle in the slightest.

Darla flipped her phone shut then flipped it open immediately and punched some buttons. She put it to her ear and I knew she engaged when she spoke.

"Yeah, Dog, you saw it, she's with me and Skull," she snapped into the phone. "You tell Tack two hundred and fifty Gs. He's got an hour or we shop her out."

She didn't wait for a response, she flipped her phone shut. Then she glared at me a second, turned and walked to the cocaine station.

I avoided Skull's eyes, stared at the filthy comforter and wondered if Hawk still had eyes on my house, saw that Skull, Darla and her crew entered and therefore he mobilized immediately. I wondered if there were any neighbors at home who heard the gunshots and called 911 and therefore, whatever happened to Brett, there was someone seeing to him and he wasn't bleeding to death in my living room meaning his baby would grow up fatherless, never knowing his dad's voice got soft when he talked about his mom and that he was ripped and bulky and kind. And wondering, if Tack came up with the money, what that would mean for me.

The man from the bathroom came out, lit a cigarette, and at the sound of the lighter catching, my eyes lifted to him only to see cocaine kidnapper headed my way. My eyes locked on him as he approached and his eyes scanned my body as he did it.

He, on the other hand, wasn't hot. He needed a shower and a sandwich. He was way too skinny and not in a slinky, ultra-cool, rock 'n' roll Steven Tyler way but in a need to lay off the coke in a serious way way.

He put a hand in the bed and leaned over me, his fevered, cocaine-brightened eyes on my breasts.

"I like this," he muttered, reaching out a hand to run it down my arm as I tried to scoot away. I succeeded in shimmying back a few inches but he just leaned in more. "We got an hour," he noted, "maybe we can take turns."

I made a small, involuntary, terrified noise against the gag and shimmied back further.

"Lay off, Skeet," Skull warned low.

"C'mon, man," Skeet cajoled, his eyes not leaving my chest, his fingers trailing down, coming close to the side of my breast as I frantically shimmied back further, his knee hit the bed and he followed me. "This cunt looks like sweet cunt. Haven't had sweet in a while and, dude, I earned it."

Oh God.

I shimmied back further, he followed me then he wasn't there.

I arched my back and my neck, my eyes following the sound of a body thudding violently against the wall.

"Tack's rabid for that cunt," Skull ground out, his long, lean but fit frame pressing deep and predatory into Skeet's slight one. "You think he'd be rabid for it, pay his fee for cunt dirtied by you?"

I didn't think so and I would have shared that if I wasn't gagged.

"Tack doesn't pay," Skull went on, "you think, we put her out to bid, they'd pay for somethin' broken? You got a vase worth three hundred large, it's worth three hundred large because it's clean and unbroken. You break it, you fuckin' moron, it ain't worth shit."

Skeet didn't answer. Skeet was busy pushing against the

hand wrapped around his throat at the same time beginning to gag.

Skull got closer to Skeet's face. "Get me?"

Skeet nodded.

Skull shoved Skeet off and Skeet's head smashed against the wall when he did. Skull didn't even look at him as he turned away, walked across the room, resumed his seat by the bed at the same time he resumed his unhappy contemplation of me.

I watched him, thankful. My hope was I'd be rescued and when I was rescued I didn't want to be dirty and broken. I didn't want that in a *big* way.

Darla wandered over to Skull, sniffing and rubbing her finger under her upper lip, against her gums. When she got close, Skull leaned back and hooked an arm around her waist. He pulled her into his lap and looked at her.

"You good, baby?" he asked softly, and Darla's face gentled at his voice.

"Yeah, baby," she replied, melting into him.

Then they started making out.

I looked away deciding to focus, not on my current predicament, but on the fact I was perplexed.

Okay, clearly he was a felon since I was pretty certain that kidnapping was a felony. But he was also hot. He *did* have that ultra-cool, rock 'n' roll thing going on. His look wasn't slinky, it was cut and sinewy, he had great forearms (aside from my scratch marks), veined and contoured. He had a mass of messy, thick, dark hair. His eyes were scary, sure, but they were also an interesting, silvery, light gray. And he wore those faded jeans really well.

Even in the dark underbelly of the Denver they lived in, I figured he was out of Darla's league. She wasn't exactly ugly but she was a skank of the highest order. I could see Skull liking rough and ready but Darla took that to extremes.

Welp, to each their own.

They made out for a while then stopped so Darla could revisit the cocaine station. Skeet and cigarette kidnapper stayed silent and wired. I knew this because Skeet regularly visited the cocaine station and paced while cigarette kidnapper chain smoked.

Time slid by and I tried to force my head into daydreams of beaches, bikinis and Hawk but instead I couldn't stop the day-nightmares of my sister not having the money, or miraculously having it and not bothering to help me out even though I'd stepped in on more than one occasion in her miserable life. I also had day-nightmares of Tack deciding I wasn't worth the effort since one Kidd sister cost him over two million dollars so he wasn't going to pay over two hundred thousand for the other one.

During this, as my eyes frequently scanned the space, they also frequently caught Skull's.

And when Darla wasn't in his lap, I found his focus always on me. It was always unhappy and it was also unwavering, intense and patient. Incredibly patient. He was not wired. He did not visit the cocaine station. He did not smoke. He did not leave his seat and it began to feel like he was some kind of sentry, a guard. Not a good one but one all the same. And I knew instinctively that Skeet and/or cigarette kidnapper were unpredictable and he needed to guard his vase or they would have expended their effort, done whatever they'd done to Brett and bought Hawk's displeasure for no payoff.

The other thing was, although he seemed pissed at me, he didn't seem edgy. For Skull, what would be would be. Whatever deal they sealed, it didn't matter to him and it was worth the wait.

Finally the phone rang. Darla sauntered over to get it

from where she left it at the cocaine station. She flipped it open and put it to her ear.

She answered with, "This better be good news, bitch."

Ginger.

I closed my eyes and listened.

"Fuck you," Darla snapped acidly and I closed my eyes tighter. "You got it. I *know* you got it. What I went through for you? You offer a hundred? Fuck...*you*. Say good-bye to Gwennie as you knew her." And I heard the phone flip shut.

Well, the good news was, my sister pulled together one hundred thousand dollars for me, which was a nice thing for her to do. The bad news was, I liked me as I knew me and I didn't want to be any different kind of Gwen.

"I say we put her out to bid," Darla suggested, and my eyes opened to see she was standing beside Skull and he was looking up at her.

"Patience," Skull muttered.

"Fuck patience," Darla returned. "Ginger is probably goin' through her pile, keepin' her ass alive. Maybe she doesn't have the two hundred. And Tack hasn't had a taste of that *and* she's spreadin' 'em for Hawk. Maybe he's not gonna go there."

"Patience," Skull repeated.

"Dude," Skeet put in, getting closer to the bed, "I just drilled three rounds into Hawk's man. He's probably tearin' Denver apart, I did that and we got his pussy. We don't have *time* to be patient."

I closed my eyes again.

Three rounds.

Brett.

I sucked in breath through my nose as I felt tears stinging my sinuses.

"Patience," I heard Skull murmur.

"This is bullshit," cigarette kidnapper entered the conversation, and I opened my eyes to see he did it from his place, leaning against the wall, one knee cocked, sole of his boot to the wall, smoking another cigarette. "We shouldn't've dicked around with fuckin' Ginger and fuckin' Tack in the first place. Those assholes who want Ginger, they'd pay huge to have a tool to use to lean on that stupid bitch and get her outta hidin'. No more waitin'."

"Patience," Skull said yet again, not moving.

"Fuck patience!" Skeet, the most coked up, the one who bought Hawk's extreme displeasure and therefore the one most wired, shouted.

Skull slowly stood and the room tensed even further. I understood why. He just straightened from his chair but he did it in a way that was scary. I couldn't describe how but the way he did it was a physical threat, one you just simply didn't want carried out. He was not happy he was forced to move and no one in that room was unaware of that fact.

"Patience," he whispered.

That was when the door crashed open *and* both the windows on either the side of the bed exploded inward because men rappelled through them. Jorge was one, I didn't see the other but the man through the door was Hawk and he was followed by a man I didn't know but was somehow familiar to me.

Darla screeched. Skeet and cigarette man flew into action but it was way too late and they were way under-trained to take on Hawk and his commandos. In no time at all, the four of them were on the floor, on their bellies, wearing plastic restraints like mine and the man who came through the other window, another man I did not know but he also looked familiar and he wasn't one of Hawk's commandos, was training a gun on them.

If I had allowed myself to feel anything other than relief at that moment, I would have found it strange that, even in the quick, brutal commotion, Skull didn't put up a fight. He seemed like a fighter to me, a fight-to-the-death kind of fighter.

Instead my eyes followed Hawk who, after he subdued Skeet with laughable ease (not that I was laughing), came direct to me. He pulled something out of a pocket of his cargoes and his knee went to the bed.

"On your belly, baby," he whispered even as he gently put pressure on me to take me facedown on the bed. I felt his warm, strong hands working at my wrists and they were released.

When they were, I whimpered behind my gag, pulled them around and pins and needles shot through my arms. Hawk moved down the bed quickly and my ankles were freed.

I rolled to my back and Hawk helped me into a sitting position then both of our hands went to my gag. Mine were shaking so I let him pull it out and up over my head after which he tossed it aside.

Then his eyes came to mine.

"Brett," I whispered.

"Critical," he whispered back.

I never thought I would have to worry about what kind of woman I was. You never think you'll have to worry about that because you can never imagine life will lead you to times where you'll have to learn that knowledge. And, later, I would give headspace to wishing I were a stronger woman. One who could nod, keep her shit together and take the hit to her soul that came from knowing a human being took bullets to keep her safe.

But I wasn't that kind of woman.

I was the kind of woman who launched herself in a full frontal assault at her new boyfriend, connected so violently his powerful frame rocked back, shoved her face in his neck, wrapped her arms tight around him and burst into tears.

CHAPTER TWENTY-FOUR

Skull

I SAT IN the hospital waiting room, leaning against Meredith, Elvira on my other side, her hand holding mine firm and strong.

Dad was standing across the waiting room with Hawk, a handful of Hawk's commandos and other men. One was Lee Nightingale, another Luke Stark, the third Hank Nightingale, the last, Eddie Chavez. Lee and Luke were the two men who assisted Hawk in the rescue effort. It came to me after I'd been swept from the apartment how I knew them. Lee Nightingale owned a private investigation service whose action had caught the attention of the media. I knew all about him and his friends, including Luke, Hank and Eddie. Luke worked with Lee. Hank was his brother and a cop. Eddie was his friend and also a cop. The newspapers had broken the stories of their adventures, and their love lives, some time ago. This was followed by a bunch of books, a series entitled *Rock Chick*, that were released sharing intimate detail of these hair-raising yet romantic adventures. Books, incidentally, I owned, read repeatedly and wished I'd edited.

Lee and his men were all famous in Denver.

They were all, upon inspection, also badasses and extremely hot.

Even so, this was lost on me because I'd met Betsy and she was currently visiting her unconscious fiancé in his hospital room and I knew conversation was one-sided not only because Brett was unconscious but also because he had a tube down his throat.

I closed my eyes but opened them when I sensed a quick, intense danger permeate the room. Then my body tensed for flight when Skull, followed by Lawson, Leo and two other men, stalked into the room.

His eyes were on Hawk and it appeared he was even *more* unhappy than he was prior to my rescue. Then again, he would be seeing as I was rescued.

My eyes were on him, my skin was tingling, my mind was paralyzed with fear and even in the presence of a goodly number of badass commandos and just plain badasses my body was ready to take flight.

What was he doing there?

"What the fuck?" he clipped at Hawk, that threatening energy shifting off him in sinister waves.

I saw all the badasses go on instant alert.

"Come again?" Hawk asked quietly, his eyes locked on Skull, his expression showing he was vastly unhappier than Skull was.

"A year and a half," Skull replied, assuming a hostile stance way too close to Hawk. "I spent a year and a half of my fuckin' life on this fuckin' shit, the last month bangin' that piece of trash, pretendin' I got off on it, all the time tryin' not to vomit and prayin' my dick'll stay hard at the same time prayin' that stickin' it in her wouldn't buy me some disease where it would fall the fuck off and I was this close, this fuckin' close." He held up a finger and thumb less than an inch apart in Hawk's face which I, personally, didn't think was too smart. "You bust in there and that year and a half goes down the fuckin' toilet."

Hawk's body shifted in a scary way and he invited, still using that terrifying quiet voice, "Maybe you'll explain."

"He's DEA, Hawk," Lawson put in, this news making my body relax but that didn't mean I didn't feel shock.

Hawk's body didn't relax.

"You were involved in an operation where one of my men went down," Hawk pointed out.

"I was involved in an operation where I finally got close to a skank who I could use to nail down another skank who I could use to nail my man. When that didn't work, she still proved valuable to get me that other skank because she got me close to that skank's sister who I could then use either to out my tool who would help me take out the players who supply half the shit circulating Denver or who I could use directly to take out the players who supply half the fuckin' shit circulating fuckin' Denver," Skull returned.

I was slightly confused by his statement but I knew the others were not. I knew this because Skull's statement was met by a significant intensification of unfriendliness. So significant, the air became hard to breathe.

"You're tellin' me, you downed my man *and* were gonna use my woman as bait?" Hawk whispered, and Elvira's hand clenched mine.

"Uh-oh, I see psycho badass comin' on," she muttered.

"She was covered," Skull shot back.

"By who?" Hawk asked.

"By *my* man inside Roarke's crew," Skull answered.

"Roarke?" Hawk said and how he managed to get his lips to move when his face had turned to marble was a miracle.

"Yeah, I see it's sinkin' in," Skull ground out.

"You had to use Gwen, Roarke would have cut her up, Ginger knows it so she'd step in then he'd keep Gwen and enjoy his shit with Ginger and if he left either of 'em breathin', they would live the rest of their lives wishin' he didn't," Hawk clipped back.

Oh boy. That didn't sound good. That sounded very, very bad. That sounded get my ass to the mall instantly and buy sexy underwear as a reward for my rescue bad.

"I had it covered," Skull returned.

"Your man inside?" Hawk asked, edging toward sarcastic but still extremely displeased.

"Yeah," Skull answered.

"They scented him, they wouldn't play. They'd cut his fuckin' throat and dump him in the Platte," Hawk growled. "In *no* way did you have this covered."

"I had to use Ginger *or* Gwen, before I handed her over, I woulda wired her and tagged her so we'd know exactly where she was and could hear everything goin' down," Skull hit back. "And, by the way, it woulda helped, she was in on this shit but you and Wonder Cop here," he jerked his thumb at Lawson, "were breathin' so hot and heavy down her neck, the night I broke in to have my chat with her to give her a heads up, sirens sounded before I could get her goddamned bedroom door open."

Well, that explained that which, for me, was somewhat of a relief. At least that meant there wasn't another unknown person out there after me for nefarious reasons.

Hawk, nor Lawson, it was clear to see, felt relief.

"What?" Hawk whispered.

"You heard me, man, with your knight-in-shining-armor bullshit, you fucked this every way you could fuck this," Skull returned.

"Maybe, you let Hawk and me in on this shit, it wouldn't be fucked," Lawson suggested angrily.

Skull leaned back and his eyebrows shot up. "Yeah, I woulda kept my cover havin' sit-downs with The Rock and John McClane." He leaned back in. "Did you *miss* me tellin' you how far beyond the call of duty I had to go to keep my cover, bangin' that filthy, foul-mouthed, drug-addled piece of ass?"

Sarcasm, and it was clear neither Hawk nor Lawson appreciated sarcasm much.

"Roarke would uncover a wire and a tag in a split second." Lee Nightingale entered the conversation, throwing down on Hawk's (and my) side.

"My man was primed," Skull retorted.

"He'd out Ginger and he wouldn't do it with a threat on Gwen, he'd do it with a blade slicing through her skin," Luke Stark put in, and he appeared to be unhappy too.

"I'll repeat," Skull clipped, "my man was primed."

"You took a big chance without the primary player knowin' you were usin' her for this shit," Eddie Chavez growled as he pointed at me.

"I think you know more than anyone, Chavez, that the streets of Denver have been flooded with product. You boys on the force were so far over your heads keepin' on top of that shit, you petitioned the Pope to declare a miracle when Kane Allen backed out of the safety business," Skull returned. Eddie's face got tight and a muscle clenched in his cheek. "And Gwendolyn Kidd was the second part of that miracle."

Okay, firstly, if I was given a chance to decide if I wanted the opportunity to participate, I wouldn't have wanted any part of that miracle not only because I was a scaredy-cat but also because I felt that perhaps someone trained should have that job. Secondly, I didn't know if it was annoying or comforting to know all this shit tied together.

"We don't play it that way in Denver," Hank Nightingale clipped.

"Yeah, and that's why you got so much product flooding your streets," Skull clipped back, and Hawk moved.

Closing the distance between him and Skull in a way that could not be misinterpreted, he got chest to chest and eye to eye with him.

"Let's go back to talkin' about you downin' my man and targeting my woman. I wanna hear a little more about that," he said quietly in a way that stated clearly he didn't actually want to hear about that, he wanted to rip Skull's head off.

"Uh-oh," Elvira mumbled.

But it was safe to say I'd had enough. I'd been broken into, firebombed, shot at, abducted and imprisoned, kidnapped, tied up, targeted and almost used as bait by an undercover DEA agent who was obsessed with getting the bad guy. I was *not* going to let my new boyfriend get arrested for assault and battery.

Enough was e-fucking-*nough!*

I let go of Elvira's hand, stood and shouted, "Stop it!"

Hawk and Skull didn't separate but both their heads turned to me.

My eyes went to Skull.

"I understand and admire your mission but this is America, which means I'm free to choose if I wish to participate in your mission. And should I choose to do so I'm entitled to the training I'd need to maybe make it out the other end alive. You didn't give me that choice which is *not cool*. But, FYI, I would have chosen no. I wear high heels, drink cosmopolitans and edit books. That's my life choice. I don't go undercover. I have no desire to do that. The streets may be flooded with drugs, I'm sorry to hear that. I wish it wasn't true and I want to express my best of luck to you on seeing that situation altered but I know enough about myself to know I wouldn't have been able to help much in that situation even if I would have wanted to. I would have messed everything up. But there *are* people, like *you*, who would make a different choice, they would have been able to help and, bottom line, you should have found another way."

I sucked in breath and continued.

"Now, my sister is tied up in this shit, I knew it was bad, but now I know it's worse so if you wouldn't mind controlling your testosterone, standing down and regrouping in order to fight another day, I'd appreciate it. I've had a pretty bad day, Brett's and Betsy's have been worse, and we don't need anything to make it suck any more than it already does."

This was received quietly, all the badasses and badass commandos simply staring at me, so I went on.

"And baby," I said, my eyes going to Hawk, "I can appreciate you're upset about Brett and having to rescue me again but if we find out Brett's going to be okay, you promised me a night out. I don't think you meant that night was me visiting the police station to talk to you on a phone through glass. I don't have a visit-your-incarcerated-boyfriend outfit and," I leaned in, "*I don't want one.*"

"Tell it like it is, hon," Elvira muttered, and I could tell it was through a smile.

Hawk didn't move and his expression didn't alter; the same held true for Skull.

"Stand down from the DEA agent, Hawk," I ordered, and he continued to scowl at me so I quieted my voice and urged, "Baby, Betsy needs you now."

Hawk scowled at me some more then he stepped away from Skull but demanded to me, "Come here."

He may have stepped away but none of the tenseness left the room. I briefly debated the merits of running for my life rather than approaching Hawk but when his eyebrows went up I decided to take my chances and approach Hawk.

The second I did, his hand hooked around my neck, he yanked me toward him so my head collided with his chest, his arm locked around my shoulders and his other hand wrapped around my wrist. He pulled it up so it and its red welts and bits of broken skin were level with Skull's eyes.

"This is on you," he said quietly, and released my wrist but his fingers slid down and curled around my hand so he could pull it around his middle and he left it at the side of his waist. "She loses sleep, that's on you. I lose my man, that's on you. Either of those last two happen, I'll make it my mission that you never forget they're on you. We clear?"

Apparently they weren't for Skull returned, "My play was allowed to go down, I woulda kept her safe and I would have saved her sister."

Hawk pulled in his lips and bit them at the same time his arm tightened around me and I knew both of these were efforts at control. What he didn't do was respond, so Skull's eyes came to me.

"I would have kept you safe," he repeated.

"And I would have appreciated a choice in whether you had to expend that effort," I replied.

"Gwen, the work I do saves lives, but don't think you watched this play out and can mistake me for a man who doesn't understand that those lives I'm savin' are worth the exchange of a good woman," Skull returned.

"Thanks for that but if that's true, how do you explain Brett?" I shot back, and Hawk's arm got even tighter around my shoulders.

"Because," Skull said gently. His face had changed, he

still looked rough, rock 'n' roll, ultra-cool hot guy but the way his face changed and his voice gentled, his hotness quotient, I, unfortunately and automatically, due to vast amounts of study on the subject, noted entered the stratosphere. "He works for your man so I know he's a man who puts on his boots every day understanding what happened to him today is always an eventuality, and knowin' that, he'll have planned for it. And I also know, he works for your man, he had that choice you're pissed I didn't give you, he wouldn't have even taken the time to blink before he decided he was willin' to take his chances to play my play."

Shit. I was guessing he had a point there.

I decided to stop talking. Skull waited for me to say more and there was something about that, him giving me the time to speak my piece, say what I had to say that I didn't want to admit, because he was *not* my favorite person, was nice.

And it was then I realized that the entire time he had me in that filthy apartment, he actually was standing guard protecting me, but in a good way. And the reason he looked so unhappy wasn't because I scratched his arms. It was because he was a good guy who, for the greater good, was enduring a life pretending to be a bad guy. He'd been involved in an operation where one on his side went down, and for that greater good, he found himself in a circumstance which was much like I suspected many circumstances he'd come up against the last year and a half in order to maintain his cover. He had to make a decision, let it happen and was powerless to do anything about it.

I had to give it to him. That would make me unhappy too.

When I didn't speak, he tore his gaze from me, his eyes caught Hawk's for a brief moment, he turned and disappeared.

Lawson filled his space and I looked up at him.

"Sweetheart, I hate to say it, but I gotta take your statement."

I sighed.

Then I remarked, "We have to quit meeting like this."

Hawk curled me closer into his side.

Lawson smiled.

CHAPTER TWENTY-FIVE

You Promised

I OPENED MY EYES.

There was mostly darkness in Hawk's loft but a soft light was coming from somewhere close.

I was in his bed and he wasn't. There was no weight, no warmth, no presence. Hawk had a presence. Even if he wasn't touching me, I knew he was there.

This meant he wasn't there.

Earlier we all waited at the hospital until Betsy wandered out of Brett's room. She looked shell-shocked, I knew this and I didn't even know her but it wasn't hard to read. Hawk, Dad, Meredith, Elvira and me, along with Betsy and Brett's parents, all waited until the doctors did their rounds and told Betsy there was no change, he was stable but critical and she should go home and come back in the morning.

Even though her parents were there, Hawk told Dad to take me and Hawk took Betsy home. Her family may have wanted to quibble but Hawk, being Hawk, they didn't. Elvira followed them because she was spending the night with Betsy.

Dad and Meredith took me to Dad's friend Rick's house, because Meredith and Dad were staying with him until their house was livable again.

Rick's wife Joanie and Meredith tried to get me to eat but I said I'd wait for Hawk. He finally showed, Joanie whipped up some grilled cheese sandwiches under Hawk's edgy, impatient stare, she wrapped them in foil then put them in a bag. Hugs and kisses were exchanged and Hawk whisked me off to his lair.

On the way he didn't talk, not even a word. I figured this was because his man was down, lying in a hospital bed, condition critical and his unconscious body was going about its duty of fighting for his life. I figured Hawk was hoping Brett's body would win that battle because I hoped the same. Because this stuff filled his head the same way it was filling mine, and I knew Brett a lot less than Hawk did, I figured he needed to brood so I let him.

When we entered the lair, suddenly finding myself starving, I went direct to the kitchen while Hawk turned on lights. I unwrapped the sandwiches and put them on plates, cutting them on the diagonal. Hawk went to the fridge and got a bottle of water.

When he closed the fridge, I offered him his sandwich with a quiet, "Baby."

He looked at me, looked at the plate, took the plate, went direct to the garbage bin, opened the pedal with the toe of his boot and dumped the sandwich straight in. Then he dropped the plate to the counter. I watched him prowl to his desk, turn on the laptop, turn on the desk lamp, sit down, snap open the top to the water and down a huge gulp.

As I watched this I realized I did not know him at all. I'd *known* him for a year and a half but I'd only been *getting to know* him for a week.

It appeared, when one of his boys got hurt, he got moody.

Understandable and good to know.

I ate my sandwich and gave him his space. Then I did the minimal cleanup.

Then I stood in the kitchen and called, "Hawk, baby?"

His head came up from his study of the laptop screen but he didn't speak.

"Do you mind if I watch TV?"

He shook his head once and looked back down at the screen.

Okey dokey.

I watched TV until I was about to fall asleep. I turned it off, turned off the lamps in the seating area and wandered to Hawk's desk.

His eyes didn't leave the screen.

I stood at the opposite side of his desk from him and waited to get his attention. After several long seconds, his head tipped back and his eyes came to me.

"I'm going to bed," I informed him.

He nodded his head once and looked back at the screen. I bit my lip and tried to decide what to do.

Then I decided to do what I'd want someone to do if I were in Hawk's position. I rounded the desk, got close, leaned into him and wrapped my hand around the opposite side of his neck. That neck twisted, his head dipped back and his eyes locked on mine.

"He'll be okay," I whispered with a squeeze of my hand and more hope than certainty.

Hawk didn't respond and when I say this, he didn't respond in any way. No hardening of the jaw. No muscle moving in his cheek. No flash in his eyes. Nothing. Zip.

So I pulled in breath, dropped my head and touched my lips to his then I moved them to his ear. "Come to bed soon, yeah?"

I gave him another squeeze, let him go, turned and moved away. I got ready for bed, climbed in and it took me a while to find sleep but it came. Sleep escaped me when Hawk's weight hit the bed, his warmth curled into me, his arm slid around me, his knee hitched mine up and I felt him settle.

Tension I felt even in sleep eased from me. I relaxed into him knowing, with him curled into me, his heat seeping in, his power enveloping me, everything was going to be all right.

And now I was alone in bed, it was still the pitch of night and Hawk was gone.

I threw the covers back and slid out of his big bed, heading directly to the stairs. I knew that the light by the battered chair was on as I headed down them even though I couldn't see it. I turned at the foot of the stairs, took two steps toward the chair and stopped dead.

Hawk was sitting under the light in that chair. He was wearing nothing but cargo pants and he was bent nearly double. He had one elbow in his knee, hand dangling between his thighs. The other elbow was also to his knee but his forearm was lifted so he could curl his hand around his neck. His head was dropped and it stayed that way.

"Baby," I called softly and his neck bent back, his eyes coming to me but his hand didn't drop.

Something was wrong with his eyes. Very wrong.

"Baby," I whispered and started to walk to him.

"I was wrong," he said quietly as I approached.

"About what?" I asked.

"Us," he answered and I stopped.

"What?" I was still whispering.

"I was wrong about us," he replied.

I felt my heart squeeze, and God, did it hurt.

"You were wrong about us?"

He dropped his hand from his neck, lifted his torso partially up but kept his elbows to his knees.

"Can't do this, Gwen," he stated.

"Do…" That word came out strangled so I cleared my throat and finished, "What?"

"This shit, can't do it."

"This…" I paused this time because it was difficult to bring myself to say it. Then I said it, "*Shit?*"

"Yeah, this shit," he replied, not having trouble saying it at all.

I moved to the side where luckily a big iron column stood and I wrapped my hand around it, leaning my body into it to hold myself up.

"What do you mean?" I asked, finding it difficult to breathe mainly because my heart was lodged in my throat.

"You and me, I was wrong. I thought I could do it but I can't do this shit."

"Are you…" That sounded strangled again so I swallowed and continued, "*Ending* things?"

"Yeah." His answer was instant and unwavering.

"You're ending things," I repeated just to confirm.

"Yeah," he repeated, again instant and unwavering.

I felt the tears hit my sinuses.

Boy, Troy was right. It hurt a lot more when a man walked all over you wearing combat boots.

"You promised," I whispered, and he did. He promised. Not even twenty-four hours ago, he fucking *swore* he'd handle me with care.

He stood and I released the column and stepped back.

"This is me keepin' that promise, Gwen."

"You are so full of shit." I continued whispering.

"Better now than when you're tied tighter to me, babe."

"You…are…" I leaned forward, lost it in the middle of a sentence and shrieked, "*So full of shit!*"

"Sweet Pea—" he started, but I cut him off, still shrieking.

"Don't call me that, you fucking *asshole!*"

Then I whirled on my foot and raced to and up the stairs.

Hawk followed and he didn't do it slowly but by the time he made it to the bed platform, I was pulling up my jeans.

"Gwen, listen to me," he demanded.

"Fuck you," I spat, zipping my jeans.

His fingers wrapped around my upper arm and he gently turned me to him but I twisted my arm out of his grip, put both hands to his chest and pushed.

He caught my forearms and shook them between us.

"Gwen, look at me."

I looked at him and hissed, "You orchestrated this. You worked for it. Then I gave you me and you didn't have it *a day* before you *threw it away.*"

"Listen to me, babe, and you'll—"

I yanked at my forearms and snapped, "Go to hell, Hawk."

"Babe, listen," he growled, shaking my arms again. I yanked again, one of his hands slid down to the bruises and cuts on my wrist, a small, sharp, involuntary cry of pain escaped me and he released me instantly.

I took advantage and dashed around him toward my suitcases. I bent over them but was pulled up and in with an arm around my waist, my back hitting Hawk's front, his other arm wrapped around me and his mouth came to my ear.

"Baby, listen to me," he whispered.

Something about that shredded me. Everything inside me. All that was me instantly in tatters. I tore violently from his arms, whirled and advanced into his space, finger out, up and pointed in his face.

"Don't call me baby. In the five minutes we have left together, Cabe Delgado, don't even fucking *think* about calling me *baby.*"

And I knew what it was. I knew why that destroyed me. I knew I loved that. I knew the first time he called me baby in my kitchen the hope I wasn't allowing myself to feel for a year and a half was not only real but what I hoped for was possible.

And just like with Scott, *exactly* like with Scott, I was wrong. *Way, way, way, way wrong.*

He opened his mouth to say something then he stopped, his tense body went statue still then he muttered an enraged, "*Fuck.*"

That was when I heard it. Pipes. The roar of Harley pipes. And it wasn't one bike. It wasn't two. It was a lot of them.

Hawk turned, bent and tagged his tee off the floor. He'd yanked it over his head and was pulling it down his abs when he lifted one finger toward me and ordered, "Stay here."

I didn't respond but there was no way I was staying there. As far as I was concerned, the cavalry had arrived and I was getting the fuck out of Dodge.

I bent to my suitcase, pulled on socks, my boots, then grabbed panties, a bra, a tee and then raced to the bathroom, snatching up shit I needed then I raced down the stairs, shoved it all in my purse, I hitched it over my shoulder and raced out.

When I got outside I saw that Hawk, being Hawk, was standing in cargoes, a tee and bare feet in what appeared to be a standoff with Tack in front of a shitload of Harleys, their headlamps illuminating the scene. Some boys were standing by their bikes, some were astride them. Only Tack was facing off against Hawk.

I located Dog and ran straight to him, not even looking at Hawk and Tack as I raced by.

Dog looked down at me. "Babe, maybe you should go inside."

"Take me with you," I begged, his body jolted and he asked, "What?"

"Take me with you," I repeated, reaching up to grab his arm in an effort to convey my seriousness.

He stared at me half a beat before his head lifted and he whistled sharply. I didn't look behind me. I was trembling and holding onto his arm for dear life. I was also holding back tears by the skin of my teeth.

I watched him jerk his chin up then he moved, swinging his leg over the bike. I guessed this meant he was taking me with him and I didn't waste time or squander the opportunity. I jumped on behind him, wrapped my arms around him tight, put my cheek to his shoulder and closed my eyes hard.

I felt the Harley roar and then I felt us move, he did a wide arc in the massive, cracked cement area beside Hawk's warehouse, an area that once housed semis and employee parking and now housed nothing. He straightened out of the curve and we roared away.

I didn't open my eyes once. With the wind whipping around me and a body that had gone totally numb in an effort to keep the pain at bay, it took a while for me to realize I was crying.

Suddenly he pulled over and Dog's hands gently pried mine from his belly.

His torso twisted, my head came up and my eyes finally opened.

"Babe, switch bikes," he ordered.

"What?"

He jerked his chin. I turned my head and I saw Tack beside us, his head turned our way and even in the dark I knew his eyes were on me.

Shit.

I wanted to stay on Dog's bike but I didn't want the

drama. No, I couldn't handle the drama. I'd had enough drama for one day, thank you *so* very much. In fact, I'd had enough drama in the last week to last me a freaking lifetime.

So I swung off, moved between bikes, hitched my purse more firmly on my shoulder and swung on Tack's.

The minute my arms closed around his middle and my cheek hit his shoulder blade, we shot off.

CHAPTER TWENTY-SIX

Not Worth the Risk

I FELT WEIGHT hit the bed, my eyes opened and slid up.

Tack was sitting there, wearing a skin-tight tee and faded jeans. His hair was wet from a shower. His blue eyes were on me.

I was lying in his bed, not at the Chaos Compound, in a rather nice house in the foothills outside Denver. It was built just up the mountain. It was one story, long and had a deck that ran the front of the house. I knew it would have great views in the daylight but I didn't take much in when we got there mainly because I was numb, exhausted and desperately fighting back hysterical tears, a tantrum and the desire to commit murder.

Tack led me to his bedroom, dumped my purse on his nightstand and ordered, "Sleep, darlin'."

Then he left.

I took off my boots, socks, jeans and since I conveniently was wearing my nightshirt, I climbed into his unmade bed and did exactly as I was told.

Now it was now and I was curled into a protective ball, my hands in prayer position under my cheek.

Tack spoke. "Mornin', Peaches, you want breakfast?"

"Do you cook or do you have a biker babe that makes breakfast to order?" I replied and there it was. Automatic. The smartass.

Would I ever learn?

Tack grinned. "I cook. Best pancakes you'll ever have, you get your ass outta bed," he answered.

For the first time in my life, I wasn't hungry.

No, that wasn't true. After I found my husband in bed with my sister and kicked his ass out, I didn't eat for three days. I didn't realize it, Troy did, and he made me eat. But that was the last time I lost my appetite.

"Sounds good," I lied but didn't move.

When I didn't Tack reached out, curled his fingers around my forearm and gently pulled my hand from under my face. Then he lifted my arm and his eyes dropped to my wrist. His hand slid up carefully so he could wrap his fingers around my palm. I watched as he lifted my arm further up...up... until he bent his neck and his lips touched the bruised and torn skin at my wrist.

My breath seized.

Hawk should have done that. But Hawk was so busy brooding about Brett, or more likely trying to figure out how to end things with me since he conquered the challenge and was ready to move on, that last night he completely forgot I was kidnapped, bound, gagged and targeted as bait.

Tack's head lifted, his body leaned in and he pressed my hand to his chest.

"My girl had a bad day yesterday," he said quietly.

Hawk should have said that too.

"There's bad and there's bad and I'm discovering the many nuances but, yes...yesterday introduced me to a new level of bad."

"Then you need pancakes."

Finally, a man who understood the healing properties of food.

"Pancakes would be good," I replied.

His hand squeezed mine. "Ass outta bed, babe. I'll be in the kitchen."

Then he lifted my hand, touched his lips to my knuckles, released it, got up off the bed and sauntered out of the room.

I took my time, got out of bed, dug through my bag, found my toothbrush and face wash, went into the bathroom off his bedroom and did my business. I didn't bother dressing, my nightshirt covered me more than most dresses I owned. I walked out of the room, and since the house was built into the hill and all the rooms were to one side, the hallway filled with windows, I saw the view.

The good news was there was a sheer drop-off beyond the deck; therefore difficult to execute a successful drive-by. The other good news was the view was unbelievable. And for the first time in over a week, there was no bad news.

I walked down the hall looking into rooms to my left. A bath and two other bedrooms, one that had a bed and dresser, one that was a messy office. Then I entered the open space. An open kitchen with bar delineating it from internal walkway was opposite sliding glass doors to the deck and the kitchen fed into a massive living room that jutted out a bit at the front of the house.

Tack was in the kitchen at the stove.

I moved to stand by him, not too close, and once there I leaned against the counter. I looked down and there were six perfect silver-dollar pancakes cooking on a griddle.

His head turned to me.

"Looks like you're good at that," I remarked.

He didn't respond to my remark. Instead he asked, "Do you need coffee?"

"Am I Gwendolyn Kidd, am I breathing and is it morning?" I answered.

Shit! There it was again. The smartass.

Tack grinned. Then he jerked his head to the counter behind me.

"Make yourself at home, Peaches," he invited.

Oh boy.

"Do you need a refresh?" I asked.

"I'm good, babe," he answered.

I moved to find mugs while speaking. "You want to tell me what that was about last night?"

"Seems we got the same thing on our mind."

I had my hand wrapped around a mug and I turned my head to look at him as I closed the cupboard door. "What?"

"Babe, you came racin' outta Hawk's like the fuckin' place was haunted and jumped on Dog's bike."

"Um..." I answered, dropped my head, grabbed the handle of the coffeepot and started pouring. "Why don't you answer my question first?"

He didn't hesitate. "I was there 'cause I wanted an explanation of why you got kidnapped and not an hour later put up for bid. Hawk and I made a deal and the deal was he's supposed to have your back so that shit *doesn't* happen and it did. He fell down on the job."

I looked at Tack. "His man got shot three times protecting me," I said softly.

Tack's eyes locked to mine. "Like I said, fallin' down on the job."

Hmm. This was unfair and heartbreakingly true at the same time.

I went to the fridge and found milk. "Do you have sugar?"

Tack was flipping pancakes. He finished this task,

reached into a cupboard and pulled out a half-full bag of sugar, putting it down by my mug. I searched for spoons, sloshed in milk, did my sugar, put back the milk and stirred. Then I set the spoon aside and sipped the coffee.

Tack made good coffee too.

Hmm.

"Peaches," Tack called. I looked and saw he was watching me.

"Yes?"

"I answered your question, now's the time you answer mine."

I took another sip and studied him over the rim of my mug. His eyes didn't leave mine so I sighed.

Then I shared, "Hawk just ended things with me so I really, *really* needed a ride."

"Hawk ended things?" he whispered, and even though I was studying him, I almost missed the change in him but when I caught it, my body got tight.

Shit!

"Um…"

"He ended things the night you got kidnapped, your fuckin' wrists torn up and your picture, bound and gagged, farmed out for bid."

That didn't sound good, but then again, it fucking wasn't.

"Um…" I mumbled.

Tack turned to his pancakes. "At least he fuckin' ended things. Clean go."

Tack scraped pancakes off the griddle onto a waiting plate as I asked, "Clean go?"

His head turned to me. "Clean go. For you. He's outta the picture, I don't have to deal with his shit anymore."

Uh-oh.

"Tack—" I started, uncertain how to say what I had to

say and that was I was *so* done with men. Seriously done with them. Forever done with them. I was not going to go there again. The problem was, according to Hawk, saying something like that to Tack was like a challenge and I really didn't need that.

Tack dropped the pancake flipper on the counter, turned and closed the distance between us before I could blink.

Then he started speaking. "Gwen, people talk and the last week, most 'a the talk on the street that's not about your fuckin' sister has been about you and Hawk. I know your shit's been linked to his for a while. I know you're different from the rest. And I saw your face last night, babe, so I know you're feelin' this deep and, believe me, it gives me no pleasure sayin' this, but I also know when he's done, he's done and if he said he's done with you, he . . . is . . . *done*."

I felt the sting in my sinuses heralding tears.

Tack went on, "I also know what I saw when you first saw me, I know what I felt when I saw you and I know *exactly* what you felt when I first touched you. That said, I ain't stupid and I ain't an asshole. You aren't ready. That don't mean I don't want in there enough to wait. So," he moved in closer and his hand came up, curled around my neck as his head bent, his face got in mine and his voice went gentle, "you take your time, darlin', you lick your wounds and you got me at your back while they heal. You feel like explorin' more energetic ways to wipe him outta your mind, I'm here. And when you come out the other side, I'm waitin'."

"Tack—" I started on a breath, my eyes staring into his and I could feel the tears trembling at their edges. Tears for the end of my living daydream with Hawk and tears because, standing in front of me, apparently, was a good man. A dangerous one, but a good one and still, there was no way in hell I was ever going there.

His head bent further, his mouth touched mine and since my lips were parted, he took that opportunity to slide his tongue in my mouth. Reflexively, the tip of mine moved to meet the tip of his and an electric shock of surprise and something a whole lot different bolted through me, causing another bolt to shoot somewhere else.

Even though he didn't miss his opportunity, he didn't take advantage, his head lifted and my eyes opened to see his staring into mine.

His hand at my neck squeezed reassuringly and he ordered gently, "Now, eat your pancakes, babe."

I did as I was told. I took the pancakes and he got me butter and maple syrup. I sat at a stool at his bar, readied them and ate them while he made some for himself.

He was right and I was surprised.

They were the best pancakes I'd ever had.

* * *

It was just after noon and I was spent.

Tack had gone down the mountain to see about getting my things. He had decreed that I was staying at his place. Thinking about this, people were kidnapping me. Dad and Meredith were homeless, and their vulnerability had been proven by a firebomb. Leo was a cop but he had a job that he had to work in order to get paid, which meant he couldn't spend his days guarding me. I was still averse to buying a gun and, anyway, I was pretty sure there was a waiting period prior to earning a permit so that was out.

Tack had a bevy of badass bikers at his command and a mountain hideaway.

So I picked Tack.

While he was gone I called and left a message with Dad telling him where I was so he wouldn't worry and telling him I'd explain later. I also told him the dinner Elvira and I sorted out with Hawk, Gus and Maria was off and I'd explain that later too. I didn't call Meredith because I wasn't ready to go there. I did call Cam and Tracy. Cam ranted about Hawk saying how she knew, she just *knew*, Hawk was a mother-fucking asshole. Tracy sounded exactly as heartbroken as I felt.

I didn't call Troy. He wouldn't gloat, I knew that. He'd be kind. He'd also offer me a place to stay, and Troy was a great guy but he didn't have a bevy of badass bikers at his command and a mountain hideaway. He had a condo and his male friends were mostly bankers.

I was sitting on Tack's huge, slouchy, comfortable tan couch that faced the view, my mind filled with unhappy thoughts at the same time considering a nap which I hoped would last around fifty years, when I saw Tack on his bike roaring up the drive. He was alone and his Harley was not laden with suitcases.

Shit.

I got up and met him at the front door.

He looked unhappy.

"Are you okay?" I asked.

"No," he answered, moved to a door off the entry area, opened it and pulled out a leather biker jacket. He turned, tossed it to me and I caught it. "Put that on, Peaches. I hate to break this to you but Hawk's bein' a dick. He won't release your shit unless he sees you. My boys are in a standoff with his boys at his warehouse and to get your shit without unnec-essary hassle, which could mean anything from minor inju-ries to bloodshed to hospital stays, I need you to show your face."

My body had locked but my mouth moved to form the word, "What?"

Tack invaded my space and one hand went to my waist, the other hand curled around my neck. "Darlin', he's demandin' to see you. So," his hands gave me a squeeze, "we gotta let him see you. He'll see you, I'm at your back, then we take off and my boys go in and get your shit."

"He's holding my stuff for ransom until he sees me?" I whispered.

"Yep," Tack answered.

"Why?" I was still whispering.

"Fuck if I know," Tack replied.

I stood there, his hands on me, staring into his eyes.

Then I lost my mind.

I stepped back and yanked on his jacket. "That fucking *dick!*" I shouted. "God! What was I *thinking!* I must have lost my mind, getting involved with him. Temporarily *insane!*"

Then I freed my hair from the collar, stomped straight out the door and toward his bike only to be pulled up short with an arm at my belly, my foot just about ready to take the step off the decking at the side of the house and onto the gravel drive.

Tack lifted me clean off my feet, turned and put me down.

I pulled away, whirled on him, then he said, "Babe, boots."

I looked down at my feet in socks. Then I tipped my head back to look at Tack to see his mouth twitching.

Then I stomped into his house to get my boots.

*　　　*　　　*

Tack was right.

When we made it to Hawk's warehouse there was definitely a standoff. A big black van was surrounded by about a dozen bikes and a dozen bikers were facing off against an equal number of commandos. Hawk had pulled in what looked like the entirety of his workforce.

He was among them.

Tack drove his Harley between the battle lines, stopped in front of Hawk and put down a foot.

"You see her, now let my boys in," Tack growled.

Hawk looked at me. Luckily I'd spent the entire ride down the mountain nursing my snit, stoking it up so I was good and freaking angry, so seeing him didn't make me dissolve into tears or anything else equally humiliating.

"Inside," Hawk clipped at me.

"No fuckin' way," Tack clipped back.

Hawk didn't take his eyes off me. "Inside," he repeated.

Tack pushed down the bike stand and I knew he was losing it too so I hopped off.

"Gwen—" Tack started.

I whipped my head around so fast my hair flew over my shoulder.

"It's cool. I'm fine. I'll be out in a minute," I assured him.

"Peaches—"

"I'm fine, Tack, honestly. I'll be out in a minute."

I didn't wait for his response. I skirted Hawk, pushed through his line of commandos, or, more accurately, between Fang and Jorge, and stomped into the warehouse.

When I got to the area just beyond the space under the bed platform I saw that rumor and Tack were right. When Hawk was done, he was done. I knew this because my two suitcases were there, my desk, my disconnected computer and my box of desk shit.

Why he wanted me there, I didn't know. Maybe because he was an asshole. But then, most men were.

I grabbed my suitcases, lugged them up, turned and ran smack into Hawk.

My head tipped back. "Get out of my way," I snapped.

He bent, pulled the suitcases out of my hands then his hands were on me. I barely got the chance to struggle before I was up against the paneled room under the platform and I was held there with his hand at my chest.

"Now, babe, you're gonna let me explain."

"Take your hand off me."

"Her name was Simone," he stated bizarrely.

"Who, your new toy?" I shot back.

"No, my dead wife."

My stomach clutched, my heart stopped beating and I stared.

Then I whispered, "What?"

"My daughter's name was Sophie."

His daughter. His daughter. His fucking daughter.

Was.

He said *was*.

He kept talking. "She had a brother, Simone did, and he was just like Ginger. But there was a reason he was a total fuckin' piece of trash shithead. Their parents were nightmares. Made your mom a candidate for Mother of the Year. Simone, she was smart, she got out from under that shit as soon as she could. But for good reasons, reasons that made her make fucked-up decisions, she was tight with her brother. Too tight. And they stayed tight. I told her, unless she was with me, she didn't go visit him. But his woman was pregnant, I was away on assignment and he called because his woman was in labor. Simone, she loved kids, she loved her brother, she loved his woman, she was so fuckin' excited to be an aunt. So she went to their place and took Sophie with her. He walked out of the house, his woman walked out and Simone was walking with Sophie up to the house to meet them. He had some of his boys with him. They were all out on the lawn. Easy targets. Simone didn't know he was in the middle of a war and died not knowin' it. Doesn't matter, that entire neighborhood was a war zone and she knew it because she grew up in it. The enemy took their shot and did their drive-by and didn't hesitate to add collateral damage to their play. Simone went down, Sophie went down, Julian, Simone's brother went down and his woman went down. She died before she gave birth but they saved the baby. That kid was the only one who survived that massacre."

I was listening at the same time trembling and I wondered if my ears were bleeding but I knew my heart was, or at least it felt like it.

"Hawk," I whispered.

"I can't go there again. I can't do it again. Trust me, babe, I promised you I'd handle you with care and when I say I'm doin' it, I'm not lyin'. This ends now before you get too deep."

I stared up at him and it hit me.

He was so full of shit.

Therefore I informed him of that fact. "You are so full of shit."

His face went hard, his hand left my chest and went to his cargos. He pulled out a wallet, his thumb sifting through it until he yanked out a folded bit of paper. He opened it and held it in front of my eyes.

In it was a younger Hawk wearing fatigues, smiling at the camera while holding two girls. One, in the curve of his arm, an extremely beautiful dark-haired woman who was also smiling at the camera, resting her head on Hawk's shoulder, her arm around his back, her other hand on his abs. The other, held up against his side, was a two- or three-year-old extremely beautiful little girl, her face in profile a perfect blend of everything that was beautiful about her mom and dad. She was wearing an adorable outfit. Pink. Her little hand was resting on Hawk's throat. She wasn't smiling at the camera. She looked like she was giggling and her eyes were on her father.

Yes, my heart was definitely bleeding.

He was still full of shit.

He pulled the picture from my face, folded it, shoved it in his wallet and shoved his wallet in his cargoes, saying, "That was the day I was shipping out and that was the last time I saw them."

"I caught my husband fucking my sister," I reminded him.

His eyes locked to mine. "Yeah, babe, that sucks, but you need to wake up and get over it."

Was he *insane?*

"You're unbelievable," I hissed.

"My wife and kid were murdered in a drive-by, Gwen, when I was thousands of miles away. What happened to you sucked but do not stand there and throw that shit in my face when it in no way, in no *fuckin'* way, compares."

"You're right, it doesn't. Absolutely. It doesn't. That doesn't mean what you said to me doesn't hold true."

"And what'd I say to you, babe?"

"You said to me, I didn't take the risk in giving myself to you that meant I was saying you weren't worth the risk. And that holds true the other way around. What happened sucked, Hawk, beyond sucked. I'm pissed at you and my heart still bleeds for your loss. But even so, you're standing right there saying I'm not worth the risk."

I knew my point was made when I watched his face freeze into a blank mask, and I took that opportunity to walk right around him, go back to my bags and heft them up. Then I stomped to the door.

At the door I turned to see his eyes on me, his face still frozen in that mask.

"Tack's boys'll be in here to get the rest and don't stop them. You want this to end, you release *all* of me."

His face unfroze and it did this in order to gentle and watching his beautiful face gentling was like a punch in the gut.

Jerk!

"Gwen—" he started.

I shook my head. "No, you said what you had to say. And you proved my point. I have no fucking *clue* how to live my life. I'm not special to you no matter what my instincts and those butterflies I got in my stomach every time I saw you before we became us, but mostly after, told me. And you're not special either, precisely because you made me feel like shit, *again*, and I listened to my heart, followed my instincts and allowed it to happen. The decisions I make are *whacked*. Point made. Lesson learned. I can't trust my gut so I'm going to live in my head. Lucky for you, we're over and you don't have to watch me doing it."

Then I turned, dropped a suitcase, grabbed the knob, opened the door an inch, picked up my suitcase and kicked the door open further then I struggled through it carrying my suitcases and leaving Cabe "Hawk" Delgado behind.

CHAPTER TWENTY-SEVEN

Disappointed in You

"IT'S SAFE TO say, Tack, I'm a little freaked out," I announced from behind my blindfold.

"Just a little longer, Peaches," Tack replied.

I was in an SUV. Tack didn't only have a Harley, he had a big Ford Expedition. About five minutes ago, when we left the highway coming from his house and hit Denver, he pulled over and talked me into wearing a blindfold. He had a surprise for me and he'd been so nice the last week, I accepted the blindfold even though it freaked me out.

The last week at Tack's had been like being on a mini-vacation. It might make me selfish, and an idiot, but when you needed time to get your head together after you'd had your heart broken by a commando, hanging at a mountain hideaway with a biker was a good way to heal.

During my mini-vacation I also took a time-out from Dad, Meredith, Cam, Tracy and Leo. I explained this briefly and they retreated, albeit unhappily. Troy called and I didn't take the call. I knew either Cam or Tracy had informed him of the state of play and I knew he was feeling for me but I couldn't face that. Elvira called too, several times, and I didn't take those either for reasons that didn't need to be explained.

Tack's boys took my desk and desk shit to my house but my computer and suitcases to his. They set up my computer in his office. I spent my days working and tidying his office. Then I cleaned his house. On day two Tack took me to the grocery store, we stocked up with a mountain of food for his mountain hideaway and I started to cook fantastic meals for when he got home that took ages to prepare. This included desserts and lots of them.

If I wasn't working or cooking, I read. At the grocery store I bought five romance novels and at Tack's house I curled up in his big, slouchy couch and lost myself in someone else's daydreams. I couldn't be in my head, not just yet. This was because for the last year and a half most of my daydreams centered around Hawk and I didn't know where to go from there because I never intended to hope for my perfect man ever again. So I needed new fodder for my daydreams and dreaming of being alone, planning hiking excursions and starting a ferret rescue didn't do it for me.

I started my days wrapping up tight and sitting in the cold on Tack's deck staring at the view while drinking coffee and battling the ache in my heart.

I ended my days in Tack's bed.

Day one and two, I did this alone. Day three, when I had dinner alone, went to bed when the house was empty and he came home late, he joined me. He didn't do it the same as Hawk. He didn't touch the small of my back, turn me into him and kiss me. He also didn't curl into me, hold me close and hitch my leg with his. Instead, he rolled me to facing him then he dropped to his back and tucked me to his side.

I should have pitched a fit or moved to the other bed. But because I was Gwendolyn Piper Kidd, and thus a stupid idiot, I didn't do either of these. I rested my head on his shoulder, curled my arm around his belly and fell asleep.

Tack slept with me every night after that and came home for dinner every night too. I didn't argue. I didn't discuss. I just went with the flow. I didn't have it in me. I couldn't say I wasn't a smartass when he was around, I was because that was me and I knew he liked it but I just kept doing it. But I also didn't give him any in or any vibes he could misinterpret. I didn't flirt. I just was me.

Except, of course, letting him sleep with me.

Hmm.

He mostly gave me my space, giving me my days and being there at night but not in an invasive, predatory way. He'd kissed me once, waking me up doing it. It wasn't a tongue-touch kiss, it was a *kiss*, tongue, heat and arms locked around each other. It sent a stronger electric bolt through me with other, no less strong, definitely sharp bolts searing through specific parts of me. It wasn't a Hawk kiss which made me lose my head *and* my control but it was a freaking great kiss.

He'd lifted his head and whispered, "Gotta be out early, Peaches, but thanks for settin' me up for the day." Then he'd kissed my nose, his ultra-cool goatee tickling my skin, and left the bed. No pressure, just a thinly veiled promise.

The kiss was great, the kind of great that, back in the day, would launch a thousand daydreams. But I was done with promises.

Now he was taking me to Denver for reasons unknown but whatever they were, they required me being blindfolded.

The Expedition stopped and I asked, "Can I take it off now?"

"In a minute," Tack answered.

I waited impatiently and felt my door open. Tack carefully guided me out of the SUV to my feet and he kept guiding me as we walked. He stopped, turned me and his arm wrapped around my ribs, pulling my back into his front as his other hand went to the blindfold and pulled it up and away.

We were standing in front of my house. There were new windows, a new door and no visible bullet damage. The big bricks that had been painted maroon prior to my habitation looked like they'd been filled and the entire front of the house had a new coat of maroon paint. It looked like a house, not the by-product of the aftermath of a battle.

"Surprise, darlin'," Tack whispered in my ear.

"Oh my God," I whispered back.

I heard his soft laugh then he took my hand and guided me up the steps. On my porch, he inserted a key into the lock, moved it to the other lock and then swung the door in. He maneuvered me in front of him as we walked in and I saw that what had been done outside had been *way* done inside. The plaster bits and bullet holes were gone. The walls were newly skimmed, smooth and had a fresh coat of white paint, so fresh, I could smell it in the air. But it was more than that. My damaged furniture had been carted away. The floors had been sanded and refinished. The mantels of the fireplaces on each side too. It was clean and sparkling and, with some furniture, habitable.

"These are yours," Tack said, lifting my hand palm up and dropping the keys in it.

I looked at the keys. Tack kept talking.

"You can paint it any color you want, it's primed."

I tipped my head back to look at him and I felt the tears stinging the backs of my eyes.

"Tack..." I whispered, "I don't know what to say."

He grinned. "Welcome home, babe."

Not thinking, I moved into him, wrapped my arms around him and gave him a hug.

"Thank you," I whispered against his chest.

His arms were wrapped around me and they squeezed tight.

Then he said, "I don't think you get what I'm sayin' to you, Peaches."

My head tipped back but I didn't let him go. "What?" I asked.

One of his arms left me so his fingers could slide in my hair at the side and hold it at the back of my head.

"You don't feel safe down here, you're welcome to stay at my place, long as you like. But we been listenin' and we been diggin' and your sister has gone to ground. Things have cooled down on that and you're safe to come home if you want."

I was certainly glad things had cooled down though a little worried about what Ginger "going to ground" meant, but I knew what Tack was saying had two meanings.

"You're giving me space?" I asked quietly.

"When you come to me, Gwen, it's gotta be because you wanna come to me, not because you need to come to me. And it's gotta be that way not just for me but for you."

God, he was a good guy.

I dropped my head so my forehead rested against his chest and his hand curled around the back of my neck.

"Thank you," I repeated into his chest.

"I see you wanna come home," he noted, and I nodded against his chest. "All right, darlin', you get settled. I'll go get your computer. Sheila can come by and pack up your shit. I'll bring it all back down."

I tilted my head back. "I can come up. You don't need to be driving back and forth for me."

"You need to settle, babe."

He was right. I did. I *so* did. I'd been unsettled for so long, I didn't remember settled.

And he was such a good guy.

I leaned into him. "Thanks."

His head dipped, his mouth hit mine and I felt his lips open. Stupid me, stupid, *stupid* me, I opened my own, his tongue slid in and my tongue moved to touch tips.

Nice. Way nice.

He tasted really good.

His lips released mine and lifted up to kiss my nose.

Then he looked in my eyes and said gently, "Anything for you, Gwen."

Such a good guy.

I shoved my face in his neck and held on tighter. He let me do this until his arms gave me a squeeze. I understood what that meant, let him go and stepped back.

"Later, babe," he murmured.

"Later, Tack," I replied, he turned and walked out of my house.

* * *

A couple hours later Tack delivered my computer and hooked it up. He also brought my suitcases. Then he left probably because he had a life, I had a decision to make and although my life revolved around me, that didn't mean everyone else's did.

I unpacked and started laundry. I made a grocery list. Then I texted Meredith, Cam and Tracy and told them I was back home but I needed the night to get settled. Cam texted back that it was cosmos at her house the next night, no excuses, no lip. I returned the text saying I'd be there. I wasn't certain I was ready but I had to live my life and I might as well start now.

I was heading back upstairs from the kitchen when I heard the chime and clunk of the doorbell.

I froze as unexpected pain sliced through me.

The last time I heard the chime and clunk of the doorbell, Hawk was coming over and taking me to dinner. Dad had called out to me to tell Hawk not to worry about the doorbell. Then Hawk had given me shoes. After that, hope had budded.

I sucked in breath to control the pain and stared at the door knowing one thing was for certain, it wasn't Hawk.

Cam, Tracy and Meredith would give me space. Dad and Troy would not. Dad could get impatient and he was protective and after all that went down, and the obvious fact I was no longer with Hawk, he would be concerned and not happy to be kept out of the loop. Troy had been a fixture in my life and being thus, I was one in his. With Hawk out of the picture, he'd make his approach.

I wasn't ready for either of these.

I still went to the door because, even if I wasn't ready, I loved them both and I couldn't leave them hanging. It wasn't nice.

When I looked through the side window I stared at who was there.

Okay, I wasn't ready for Dad and Troy but I *really* wasn't ready for a surprise visit from Maria Delgado.

She moved, caught sight of me at the window and focused on me.

I jerked away from the window.

Shit!

The doorbell chimed and clunked again.

Shit. Shit. *Shit!*

Well, she saw me. I couldn't ignore her.

Shit.

I opened the door. "Hey, Maria."

She stared up at me. Then without a word, she pushed through and into my house.

I stared out at my yard and prayed for strength. I endured and survived Hawk ending things. It tore me to shreds inside but I did it. I could endure this too.

I closed the door and turned. "This is a surprise," I noted, forcing a smile.

Her eyes narrowed on me then she demanded to know, "What gives?"

"What..." I paused for no reason then went on, "gives?"

"Yeah," she replied. "A week ago, you were dazzled by my son. A week ago, me and my boys show at his place first thing in the mornin' and you're in his bathroom. A week ago, you played hide-and-seek with his nephews. A week ago, you turned to him when you got your heart broken by your mama. Now, Elvira tells me, you're done. What," she leaned forward, "*gives?*"

Elvira. Great.

"Maria," I said softly. "He ended things with me."

"So?" she asked instantly, and I stared.

"So?" I repeated stupidly.

"Yeah," she threw out her arms, "so?"

"Um... when Hawk's done, he's done."

She crossed her arms on her chest. "His name is Cabe, Gwen."

Something about that and the way she said it made me still.

Then I shook my head. "No, Maria, he told me that man is gone. He's Hawk now."

She shook her head back at me. "No, Gwen, that man *was* gone. But I walked into his place with my boys and saw for the first time in eight years my boy Cabe was *back*."

Oh God.

"Maria—"

She took a step toward me, lifted her finger and jabbed it

at me. "You listen to me. You're not a mother but I'll tell you, when your child experiences pain, you experience it right along with him. My son has been in pain for eight years. Not a little pain, the kind you learn to get used to, a lot of pain, the kind that brings you to your knees. Eight years. Eight years I watched him endure that and me, Gus and my boys endured it right along with him. And the first time in eight years I saw him healed and whole was that morning with you."

Oh *God*.

I couldn't listen to this and I couldn't listen to this because she was way, way wrong.

"He's not done enduring that pain, Maria," I explained quietly.

"No, and he won't ever be," she agreed. "And you obviously don't know it but you took on the job of making him see that when he lost Simone and Sophie, he didn't lose himself. He could feel their loss and still manage to heal. You take on a job like that, you don't throw it away."

"He threw it away," I told her, because he did!

She shook her head. "I see you don't understand how important you are to him."

"If someone's important, Maria, I'm sorry, really, really sorry to say this but you don't treat them the way your son treated me. There's more to what happened that you don't get and I can understand you'd stand behind your son. I'm all right with that. But you don't know all that happened."

"You're right, I don't know what happened but something else a mother wants for her child is for him to be happy. And you clearly don't realize this but you gave him a promise to make him happy and when you gave it to him, you gave it *to me*."

"You don't understand," I whispered, she shook her head,

hitched her purse up on her shoulder and marched to the door.

Hand on the handle, she turned to me. "I understand, Gwen, and I'm sorry. I can see you're upset. I can also see just how upset you are, which makes me think and what it makes me think is that I'm disappointed in you."

God! Shot to the heart. I barely knew her and it killed that she was disappointed in me.

And then, before I could say a word in my defense, just like a Delgado, right in front of me she disappeared.

Shit!

CHAPTER TWENTY-EIGHT

Boston

A WARM HAND hit the small of my back, weight hit the bed, I opened my eyes, saw dark and my body was turned, hitting the hard wall of Hawk's.

What on earth?

He shifted into me so I took the weight of him and I didn't have the chance to say a word when his mouth was on mine.

What. On. *Earth?*

Before I could lose my head and my control, my hands went to his shoulders and I pushed. Then I tore my mouth from his by wrenching my head to the side.

"Get off me!" I demanded, pushing again.

"He fuck you?" Hawk growled into my ear, his hands moving down, going in, fisting in my nightshirt, pulling it up.

What was happening? Why was he there?

"What?" I snapped. "Who?"

His hands pulled my nightshirt up further. "Tack, babe, you let him fuck you?"

My head righted and I squinted my eyes at him in the dark. "That's none of your damned business!"

"You let him kiss you, right in your fuckin' living room."

Um...what?

"What?" I whispered.

"Got cameras in your house."

My body stilled. "Since when?"

"Since the kidnapping, Gwen."

Oh my God. I didn't know what to do with this. What did I do with this?

"You can't have cameras in my house!" I yelled, shoving at his shoulders again. "You can't watch me anymore!" I kept shouting. "And you can't *be* here!" I finished shouting.

"I'm here," he growled, the nightshirt now up to my ribs.

"I see that and *feel* it but I want you to go."

One of his hands left my nightshirt so he could wrap his fingers and thumb around my jaw, positioning my face, his entire weight on my body pinning me down, my hands were useless, totally. I was no match for his strength when he held me steady and kissed me.

But this wasn't going to happen to me again. Not again. He wasn't going to think he could start this up again. Taking what he wanted and holding everything back.

No way. No fucking way.

So I fought him. I fought his mouth and his hands and his body.

He was too strong and he knew what he was doing. But he also knew he was a lot stronger than me so the one advantage I had was that he didn't want to hurt me.

I didn't share the same desire.

So I didn't fight fair. I was vicious and I was determined and I used everything I had.

Unfortunately, when I was biting him, I tasted him and smelled him. Then, also unfortunately, somewhere along the way he quit trying to contain me and started doing other things to me. Therefore, somewhere along the way, I lost my nightshirt. Then I lost my determination. Then my fighting became something just as strong and overpowering and that something was hunger.

I had him on his back and I didn't jump away. Oh no, not me. Not stupid, stupid me.

I used my hands, lips and tongue to touch him, taste him, his chest, his nipples, down, his abs, down, I wrapped my hand around his hard cock and circled the tip with my tongue.

Mm.

Then I was in the air a brief second before I was on my back, my panties were gone a second later and my knees were lifted high with Hawk's hands at the back of them, then they were spread wide. Then his mouth was on me. He wasn't feeling insatiable. He was feeling in the mood to savor. So he did. He savored me and I not only let him, I slid my fingers over his hair and held him to me, it felt that good.

He took me close, God, so close, unbelievable and I was about to come, whimpering and whispering, "Baby," when his mouth went away. He turned me to my belly, spread my legs again, positioned between them and yanked up my hips so we were both on our knees.

Then he was inside me, pounding deep. Beautiful.

I arched my chest into the bed and stretched my arms out in front of me, palms into the headboard as I reared back to meet his thrusts. God, I loved this. Fucking loved it.

"Touch yourself, baby," Hawk ordered, his voice thick, and one of my hands moved from the headboard and slid between my legs. "That's it," he growled, "help me out."

I helped him out, whirling as he thrust, my moans drowned by the pillow, it didn't take long before I came and I did it *hard*.

It took Hawk longer, his grip tight on my hips, he pounded in as he pulled me back and, even coming down, I loved the feel of him.

Then he groaned as his thrusts magnified, driving deep, he kept taking me as he climaxed.

The power of his movements gentled but he kept moving inside me, gliding in and out slowly, an intimate caress, the most intimate there was. His fingers stopped gripping my hips and slid soft against the skin of my ass, my lower back, hips, down the sides and back of my thighs and it felt nice. Sweet and nice.

I closed my eyes, my face still in the pillow.

I was such...a...*slut*.

How humiliating was this? There was no degree. It was off the charts. They had to make new charts to measure this kind of humiliation.

Finally he slid out and started to drop to his side at the same time I felt his hand curl around my waist to take me with him, but quick as I could, I slid away. Jumping off the bed, I bent, snatched my nightshirt off the floor and I pulled it on while I raced from the room.

I went to the bathroom and locked the door. I turned on the light and stood there shaking.

What was *wrong* with me?

The tears threatened but I beat them back by deep breathing. I snatched a washcloth out of my bathroom closet, turned on the faucet until the water was hot and I cleaned him from me.

He would leave. He would leave. He always left.

Then I needed to move. Not houses, to a different state. I could work anywhere. I was free to go. It would suck, leaving everyone behind, but I was up for the adventure. Dad had taken us to Boston when I was a kid. We toured the USS *Constitution*. We went to Lexington Green. We ate clam chowder and I loved it. We had lobster and that was still my most favorite thing. I was into history. I was into lobster. I could do Boston.

I sat on the toilet, thinking of Boston. I was listening but I wouldn't hear him leave. But he'd leave. He'd go. I knew it.

I waited and listened to silence.

I sucked in breath and went to the door. I had my hand on the light switch when I opened it but I stopped dead because Hawk was in the hall. He was wearing nothing but his cargoes, his ass was to the wall, his legs slightly out in front of him, his head bent, he was contemplating his feet.

Shit. He didn't go.

He kept his head bent but twisted his neck and his eyes came to me.

"You need to go," I announced, flipping off the switch and entering the hall.

Then I found my back to the wall and I was pinned there with Hawk's body. One of his hands was at my neck, thumb in my jaw to force me to look up at him, the other one was at my hip. Mine went to his waist and I pushed, to no avail.

"You need to go," I repeated.

"I was in the middle of an operation, an important one, they needed me. So when my wife and daughter died, they couldn't tell me, they needed me focused. They were dead two days before I knew I'd lost them."

Oh God.

"I don't want to hear this," I told him. "I have no interest in this," I went on, but I said this in an effort not to convince him but to convince myself.

Hawk ignored me. "I was thousands of miles away. Thousands of miles away when I lost my family, Gwen."

"You need to go," I said again with another push of my hands.

"I loved her," he announced, and I stopped pushing.

"Hawk, really, I don't—"

"But I was fuckin' pissed at her. Jesus Christ, so fuckin'

pissed. How fuckin' stupid could she be? Not only goin' there herself but taking our daughter?"

I closed my eyes and turned my head away.

"You should talk to someone about this," I said, looked back at him and suggested, "Elvira. She's a good listener."

He ignored me again. "I was at base when Lucas, Darla and their crew entered your house. I was in the surveillance room and one of my boys whistled to me and I looked at the screens. I called the order to mobilize on your house, got my shit sorted and started to go myself but before I reached the door, I saw Lucas carrying you out over his shoulder. You weren't moving."

"Lucas?"

"Brock Lucas, you know him as Skull."

"Oh," I whispered.

"You weren't movin', Gwen."

"They'd stun gunned me," I told him.

"I didn't know that," he told me. "All I knew was that 911 had received a call from one of your neighbors, shots fired at your house, and you were carried out not moving. That's all I knew."

"They'd stun gunned me, Hawk," I repeated.

"I didn't know that, Gwen," he repeated back and continued, "I was in the car when the call came in that Brett was down, three to the chest. I knew the players. I could see the play. They took your body as proof of death, the beginning, you first, then your stepmom or your dad. They'd go through all of you and Ginger would need to step up to stop that happening."

"It didn't happen that way," I informed him of what he already knew.

"Yeah, but for two hours, I didn't know the state of you. Lee got a lock on your location, we went in and I had no idea what I'd face when I walked into that room."

"I was fine," I lied.

"You were bound and gagged, Gwen."

"Yes," I returned, "but otherwise fine."

He kept going. "Days earlier you were caught in a drive-by. Your car at the curb, your purse on the couch and you were *gone*. For fuckin' hours, babe. The only thing I had to hold onto, seein' as another woman of mine had been caught in a drive-by, was that no blood was at the scene and my boys saw Tack drag you out. Camera angles weren't good so we couldn't see for sure you'd not been hit but at least you were standing."

Shit, that hadn't occurred to me. Why hadn't that occurred to me?

"I was fine then too," I reminded him.

He pressed in deeper. "Yeah, Gwen, but I...didn't... *know that*."

All right. I had to give him that.

Still.

"You're telling me all this because...?" I prompted.

His hand left my hip and went to cup the other side of my jaw as he said, "Jesus, Gwen, I'm tellin' you this so you'll know where my head was at."

"Okay, now I know. Thanks for story time, Hawk. Now are you going to go?"

His hands tightened and he whispered, "Don't do that, babe."

"Do what? Be an unfeeling bitch in the face of your pain? Sorry, is that not okay? Because, see, the day I was kidnapped and a man was shot protecting me, after a week of dealing with a bunch of really bad shit at the same time you came at me and got me to trust you, you ripped me to shreds Hawk. Firm and unwavering. You tore right through me, leaving me in tatters, and you didn't even fucking *blink*."

"And now you know where my head was at and why I did that shit."

"No, now I know that you saw Tack playing with your fuck toy and you don't feel like sharing."

His body froze and his fingers flexed. I could feel his fury but I didn't care. I wasn't done. The hurt he inflicted went too deep and I had to protect myself at all costs.

"That's okay, baby," I whispered. "There's plenty of me to go around. But, rules are, you come, you make me come, and then you *go*."

He didn't move and I felt his anger beating against me as he held me pinned against the wall. Then suddenly his body relaxed, the anger vanished and his thumbs swept my jaw.

"I cut you," he murmured.

"Nothing a little cookie dough can't cure," I returned.

"Bullshit, Sweet Pea."

It was then my body went still.

"Don't call me that," I snapped.

He ignored me again. "We were us for a week, a fuckin' week, and I cut you deep."

"God!" I exclaimed pushing against his waist again. "Are you ever going to go?"

He surprised me by moving back. Then he surprised me again by bending and putting a shoulder in my belly and I was lifted up.

"Hawk!" I cried, pushing against his hips and kicking with my feet as he walked me into my room. "Put me down!" I demanded.

He did. He bent, bumped his shoulder, I flew through the air and landed on my back with a bounce on my bed.

I got up on my elbows and opened my mouth to speak, or more accurately yell, but I saw in the shadows that his hands looked to be at his cargoes.

Shit!

I turned to escape and nearly got to the other side of the bed when I was caught with an arm at the waist and hauled back.

"You're not welcome to spend the night here," I informed the room because my back was to him.

He let me go just long enough to flip the covers over us but not long enough for me to make good an escape. He curled into me, deeper than normal, pinning me to the bed with his torso, his leg hitched in mine, keeping me secured to him with his arm tight around my belly.

He lifted his head and his mouth was at my ear. "Go to sleep, Gwen," he ordered.

Oh my God!

"Are you *high?*" I screeched.

His response to my query was to touch his tongue to the skin at the back of my ear then he settled into the pillows and further into me.

He was. He was high. Totally.

"I can't believe you," I hissed.

"Go to sleep, babe."

I strained against his arm but it got super tight so I gave up and repeated, "I...cannot...*believe* you."

"Baby, go to sleep."

I stilled at his use of the word "baby" because I had to. The slightest movement I knew would shatter me.

When I fought back the pain, I announced, "I'm moving to Boston."

He chuckled, deep and manly, and I felt his face in my hair at the back of my head where he said, "Babe."

God!

I tried again. "You can't stay here, Hawk."

His arm gave me a squeeze, his head lifted and his mouth

came back to my ear. "You're livin' in Badass World, baby," he whispered in my ear. "Fair warning, until I fix what I cut in you, you're there to stay."

Oh.

Shit.

CHAPTER TWENTY-NINE

I Was Wrong

I WOKE PRE-DAWN, I could see a bit of light in the sky and I could feel Hawk's heat at my back.

Damn.

I scooted out from under him, carefully but quickly, successfully made it off the bed and I grabbed my undies and rushed to the bathroom. I put them on, used the facilities and then walked out, going to my thermostat. It was on a timer and went down way low at night. It wouldn't kick in for a while. I turned it up and went to my office. I arranged the toss pillows on the armrest on the couch, lay down and then pulled my chenille throw over me. It would take a while for the house to heat up. The chenille was snuggly soft and nice to cuddle under while watching TV but it wasn't exactly ultra-warm.

I lay there and my mind was filled with possible strategies of how to get out of my current predicament. I could go to Tack but that might send mixed messages, and anyway, I needed to sort myself out. I could report Hawk to Lawson but I might have difficulty explaining why, after Hawk broke in, I let him fuck me.

Hmm. Not good.

Hawk told me he'd come after me even if I stayed at Leo and Cam's. Meredith and Dad were back home but Hawk had already proved he could infiltrate their house and would. Troy lived on the seventh floor in a secure condo building but I figured Hawk could beat a security system or scale walls.

Hmm. More not good.

Then, totally against my will, my mind slid to Simone Delgado dying because she loved her brother and was excited to be there when her niece or nephew entered the world.

I could see that.

I could also see Hawk's grief swinging to anger because she let love veer her away from caution and she dragged their daughter into it, something, as a mother, she should never do. I could also see that would make him feel guilt, the extreme kind, loving her, his grief at her loss mixing with anger. An innocent decision, but he knew the danger and warned her against it. She didn't listen and that happy beautiful family in that photo he showed me was gone. *Poof!* He had the memory of their farewell and left to do his job not knowing it was the last memory they'd ever make.

And he was thousands of miles away. Simone and Sophie dead for days and he was thousands of miles away. Hawk, who controlled every nuance of his life, completely removed, powerless and thousands of miles away.

I tried not to think of this. I tried to force my mind back to ways to keep him out of my life, stop him from hurting me again, but all I could see in my head was that picture.

You weren't movin', Gwen, he had said.

Firebombs. Drive-bys. Kidnappings. He'd been through it all with me.

And he saw Brock Lucas carry my immobile body out of my house and he decided he wasn't going to go there again, and damn it all to hell, who could blame him?

"Shit," I whispered into the room, tucked my hands under my cheek, curled my knees to my chest and felt the heat seep into my house.

Then I fell back to sleep.

*   *   *

My knees were gently pushed down and this woke me up.

My eyes opened as I felt Hawk's hips fit into the curve of mine then my gaze slid up to look at him sitting on the edge of my couch.

His hand came out and he shifted the hair off my shoulder then his hand curved warm against my neck.

"Not a big fan of bein' the reason you're curled into a protective ball, babe," he murmured as a good morning.

He was fully dressed, his face unhappy.

I had no response. I was still sleepy and having trouble getting my guard up.

He held my eyes as I mentally struggled. Then suddenly he moved, I was plucked out of the couch, planted in his lap and his arms went around me.

"Hawk," I whispered.

"You could have anything, babe, anything in the world, what would it be?" he asked.

I blinked. "What?"

"Anything you want, it's yours. What would it be?"

"Um...I don't—"

His arms gave me a squeeze. "Anything, Gwen."

"Ginger out of trouble and safe," I answered.

His eyes studied my face for a while after I answered. Then he said, "Next up."

"Next up?" I repeated, confused.

One of his arms left me so his hand could bunch the hair at the side of my neck. "Next up, Gwen, the next most important thing you could have if you could have anything."

"Hawk, I don't understand."

"Anything, no matter what it is."

"Hawk—"

"Answer me, Sweet Pea."

"Hawk, I don't—"

"Gwen, answer me."

"Simone and Sophie alive and you with them and happy like you were in that photo," I blurted, and his face froze into that blank mask.

Staring at him, sleepy and confused, I suddenly understood that mask. It slotted into place when he was hiding something important from me.

"Which would mean, of course," I kept blurting, "that you would never darken my door."

The mask fell away instantly and he grinned, huge, his dimples popping out and dang, it killed me, but I had to admit I really missed those dimples. Then he twisted his torso and I was on my back in the couch, his upper half on top of me, my hips in his hips, my legs dangling over the back.

His fingers trailed my hairline and tucked my hair behind my ear as he went on, "What's next?"

I felt my eyes get squinty. "Why are you asking me this?"

"What's next, Gwen?"

"I'm still sleepy," I dodged.

His face came closer and his thumb stroked my jaw when he whispered his demand, "Baby, what's next?"

God!

Okay, he wanted to play this game, whatever. I'd play.

"Meredith being my real mom, not my stepmom."

He nodded and his thumb swept my lower lip. "What's next?"

"You want to clue me in, Hawk?" I requested.

"What's next?"

Apparently, he didn't.

"There isn't anything next," I declared.

"Bullshit, Sweet Pea, a woman who wants a pair of seven-hundred-dollar shoes, she's gotta have a next."

"A diamond bracelet from Tiffany's," I replied then went back on it. "No! Wait. Leo to get Cam an engagement ring *then* a diamond bracelet from Tiffany's."

His head dipped and his mouth touched mine before he moved back and murmured, "All right, baby, that'll do for now."

What'll do? And for now?

No. No. I didn't want to know.

Time to move on.

"Since you're here and don't appear to intend to leave anytime soon, I might as well ask you something," I announced and got another grin. "Tack says that things have cooled with Ginger. Does your intel confirm that I'm safe?"

"Ginger's gone to ground," Hawk repeated Tack's words. "Darla, Skeet and Fresh were facing kidnapping charges, and luckily they all signed confessions so they won't breathe free for a while. This is good because it's good. This is also good because their incarceration is an added deterrent to anyone who might think of fuckin' with you. Lee entered the game, which is further inducement for someone to avoid fuckin' with you. But, no, you're not safe."

Dammit!

"So I take it that means I can't go to the grocery store."

"You can go to the grocery store but you'll do it with one of my boys at your back."

My body froze under his and my heart slid into my throat.

Then I forced out, "No."

His hand at my neck moved so his thumb could lightly stroke my throat.

"Brett's recovering, babe," he whispered. "It'll take time but it'll be a full recovery."

"No more of your boys at my back."

"Gwen."

"No, Hawk," I denied, made a decision and then proclaimed, "I'm buying a gun."

He burst out laughing at my words, no hesitation, like they were beyond hilarious and I glared at him.

"I'm not joking."

He controlled his laughter and stated, "Babe, you want a gun, I'll give you one. but you won't be let loose on the unsuspecting population of Denver until I train you how to use it and you get comfortable with it, so no gun."

"I don't need your permission to buy a gun, Hawk."

"Yeah you do, Gwen, seein' as you're livin' in Badass World now."

"Well, I'm taking a vacation from Badass World and visiting Zip's Gun Emporium," I shot back.

He smiled at me, dimples and all. Then he changed the subject.

"We're goin' out tonight."

Oh no we were *not*.

"No we're not. It's cosmos at Cam's tonight."

"Then I'll take you there and bring you home."

That's when I made another decision.

"No, I'm spending the night so I can get as drunk as I want."

"Babe, warned you about that shit."

Something about that pissed me off. Likely it was the reminder of how the us we came to be used to be. Something he seemed totally okay with resuming and something I was really not okay with.

In other words, that was when my mouth ran away from me.

"Yes, you did, but you did that before you destroyed me. See, Scott crushed me but *you* destroyed me. It was just a week, I know that, so here's something to freak you out. You got it wrong, in only a week I was already tied to you. I was already in deep. It was only a week but it happened, you didn't see it and you went in for the kill. So I'm getting from you that you've had a chance to rethink things. But for me, you not reading how precious it was, what I gave you, and even for self-preservation's sake, walking all over that is a red flag, Hawk. And that red flag says to me it could happen again and I've had enough in my life, I don't need any more of that shit."

"I'm not your fuckwad ex, babe, my shit's not about bangin' any woman I can to prove I'm a man," he returned, and I noticed he looked just about as pissed as me.

"I'm aware of that, Hawk, that doesn't change the fact you walked all over me."

"I didn't, Gwen. I explained that shit to you then and again last night. And, newsflash, Sweet Pea, outside my family, you're the only one in Denver who knows anything about it."

Wow. Interesting.

So interesting, I gave a little but I didn't give in.

"Okay, I understand where you're coming from but can you at least take a second to understand where *I'm* coming from?"

And it would appear, from a response that gutted me, that I was so deep in my own efforts at self-preservation that I wasn't paying enough attention. I vastly underestimated just how pissed off Cabe "Hawk" Delgado was.

"I know where you're comin' from and what I see is that you haven't dropped that hand, Gwen, and you never did. I came clean and you're usin' some seriously bad shit against me to fend me off. He taught you to curl up tight and keep everything out. You threw it in my face that I called you on what it would mean, you don't take a risk on me. Now you're blinded to the fact that you're doin' the same fuckin' thing I was but I'm strugglin' to get past it and move on. But you, babe, not you. You're hell bent on holdin' on. My wife and daughter were *murdered*, Gwen, and I found myself, eight years later, in the same fuckin' mess with a woman who had a sibling that put her in extreme danger. I took that risk and in a week, *I* was so tied to you, *I* was in so deep, I faced that shit again, was confronted with the possibility of that kind of loss, and I couldn't deal."

He lifted up suddenly, taking me with him, standing and putting me on my feet in front of him.

Yes, definitely pissed, and if I could get beyond the justified jab wounds he inflicted with his words, I would come to realize he had a right to be.

Unfortunately, he kept speaking. "So, yeah, I get where you're comin' from. Jesus, I understand protecting yourself from pain. But standing in front of me is a woman who can't see beyond herself and her own fuckin' issues to recognize that the man she was tyin' herself to needs some understanding or, if that's too much for you, some fucking compassion."

I realized I wasn't breathing as I stared up at him because he was right. Damn, he was right.

I wasn't just a slut, I was also a bitch.

"So thanks for the heads up, babe. Everything you did that week we were together, every reaction you had to the shit swirling around you, everything out of your mouth, the way you were with the people who love you indicated to me I'd found treasure. It's good to know early that I was wrong."

After he sunk that last blade into my flesh or, more accurately, I positioned it, held his hand and did the deed, Hawk vanished.

CHAPTER THIRTY

TMI

IT WAS EARLY afternoon when I took a huge breath, flipped open my phone, went to the contact list, scrolled down and hit go.

"Talk." Hawk's voice came at me and I started to talk and then I heard a beep and I realized that Hawk demanding the caller to talk was his voicemail message.

I'd been skating the edge of hysteria all day. Confronted with my selfish bitchiness in the face of the man who I wanted to be mine's attempt at letting go of a tragic past and moving on with me, the only reason I didn't make four batches of cookie dough and eat through them all was because I was out of butter.

And his voicemail greeting sent me over the edge.

It was inappropriate considering he walked out on me with a parting shot that pretty much equaled good-bye but I still started giggling.

And through my giggling, I forced out the words, "Baby. Your voicemail message is 'talk.'" Suddenly my laughter died away and I whispered, "That is *so* you." I closed my eyes tight because it *was* so him and I loved that about him and I finished, "Please call me so I can say I'm sorry."

Then I flipped the phone shut, placed it on the kitchen countertop, lifted both hands and pressed my fingers in my cheeks. Then I closed my eyes again and sent a wish into the universe that Cabe Delgado would call me back.

Then I grabbed my phone, grabbed my purse, grabbed my net bags to put my groceries in and headed out the front door to my car, which was still at the curb where I parked it prior to the drive-by. It hadn't moved in over a week. I was halfway down my walk when Detective Mitch Lawson slid up and parked behind my Hyundai.

I stared at him in his car.

Why?

Why me?

His being there could only mean, firstly, something was wrong with Ginger and/or I was in some peril or, secondly, he'd heard things were over with Hawk, I was down the mountain from Tack and he was moving in.

Why…me?

I buried this reaction and met him on the sidewalk, wishing he wasn't so freaking hot.

"Hey, Mitch," I greeted.

"Gwendolyn." He smiled.

I stared at his smile.

Why, I will repeat, me?

"I've managed not to get shot at or kidnapped for a whole week," I bragged.

"Good for you." He kept smiling.

"Please tell me you're not here to inform me my winning streak is ending and another incident is imminent."

He shook his head. "Not here for that, sweetheart."

I tipped my head to the side. "Then why are you here?"

"'Cause Leo spoke to me this mornin' and he gave me a surprise invitation to girls' night in with cosmopolitans."

I stared at him.

I was going to *kill* Cam.

"Mitch," I whispered.

"Honey, I said no," he replied gently.

I felt relief and loss, the first more than the last but I felt loss all the same mostly because he was hot, partly because he was gentle and partly because I really liked his eyes.

He got closer and I held my ground as his soulful eyes that I liked so much locked with mine.

Then he shared, "Every instinct I got is tellin' me to move in and protect you not only from everything that's happening with your sister but from two men I'm uncertain are good for you."

I sucked in my lips and bit them.

"At the same time," he went on, "I'm sensin' that you need space to do whatever you're gonna do."

I let my lips go and nodded my head.

"That said, I'd be a fool not to tell you where I stand."

Uh-oh.

"I was another type of man, the type they are, I wouldn't hesitate gettin' in there and muddling your head by making my play."

At that point, I felt I should intervene.

"Hawk is...well, Hawk," I lamely defended him. "And Tack is giving me space."

"It isn't space to install you in his house, sweetheart."

Well, that was semi-true.

"But—"

"He's makin' his play," Lawson said firmly.

"Uh...okay," I agreed since he would know because he was a man and I, obviously, wasn't. "But I'm home now."

"Yeah," Lawson agreed. "You're in a home that every

time you walk up your walk or into your livin' room, you'll be reminded of Tack's play."

Hmm. This was true. I hadn't thought of that.

Still, what Tack did was nice.

"Mitch—"

He cut me off. "Remember what I said to you, Gwendolyn. Head up, eyes open and I'll go on to say be happy. And I'll finish by tellin' you, you're willin' to give me a shot at makin' you happy, you call me because I'm willin' to take that shot."

Wow.

"Mitch," I repeated, and his hand came up to cup my jaw so I blurted, "Please don't kiss me. I like kissing and if you're a good kisser that'll definitely muddle my head. No joke. And, honest to God, I don't need that right now."

His head dipped toward me, I braced, but his face stopped an inch away.

"Okay, honey," he whispered, "I won't kiss you, but just for your information, I've had no complaints."

I bet he hadn't.

"Great," I muttered. "Now I'm curious."

He grinned and his thumb moved over my cheek. "You ever wanna assuage that curiosity, find me. Yeah?"

"You're muddling my head," I warned.

His grin got bigger and I knew he knew he was and I also knew he intended to, so I knew that whole speech about not muddling my head was a big, old play.

"Your eyes say you're soulful but you're actually dangerous," I whispered.

"A man can be both," he replied, his fingers slid back into my hair, he tipped my head down, kissed my hair at the top, let me go, and when I looked up at him, he winked at me and walked away.

I watched him drive away and then I wondered about the angles of Hawk's cameras and then I worried that he'd seen that or it would be reported and then I got in my car and checked my phone.

Nothing.

I drove to the grocery store. Considering my recent past, I did this vigilant so it wasn't lost on me that the minute I pulled my Hyundai away from the curb, a shiny black SUV pulled out with me and followed me to the store and in the driver's seat was Mo.

Shit. Even if the cameras hadn't seen me, Mo had and Hawk would get a report.

Shit!

Well, the silver lining was, Hawk had sent Mo to have my back. which didn't exactly equal good-bye forever and ever, you thoughtless, selfish cow.

But it didn't say I forgive you either.

*   *   *

"I'm a thoughtless, selfish cow," I announced to Cam, Tracy and, somebody kill me, Elvira.

Then I leaned forward and banged my head on Cam's kitchen table.

"I think maybe this means cutoff time," Elvira muttered.

I was on cosmo four and I was drinking fast. Firstly, because Hawk hadn't called back. Secondly, because I spent the entire afternoon obsessing about the fact he hadn't called and whether or not I should leave another message. And thirdly, because Elvira showed at girls' night in.

Luckily after reading me the riot act for not returning her calls, Elvira was just Elvira. She didn't get into Hawk, she didn't press and she didn't pry. She just dug into Cam's famous spicy red beans and rice (well, actually, it wasn't

Cam's recipe, it was her great-grandmother's and I tried to get her to give it to me but she said we had to exchange blood transfusions and go through adoption proceedings for her to do that without getting disowned so I just ate hers and considered myself lucky) and sucking back her cosmopolitan so I was free to continue obsessing because Hawk *still* hadn't called me. Something I did, barely participating in girl talk until I made my insane announcement.

"I'm actually surprised the meltdown hasn't occurred before now," Cam remarked.

"Cam!" Tracy cried.

"Oh shit, woman down," Leo muttered, and I looked up to see he'd come into the room probably to get a beer.

Very bad timing.

"I slept with Hawk again last night," I told Leo, avoiding directly telling Cam, Tracy or Elvira.

Leo's eyes got big and he made a strangled noise.

"You *what?*" Cam screeched.

"Well, all right," Elvira stated.

"Oh boy," Tracy mumbled.

"I did," I told Leo, who still had his deer-caught-in-headlights look going. "He came to my house in the middle of the night and—"

Leo's hand shot up. "Stop right there, darlin'," he interrupted me. "Last time I looked, I still had a dick."

"Leo!" Cam snapped, and Leo's eyes went to her.

"And the last time you looked, I had a dick."

"We all know you have a dick, Leo," Cam flashed back.

"All I'm sayin' is, I got a dick and I'm in here for a beer and that means I'm invisible during this discussion. Yeah?" And with that, he got his beer and walked right out.

"I'm sorry about my man," Cam said irately to Elvira.

"I'm not, girl. A, he's hot and B, he's got a dick and C, his not wantin' any part in girl talk states he knows how to use it. Now," her eyes swung to me, "movin' on to the good shit. You slept with Hawk? Word was it was over."

"Well, it was, then it wasn't and now I think it is again."

"Uh... what?" Elvira asked, her brows drawing together.

I sucked back my cosmo then I told them everything. Cam and Tracy knew the first part, so I didn't get into that, I just got into last night and this morning finishing with "And now I think he thinks I'm a thoughtless, selfish cow."

I got silence as they all stared then, as usual, Cam spoke first.

"Hate to say this to you," she straight-talked me albeit gently, "but, babe, sounds like it to me too."

Great. Just freaking *great*.

"My God, I had no idea," Elvira stated, sounding stunned, and Tracy nodded.

"Actually this whole week I was thinking it sucked that it didn't work out but I got why it didn't, his tragic past and all," Trace added.

"You did?" I asked her.

"Yeah, Gwennie, but you wanted space so I gave it to you and couldn't tell you that."

I stared at her. Then I dropped forward and banged my head against the table again.

"Gwen, calm down. If he's into you, which he obviously is, he'll get over this," Camille pointed out.

I lifted my head. "I called him at one thirty."

"Maybe he's busy," Tracy suggested.

"He's busy," Elvira confirmed. "I wasn't let in on what he's workin', top secret, and he selected his top boys to work with him but he's been incommunicado all day."

A ray of hope.

"I thought he forwarded his phone to you," I said.

"He didn't today. He went off-line," Elvira told me.

"Why didn't he forward his phone to you?" I asked.

"Why does the earth go round the sun? Because he's Hawk. You don't question Hawk. He just does what he does when he does it and you go with the flow," Elvira answered.

"Is this operation so intense he can't call back?" I pressed.

"Don't know, hon, sorry to say," Elvira replied, and sounded like she was.

"Should I call him again?" I asked. "Does he check his voicemail?"

"Sure, if I'm not takin' messages for him," Elvira responded.

That ray of hope died.

I'd said I was sorry. I didn't know much about his operations but anyone had a moment in their day to check their voicemail and mine said I was sorry. If I cared about someone and they told me they were sorry in a voicemail, I would call them and put them out of their misery. It had been seven hours and he hadn't put me out of my misery.

Maybe the giggling pissed him off.

I dropped my head to the table again.

"Gwen," Cam said softly.

"I was falling in love with him," I told my lap, and I heard three quick, feminine intakes of breath. "Deep," I finished on a whisper, then lifted my head, "and I fucked it up."

"He's busy, babe, don't jump to conclusions," Cam stated.

"Every time I see him, every time he touches me, I get butterflies," I whispered.

"Oh boy," Elvira murmured.

"Scott didn't even do that to me," I shared.

"Who's Scott?" Elvira inquired.

"Her ex-husband and Denver's Patron of Dickheadedness," Tracy answered.

"Ah," Elvira replied, that one syllable full of under-standing.

"You didn't tell me about the butterflies," Cam whispered.

"I denied them," I whispered back. "They scared me."

Cam's face gentled. "Oh babe."

"He's bossy and annoying and intrusive and lives a nar-row life and demands emotional closeness but keeps distant but that last part is because he lost his wife and his little *daughter*," I went on. "And she was cute. He showed me a picture. She was wearing pink. She looked like him. She had the best of both of them in her."

Cam, Elvira and Tracy kept gentle eyes on me as I kept on.

"But he thinks I'm funny and Dad and Meredith adore him and we banter and I like it. It's fun and it's safe, though I didn't know it at the time, and he holds me while we sleep and he's an unbelievably good kisser and even better in bed. He gave me four orgasms in thirty minutes and I didn't even know that was physically possible."

"*Four* orgasms in *thirty* minutes?" Elvira breathed.

"Four orgasms in thirty minutes," I confirmed.

Elvira put her hand flat on the table and her upper body started teetering as she mumbled, "Lordy."

"Maybe we should get the smelling salts," Tracy noted, her eyes on Elvira.

"Babe, I don't have smelling salts," Cam returned.

"I need to quit," Elvira announced. "I gotta turn in my resignation. I can't work with a man knowin' his capacity to give pleasure. I mean, I can work with a man *guessin'* his capacity to give pleasure but not *knowin'* it. This is it. I hit the threshold. I never understood TMI. In my opinion, no amount of information is too much information but I've found it. I'm here."

"You can't quit because of me!" I hissed. "I get the sense

that Hawk likes you and depends on you. If you have someone like that, you don't want to lose them. He can't lose you
because I told you he can give multiple orgasms!"

"Those four orgasms were a multiple?" Elvira asked.

"No, those were mostly separate. He can only pull off
three in a one-go multiple," I answered.

"Holy crap," Tracy breathed.

"No joke?" Cam asked.

Elvira teetered so I put my hand on her so she wouldn't
go down and looked at Cam. "Why do you think I let him
keep coming at night? I told you he was good but he's not
good. He's *good*."

"Stop talkin'," Elvira whispered. "Where's the martini
shaker? I need a reload."

Cam got up and sauntered to the counter.

Then it hit me. "My God, if he doesn't forgive me, I'm
ruined for all other men."

"Gwennie, honey, really, don't stress. It hasn't even been
a day," Tracy soothed.

Cam started pouring vodka into the shaker and decreed,
"All right, this is serious for you and obviously he had reasons to be a motherfucking asshole meaning he actually
never was one. So, you called, left a voicemail, said you
were sorry. You wait. He doesn't call you back by one thirty
tomorrow, you call again. Voicemails can get missed. He's
there, you explain and apologize again. He's not there, you
leave another voicemail. He doesn't call back, say, for two
days, you know where he's at, you make a batch of cookie
dough, you call us and we'll all come over and eat it."

Thank God. A plan.

That was all I needed.

I took in a breath, checked Elvira to make sure she was
steady, let her go and looked at Cam.

"Thanks, babe."

Camille nodded her head and poured in cranberry juice.

"He'll call," Tracy whispered and my eyes moved to her. She smiled her hopeful smile.

I smiled back but mine felt shaky.

CHAPTER THIRTY-ONE

She's My Sister

I LAY ON my side, my knees curled up to my chest in Cam and Leo's guest bedroom and I flipped opened the phone, went to contacts, scrolled down and hit go.

I immediately got Hawk's "Talk."

"Hi," I whispered. "I don't know if you got my other voicemail but I wanted you to know, I drove over to Cam and Leo's tonight and had enough to drink, it wasn't safe to drive home so I'm spending the night." I paused. "I just...wanted you to know where I am." I paused again, then kept whispering. "I hope, even after what happened this morning, that you managed to have a good day, baby."

I flipped the phone shut and stared at it.

God, I was such an idiot.

I tapped the phone on my forehead and then put it on the nightstand.

It was nearly midnight. Over ten hours since I called.

Shit.

I tucked my hands under my cheek and closed my eyes tight thinking maybe I should have texted.

Then I heard a scratching at the window.

My eyes flew open and I shot up to an elbow in the bed. I stared out the opened curtains and my heart squeezed.

Ginger was standing there, partially illuminated by streetlights, and the entire left side of her face was swollen, bruised, bleeding and mangled.

"Gwennie." I heard her pained whisper.

I didn't think. I threw the bedclothes back and raced from the room. The panels of Cam's long, sexy satin nightgown that would make Meredith's mouth water and had slits up each side practically to my hips were tangling with my legs. I went straight to the front door, unlocked it, threw it open and dashed out, running and frantic. I made it to the edge of the house, turned and collided headlong with something big, hard and solid.

I looked up into Hawk's face.

"Gwen," he said, "get back in the house."

"Ginger," I whispered worriedly, rounded him, started to fly and stopped dead.

Ginger was down on her ass, back to the house under the guest bedroom window. Her knees up, her head bowed.

I ran to her, yanked up the panel to my nightgown and dropped to my knees beside her.

"Honey, look at me," I whispered, but she didn't raise her head and she was breathing funny. "Ginger, honey, please," I begged, reaching out to take her chin gently and lift her face to me.

I saw it and sucked in breath. It was worse close up. *A lot* worse.

Hawk crouched low at her other side, took her chin from my hand into his own and carefully pulled her head his way. He had his phone at his other ear and he spoke as he scanned my sister's face.

"I need a pickup at Freeman's for Gwen and guards to

stay with her at the warehouse until I get there. We were right, Ginger was going to her and she's here. Call Doc, he needs to head out, she's a fuckin' mess. Safe house. Then call Lawson, he's up." He stopped talking a moment then said, "Out."

He flipped his phone shut and shoved it into his cargoes.

"You havin' trouble breathin'?" he asked Ginger.

"Ribs," Ginger replied.

"Fuck," Hawk muttered. "Can you handle me carrying you into the house?"

Ginger ignored him. "No cops."

"Your plays aren't workin', Ginger, you're gonna try mine."

"No cops," she repeated, and I reached out and grabbed her hand, holding on tight.

"You love your sister?" Hawk asked suddenly. Ginger pulled her chin away from his hand then she whimpered. "I asked you a question," he pushed.

"She's my sister," Ginger answered and the tears hit my eyes, no warning this time, they just hit them and spilled over.

And they did this because this meant yes.

I moved closer and held her hand harder.

"Then trust me to do right by you," Hawk replied, knowing what she meant.

"You can't fix this," Ginger told him.

"I sure as fuck can try," Hawk returned and looked at me. "Let her go. I need to get her up."

I let her go. Hawk leaned in and lifted Ginger in his arms. This didn't cause whimpers, it caused moans. I raced ahead of him, swiping at my face, opened the front door and left it open while I moved around the room turning on lights. Hawk came in and lay Ginger down on the couch while I moved down the hall. Leo was already out of his bedroom and I rushed to him.

"I'm so sorry. She found me. Ginger's here," I told him quietly.

"Fuck," he muttered, and Cam came out, her eyes alert.

"Ginger's here," I told her.

"Fuck," she muttered.

I raced away. Leo and Cam followed me. Ginger was on the couch. Hawk was nowhere.

This alarmed me but I moved straight to Ginger and got down on my knees by the couch. I took her hand again and she turned her head away.

"We'll get you sorted, honey, promise," I whispered.

"Don't call Mom and Dad, Gwen," she told the back of the couch.

"Right now, I'm about you, Ginger."

She turned to face me. "Don't call Mom and Dad."

"I won't," I promised.

"Promise it and mean it and not like you meant it when I told you I snuck out and met Darren Petri and then you heard he had the clap so you told on me. Promise it and mean it."

Jeez. Darren Petri was ages ago.

"Ginger, you kept sleeping with him and he had the clap," I reminded her.

"He was cute," she reminded me.

She was right. He was. Still, he had the freaking clap and she told me they didn't use protection. What was I supposed to do?

Suddenly Hawk was crouched at my side. "Gwen, reunion later, if you're lucky. Go get your shit," he ordered, and held a dishtowel with ice to Ginger's swollen face.

I watched her eyes close when the towel gingerly hit her skin and I could tell that felt good.

"I'm staying with Ginger."

"Go get your shit," Hawk repeated, and I looked at him.

"Baby, I need to stay with my sister," I whispered.

"No, Gwen, you need to trust her to my care and go get your shit," he stated and scarily went on, "My boys'll be here in five to take you to my place and I'm takin' care of her. I followed her here and others followed me. She needs to be gone so your friends'll be safe and *you* need to be gone. Get me?"

Oh shit. I got him.

"You'll keep her safe?" I asked.

Hawk just looked at me.

He'd keep her safe.

I didn't know where he and I were with our relationship, but still, I lifted my hand, curled my fingers around his neck and leaned in to touch my mouth to his as my show of gratitude.

"Fuck me, I'm gonna be sick," Ginger groaned, and my mouth left Hawk's, my hand went away from his neck and I turned to Ginger.

"Do you need a bowl?" I asked, squeezing her hand which I still held.

"No, Gwen, fuck, *at you. You're* makin' me sick." Her one unswollen eye not covered in an iced up dishtowel slid to Hawk. "She's always been gushy. It's sick. Even somethin' stupid, like watchin' TV, she'd curl up to me. Fuck."

Hawk had no response.

"I thought you liked cuddling," I stated.

"Yeah, when I was *five*," Ginger replied. I sucked in breath and prepared to retort.

"Gwen." Hawk spoke in a warning low voice and I looked at him.

"Right," I whispered, turned back to Ginger and pulled

her hand to my mouth. "Whatever happens next, honey, and whatever we left behind, I love you and I always have. You can believe me or not. I don't care. I need to say it and tell you I mean it. It's your choice whether you believe it."

Then I kissed her knuckles, let her go and raced through Cam and Leo to the guest room.

CHAPTER THIRTY-TWO

Is Everything All Right?

My GUARDS WERE Fang and a man named Suarez.

Suarez was a mini-commando in the sense that he was younger than the rest, not in the sense he was less scary than the rest. His body was such that they could use it in anatomy class to teach musculature, such was the definition.

When we made it to the warehouse, Fang took his position outside, Suarez took me inside then positioned himself at the door.

I asked if he wanted coffee. He said no.

That was the extent of our conversation. This was because Suarez was clearly a conversationalist of the Fang variety but also because I didn't have conversation in me.

I paced. After I paced for a while I realized I was trembling. I wasn't trembling because I was cold. I was trembling because I was scared. So I raced up the iron steps and went to Hawk's wardrobe. I should have gotten dressed. But being in a Do As I'm Told mood, my clothes, jacket and shoes had hastily been stuffed in plastic grocery bags so I could carry out Hawk's orders and I was too wired to get dressed. I searched and found a navy blue flannel shirt of Hawk's. I put it on. After I put it on, I stopped trembling.

There you go. Hawk's superhero superpowers extended to his clothes.

Good to know.

I walked back down the stairs and started pacing again.

After I did this for a good long while, Suarez spoke.

"Maybe you should try to sleep," he suggested.

Yeah, like that would happen.

"I'm not thinking that's a possibility," I informed him, then asked, "Can I watch TV?"

"Rather be able to hear," he answered.

Right. It was probably better that, if bad guys approached, he had advance warning.

I nodded.

Then I paced some more.

Time slid by, adrenaline seeped out and exhaustion seeped in. So I lay down on Hawk's couch, curled up and stared at the moonlight on the scrub opposite the small-river-maybe-large-creek and thought about breaking my promise to Ginger and calling my folks. Then I thought about Ginger's face. Then I thought about how I'd never forget Ginger's face. Then I hoped that I'd see it again when it wasn't bleeding, mangled and swollen.

After thinking all that, I fell asleep.

My body jolted awake when I heard the loud creak of the garage door going up. Sleep shot from me and I jumped from the couch, rounding it to see Suarez facing the door looking like he was standing at modified ease, feet planted wide, hands on hips, which brought one closer to the gun on his gun belt.

The garage door creaked again, the inner door opened and Hawk walked in, my heart shifted, my stomach clutched and his eyes went to Suarez.

"Relieved," he muttered, and Suarez took off, not glancing back.

Hawk walked to me. I ran to him.

I stopped and put my hands on his chest. "How is she?" I asked.

He'd stopped and he put his hands to my upper arms. Then he lifted me right up off my feet and planted them down so I was outside touching distance. That not being enough, he let me go and took a step back himself.

I stared at him as my insides paralyzed.

There it was. My answer. He didn't call back because he didn't forgive me. He so didn't forgive me, he didn't want me touching him or even close to his space.

At that, it was my heart that clutched to protect itself from the searing pain burning through my insides.

"She's in the hospital under guard," Hawk replied. "She has facial fractures, a concussion and seven broken ribs. No internal damage but the injuries to her face will require plastic surgery."

I swallowed as new pain seared through me. Then I nodded.

"Is she..." I swallowed again, "is she safe?"

"Had a deal with Lawson," Hawk answered, crossing his arms on his chest. "I get Ginger, I give her to him only if he brokers a deal with the Feds. She testifies and goes into protective custody. We took her to my safe house, Lawson met us there and we had a chat with her while Doc looked at her. Took a while for Lawson and me to talk her into testifying. Then it took longer because the Feds wanted to know what she knew because she isn't a good enough witness to merit the resources they'd need to expend to put her into protective custody and then get her into the witness protection program. She's got a rap sheet, just misdemeanors but she's a known drug user, hasn't kept good company, actively participated in some not very good shit and the longest time she's held down a job was four months workin' at a convenience store. Not exactly an ace-in-the-hole witness, the defense attorneys would chew her up and spit her out."

Unfortunately, this was true.

I sucked in my lips.

"The surprise was Ginger isn't as stupid as we thought. Ginger doesn't only know a lot, Ginger's been playin' it safe and gathering insurance. She told us she's been keepin' diaries, she stole documents, she took pictures and even sometimes wore a wire. She might not be a good witness if she only had her word against theirs but she also has physical evidence to back up her shit. Roarke and the others knew this and this was why they were rabid for her. She was trying to use it as leverage to buy her way out but they didn't feel like payin' when she'd fucked them over and even if she turned over the shit, she couldn't wipe her memory and Ginger, bein' Ginger, would always be a threat. She gave up the location of some of it but says she has more and kept that back as incentive for the deal. Lawson and the Feds went to her location, found the shit and spent about half an hour sorting through it before they offered her the deal. I handed her over and they took her to the hospital. That means, until the trials, you won't see your sister and she's in the wind after."

I pulled in an audible breath and Hawk kept talking.

"She's got shit on three big players, two into drugs, one runs guns. Tonight, Ginger Kidd and Mitch Lawson significantly cleaned up the streets of Denver. But these men, they got armies and they got reach. Before they go down, they'll do everything they can to take her out. And even if they go down, they'll want retribution. She's gotta disappear."

I took that hit and nodded.

Hawk went on, "I know you promised not to call Bax and

Meredith but I advise that you let them have a good night's sleep then you phone them and share. They should know."

I nodded again then whispered, "Thank you, Hawk."

He lifted his chin then ordered, "Go to bed, get some sleep. I'll take you home after I get some rest. You take the bed. I'll take the couch."

It took everything but I didn't even twitch when he said that but that didn't mean my body didn't bear the brunt of this powerful blow.

"I'll call a taxi," I offered quietly, "get out of your hair."

"Take the bed," he replied.

"It's okay. I'll—"

"Gwen, I'm wiped. Take the fuckin' bed."

I nodded again. I wanted to search his eyes, see if something was there, anything, but I was too much of a wimp. I didn't want to witness it if there wasn't anything to be found. All I knew was that his manner, his voice and the fact he didn't call me "babe" or "Sweet Pea" meant there wasn't.

So I looked away, muttered, "Sleep well," and walked quickly to the steps.

I heard the beeps of his phone as I went up them but my mind was in a foggy, painful haze and I tried to force my body to go numb. I took off his flannel and missed it the instant its warmth left my body. I dropped it to the foot, slid into his big bed, my lips quivering, my sinuses tingling, fighting back the tears as I heard his voice talking on the phone. I pulled the covers up and curled into a ball, yanking a pillow to my chest to anchor it against me with my legs, and I bent my neck and shoved my face into it. My body was refusing to go numb because I had to force all my energies not to burst into loud, uncontrollable tears Hawk would definitely hear.

My sister was still a marked woman, but at least under

protection. Nevertheless, she wasn't safe until the trial and she'd never really be safe, not for the rest of her life.

That really sucked.

And I'd fucked things up with Hawk. Broken it beyond repair. When he was done, he was done but he wasn't done, not with me. I'd somehow got him tied to me, in deep, but it was me who cut him away and yanked him out of me and now he was definitely done.

I closed my eyes and heard he'd stopped talking. I pulled in a deep breath, wondering, hysterically, if ferrets were friendly.

I heard his feet on the stairs. It was impossible even for Hawk to walk up those stairs silently.

I figured he was going to use the bathroom and, again hysterically, I thought he should put in a bathroom downstairs. He had the room for it. If it was me, I'd put it at the other end of his lair, behind his desk, once I moved that closer to the kitchen and installed the Ping-Pong table, pool table and air hockey table.

I focused on air hockey, not on Hawk's presence on the bed platform, and I forced my body perfectly still.

I heard some beeps from what I guessed was his phone and they were coming from close to the bed.

I stayed immobile.

Then I heard him flip his phone shut, it clattered to the nightstand, I tensed and my eyes flew open. There was nothing for a moment then the light by the bed switched on. I uncurled and turned to my back to see he was standing by the bed, tugging off his tee.

My breath froze in my throat.

Then I forced out, "Is everything all right?"

He dropped his tee on the floor, turned and sat, his back to me. He bent forward and I heard one boot drop, then the other. He stood and turned back to the bed and his hands went to his cargoes.

My breath instantly heated and I found it hard not to pant for a variety of reasons when he tugged them down.

"Hawk," I whispered. "Is everything all right?"

"It wasn't," he replied, leaned in, grabbed the covers, pulled them back and I tensed as he slid in. His arms reached out, he turned me and then I was plastered to his body and his mouth was at my ear. "It is now." His arms got tight. "Just got your voicemails, babe."

He just got my voicemails. He just got them and I was in his arms.

My relief was so deep, so sweet, I couldn't hold back the tears as my hands went hesitantly to his chest.

"Hawk," I whimpered through my tears.

He leaned in; taking me to my back, his torso on mine and his head came up. The tears slid out of my eyes, his hand came up and his fingers moved through the wetness at my temple.

His gaze came to mine. "Baby," he whispered.

"I was a thoughtless, selfish cow!" I wailed, lifted my head and shoved it into his neck as I wound my arms around him.

"Sweet Pea."

"I'm sorry. I'm so, so sorry. It hurt, what you did to me, and that was all I could think about," I told him, dropped my head back to the pillows and looked into his black eyes. "You were right. I couldn't see through that to see what you were going through. It was thoughtless and selfish and—"

He rolled to his back, his arms around me taking me with him and when I was on top, his hand came up and pulled back one side of my hair, holding it at the back. He pulled my face down to touch my mouth to his. He let me back an inch and spoke.

"I cut you," he said softly. "You moved to protect yourself. It's a natural reaction, babe."

"It was mean and...and...*bitchy,*" I replied, still crying.

"Yeah, babe, you can maintain mean and bitchy for about ten hours and then you call and apologize. I think I can handle that. I left you hangin' for a week."

This was true.

"This is true," I muttered, the tears subsiding, and I watched his dimples form.

Then they disappeared, his hand left the back of my head so it could move to my face, his thumb sliding along my cheekbone, my jaw then my lips as his eyes followed its path. Then those eyes locked on mine.

"I'm sorry I cut you, baby," he whispered. The tears that had subsided welled up again and slid down my cheeks and his thumb moved instantly to glide through them as they did. "I'll do everything I can not to put you through that again," he promised.

"'Kay," I whispered back, and then my hand went to his cheek. I thought about his mom's visit. "And I'll do everything I can, if you do it again, not to give up on you and be a mean, bitchy, thoughtless, selfish cow."

His fingers slid back into my hair, he pulled my head back down and he touched my mouth to his where he murmured, "That'd be good."

Then the touch became a short, light kiss before he again let me back an inch.

"Glad that's done, Sweet Pea," he whispered.

I took my hand from his face and wiped my own, agreeing, "Yeah," but thinking "glad" was a mammoth understatement.

"Though that's done, we're not done talkin'," he told me, and the tone of his voice had changed.

I studied him and the look on his face had changed too. No longer gentle, it was firm.

Uh-oh.

"Um…" I mumbled, trying to find words to get out of a talk I was thinking I might not like.

"I'll remind you you're livin' in Badass World," he declared, and I didn't think this reminder boded good tidings.

"Um…" I mumbled, wondering what was next, however, although wondering, from his look and tone, not actually wanting to find out.

"And in Badass World, even when shit's unsettled between us, you don't meet another man on the sidewalk in front of your house and let him touch you and put his mouth on you."

Oh boy.

"Mo told you," I guessed.

"Another voicemail I just got."

Shit.

"He kissed my hair," I defended myself. "I don't have a brother but I would guess that would be how a brother might kiss me."

"Mitch Lawson does not feel brotherly love for you, babe," Hawk returned.

This was true.

Shit!

"Um…"

"Gwen, you made that sweet call, you told me you were sorry and when you did, you dropped that hand and gave yourself back to me. That means you just entered Badass World for good, you did it on your own and you gotta know there are rules. You stick to those rules or bear the consequences. Understood?"

Uh-oh. He was being bossy and it was kind of making me mad.

"I didn't throw myself at him and start making out with him on the sidewalk, Hawk."

He ignored my reassurances. "No hands and *definitely* no mouth, Gwen, no man but me. No man. At all. No excuses. Yeah?"

"Hawk—"

"And you don't jump on the back of a bike unless I'm on that bike," he went on.

"Hawk—"

His arm at my waist and hand at my head tightened. "Babe, you need to confirm you *get me*."

"God!" I exploded. "Yes, okay, I *get you*. Yeesh!"

The dimples popped out, he rolled me again so he was on top, his face was at my neck and his hands started sliding against the satin of Cam's nightgown.

Mm. Guess that subject was closed.

"Hawk, I thought you were wiped," I remarked.

"Yeah, I was, but this thing is soft and what's under it softer, didn't have either pressed against me when I said that so now I'm not wiped anymore," he said against my neck.

Mm!

He touched his tongue to the skin behind my ear.

Mm!

My hands went to his back, which wasn't soft, it was hard and that hard was the nice kind of hard so they explored.

Then he whispered, "Your sister's out of trouble, babe, and as safe as I can make her."

My hands stilled as it hit me.

Top-secret operation according to Elvira. He'd put his

top men on it. He'd gone off-line and hadn't checked his voicemail all day. He'd been there when Ginger showed at Leo and Cam's. He'd been following her, guessing she would come to me.

He'd spent his day, after how I treated him, going all out, likely putting himself and his boys in danger in order to give me what I wanted most in this world.

Oh my God.

His head came up and he looked down at me.

"Woulda made a deal with the devil to get my wife and daughter back." He was still whispering and my breath stilled. "Don't have that chance so nothin' I can do about that. But I darkened your door, baby, and you lit up my life again, so I'm not lettin' that go."

Oh my *God*.

He continued, "And Meredith is already your real mom. You want that legal then call an attorney. But, I'm tellin' you, it's already there, you just need to embrace it. So, I can't give you that 'cause you already have it."

Tears stung my eyes again.

"Hawk—" I whispered, my arms tightening.

Hawk kept talking. "Don't know Freeman and because of that, I figure he'd be unreceptive to me gettin' in his business, but you want me to have a word with him about puttin' a ring on his woman's finger, I'll do it."

"Stop talking," I begged.

He didn't.

"Tomorrow, we'll go to Tiffany's and you can pick out what you want."

I wrapped a leg around him and held on tight.

"Stop talking, Hawk."

His hand slid up the satin to cup my breast as his face got closer.

"Does that fix what I cut up inside you?" he whispered. "Or do you wanna give me a new list?"

It didn't but only because he'd already fixed it when he forgave me.

One of my hands slid up, over his hair, cupping the back of his head to pull him down as I lifted and turned my head so my lips were at his ear.

"Yes, baby, you fixed it but prepare to be freaked," I whispered back. He started to turn his head but I quickly kept talking before I lost my courage. "I'm falling in love with you, Cabe."

He stopped turning his head as his body froze and I held my breath.

Maybe that was too much too soon. We'd made up, we'd gone back to us, maybe I was pushing it.

And maybe I shouldn't have called him Cabe. I didn't do it purposefully, it just came out. And maybe this was because a man named Cabe would be as sweet as the man in my arms.

Then again, I'd learned a man named Hawk could be just as sweet.

Suddenly he rolled to his back with me on top of him. Just as suddenly Cam's nightgown was pulled up and off and tossed aside. Then I was on my back and his mouth was on mine.

Totally a take-it-off-because-it-was-in-the-way man. Cam's nightgown was hot.

I had a nanosecond to realize he really didn't mind me calling him Cabe, nor did he think my declaration was too soon if what he was doing to me with his mouth and the path of his hands were anything to go by. Then I lost the capacity to think.

After he kissed me, his mouth went to my neck. His

hand, which was cupping my breast, became fingers rolling my nipple and I gasped.

I planted my foot in the bed and tried to roll him to his back, an effort that failed.

"I want you on your back," I said in his ear.

"Not done," he muttered against my neck then his tongue glided across my throat.

I shivered.

"Hawk, I only got one lick in last night. That isn't fair."

At my words his fingers at my nipple squeezed and I gasped again as my hips bucked and his head came up.

Then he rolled to his back, me on top again, but both his hands went to the sides of my head and he held it over his.

"Your mouth can have me, babe, but you aren't bringin' it home. I'm comin' inside you, get me?"

"'Kay," I agreed instantly. I got more dimples before he brought my mouth down to his and kissed me again, hard and long and beautiful. I let him then his mouth released mine and I used it on him, all over him, taking my time and enjoying it until I got to the prize.

There I took more time and enjoyed that too, though it was safe to say, not as much as Hawk.

But, as agreed, I didn't bring it home. As usual, Hawk did and he did it connected to me.

And, as usual, it was unbelievably *good*.

CHAPTER THIRTY-THREE

Air Hockey

I WOKE ALONE in Hawk's bed.

The sun was shining bright through all the windows and I tipped my head back to look at Hawk's alarm clock. It was nearly eleven. I hadn't slept that late since I was a teenager.

I heard kitchen noises and smiled. Then I lifted up, reached to the foot of the bed, grabbed Hawk's flannel and shrugged it on while in bed. I threw my legs over the side, nabbed my panties from the floor and shimmied them on.

I wandered to the iron railing and looked down to see Hawk wearing a tight white tee and black track pants with a wide white stripe up the side. He was in the kitchen but his eyes were on me.

"Hey," I called and I saw, even at the distance, his small smile.

"Mornin', babe."

I grinned at him then walked to the bathroom. I had to open the second extra toothbrush but I didn't expect Hawk would mind. I went to town on my teeth, flossed, splashed warm water on my face, wiped it dry and walked out of the bathroom where I spied his cargoes on the floor.

The idea hit me, and before I could chicken out, I went to

his cargoes, pulled out his wallet and pulled out the photo. I returned the wallet, dropped the cargoes and unfolded the photo.

Sophie really was adorable. An unbelievably beautiful child. And Simone was stunning. Looking at her it was clear Hawk didn't have a type because she looked nothing like me. She had a hint of exotic ethnicity to her and I was as WASP as they came.

I folded the photo back into quarters and palmed it then walked down the stairs.

Hawk was at the stove but he turned to me when I hit the seating area. I kept on going until I collided with his big, hard body, put my arms around his waist and my cheek to his chest.

His arm curved around my shoulders.

"Sleep well, baby?" he asked into my hair.

"Yeah, baby, you?" I asked back.

"Yeah," he answered.

I gave him a squeeze and he returned it. Then I focused on the skillet on the stove. In it was an egg-whites-only omelet that had yet to be folded over but had mushrooms and various green bits on one side.

Tack appreciated food and consumed it in a way that I suspected he lived his life. Not safe and controlled, but with pleasure and abandon. Tack had a mountain hideaway with a fabulous view. Tack was a great kisser. Tack didn't pin me to the bed in a way that demanded closeness and promised safety but he expected closeness all the same, just not the same way.

That was all good but I still wouldn't be anywhere but where I was right then.

Even so, I wondered if Lawson was a cuddler.

I watched Hawk expertly flip one side of the omelet

over, drop the spatula, turn off the stove and grab the skillet to slide the omelet on a waiting plate. He did this all one-handed, not letting me go.

"You left out the yolks," I informed him.

"Babe," he replied, then he shuffled me a few feet in order to get to a drawer. He opened it, grabbed a fork and shuffled me back to his plate. I watched him cut into the omelet and then I watched the fork as he lifted a piece to his mouth. I kept watching as he chewed and swallowed, his eyes on me. "You want one?" he asked.

I fought back a lip curl by pressing them together and shook my head.

He chuckled, deep and manly. Then he went back to his omelet.

I slid out from under his arm and walked to the fridge. There was a big, rectangular magnet on the side, printed on it a tiny calendar (and, incidentally, this calendar was two years old). On top of the calendar it said "Zip's Gun Emporium" and under that in italics *For all your gun and ammo needs.* It was my only choice. Hawk didn't decorate his fridge with cute magnets and photos and stupid shit like I did.

I resolved to buy a good magnet, one of those clear plastic picture frame ones or maybe one that had a nice edging, and before I could lose my nerve, I unfolded the photo and stuck it to the fridge with Zip's calendar magnet.

I slowly turned to face Hawk and braced.

My eyes hit his, his eyes were on the photo and his face was that blank mask.

"Drop the mask, Cabe," I ordered gently, and his eyes sliced to me.

"I appreciate what you're tryin' to do, Gwen, but not ready for that shit," he replied.

"You carry them in your wallet," I pointed out, still speaking gently.

"Not ready for that shit, Gwen," he repeated.

"Then you need to get ready," I returned quietly, "because, see, last night, when you forgave me, I entered Badass World but *you* entered Cosmo Girl World and in Cosmo Girl World, there are rules. You don't live a narrow life that includes nothing but work and work-related leisure activities. You don't wipe your environment clean of personality. And you don't keep your emotions in a stranglehold. You go to movies. You go out to nice restaurants. You go out to not-so-nice restaurants if they have fantastic food. You sit around with friends doing nothing but drinking, eating, laughing and bonding. You inject your personality and taste in your surroundings so when people who care about you visit you, they can be surrounded by you. We're starting with that," I pointed at the picture, "by bringing Simone and Sophie into the light because there are people in your life who miss them, not as much as you do, but they do. And you miss them and they don't belong folded up and hidden in your wallet, they belong out in the open." I paused, sucked in breath and finished. "We'll graduate to the air hockey table."

The mask cracked when his lips twitched and his eyebrows went up. "Air hockey table?"

"I vote that first, pool table next and then Ping-Pong. Along the back wall. That is, after you put in a downstairs bathroom, maybe a sauna and also a hot tub," I added extras as they came to me.

He lost his fight with his smile and ordered softly, "Come here, Sweet Pea."

I walked to him and he folded me in his arms.

I tipped my head back just in time for his mouth to touch mine.

When he lifted his head, he whispered, "All right, they can come into the light."

"Thanks, baby," I whispered back. "But they already are, aren't they?"

His brows drew together. "Come again?"

"That chair, rug, table and lamp," I replied. "That's from your life with them."

His arms got tight, super tight, and I held him close as he battled. Then he relaxed and nodded.

"Her parents were nightmares so she pretty much grew up with her grandparents. Those are from their house. They were movin' to Florida when we were startin' out so they gave them to us and Simone liked havin' them around so even when we started gettin' our own shit, she never got rid of them. When she was nursing Sophie, she always sat in that chair and if I was feedin' her, I always took my girl and did it in that chair. We didn't live in Denver, we lived in South Carolina but when they died, I got out of the Army first chance I could get and moved back to Denver. Before that, I sold everything, everything from our life, except that chair and everything around it."

I closed my eyes, planted my face in his chest and sighed.

Well, I guess if he was going to keep something, he picked the right things. The things Simone treasured and the things that surrounded him with memories of his wife and himself nurturing their baby daughter.

God.

"I can't imagine carrying the weight of your loss, baby," I whispered into his chest, and his hand came to the back of my neck and gave it a squeeze.

"Hope to Christ you never do," he whispered back.

I nodded. I hoped so too.

His hand left my neck and came to my chin, lifting it up. I opened my eyes and his knuckles swept down my cheek.

I really liked it when he did that.

"Speakin' of that, Sweet Pea, you got a call to make."

I sighed again. Then I nodded.

"One thing," he stated when I started to pull away.

I stopped and tipped my head to the side.

He grinned and decreed, "We're startin' with the hot tub."

I pressed my chest deep into his and grinned back.

CHAPTER THIRTY-FOUR

Drowning

"BABE, SERIOUSLY?"

I jumped and whirled to see Hawk standing in the bathroom door looking hot wearing a dark gray suit and deep red shirt open at the collar.

"Jeez, Cabe, you scared the crap out of me."

His eyes shifted the length of me then came back to mine.

"I'm twenty minutes late and you're still not ready?"

I turned to the bathroom mirror, lifted my mascara wand and ignored his impatient question. "How *do* you do that anyway?"

"Gwen, babe, we gotta go. Why are you runnin' so late? You aren't even dressed."

"Well, I made a shoe decision change." I stroked mascara on my lashes. "I'm not wearing the Choos. I'm wearing the Valentinos."

"A shoe decision change leads to bein' more than twenty minutes late?"

"The Choos are silver. The Valentinos are a blush. Sure, the Valentinos have crystal and mesh but I'd gone gray, smoky and drama. The blush requires soft pink, glimmer and dewy. That required total cleanse off and reapplication of makeup," I explained.

Hawk was silent and my eyes shifted to him.

Nope, no less impatient even with an explanation.

I tried a different tactic.

"I won't be a minute," I assured him on a complete lie.

He dug his phone out of the inside of his jacket pocket, flipped it open, hit some buttons and put it to his ear. His eyes came back to me. My eyes went back to the mirror and my mascara wand went back to swiping.

I felt his presence leave and I heard him say, "Bax, Gwen's runnin' late. We're still at her house but leavin' in five."

I finished my makeup and went to my bedroom. Hawk was whereabouts unknown. This happened a lot even though my house wasn't a rambling mansion. Hawk, I'd discovered, could disappear yet stick around just as easily as he could vanish into or appear out of thin air.

At first I found this disturbing. Now I was used to it.

I spritzed with perfume and put the diamond studs in my ears that Dad and Meredith gave me upon graduation from U of C. Then I slipped off my robe and started to dress.

As it was a special occasion, I'd, of course, made a new purchase. I'd done the unthinkable and moved away from the little black dress. This was a little shimmery *dove gray* dress. It had barely there straps that held up a draped bodice and the rest of the dress to my sides just behind my arm-pits. It had no back. At all. The little drape at the back rested against my upper ass. It was short, the skirt hugged my hips, the material clingy on the rest of me.

It was perfect for the Choos. The thing was, three weeks ago, I was shopping with Elvira and I tried on the Valentinos. The Valentinos were the dream, la-la land of shoes. Blush satin. Four-and-three-quarter-inch spiked heel with platform at the sole. Peep-toed pump with a huge see-through, multi-layered mesh bow lined in satin and crystals with more crystals leading up in bands around the foot to the bow on the toe. They were to die for. They were to kill for. They were the impossible dream.

That was until I thanked the shoe person and started to put them back in their box, Elvira whipped out her phone, called Hawk, got the go-ahead and then whipped out the company credit card.

She was in throes of ecstasy. I called Hawk and told him he couldn't possibly, considering they cost nearly double the price of the Choos.

His reply, "Babe," then disconnect.

Elvira bought the shoes. Thirty minutes later, I bought a boatload of sexy underwear, the sexiest of which I put on under my clothes so Hawk could discover them, like unwrapping a present. When he did, he took one look, his pupils dilated instantaneously and it took him approximately three point two five seconds to take them off.

At that point, I decided that I'd have to find another form of gratitude.

I was still searching.

I pulled on the dress and sat on the side of the bed, opening the shoebox and unveiling the Valentinos.

I had vowed to myself to take them back and return them.

I changed my mind.

Then I had vowed to myself I would never wear them. I couldn't possibly walk on what was more than most people's monthly mortgage payments.

However, I again changed my mind.

I was sliding on shoe two when Hawk walked in my bedroom door.

I put my foot to the floor and looked up at him, standing. "Glad you're here, baby. I need you to help me with my bracelet."

I walked to the dresser and opened my jewelry drawer, unearthing the Tiffany's box.

He'd bought me a diamond bracelet too, just as he said, that very next day after we became us for the second time. I told him he couldn't possibly do that either and, when in the store, refused to pick one. So he did.

I pulled the bracelet out of the box and shut the drawer just when I felt Hawk's fingertips on the skin of my side right where the material started. Those fingertips became a hand gliding into my dress, across my ribs and then up where they cupped my opposite breast. Then he pulled me into his front.

"Hawk," I whispered, my head falling back to his shoulder as his thumb swept my nipple and I repeated, "Hawk."

"Hold onto the dresser, baby," he muttered into my ear.

"What?" I breathed as his other hand tugged up the skirt of my dress.

"Hold on," he ordered.

"We're late," I reminded him then sucked in breath when I got another nipple swipe.

"We're gonna be later," Hawk replied.

"But—"

"Hold on," he repeated, his hand sliding into the front of my panties.

Oh God.

He hit the golden spot.

Oh *God*.

My head turned so my forehead was pressed to his neck.

"We'll be quick now," he whispered. "But later I'll show you how I really feel about this dress."

"'Kay," I agreed but I did it on a moan because the fingers on both his hands moved.

*   *   *

I crossed my legs in the Camaro, studying my shoes at the same time adjusting my bracelet on my wrist for no reason except I liked to remind myself it was there.

"Okay, well, we have to come up with an excuse. You needing to work and me needing a makeup change isn't going to cut it. We're seriously late," I said into the car.

"Babe, we don't need an excuse. Anyone who sees you in that dress and those shoes will know exactly why we're late."

I felt my face pale, actually felt it, and turned my head to look at him. "That isn't true."

"Okay, I'll amend my statement. Any *man* who sees you in that dress and those shoes will know exactly why we're late. Including your dad."

"Ack!" I gagged then put my hands up to my ears and chanted, "La la la."

Through my chanting I heard Hawk laugh.

When it seemed it was safe, I stopped chanting and dropped my hands.

Hawk started speaking. "Got an interesting call today."

"Yeah?" I prompted when he said no more.

"Developers," he replied, and I turned to look at him again. "This is their fourth call in as many months. They want the warehouse and the space around it, all of which I own. They've been offering bullshit but their offer today got motivating."

"What?" I whispered.

It had been four months since Hawk and I went back to us. Four really good months. It was the beginning of July. The weather was nice. The days were long. Our passion (obviously) hadn't cooled. But things had changed.

Now I was tied so tight to him I was certain I'd never get loose and I didn't want to. The same with being in so deep, I'd never surface.

But, even drowning in Hawk, I didn't lose a hint of me.

I lived my life, edited my books, met my girls, went shopping, went out to dinner, went to movies, sometimes alone, sometimes with my friends and sometimes he was a part of that.

Hawk worked and he worked a lot. But when he was with me, I had his total focus. We'd seen several movies together. We went out to dinner often, mainly because I didn't eat like he did (and wasn't going to) and he could order food like he liked and I didn't have to cook two meals (though, on occasion, I did this too). When he had time, he'd hang at mine or I'd hang at his.

No matter if our days took us separate ways, we slept together every night. Sometimes he'd be with me and we'd go to bed together. Sometimes I'd feel his warm hand on the small of my back in the middle of the night. Sometimes he'd call and tell me he wanted me at his place and I'd go. I had a key, though he didn't have one to mine (that I knew of) but he didn't need one.

Our relationship wasn't easy. It wasn't mellow. It wasn't comfortable and sedate. He was too bossy and I was too much of a smartass. We bantered and sometimes we fought. But I'd learned I was completely unable to endure Hawk being mad at me and then I'd noticed that Hawk felt the same. No grudges were ever held. We created sparks but those sparks never caught the kind of fire that could do damage. Instead, we got over it and moved on.

And I liked this. This was good. I liked him in my space and I liked to be in his. I had sweet pea lotion and bath wash at his. My own stick of deodorant was in his medicine cabinet. He had one in mine. It stood next to his razor.

I'd bought a sweet frame for Simone and Sophie and at the same time I bought two more.

One had a picture of Hawk and me that Tracy took at Leo's birthday party. I was pressed against Hawk's side, my arms around him, my head tipped back, my nose pressed to his jaw and I was laughing. Hawk had his arm around my shoulders and he was looking slightly down and to the side, also laughing. That picture was on Hawk's fridge.

The other frame was on mine and it had a picture in it that Elvira took. We were walking through the surveillance room at his base, my arm curled around his back, his around my shoulders. Hawk's head was turned to the side and he was looking at and listening to Jorge. I was looking over my shoulder at Elvira and laughing at something she said.

I loved that photo. I didn't know why. Maybe the fact it was a candid that captured the casual way we were together, holding each other, walking together, Hawk's profile so handsome, my face looking happy. And, of course, I was having a really good hair day.

He couldn't sell the warehouse. We were settled. We had a system. We had a way that was our way.

And where would we set up the air hockey table (when he bought it)?

"You're thinking of selling?" I asked.

"Yeah, they got that kind of cake, they want it, so they'll offer more. They offer more, seriously, babe, be a fool not to."

"But I thought you liked the warehouse. I thought you needed space. There's not a lot of places you can get that kind of space, Cabe."

"Findin' I don't need that kind of space anymore, Sweet Pea, and you can't raise kids in a place like that."

I sucked in so much air it was a wonder Hawk didn't immediately pass out due to lack of oxygen.

"Gwen?" he called.

"Kids?" I choked.

He was silent. So was I mostly because I was struggling for breath as visions of dark-haired, dimple-faced baby commandos wearing miniature cargo pants danced through my head.

Finally he muttered, "Fuck."

"Fuck what?" I asked.

"Shit, babe, saw you with Crisanto and Javier, thought you liked kids."

"I—"

"Thought you liked 'em so much, you'd want 'em."

"I—"

"Fuck, Gwen."

"Fuck what?" My voice was rising mainly because I was freaking out but also because he wasn't letting me talk.

He pulled to the side of the road, stopped, turned to me and his eyes caught mine.

Then he muttered again, "Fuck."

"Fuck what!" I almost shouted.

"It isn't a good time to talk about this."

"Hawk, you need—"

"It's your parents' anniversary."

"Hawk!" I snapped. "You need to tell me what's flipping you out."

"I want kids."

I stared at him, my heart beating so hard I could swear my dress fluttered.

He wasn't saying he wanted kids as much as he was saying he wanted kids *with me*.

I mean, he wanted kids, but he was saying *he wanted kids with me*.

Cabe "Hawk" Delgado wanted kids with me!

Yay!

Oh shit. I was going to start crying and ruin my makeup.

"It's important to me, baby," he said softly.

I swallowed. Then I asked, "How many do you want?"

"Two or three."

"Boys or girls?"

"Don't care."

I didn't either. I didn't care. I didn't care at all.

My vision went blurry as my mind filled with Hawk holding our child and feeding it a bottle.

Then my belly got squishy.

Then I felt his knuckles glide down my cheek and I refocused when he said quietly, "I'd be happy with one, Gwen."

"Only children can get spoiled. You have to have at least two. Siblings are important. And if we start with two boys, we have to have a girl because brothers should have a sister. But if we start with two girls, we have to go for a boy because sisters should have a brother. I always wanted a brother. A son of my father would have been able to beat the shit out of boyfriends that broke my heart. I wouldn't have had to resort to cookie dough and it would have saved Scott a lot of money in divorce attorneys, seeing as he'd still be in a coma."

I stopped talking and felt it. The air in the Camaro had turned electric.

"You sayin' that for me or do you want kids?" he asked.

"Both," I answered.

Suddenly my seat belt was undone and zipped back so fast I cried out in surprise. Then Hawk's did. I was then plucked right out of my seat and wedged between him and the steering wheel, my ass in his lap, his hand in my hair, his other arm around me and his mouth hot and heavy on mine delivering a very wet, very heated kiss that included some hand action when his started to roam.

He released my mouth but kept me wedged and I blinked as he spoke.

"They offer higher, I'll accept."

"Okay," I breathed.

"You got a problem with me movin' into your place?"

"No," I replied instantly, my heart beating, my belly squishy, my mind spinning cartwheels of joy.

"All right," he whispered.

"You sure you don't need space anymore?"

"That kind of space means, you're there, you need to go somewhere, anywhere you go is far away from me so, yeah, I don't need that space anymore."

Oh my God.

I knew what he was saying. I knew what he meant and I lifted my hand to his jaw.

"You're in deep with me, aren't you, baby?" I whispered my question just to confirm.

"Drowning," he whispered back.

Oh my *God*. He felt the same as me!

"I love you, Cabe."

The minute I said it, he curled me into him so we were pressed together and his face was in my neck.

"Love you too, Sweet Pea."

He loved me.

Thank God, he loved me.

I relaxed against him but slid my hand from his jaw to the back of his neck.

"Yay," I whispered in his ear and felt him smile against my neck.

He kissed me there, his head moved slightly, his tongue touched the skin behind my ear then his head moved again. He kissed my lips lightly, once, twice, again before he nipped my lip, unwedged me and deposited me in my seat.

He rebuckled, I followed suit and I took a moment to feel my joy.

Then I grabbed my clutch from the floor, opened the clip, pulled out my lip gloss and flipped down the visor, muttering, "Twice tonight you've ruined my lip gloss and we're not even at the restaurant."

He pulled into traffic, muttering back, "Babe."

*   *   *

Meredith celebrated her and Dad's anniversary like it was a national holiday. She didn't focus on the special ones, she had a party every year.

When I was a kid, and money wasn't as plentiful, if the anniversary fell on a weekday, Meredith took the day off to cook and had friends and family over for a huge, buffet extravaganza. After Ginger and I left the house and things got more comfortable, these celebrations moved to a variety of locales in Denver.

Tonight's was at McCormick's Fish House and Bar at the Oxford Hotel. Fantastic seafood and steaks. It was elegant but still Old West Denver atmosphere, great bar and just a short walk away was Oxford's Cruise Room, arguably *the* coolest bar in Denver due to its art deco décor and the talent the bartenders had with a martini shaker.

Hawk and I walked, arms around each other, into the private room and saw the gang was all there.

Since Meredith adopted all my friends, Tracy was in attendance although I didn't see one of her jerky boyfriends with her. I couldn't spy Cam and Leo but I knew they had to be there somewhere. Elvira was also there. And so were Gus and Maria, Jury, with a lush, gorgeous Mexican American woman wearing a fabulous red and black dress and Von and his wife, Lucia.

And I saw straight away Troy and his whiny girlfriend, Hanna were there.

The past four months had not been good between Troy and me. He was not pleased that Hawk and I became us again and he told me so, giving dire warnings that if it happened once, it would happen again. I figured Troy was just trying to be a friend, he and I were solid deep down and he'd get over this.

He hadn't.

We saw each other, mostly him coming over. But, when he came over once and Hawk was there, he left immediately and made no bones about why he was doing it. From that point on, he called before coming to be certain Hawk wasn't there or intending to be there. I gave him these assurances, even though this annoyed me. Sure, what Hawk said to him was harsh but weeks were sliding into months, Troy had to see Hawk was making me happy and if he gave Hawk a chance, like everyone else was, he'd see Hawk was a good guy. And, bottom line, if he was a true friend, he'd get over it, for me.

I mean, I put up with Hanna with not a word and she was whiny and annoying and I wasn't the only one who thought so.

Unfortunately, during one of the times I assured him Hawk wasn't coming over, Hawk had surprised me by showing. Even after Troy had just opened a beer, he left it unsipped, glared at Hawk, told me he'd see me later and left.

What surprised me about this was more than Troy's behavior. It was Hawk's. Hawk was like Camille. If he had something to say, he'd say it. He was straight and could be gentle, but he didn't hesitate communicating what was on his mind. But he left me to deal with Troy without a word or comment. I thought this said a lot, mostly that Hawk knew Troy meant something to me and he wasn't going to try to sway me either way, just let it play out and he'd be there at the end. But it wouldn't be an end where, if Troy and I sorted things out, Hawk had said something about a friend I cared about that he couldn't take back.

"You're wearing the Valentinos!" Tracy shrieked, half dashing, half dancing to us, clapping her hands, Elvira following her.

I gave her a hug and she moved to Hawk to kiss his cheek as I gave Elvira a hug. Elvira didn't move to Hawk to kiss his cheek. She just nodded to him, stepped back and gave me an eye sweep

"Girl, you are hot!" she declared. "That dress is hot. Those shoes are hot. And that expression on your face that says you just got you some is *hot!*"

I froze. Hawk chuckled and pulled me closer.

"Told you," he whispered in my ear.

Before I could reply, Meredith and Dad approached, Gus and Maria bearing down behind them.

"Hey, sweetie," Meredith said as she got close and gave me a hug.

"Sorry we're late," I told her while hugging her. She stepped back but kept hold of my upper arms.

"It's still cocktail hour. We don't sit down for twenty minutes so you're not late." She smiled and turned to Hawk while Dad turned to me.

After Dad, I got hugs from Maria and Gus then everyone assumed their places in our huddle, Gus staring at me with a wicked grin on his face.

"Nice dress," he observed, his meaning clear. I closed my eyes and Hawk chuckled again.

Moving on!

I turned to Dad and Meredith. "Can we give you your presents now?" I asked.

"Sure, honey," Meredith replied. I opened my dark gray satin clutch with its crystal clasp while juggling the large manila envelope.

I pulled out the smaller white envelope and handed it to Dad.

"Season tickets to the Broncos," I announced, and Dad stared at me. "Forty-yard line. Hawk knows someone." That was when Dad turned his stare at Hawk. "Happy anniversary, Dad," I finished.

"Holy fuck," Dad muttered.

"They're from me and Cabe," I replied, even though Hawk knew someone, I bought the tickets. This caused a fight which I won. Hawk could spoil me but I put my foot down about spoiling Dad. It cost a whack but the simple matter of fact was that Dad was worth it.

"I don't know what to say," Dad whispered.

"Don't say anything and give me another hug." I smiled at him.

He turned his eyes to me but he didn't smile. He lifted his hand and cupped my cheek and the expression on his face caused tears to sting my eyes. He had a daughter he could not see in protective custody and a daughter who had gone through hell because of her. That said, I was alive, breathing, wearing a fantastic dress and fabulous shoes, happy and I loved him enough to get him season tickets to the Broncos, something he'd always wanted. His eyes hit mine and I knew from the look of them that he was counting his blessings and I could see that the Broncos tickets weren't high on that list but I definitely was.

Then he dropped his hand and shook Hawk's, clapping him on the shoulder at the same time.

Again, moving on.

I handed Meredith the manila envelope. "That's for you."

Her brows drew together, Dad looked down at her and she opened the clasps on the envelope.

"It's just a formality," I stated, suddenly feeling nervous. "And it was Cabe's idea. I mean, really, it happened on your wedding day when you let me walk down the aisle with you. I'm just making it official."

She pulled out the papers and looked at me. "Making what official?"

"Those are adoption papers. If you sign them, I'm legally your daughter."

Everyone sucked in breath but Meredith's mouth dropped open and her eyes got big. I could usually read Meredith, heck, anyone could, but I couldn't read that. I didn't know what to expect when I gave the papers to her but I'd day-dreamed about it a lot. I knew she loved me but it was a posh anniversary party at McCormick's, she wasn't going to do cartwheels. She couldn't, not in four-inch heels. But I'd hoped at least for a smile.

Therefore I rushed on. "I know, it's kinda loopy, adopt-ing a thirty-three-year-old woman but...um...why not?" I faltered when she just stared at me and I wondered if I'd insulted her. "I mean...I don't want to imply that I haven't always thought of you as my mom but I just want to...I don't know, make sure you know that, uh...that's how I feel and it always has been."

Meredith didn't move, nor did she speak.

"You don't have to sign them," I assured her. "It's okay. Nothing between us changes. I—"

I shut up when she jerked her body toward Dad and whis-pered, "Find me a pen, Bax."

She asked Dad but it was Gus who took off. Hawk's arm curled around my neck and he pulled my front into his side as the tears filled my eyes.

Meredith looked up at me. "Now...sweetie, now *I* don't know what to say."

"Sign the papers, that says it all," Hawk replied for me, but he did it gently.

Meredith looked down at the papers and when she lifted her eyes back to me they were filled with wet.

"This is the best present I've ever had," she whispered.

Tracy emitted a muted sob. I moved away from Hawk and hugged Meredith as a tear slid down my cheek.

"I've always loved you," I said quietly in her ear, and her arms spasmed around me. "I think I fell in love with you the first time I saw you."

"Oh, sweetie," she whispered, holding on tighter, so I did too.

We hugged for a long time then I pulled away and Meredith moved into Hawk and gave him a squeeze and kiss on the cheek. Gus showed with a pen, she signed the papers, put them in the envelope and when she handed them to me, I handed them to Hawk. He folded the envelope double and slid it into his inside jacket pocket. It was his attorney's firm that had drawn up the papers and it would probably be Elvira who returned them to be filed.

"I need a reload," Elvira announced, and I looked at her to see her eyes were on Hawk. "And your woman has been here all of five minutes and she doesn't have a martini glass in her hand. What? You think you can buy her twelve-hundred-dollar shoes and that gives you the right to slack on bein' a gentleman?"

Tracy giggled.

But I turned, leaned into Hawk and looked up at him. "Actually, just FYI, giving me twelve-hundred-dollar shoes *totally* gives you the right to slack on drink deliveries."

Hawk's dimples made an appearance then disappeared

when I couldn't see them anymore because his head dropped and his lips gave me a light kiss.

He lifted his head and asked all around, "Anyone else?"

"Me," Tracy put in.

"I already gave my order," Elvira added.

"A white wine, honey, if you don't mind," Meredith stated.

"Cuba libre, *querido,*" Maria muttered.

"I'll go with you," Gus offered, and Hawk and Gus walked away but Maria got in my space, so close it was surprising, and I looked down at her.

"My boys," she started, "look like their father, act like their father and he gave them something else." She paused then finished on a huge grin, "Good taste."

I stared at her a second then threw my head back and laughed.

                    *   *   *

Dinner was over but the party (in other words the drinking) was not.

I was sitting beside Leo but listening to Mrs. Mayhew and Erma, both hilariously tipsy, as they shared stories of Dad and Meredith's anniversaries past with their other audience member, Elvira.

Suddenly, Leo took my hand and my head turned, my eyes going to his face to see he was gazing across the room.

My eyes followed his and my heart warmed. Cam was standing with Meredith who was holding Cam's hand by the fingers, admiring the diamond Leo had slid on earlier that night when he'd asked her to marry him.

The reason they were late.

"Lingerie parties, darlin'," I heard Leo whisper in my ear. I smiled and turned to face him. "You promised," he finished when he caught my eyes.

I squeezed his hand and whispered back, "You happy?"

"She is, so, yeah," Leo answered.

That was a great freaking answer.

"Love you, babe," I told him softly.

"Lingerie," he replied.

"Gotcha," I whispered on a smile.

"Gwen, can I have a moment?"

Leo and I both twisted our necks and tipped our heads back to see Troy standing there, his face set, looking unhappy.

Shit.

I nodded, squeezed Leo's hand again and stood. Troy moved in, putting his hand to the small of my back and leading me out of the room. I searched for Hawk as I went so he'd know where I was going and who I was with but I couldn't find him.

We made it to a hallway and I turned to Troy.

"Troy, I—"

"Just wait a second, Gwen, would you?" he asked tersely, and I wondered what was on his mind and why he seemed in such a foul mood.

Though it wasn't hard to guess. Hawk was not shy with public displays of affection. This was coupled with him being an alpha male which meant PDA was liberally mixed with possessive branding moves, such as curling his arm around the back of my chair while we were seated or running his hand over my ass when he saw a man's eyes on that ass. Shit like that.

Shit that I'd noticed, as the night wore on, Troy didn't like much.

We turned a corner and both of us stopped dead on the carpet when we saw Hawk, his back to us, about eight feet down the hall. There was one female hand at his bent head, one arm tight around his back.

I sucked in a silent, searing breath and felt my head reel as Troy's arm curled around my waist and held tight.

Maybe a nanosecond later Hawk moved, the woman's arms disappeared and it hit me that he'd set her away and he'd done it roughly.

"What the fuck?" he clipped, his voice so harsh, it was acid and it was a wonder the wallpaper didn't melt off the walls.

"I—" a woman replied.

"You told me you wanted to talk about my woman and your man," Hawk went on.

"I—" she repeated.

Hawk cut her off again. "Jesus, fuck, what's the matter with you?"

"I—" she tried yet again and failed yet again.

"Give me one good reason not to go back into that room and tell your man you put your hands and your fuckin' mouth on me," Hawk demanded.

"He won't believe you," she got out. My body froze solid as Troy's did the same at my side.

That voice was Troy's whiny, annoying, *grasping* girl-friend, Hanna.

"You're right," Hawk replied. "He won't, which, I gotta tell you, woman, sucks because he's a good man and he could do a lot fuckin' better than *you*."

Oh God.

I had to end this for Troy and I had to do it now.

"Cabe, honey," I called, and Hawk's body jerked around to face us. I saw his eyes were narrow, his jaw hard and his gaze slid over me to Troy.

"Fuck," he muttered.

Hanna was staring at Troy, her eyes huge, face pale.

"Troy," she whispered.

"I hope you have money for a cab," Troy replied.

"Uh..." She took a step forward but I moved into Troy, turning into his side, my arms going around his middle. I pulled him a step back so she stopped. "Troy, it isn't what—" she tried.

Troy interrupted, "Stop, Hanna, it was. Don't add being a fucking liar to being a fucking slut."

Hanna winced. I gave Troy a squeeze. Hawk studied Troy and when no one said anything further, his head turned to Hanna.

"I think that's your cue to get the fuck outta here," he prompted. She looked up at him, her pale face got whiter and she nodded.

Then she scurried toward Troy and me as I glared sharp, lethal daggers at her, none of which, unfortunately, formed and drew blood. She skirted us because neither Troy nor I moved and she hustled around the corner.

Hawk approached, his eyes on Troy, and he stopped in front of us.

He looked down at me and asked softly, "You got this, baby?"

I nodded up at him. He lifted his chin, glanced at Troy and walked around us on my side, his hand sliding along my hip as he did it.

See. Total alpha male possessive branding moves even when no one was around to see them!

Hawk disappeared.

I moved into Troy's front, not letting him go, and looked into his stony face.

"Do we need beer, tequila or a trip to the firing range?" I asked quietly, and Troy's arm around my waist gave a reflexive squeeze.

"Shit, Gwen," he whispered.

I pressed my cheek to his shoulder and held on tighter.

"Shit," he repeated over my head.

"Hawk's right, honey, you can *so* do better than her."

His other arm slid around me and it was his turn to hold on tight.

We held each other for a while in silence before Troy broke it to mutter, "Maybe he isn't a dick."

I pressed my lips together but relaxed in his arms.

Then I lifted my cheek from his shoulder to put my lips to his ear.

"Missed you," I whispered. "So much, Troy. So *freaking* much. It's good to have you back, babe."

Troy buried his face in my neck and I closed my eyes as I felt the heady sensation of everything in my world, everything (save my sister being in protective custody, though I focused on the word "protective" when I thought of that) turning into the absolute, most perfect daydream. Better than any daydream I could imagine and not only because it was better but also because it was real.

Then I gave Troy a squeeze, decided for him and therefore announced, "Tequila."

Troy's face came out of my neck, he looked at me, gave me a small, not very happy smile and whispered, "Right."

I sighed then I turned my friend in the direction of the bar.

* * *

Oh God.

I was going to bring it home!

"Baby," I whispered, my face in Hawk's neck, my arms around his shoulders, his hands were at my hips and I was riding him hard.

His head turned so his lips were at my ear.

"Mouth," he growled, I lifted and twisted my head instantly, my mouth going to his as a moan slid up my throat. "Harder, baby, you're almost there."

"Hawk," I whimpered into his mouth as I drove myself down on him harder and both my hands went to his head.

"Cabe," he corrected on a thick rumble. "You call me Cabe when you bring it home."

"Cabe," I whispered then gasped, my back and neck arching as it burned through me.

Hawk's hand slid into my hair, fisted and tugged gently, making my back arch further. I felt his mouth close over my nipple, sucking it deep, prolonging my orgasm as new heat blistered through me. Then he released my nipple, his other hand yanked me down hard on his cock, he buried his face between my breasts and groaned.

Beautiful.

We came down and when he finished, his lips slid along the inside of my breast and he kissed me there. I put pressure on his head, it tilted back, mine tipped down and his hand in my hair guided my mouth to his where he gave me a sweet, hot, wet, delicious kiss.

When he was done, I bragged on a whisper, "I brought it home."

I felt his mouth smile against mine. "Yeah you did, baby."

I lifted my mouth an inch from his and slid one hand to his neck, the other to his jaw.

"Did it work for you?" I asked softly.

The dimples, already there, got deeper. "You seriously askin' that shit?"

"Um…" I replied.

His hand in my hair brought my lips back to his and he responded, "Yeah, Gwen," he gave me a light kiss then his head dropped and he kissed the base of my throat where he murmured, "Oh yeah."

"Yay," I whispered.

He ran his nose along my jaw then he pulled slightly away, his hands going to my dress, which was bunched at my waist. He pulled the wisp of material up, my arms went up with it then he tossed it aside.

Normally, I would have concerns about an expensive satin dress being tossed to the floor.

At that moment, I didn't give a shit.

Hawk fell back, taking me with him, then he rolled me to my back, unfortunately disconnecting from me but I took that loss because I gained his heat and weight.

His mouth was at my neck and he started speaking. "Next time you wear those shoes, babe, takin' you on your knees and you're not takin' 'em off."

I twisted my neck and his head came up so he could look at me.

"Do you like those shoes that much?"

"Like the dress more, Sweet Pea, but those shoes are hot."

I blinked at him. I could understand the dress. It showed more skin than it covered and the parts that covered skin clung to flesh but I was shocked a badass could like Cinderella-perfect shoes.

"Seriously?" I asked.

"Why are you surprised?"

"Um...they're satin and have crystals and if the Brothers Grimm were clairvoyant and knew they would one day exist, Cinderella would have those shoes. Those are not commando shoes."

"No, they're commando's woman's shoes. The heel is high and you got great legs, babe, and the perfect ass but those shoes do the impossible and make your legs and ass even fuckin' better."

This was true.

Though I wouldn't describe my ass as perfect, it made my belly squishy to hear Hawk do it.

"So," I slid my hands down his back to wrap my arms around his waist, "you're saying you bought me those shoes because *you* like them."

"No, Sweet Pea, I bought you those shoes because when I saw you after buyin' them, the minute you looked at me I knew it meant a lot to you. Your face was gentle." His finger came to my temple and then slid down my hairline before his hand curled around my neck and when he spoke again, his voice was soft. "I'd do just about anything to make you look at me like that, Gwen. And I'll keep doin' it as long as I can surprise you and know, from that look, you like me spoilin' you, it means somethin' to you and I'm gonna keep doin' it and only stop when I don't get that in return."

God. *God.* I loved this man.

"Hawk," I whispered.

"Helped that you gave great underwear as a thank-you."

I grinned at him. Then I reminded him, "You took it right off."

"Babe, your body in that underwear, burned on my brain. Fuck, I can still see it."

I giggled and Hawk gave me his dimples.

"Well, this is good to know," I informed him. "I thought you were a take-it-off-because-it-gets-in-the-way man. I'm pleased to know my efforts were appreciated."

His head dipped and his mouth touched mine before he whispered, "Everything about you is appreciated, Gwendolyn."

My stomach melted, my heart skipped and I felt a tingle in my throat.

"Cabe," I whispered back then my arms left his waist, my hands went to either side of his head and I shared, "You should know, I'm living in a daydream. A real one. I've never been this happy. Not ever, baby, not in my whole life." I lifted my head, slid my arms around his shoulders and kissed his jaw then said in his ear, "Thank you, Hawk."

He rolled us to our sides, his arms closing around me, his mouth going to my ear in return and he murmured, "You're welcome, Sweet Pea."

I sighed into his throat.

He touched his tongue to the skin behind my ear then turned me in his arms so my back was to his front, he separated from me only to turn off the light and then curled into me, saying his nonverbal goodnight.

I made mine verbal.

"'Night, baby, love you."

His arm gave me a squeeze and I felt his face in my hair.

"Love you too, Gwen," he said quietly then ordered, "Go to sleep."

So bossy.

But seriously, did I care?

The answer to that was a big fat *no!*

Therefore I snuggled my ass into him and replied, "'Kay."

And, about five seconds later, I did what I was told.

CHAPTER THIRTY-FIVE

Deal?

I FELT HAWK's lips at my hip, they disappeared but his hand moved up, taking the covers with it and I opened my eyes to see the day had just about dawned.

I twisted my neck and saw he was bent over me in the bed, fully clothed.

"Shit to do, Sweet Pea," he muttered, then dropped his head to give me a light kiss.

"'Kay," I muttered back when his mouth left mine.

"See you tonight," he went on, pulling the covers up to my shoulder.

"'Kay," I replied, turning back, tucking my hands under my cheek and closing my eyes.

I felt him shift my hair from my neck and then his lips at my ear.

"Love you, baby," he whispered.

"Love you too, Cabe," I whispered back.

Then he was gone.

* * *

My cell chirped telling me I had a text and my eyes opened again to see the day had now fully dawned.

It was Friday. I had work. I was facing another deadline on Monday. I was close to finishing and if I hit it that day, I'd have the weekend to do whatever I wanted. And I needed to get my work done and have the weekend to do what I wanted, most of this being relaxing. Some preliminary stuff for the first of Ginger's trials was close to starting and Meredith, Dad and I intended to be there when she was in the courthouse. This meant I needed time to be able to be there and this meant I needed a life devoid of stress.

Luckily, and unusually, the second part of that was already the case. I just needed to hit it to make the first part true.

I turned in bed, lifted up and reached for my phone which was sitting by my happy kitty snow globe.

Then my eyes spied the Polaroid that Hawk must have taken out of his jacket pocket and put on the nightstand.

I picked it up and looked at it. Jury's girlfriend, Gloria, had taken it last night. It was me in my fabulous dress with my infinitely more fabulous shoes sitting in Hawk's lap, my arms around his shoulders, his arms around my waist. My head was tipped back because I was laughing hard at something Elvira had said. Hawk was laughing too but he was doing it looking at the camera.

It was a great picture and I wished it wasn't Polaroid because I wanted to blow it up and put it over my fireplace.

I dropped the photo, a smile playing at my lips and picked up my phone. I opened the text and my body froze but as it did, heat seared through my lungs at the same time every inch of skin tingled as if encased in ice.

It was a picture text but there was a message. The message said, *Trade for Ginger*.

The picture was tiny but I could see it. With a trembling body and shaking hands, I sat up in bed and touched the button on my phone to zoom in and enlarge the photo.

Then the whimper of fear slid up my throat.

Hawk.

Oh God. Oh God. Oh God. *Hawk*.

He was hanging from something. I knew this because his arms were in the frame but high over his head. It was a photo mostly of his head, tipped forward; he looked unconscious. Blood was sliding out of his ear, down his cheek, joined by blood coming from his lip and his cheekbone was red and swelling.

The phone chirped in my hand as I stared at the photo and hyperventilated and when it did, I jumped. I closed the photo and went to the texts.

I had a new one. It was only one word:

Deal?

I started breathing through my nose, not able to get enough oxygen in and my eyes, of their own accord, slid to the Polaroid.

Laughing, close, happy.

"You're in deep with me, aren't you, baby?"

"Drowning."

Oh God.

I closed my eyes and I saw the image in the Polaroid burned on my brain.

That was what Hawk saw for eight years. I knew it then. I got it. He saw that picture he carried in his wallet burned on his brain, every time he closed his eyes, every time his guard went down, every time his control slipped. That was why he shut everything out. That was why his world was void. So he'd never lose control and see that image on his brain, the last memory, the last happiness he thought he'd ever have.

I opened my eyes and hit reply.

Then I typed in *Deal* and hit send.

*   *   *

Tack was walking out one of the three big bays in the garage behind the back of Ride. He'd seen my car coming.

A miracle had happened since Hawk and I became us again, Tack and I stayed us too. Of course, this didn't include me sleeping in his bed or letting him touch his tongue to mine but I texted him whenever I thought there was something he needed to know, mostly all things smartass. Tack texted back, mostly all things biker guy smartass reply to cosmo girl smartass comment.

And also, Tracy and I went to a Chaos party that was a freaking hoot, so much fun, and most of the time we spent with Tack and his biker babe drinking tequila shots and eating fantastic barbeque pork sandwiches.

Hawk was okay with this because he knew I was in deep with him but mostly because he took us there and picked us up. He was also okay with this because Suarez sat in a black SUV across the street from Ride, his eyes to binoculars out his window trained on the big hog roast party which was taking place in the huge cement area behind Ride.

I got out of my car and slammed the door as Tack smiled at me.

"Peaches," he called his greeting.

I ran to him and when I closed the distance and he got a good look at my face, his smile died.

"Talk to me, Gwen," he ordered.

"They have Hawk, they want Ginger," I told him.

His body went tight.

"Who?" he asked on a bark.

I pulled my purse off my shoulder and dug into it, shaking my head and saying, "I don't know." I pulled out my phone, found the picture text, opened it and turned it to face Tack.

His eyes dropped to my phone and a muscle worked in his cheek.

"Roarke," he clipped.

I closed my eyes.

"Dog!" Tack barked. My eyes flew open to see he was looking over his shoulder at the bays.

"Tack," I whispered, my hand came up and I curled my fingers in his tee so his head twisted back to me. "I know that you and Hawk...you and me...I know...I..." I shook my head again. "I have to get him back."

"What'd I say to you?" His gravelly voice rumbled deep.

I blinked. "What?"

"What'd I say to you, Gwen?"

"I...I don't know," I whispered.

His hand came up and curled around my neck and it did this tight just before he jerked my neck gently and his face got in mine.

"I said anything for you, Gwen, anything. That means anything. Yeah?"

My eyes filled with tears, I pressed my lips together and I nodded.

"You willin' to give up Ginger?"

Oh God.

"Do I have to?" I asked.

"You gotta tell me what you're willin' to do."

I closed my eyes and he jerked my neck gently so they shot open again.

"Peaches—"

Was I going to say it?

I was going to say it.

"Anything," I whispered, my heart breaking.

He stared into my eyes then he nodded.

He let me go and ordered, "Get home. I'll call." I nodded

but didn't move and noticed Dog and some other bikers had surrounded us. "Now, Gwen," Tack prompted.

I nodded again then rushed to my car.

But I didn't go home.

Because if I was willing to trade my fucked-up sister, who I still loved, for my man, I was willing to do anything.

*   *   *

"Have you lost your fuckin' mind?" Cam screeched.

My eyes jerked to the commandos who were manning their stations in Hawk's command center outside Elvira's office. I'd called the girls for an emergency meeting, both Cam and Tracy were off, Elvira was working, so base it was even though I wasn't sure base was the right place for me.

And I'd just told Cam what I needed.

"Keep your voice down," Elvira ordered, and I looked back at Cam.

"I need you to do it," I whispered.

"First, babe, that info is *not* easy to come by and second, I pulled off that miracle and told you and the Feds lost their key witness in three big cases, I'd not only get my ass fired, I'd probably get it tossed into a jail cell," Cam replied.

Shit. I hadn't thought of that. Why hadn't I thought of that? *Shit.*

Cam providing the intel on Ginger's whereabouts was out.

Elvira had moved to her computer. "Let me work on this," she mumbled.

"Work on what?" Tracy asked.

"I'll pull together a file, talk to some boys, see what they got in places I can't look. There isn't much I can't access, but Hawk kept the Ginger shit and therefore the Roarke shit under heavy password. Zero access except him and Jorge.

That don't mean boys don't know shit and Jorge disappeared this mornin', off-line. He won't know I'm tryin' to hack."

I looked back out at the commandos. It seemed a skeleton crew but it was business as usual. They didn't know their boss was hanging unconscious somewhere, bleeding from his ear.

What did that mean, blood coming from your ear?

I shook my head to clear this thought and looked back at Elvira.

"Do it," I ordered. "But proceed with caution and if you think they can help, you give it to them and mobilize but *only* if you think they won't go commando and put Hawk in jeopardy." Elvira nodded her answer to me but she did it looking at the computer screen and I turned to Cam. "But Lawson doesn't know, nor Leo."

"Babe, I love you and I know you care a lot about Hawk but you gotta let the cops in on this," Cam warned.

"No!" I snapped. "No cops. I'm already taking enough chance with you being here. They're probably watching me."

"Oh God, do you think that's true?" Tracy asked.

"Yes," I replied immediately and then turned to Elvira. "You get anything, call me. I've gotta go."

"Where?" Elvira asked, her eyes not leaving the computer screen.

"Nightingale Investigations," I answered.

"Shit," Cam muttered.

"I'll come with," Tracy offered and I looked at her.

"No, babe," I told her.

"I'm coming with," Tracy repeated.

"No, Trace, this is dangerous. Stay here, maybe you can help Elvira," I suggested, knowing this wasn't true.

Elvira's fingers flew over the keyboard.

"I'm coming with," Tracy stated again.

"Trace—" I started, but stopped when she grabbed my hand.

"I'm…coming…*with*."

I stared into her eyes.

Then I whispered, "Okay."

"Shit," Cam muttered again.

* * *

Tracy sat next to me in my car. I drove and tried to be focused as panic threatened to overwhelm me. Tracy was beeping buttons on her phone.

The beeping stopped and she put the phone to her ear.

"Troy?" I heard her say and nearly ran off the road.

My eyes flew to her. "Trace! What are you—?"

She waved a hand at me and I looked back at the road.

Tracy kept talking. "Yeah, listen, now's not a good time. You know those baddies who were after Ginger?" Pause. "Well, they have Hawk."

"Tracy!" I cried.

She ignored me. "I know, I know. They want to trade him for Ginger and I need you to do your thing, find any properties owned by Nelson Roarke or any owned by any companies he's involved with."

Wow. That was a good idea.

That would also probably ping on some Federal Bureau of Investigation Super Nerd Computer in the basement of some federal building.

"Trace," I tried again.

"No, of course we're not going to do anything stupid," she lied through her teeth.

I closed my eyes then quickly opened them and turned off Speer heading to 15th.

"Okay, if you don't want to help, don't help. But if

something happens to Hawk and Gwen gains seventy pounds by going on a diet of pure cookie dough, don't come to Nordstrom and expect to use my employee discount!" she snapped then flipped her phone closed and stated, "He'll run the searches. He likes Armani suits."

"I can't believe you did that, Trace, he could get into trouble."

"Well, sure, but Hawk could also get dead."

This was true.

I whimpered.

Tracy's voice got soft. "It's going to be okay, babe."

I pressed my lips together and turned on 15th.

* * *

My phone rang when we were on the sidewalk. I saw it said "Tack Calling" so I looked at Tracy.

"Can you get us coffees? I have to take this."

She looked at my phone then at me then she nodded and headed toward The Market on Larimer.

I flipped the phone open and put it to my ear.

"Tack."

"Peaches, how long they give you?" he asked.

"They didn't," I answered.

There was silence then, "All right, babe, there's bad news and that's all I got."

My heart squeezed so I squeezed my eyes shut too to try to block out the pain.

"What's the bad news?" I whispered.

"We went in soft to every place we know Roarke works dirty. We got nothin'. We're outta leads."

Shit!

I opened my eyes. "I know someone who's a mortgage broker. He's checking databases now. If he gets anything you haven't got, can I feed it to you?"

"Don't wait, babe, get his ass on it and call me."

"Thanks," I whispered.

"Later," he replied then hung up.

I looked down the street where Tracy had disappeared.

Then I made a decision.

I flipped my phone open and went to my text screen.

Then I typed in, *I can't get to her but if you trade Hawk for me, you got Tack, Chaos MC, Hawk's boys and probably Mitch Lawson who'll find her and trade Ginger for me. No tricks. No joke. Him for me and you get Ginger. Deal?*

I hit send and stood on the sidewalk waiting. People might have passed but I didn't notice. I just stood there staring at my phone.

Then it chirped.

I flipped it open.

She's at 83 Bannock. You get her, text. That's the deal.

Shit! How did I get my sister out of an FBI safe house?

Shit!

My phone chirped again and I looked down at it.

Call off Chaos or you'll get a body to bury.

I closed my eyes.

Then I opened them, flipped my phone shut, flipped my phone open and headed to my car as I called Tack.

Tracy would find her way home. She'd be pissed but she'd find her way home. And that home wouldn't be a penitentiary which was where I was headed.

If I was lucky.

I got Tack's voicemail, left a message that called him off, flipped my phone shut, got in my car and headed to 83 Bannock.

*   *   *

I sat in my car on Bannock two houses down from 83, staring at it and thinking it was a rather nice house and didn't look like a safe house at all. Not, of course, that I knew what safe houses looked like but still.

I flipped my phone open and I went to my texts.

I typed in, *Before I do this, I want proof Hawk's all right. No pictures. I want to hear his voice.*

Then I hit send.

I sat again in suspended time as I stared at my phone.

It rang. Unknown caller. I sucked in breath, flipped it open and put the phone to my ear.

"Hello," I whispered.

"Baby, do not do this shit," Hawk growled in my ear and my eyes filled with tears as they closed.

"I'm doing it, Cabe," I whispered, the tears sliding down my cheeks.

"Do not do it, Gwen."

"I'm drowning." I was still whispering.

"Gwen—"

"In you and I don't want to come up for air."

"Fuck. Baby—"

I heard the phone jostle, then a man told me, "Do it. Text."

Then I got dead air.

My head hit the steering wheel but I didn't feel it or see it. My eyes were still closed and tears were streaming down my face.

Baby.

That was burned on my brain too.

Baby.

"Oh God," I whispered, opened my eyes and stared at my thighs. "If I pull this off, Ginger, please, please forgive me."

My breath hitched and it did it painfully, burning my throat.

Baby, do not do this shit.

Another sob tore from my throat.

Do not do it, Gwen.

My hands went to the steering wheel and held on.

Do not do it…

My fingers were curled around the steering wheel but I didn't feel the wheel. I felt fingers curled around mine, my hand was little and they engulfed mine. In my mind, I looked up and saw Meredith with her wedding veil over her face smiling down at me.

Her fingers squeezed mine, warm and tight.

I felt my tears wet on my jeans.

Shit. I couldn't do it. I couldn't turn over my sister, my dad and Meredith's daughter, for my man. I couldn't do it.

I let the steering wheel go and covered my face with my hands as the sobs burned up my throat, so powerful, they shook my shoulders.

"Baby," I cried into my hands, that picture in the Polaroid all I could see against my closed eyelids. "Oh God, *baby*," I whispered as my shoulders heaved.

The passenger door flew open, my back shot straight, my head turned and through my tears I stared in stunned shock as Ginger jumped into the passenger seat.

"What the—?" I breathed.

"Drive!" she shouted.

"What?" I asked.

"Drive, bitch, *drive!*" she screamed.

I blinked then straightened, turned the key in the ignition and shot from the curb.

CHAPTER THIRTY-SIX

Commando Woman Lesson One

"NOT MY GIG, Gwennie, but those shoes are hot," Ginger said through a mouth full of Mustard's Last Stand, Vienna beef, Chicago-style chili-cheese hotdog.

Mustard's Last Stand had always been Ginger's favorite and that was where she wanted to go after escaping her protective custody safe house when she saw my car on the street with me sitting in it having a mental collapse. So I headed to University Boulevard, bought her a chili-cheese dog and then we drove to the Target parking lot on Colorado Boulevard so she could eat it. The whole time to and from, Ginger checked for a tail and declared we didn't have one.

I figured she would know so at least that was a relief.

She had her dog in one hand, the Polaroid of me and Hawk in the other one and she was studying it.

"Ginger, we need a plan," I told her. "And I think the best plan we have is taking you straight to the police station. You can say you got a craving for Mustard's and I'll say I was just in the neighborhood having my annual nervous breakdown."

Her eyes slid to me and, again with her mouth full, she asked, "Are you *high?*"

Okay, clearly that wasn't a choice.

"How about I rent you a car, get you some money, we go to my house and get you some clothes and then you drive to Canada," I suggested.

"Gwen, your clothes . . ." She trailed off and shook her head.

"Okay, then we'll go to the nearest biker babe and stripper shops and we'll stock you up."

She glared at me then she stated, "It's cold in Canada."

"It's cold here," I reminded her.

"Yes, for a few months, it's cold there all the time."

"It is not."

"It is too."

"It's not."

"I'm not going to Canada," she snapped, took another bite and shoved the photo in my purse.

"Don't hurt my Polaroid!" I cried, my hand darting out to it to make sure she didn't bend or scratch it. I pulled it out and inspected it, taking in a huge breath through my nostrils when I saw it was fine and then taking in another one when I saw the picture of Hawk laughing.

Fuck.

"Gwennie," Ginger whispered, and I carefully slid the picture safe into my purse and looked at her.

"How about we go to Dad? Dad'll have an idea."

"I can't go to Mom and Dad. I shouldn't be here with *you* and they've got *your old man*. This shit needs to be contained. It isn't spreading any further."

Wow. It seemed like Ginger had spent her time in protective custody reflecting.

Interesting.

"We're going to Tack," she announced, and I stared at her.

"Ginger, honey, I hate to remind you of this but you owe the Chaos MC over two million dollars."

"Yeah, well, my partners on that job were Fresh and Skeet, and they got their stupid jackasses caught kidnapping you before they were able to move that shit. It was hot. Tack and his boys were all over it. We couldn't move it until it got cold, not custom-built cars and a bike, no way and none of his other shit from the garage either. That stuff surfaced, it would lead back to them, and they'd be fucked. Fresh and Skeet share a brain cell so neither of them could open a safe even though they told me they could. *I* don't know how to do that shit so all of it is sittin' in one of Skeet's sister's storage units on Evans."

This was good news.

"This is good news," I told her.

She shoved in the last bite of dog and then crumpled the messy wrapper and napkin, speaking again with mouth full. "I give you the location, you call it in to Tack, he sends boys out, they find that shit, I'm cool with Tack. Then we meet with him and you text Roarke. You tell them Tack is makin' the switch." I sucked in breath as she swallowed but before I could say anything, she kept talking. "If he can take my back after the switch is made, good. If he can't..." she trailed off and shrugged.

I stared at her.

Then I asked, "Are you nuts?"

"No, Gwen, I'm not nuts. You aren't gettin' anywhere near Roarke."

"Neither are you!" I fired back and her body jerked toward me.

"Call Tack, set up the deal," she ordered.

"No, Ginger. I like the Canada plan," I returned. "If you won't do the police station plan, we should explore the Canada plan."

"Bitch, they got your old man," she reminded me and my throat started burning again as tears stung my eyes.

"I know," I whispered, "and they're not going to get you."

"They got your old man," she repeated.

"Stop it, Ginger. I *know*, okay? And they are *not* going to get you."

She slipped her hand in my purse and then the Polaroid was in my face. "Gwen, for fuck's sake, they've got—"

I snatched the picture from her and screamed, "*I know!*"

I closed my eyes tight and looked away.

Ginger was silent as I struggled with tears.

Then I heard her whisper, "Gwennie, call Tack."

"No," I whispered back.

Then she did something she hadn't done in years. So long, I forgot she used to do it but she did it all the time when we were young.

I felt her hand curl around my neck and then I felt her forehead against the side of my hair as she sang a silly, nonsensical song she made up when she was three, "Gwennie, Gwennie, hennie, fennie, Gwennie, Gwennie, lennie, bennie, love my sissy…Gwennie."

A sob tore up my throat.

I felt the Polaroid move gently in my hand before Ginger whispered, "You aren't losin' that because of me."

My neck twisted and our eyes, an inch apart, locked.

"I love you, baby," I whispered.

"I know you do," she whispered back. "Call Tack."

I sucked in breath. Then I asked, "You have to do this, don't you?"

"I'm not supposed to look out the windows, Gwen. They've been watchin' me like…" She closed her eyes then opened them but didn't finish what she was going to say. "The shift was about to change. They got a guy, he gets sloppy around shift change, so I looked. I been lookin' awhile to find my shot and I couldn't believe I saw you. So I took it. And I took it because they can't…" She shook her head. "They'll get me, Gwen. Eventually, they'll get me. They can't keep me safe because, obviously, they can't keep *you* safe. I started this and it's gotta be me who ends it."

I stared at her. She was right.

Shit.

"I'll call—" I started but both Ginger and my doors were yanked open.

We separated and my head shot around to see a very good-looking Native American man lean in front of me and nab the keys out of the ignition. He had long hair pulled back into a ponytail and I knew exactly who he was. Vance Crowe, one of Lee Nightingale's men.

Shit!

He pulled back but his eyes came to me as I heard Ginger cry out and felt her presence leave the car.

"Lee wants a word," Crowe stated. "You come or I drag you."

"Okey dokey," I whispered, slid the picture in my purse, grabbed the strap, and when his body pulled out of the frame, I exited the car.

*   *   *

Ginger and I, escorted by Vance Crowe and Luke Stark, entered the Nightingale Investigations offices.

They were posh, all gleaming wood and bronze statues.

Nice.

"I can't believe you ditched me!" Tracy screeched after I got two feet in the door. I turned to look at her and she was advancing on me then she skidded to a halt when she saw Ginger. "Holy crap! You busted her out!" she yelled.

"I didn't bust her out. She escaped," I replied.

"Shee-it." An African American woman with a very

large afro and stunning tawny brown eyes was sitting behind the reception desk and staring at Ginger. "Little thing like you caused all this ruckus? Feds, cops, badasses, commandos all in a tizzy. Denver's underground and overground spinnin' like tops." She smiled huge and nodded once before she finished with, "You go, girl."

Ginger grinned at her.

I looked toward an inside door that had opened and Lee Nightingale and Jorge were coming out of it.

"Smoke," I whispered.

"Thinkin' we should count ourselves lucky you don't clue in that Hawk still watches your every move, babe," Jorge said to me. "And that means your *every* move. He's got a tracking device on your car."

Shit.

"And in your phone," Jorge went on.

Shit!

"And we monitor your calls *and* texts," he finished.

Shit!

"Okay," I replied. "So if you monitor my texts, does this mean you've been looking for him since this morning?"

"Lookin' and findin', Gwen," Jorge returned. "Mighta went faster we didn't have to keep your shit covered, you runnin' around Denver, findin' trouble."

My relief was so extreme, I felt light-headed.

"You found him?" I breathed.

"Rescue mission is imminent and would be under way, we didn't have to lock you and your sister down in Lee's safe room to keep your shit out of trouble."

My relief fled as my eyes narrowed. "What did you expect me to do?"

"I don't know. Hit base and tell us Hawk was compromised?" Jorge shot back.

Sarcasm.

"I didn't want you to go all commando and get him killed!" I yelled.

"Part of Hawk's business is K and R, babe," Jorge informed me.

"I don't even know what that means," I informed him back.

"Kidnap and ransom, or, for Hawk, the R stands for rescue," Jorge enlightened me.

Wow. That was cool.

"Really?" I whispered.

"Jesus," Luke Stark muttered.

"Shirleen, make our guests comfortable." Lee, clearly done with Jorge and my exchange, moved toward the outer door.

"I'm coming with you," Ginger announced.

"You're goin' back to the Feds," Lee contradicted.

"They want me," Ginger returned.

Lee stopped close to her. "They aren't gettin' what they want."

"Her old man could get hurt," Ginger told him.

"Woman, you know who I am. You know who Hawk is. You know his boys are trained. Don't talk stupid," Lee warned.

"My sister's old man can't be—" Ginger started, but Lee leaned into her.

"He's hangin' from a hook right now, Ginger. I gotta stand here listenin' to your mouth and your guilt, he hangs from that hook longer. You shut up, I can go get him and get him back to your sister. You got more to say?"

"I feel like taking a tour of the safe room," I declared quickly, my eyes going to who I guessed was Shirleen, the tawny-eyed lady behind the reception desk. "Shirleen? Do you do tours?"

She shot out of her chair. "Part of my job description."

"Yay," I said, but it came out shaky.

Shirleen rounded the desk and I looked to Ginger as the men headed toward the door. Shirleen scooped up Ginger as she passed her, hooking her arm through my sister's and pulling her along.

My eyes went to Lee who was the last one out the door and he paused before he went through, his eyes coming to me.

"Be careful," I whispered, he nodded, and I finished, "But bring him safe back to me."

"Less than an hour, Gwen, he'll be close enough to touch," Lee whispered back. Tears filled my eyes and slid down my face.

"Thank you." Those two words were barely audible.

Tracy's arm hooked me, I had no choice but to turn away from Lee, but before I did I saw his chin go up and then I saw the door close on his back.

*   *   *

Tracy, Ginger, Shirleen and I were in the safe room.

It wasn't that big but we were all scrunched in there watching the movie *300* on a flat-screen TV. This was a movie I suspected Shirleen watched a lot and I mostly suspected this because she quoted most of the dialogue while the actors were saying it. I also suspected this because it was already in the DVD player. And lastly I suspected this because she didn't ask us what we wanted to watch, she just settled us in and turned it on.

The room had a double bed, a reclining chair and shelves full of DVDs. Ginger was in the chair. I was tucked into a protective ball on the bed, pressed into the corner of the wall. Tracy was close to me, holding my hand. And Shirleen was lounging on her side across the foot of the bed.

Ginger and Shirleen were watching the movie. I didn't think Tracy was but I wasn't sure because I was suspended in time.

Suddenly and without warning the door opened, my eyes shot to it and Hawk prowled through.

I sucked in breath and my heart stopped beating.

He was clean and bloodless, his hair still wet from a shower. He was wearing a fresh pair of black cargos and a dark blue, skin-tight t-shirt. There was a raw, scary-looking cut on his lip, an equally raw, scary-looking cut and swelling on his cheek and around his eye. The cut on his cheek was taped closed by three thin, short white bandages. He also had angry red welts around both his wrists.

Other than that, he looked fine. Standing, breathing, *prowling* fine.

Except, vaguely in the recesses of my mind, it struck me he looked kind of pissed.

I didn't care.

I shot out of my protective ball and up on my feet on the bed. I took one step, jumped over Shirleen's body, my foot hit the edge of the bed and I launched myself through the air at my man.

He caught me with a grunt and went back on a foot.

My arms and legs went around him and I started raining kisses on every bit of skin my mouth could find.

"Babe," he called, one of his arms curled under my ass, the other one around my back.

I ignored him and kept kissing his neck, his jaw, his throat, his cheek…

"Sweet Pea," he called, his arm at my back becoming a hand sliding up and into my hair.

I continued to ignore him and my mouth touched his.

His head jerked back and his hand twisted gently in my hair.

"Gwen, baby, I'm okay," he whispered and my eyes moved to his.

I stared down at him, drinking him in, feeling his power, his heat, all that was him wrapped in my limbs. Then I felt my face dissolve and I shoved it in his neck right before my breath hitched loudly and my body bucked with tears.

His head turned and his hand in my hair tightened. "Baby," he whispered in my ear.

My head jerked up and I wailed, "I can't believe you took a shower before you came to see me!"

"Gwen—"

"Next time I get a scary picture text where you're *bleeding* from your ear and *hanging* from something, *new rule!*" I shrieked. "You come see me *immediately* after you're rescued!"

"It wasn't exactly a rescue effort," Luke Stark put in, and my head snapped to see him standing two feet from Hawk and my side. "More like a cleanup one," he finished.

"What?" I asked.

"Glad I work for Lee," Vance Crowe muttered, and my head snapped to the other side to see him standing two feet from us there. "Lee doesn't like mess. Fuckin' hell." Vance leaned forward to look at Luke. "Did you see Jorge? He walked into that shit and didn't even blink."

"Forgot that smell," Luke muttered and shook his head. "Fear." Then his lip curled.

Oh boy.

I looked at Hawk. "What'd you do?"

Hawk looked at me. "Not a big fan of bein' Tasered, hung on a hook and men takin' fists to me, babe."

This was not an answer.

"What'd you do?" I repeated.

"Yeah, what'd you do?" Shirleen asked from behind

me. She sounded more than a little curious. Actually, she sounded excited.

"Thought we agreed ignorance is bliss," Hawk said to me.

"What," I started. "Did," I went on. "*You do?*" I finished, and he grinned at me, the dimples popped out and seeing them again after thinking I'd never see them again, my heart skipped a beat.

"Commando Lesson One," Hawk answered. "You got a hostage you know is trained, you incapacitate him. They should have drugged me. They didn't. They tied my ankles but left me hanging. Tyin' ankles doesn't do shit. The power, babe, is in my thighs. I get a head between my thighs, the neck is vulnerable—-"

"Okay," I said swiftly, "I'm done with Commando Lessons. That was the first and last."

Hawk's dimples came back. Then he set me on my feet. Then the dimples disappeared.

Uh-oh.

"All right, Sweet Pea, Commando *Woman* Lesson One, you get a text like you got, you call it into base and you do it *immediately*."

I was right except uh-oh didn't quite cover it.

"Hawk—"

"You do *not* go visit your local friendly motorcycle club to recruit assistance."

"Ha—"

"You do *not* drag your dispatch cosmo girlfriend into your man's shit, first because it might get her ass fired but especially because it might get her ass hurt."

"Cabe—"

"You do *not* set your banker friend on a data search that'll get his ass hauled to the local FBI offices for an interrogation that will be really fuckin' uncomfortable."

Uh-oh!

"Ca—"

"You do *not*," he leaned into me, his serious face turning hard, "*ever* offer yourself up for exchange."

"Baby—"

"And you do *not* go on the lam with your protective custody witness sister."

"I—"

"Confirm you get me, babe."

"But—"

He leaned in so he was an inch from my face. "Confirm...you...*get*...me."

I stared at him.

Then my day surged through my brain which sent acid through my system and I lost my mind.

"I will do," I planted my hands on my hips and stared in his black eyes, "what I have to do first to make sure you're safe and second to make sure I get to make more memories with you. So, okay, I'll call base but then I will do whatever the fuck I have to do to make that happen so, no, Hawk, I do *not* get you!"

"Gwen—"

"I've been panicked all day!" I shouted, throwing up my hands and taking a step back from him. "You didn't give me Commando Woman Lesson One this morning. No, you kissed me good-bye and said you'd see me tonight. I went about my business of the day to make sure *you'd see me tonight!*"

"Gwen—"

"*You were bleeding from your ear!*" I shrieked.

He reached out with both hands, caught me and hauled me into his body, whispering, "Baby."

My hands clenched in his tee as his arms slid around

me. "It was you or my sister. Do you know what that kind of decision does to your head?"

"All right, Sweet Pea, I get it," he said gently.

"Yes, Cabe," I stared him in the eyes, "of anyone, you do. You know what I was facing today. *You* know." I watched his eyes close, my hands released his shirt, slid up to wrap around the sides of his neck, his eyes opened and he showed me he not only got it, he *really, really* got it. So my voice was quiet when I went on, "I can get why you're angry, honey, but cut me some slack. I was doing the best I could do so you didn't become a picture on my fucking refrigerator."

His neck bent and his forehead touched mine then slid to the side, his cheek hit mine and that slid down too. Then his face was in my neck and his arms got tight.

In return I circled his shoulders with my arms and pressed close.

"They need a minute." I heard Luke say in a way that was kind of a suggestion but more a *get your asses out of here*.

I felt people move around and I heard a door close. Then I turned my head and put my lips to Hawk's ear.

"You think you could make a call so the Feds don't do a cavity search on Troy?" I asked.

Hawk lifted his head and looked at me.

"Yeah," he answered, his lips twitching.

"You think, before Ginger goes back to the Feds, Dad and Meredith can visit with her?"

His eyes warmed and he repeated, "Yeah."

"Okay," I nodded, relaxing into him. "Now do you think, since you've been close enough to touch for at least five minutes and you're safe and healthy enough to get pissed at me, you could finally kiss me?"

His eyes got warmer and he added intense.

"Yeah."

My hand slid up to cup his head. "Then kiss me, baby," I whispered.

He stared into my eyes then his head slanted and, just like Hawk, he gave me what I wanted most in the world.

EPILOGUE

Give Me the Dimples

CABE DELGADO WAITED while the garage door opened then he pulled his Camaro in beside Gwen's Mustang. He parked, grabbed his workout bag from the seat beside him and folded out of the car.

He walked in front of the Mustang and saw the Expedition sitting on the other side of the 'Stang. Gwen called it the "station wagon" and hated driving it because it was so huge. However, Hawk had a rule. She had their boys in the car with her, she was in the Expedition. She was off on her own, she could take the Mustang. She gave him lip, told him he was too damned bossy but only because that was what she did. She knew the Expedition was safer and Gwen would do anything to keep her boys safe.

He walked in front of the Expedition, through the door that led into the house and dumped his bag in the utility room on his way to the huge, open-plan kitchen.

She'd left the under-the-counter lights on for him.

He moved through the space and turned off the lights, heading to the wide, carpeted staircase that had a nightlight lit in an outlet halfway up. He didn't need her to light his way but she did it anyway partially because, if one of the boys got up, she wanted them to have light and partially because, when her man got home, she wanted him to know she was thinking about him.

He'd lied to Gwen although he didn't know it at the time. He needed space. Or, more accurately, he needed a Hawk and Gwen zone, he needed to give his boys their zones and they all needed a family zone. So he'd moved his family from Gwen's farmhouse to this five-bedroom, three-car-garage "monstrosity" as Gwen called it. She only allowed the move because it came with Janine cleaning it. She said she had a life rule and that rule was that she refused to live in a house that it took longer than two hours to clean. Now she lived in a house that took longer than two hours to clean, Hawk just made it so she didn't have to clean it.

He silently climbed the staircase, turned right and moved through the large open space at the top, one of the many family zones. He didn't see the pictures but he knew they were there. Gwen decorated in photos. She wasn't a knick-knack sort of woman, thank fuck.

Hawk liked the way his wife decorated. There were pictures everywhere, on every surface, on all the walls, hell, you could barely see the fridge for the photos tacked to it. There were pictures of her, of him, of their two boys, their families, their friends—alone, in pairs, in huddles, all candid, nothing posed, nearly every photo everyone was smiling.

Or laughing.

And there were pictures of Simone and Sophie. Gwen had conspired with his mother and made certain Simone and Sophie had their places among her décor and his woman decorated in family.

It took a while to get used to this. It took a while for the pain of seeing them every day to dull. Then it dulled. Then he saw what was in the photos instead of feeling the loss of it. And what was in the photos were memories. Those memories were bittersweet, but with time, and with Gwen's guidance, the sweet outweighed the bitter.

Hawk turned right again at the first door.

He walked in and saw Asher asleep in his bed on his belly wearing loose shorts and a t-shirt, his black hair a mess, his limbs splayed, taking up more space than any four-year-old kid should in a double bed. The covers had been kicked off. Even as a baby, he'd kicked off his covers. Ash liked to be free. No restraints. Even in sleep. Hawk's mom said he'd done the same thing and Hawk learned not to be surprised at this.

Asher was his boy in more ways than one. Ash was intense, always had been from nearly the instant he left Gwen's womb. And if Hawk was home, Asher was with him. From the second he could crawl, when Hawk opened the door to the house, Asher would be sitting on his ass, staring at the door, waiting for his dad to walk in. It wasn't clingy. Even as an infant, Asher had been able to entertain himself.

He just liked to do it close to his dad.

Hawk walked to him and bent, doing what he did frequently, in fact every night he got home when his boys were asleep. He rested his hand light on the heat of his son's back and felt him breathe. Once his son's life communicated itself through Hawk's hand, he lifted that hand and slid it over Asher's thick hair. Then he left the room, crossed the hall and entered another door.

Bruno was on his back, one arm thrown wide, one knee up and dropped, the other leg straight, hand on his belly. Covers half on, half off. The stuffed bear with an ill-fitting Broncos t-shirt had fallen from his outstretched hand.

Bruno sat quietly on his granddad's lap during every

Broncos home game. It was fucking uncanny but Hawk could swear his two-year-old son's study of the game was more intense than Bax's. Even if a game was on TV, Bruno would stop, sit his ass down and stare at it. If he was awake, he was wearing a football helmet and if Hawk or Gwen tried to take it off him, the kid pitched one helluva fit. So they let him wear it everywhere but to the dinner table and to bed. This was a good call considering, when Bruno wasn't eating, watching football on television or wrestling with his brother, he was tackling shit.

Hawk bent, his hand going to Bruno's chest, resting lightly, and his eyes roamed his son's face as his hand felt his son's heartbeat.

Both his boys looked like him, black hair, black eyes. Bruno got his dimples and Gwen praised the Lord loudly, and hilariously, that he did and she did this often. Nearly every time she saw them, which was a lot. Bruno, like his mom, liked to laugh, and like his mom, he did it often.

At that memory, Hawk smiled at his son.

His wife liked her husband's dimples. Hawk just liked his son's.

He walked out of the room and his cell rang. He headed to the master suite pulling it out of a pocket of his cargoes. He turned the display to face him and his brows knit.

It said "Gwen Calling."

He didn't answer as his eyes went to their door, seeing weak light coming from under it.

She was awake. This was surprising. It was late.

Fuck.

She was nearly nine months' pregnant with their, what Gwen decreed, final child. She'd decreed this because the ultrasound showed it was a boy. She was done. Giving up the ghost. She had a lifetime ahead of her of fights, blood, drunkenness, puke and pregnancy scares. She wasn't going to make it worse.

This was why he let her name their kids. Deacon was gestating in her belly. Hawk didn't like the name Asher until Asher made it into the world. He *really* didn't like the name Bruno until he met Bruno. And he *seriously* didn't like the name Deacon but he reckoned he'd grow to like it.

His mother had a hand in these names but Hawk didn't complain. He saw the signs with Asher's intensity and Bruno tackling everything. Gwen was fucked.

He shoved the still-ringing phone in his pocket as he twisted the knob and opened one of the double doors to the master suite.

Hawk walked through and stopped dead.

The bedside light on Gwen's side was on. The covers thrown back. The bed empty. A pool of blood was in the bed, a trail of it leading to the bathroom.

"Cabe, honey, you get this, go to the hospital." He heard his wife's voice, jerked out of his freeze and ran to the bathroom. "Something's wrong. I'm calling..."

She stopped talking when he hit the bathroom and her head came up to look at him. She was sitting in her nightshirt on the floor, one arm around her swollen belly, one shapely leg straight, the other bent under her, her long, thick blonde hair down and tousled, her blue eyes pained, her gorgeous face ashen, blood pooling around her on the black-and-white tiles.

The minute they hit him, her eyes filled with tears. She dropped her hand and it fell limply to her lap while she whispered, "Baby."

Less than five minutes later, Hawk had his wife strapped into the Expedition, his sons safely secured in the back, his phone ringing Bax and he was backing out of the garage on his way to the hospital.

*   *   *

"Son," Hawk heard, and he tore his eyes from the window to look into Baxter Kidd's. The minute their eyes locked, Bax flinched so Hawk knew what he was feeling was written on his face.

Bax's hand came up and his fingers curled on Hawk's shoulder.

"This happened with Libby," he said quietly. "Same thing, Cabe. Same exact thing. I didn't say anything, Ash and Bruno were so easy, I thought…" He stopped, closed his eyes, sucked in an audible breath, opened his eyes and went on, "Libby was fine. Gwen was fine. And now Gwen and Deacon are gonna be fine."

Hawk nodded once and looked back out the window. Bax's fingers gave him a squeeze, disappeared and Hawk felt his presence move away.

Meredith and his mother had tried to get Hawk to agree to Tracy taking the boys away but Hawk refused to allow it. It might be the wrong decision but he didn't give a fuck. They weren't taking his boys from him. He needed his boys close.

The doctor had examined Gwen for about five seconds before he started barking orders, they urgently yanked her gurney out of the bay and rushed her down the hall. Gwen hadn't uttered a word but her eyes never left him until they had no choice because she'd lost sight of him. They'd forced Hawk out of the bay and to the waiting room where Meredith and Bax were waiting with Ash and Bruno.

It had been two hours since they'd wheeled his wife away. His mother and father showed, Von and Lucia, Jury and his wife, Gloria, Tracy and her husband, Uri, Cam and Leo, Elvira and her man, Malik, Troy and his wife, Keeley, Mrs. Mayhew—but they heard no more.

Not a fucking word.

Hawk's gaze was at the window but all he saw were Gwen's frightened, pain-filled eyes locked to his.

He closed his eyes and shit collided in his brain.

Gwen's body pressed to his, the silk of her dress under his hand, her smiling lips on his, her mouth tasting of frosting, her laughter sliding down his throat after they'd cut their wedding cake and shared bites. She'd pulled half an inch away and looked into his eyes before assuring him, "Don't worry, baby, that little piece of cake won't give you a gut." After which he yanked her right back and kissed her so hard and so long, their audience started catcalling, hooting and he heard Elvira threaten to throw cold water on them.

Gwen walking out of the bathroom when they were on vacation in Bermuda. The windows open, a breeze blowing the thin curtains in, the sounds of the ocean filling the room. She had her hands behind her back and was wearing a little sexy nightgown, a smile playing at her mouth. He'd watched her as she'd come to the side of the bed, climbed in and straddled him then whipped her hand around and showed him the white stick with a pink plus sign on it. Then she'd tossed it to the floor, plastered her soft torso to his frozen one, framed his face in her hands and announced through a grin, "If it's a boy, Maria and I have decided on Asher. If it's a girl, you get to name her." When she was done speaking, his arms went around her, he rolled her to her back and kept her occupied for the next two hours so she could say nothing more than moaning her sweet "Baby."

Coming home late to see Gwen in Simone's chair, her legs thrown over the side, her head rolled on the back, Ash cradled safe in her arms, both his boy and his woman asleep and neither had woken when he carried them in turns to their beds.

Gwen, her belly slightly rounded with Bruno but still in spiked heels, wandering The Monstrosity while Hawk, Ash at his hip, and the real estate agent watched. Then she'd walked to him, put her hand to his abs and proclaimed on a complete exaggeration, "This monstrosity is bigger than your lair." He'd hooked her around the neck, pulled her deep into his body, kissed her hard while Ash banged them both with tiny baby fists and when he lifted his head, he kept her close but looked at the agent and stated, "We'll take it."

Watching Gwen cross her legs in his Camaro while she fixed her lip gloss, staring into the mirror on the sun visor and muttering, "I think I love Meredith and Dad's anniversary more than they do." To which Hawk had teased, "Because it gives you an excuse to wear expensive shoes?" And Gwen had turned her head, he felt her eyes hitting his face and she'd replied, "No, because it's also the anniversary of when you told me you love me, which was, and even with all the beauty you've given me in between, still is the best day of my life, Cabe 'Hawk' Delgado." And Hawk had had to stop the car so he could kiss her, which meant she again had to fix her lip gloss.

He'd lived a nightmare for eight years, closing off the world and refusing to feel anything only to walk up to a god-damned restaurant and through a window see the woman of his dreams wearing a sexy little black dress and laughing with abandon. Then he'd fucked around for a year and a half. A year and a half. Every night he left her he told himself he'd never go back and then every night he fought going back until he couldn't fight it anymore and he had to taste her, touch her, hear her soft, sweet voice whisper "baby," feel her limbs hold him tight after he made her come, feel her eyes on him while he dressed and struggled with climbing right back into her bed and holding her close until he could see the sun shine on her beautiful face.

He'd had her in his arms and he had no idea he was in her heart and he'd denied she'd touched his for a year and a fucking half.

He'd never get that back and now he knew exactly what he'd been missing and he'd never *fucking* get that back.

"Mr. Delgado?" he heard, and he opened his eyes to turn and see a doctor in scrubs walking into the room.

Everyone but Tracy and Elvira stood. Tracy because she was cradling a sleeping Ash, Elvira because she was doing the same with Bruno.

Hawk didn't move as he watched Dr. Hunter walk to him and he still didn't move even when he saw the man's smile.

"Your wife is fine," Hunter stated then stopped a foot from Hawk before he finished, "As is your baby girl."

"A girl?" Hawk heard his mother cry as he heard other noises of relief and joy.

He just stared at Hunter and demanded, "I want to see my wife."

"Of course." Hunter nodded. "She's sleeping," he went on to warn.

"I want to see my wife," Hawk repeated.

Hunter nodded again. "Follow me."

Hawk's eyes scanned his sleeping sons but didn't move to anyone else in the room as he followed the doctor.

*   *   *

He saw it the minute her eyes opened.

She looked confused a moment then his hand in hers squeezed and her head turned on the pillow.

"Cabe, baby," she whispered.

He felt her words like a physical touch.

Then he felt her hand squeeze his and his thumb slipped, brushing across her wedding rings.

He closed his eyes.

Thank Christ. Thank fucking Christ.

Hawk opened his eyes. "We're namin' her Genevieve."

He watched her eyes grow round.

"Genevieve?" she whispered.

"Yeah," he whispered back.

She stared at him. Then, still whispering, she declared, "Vivi."

"Whatever," Hawk muttered.

Gwen smiled at him and, seeing it, his hand automatically tightened around hers.

Thank. Fucking. Christ.

"No more kids," he proclaimed.

"'Kay," she agreed softly.

He got up from the chair but stayed bent so his face was close to hers.

Then he admitted, "You scared the shit outta me, Sweet Pea."

Her eyes got soft and her face gentled. He'd surprised her in a way she liked.

Fuck, but he loved that look and he didn't love it any less no matter how often he saw it, which was often considering he worked hard to earn it.

"Superheroes don't get scared," she told him, and for the first time in hours, he felt his mouth smile. She smiled back. Then she asked, "Where are my boys?"

"Sleepin' in the waiting room."

"Can they come in?"

"Don't care. You want 'em, I'll go get 'em."

"I want them," she whispered.

"You got it, babe," Hawk whispered back, bent closer and touched his mouth to hers.

When he pulled away her hand got tighter so he stopped and caught her eyes.

"We have a little girl," she said softly.

"Yeah," he replied just as soft.

"Can I see her?"

"I'll bring her too."

Gwen nodded and studied his face for a while.

Then she asked quietly, "What am I going to do?"

"What?"

"I don't have anything else to daydream about. Now what am I going to do?"

Hawk felt his gut get tight, his chest swell and something stung his throat.

"I'll find a way to keep you occupied, baby," he whispered.

"'Kay," she whispered back.

His hand again tightened in hers and his other hand lifted so he could run his knuckles down her pale cheek, and when he did, her eyes closed.

"Love you, Sweet Pea," he murmured and her eyes opened.

She smiled then she replied, "Love you too, baby." He started to pull away again but she called his name so he stopped.

"Yeah?"

"Before you go, give me the dimples," she demanded.

That thing in his throat prickled and Hawk dipped his head and kissed the indentation at the base of his wife's throat. Then he lifted his head and smiled at her.

Her hand came to his face and he felt the pad of her thumb in one of his dimples.

Then her eyes moved from her thumb to his and she smiled back.

Tabitha Allen grew up in the thick of Chaos—
the Chaos Motorcycle Club, that is.
Her father is Chaos's leader, and the club
has always had her back.
But one rider was different from the start...

Please turn this page for an excerpt from

OWN THE WIND

PROLOGUE

You Don't Know Me

HIS CELL RANG and Parker "Shy" Cage opened his eyes.

He was on his back in his bed in his room at the Chaos Motorcycle Club's compound. The lights were still on and he was buried under a small pile of women. One was tucked up against his side, her leg thrown over his thighs, her arm over his ribs. The other was upside down, tucked to his other side, her knee in his stomach, her arm over his calves.

Both were naked.

"Shit," he muttered, as he lifted and twisted himself out from under his fence of limbs. He reached out to his phone.

He checked the display and touched his thumb to the screen to take the call.

"Yo, brother," he muttered to Hop, one of his brethren in the Chaos MC.

"Where are you?" Hop asked.

"Compound," Shy answered.

"You busy?"

Shy lifted up to an elbow and looked at the two women passed out in his bed.

"Not anymore," he replied.

Knowing Shy and his reputation, there was humor in Hop's tone when he stated, "Tabby Callout."

At this news, fire hit his gut, as it always did when he got that particular callout. He didn't know why, it made no sense, he barely knew the girl, but always when he heard it, it pissed him way the hell off.

"You are shittin' me," Shy bit out.

"No, brother. Got a call from Tug who got a call from Speck. She's out on the prowl, as usual. She's closer to you than me, so if you can disentangle yourself from the pussy you got passed out in your room, it'd be good you go get her."

There it was. Hop knew Shy and his reputation.

"I'm on my bike. Text me the address," Shy mumbled, shifting from under the bodies to put his feet on the floor at the side of the bed.

"Right. Under radar, yeah?" Hop returned, telling him something he knew, and Shy clenched his teeth.

Three years they'd been doing this shit with Tabby. Three fucking years. It was lasting so damned long, he knew, unless she got a serious fucking wakeup call, that girl would never learn.

But no one was willing to do it. The Club didn't normally have any problems with laying it out no matter who it needed to be laid out for, but Tab was different. She was the nineteen-year-old daughter of the President of the Club, Kane "Tack" Allen.

That meant she was handled with care. That also meant when they got word she was out carousing and needed someone to nab her ass and get her home before she bought trouble, they did it under radar. In other words, they didn't tell Tack. And they didn't tell Tack because the first time it happened he lost his shit, but worse, his old lady took off to extricate Tabby from a bad situation and nearly got her head caved in with a baseball bat.

No one wanted a repeat of that kind of mess, so the brothers kept an eye on her and took care of business without getting Tack involved.

"Under radar," Shy muttered then finished, "Later," and touched the screen with his thumb.

He rooted around on the floor to find jeans, tee, underwear, and socks. The women in his bed didn't twitch when he sat down next to them to pull on his boots.

Dressed, he turned off the light in his room and headed down the hall and into the common room of the Club's compound. The brothers' rooms were at the back, doors opening off a long hall that ran the length of the building. A doorway in the middle of the hall led to the common area, which had a long, curved bar and a mess of couches, chairs, tables, and pool tables. Off to the side through another door was their meeting room, a kitchen, and a set of locked, reinforced storage rooms.

As he moved through the common space he saw Brick, one of Chaos's members, flat on his back on one of the couches. He had one foot on the floor and was dead to the world. He also had a woman draped on him, dead to the world too. She had a short jean skirt on, and Shy saw that Brick was sleeping with his hand up the hem, cupped on her ass. Shy also saw the woman wasn't wearing any underwear.

Other than that, the space was empty and currently lit only by a variety of neon beer signs on the walls.

That night, Brick's girl had brought two friends to party.

Brick got his girl. Shy got the friends.

Shy left the Compound, went to his bike, threw a leg over, and drove the six blocks to his apartment. Once there, he didn't bother going upstairs to his place. He never bothered to go upstairs to his place.

He wondered vaguely why he kept it. He was rarely there. He ate fast food that he ordered to go. He slept in his bed at his room in the Compound. He worked in the garage at Ride or the auto supply store attached. He drank and partied wherever there was drink or party provided. He communed with the brotherhood.

All other times, he was on his bike.

This was because Parker Cage only felt right on his bike.

It started with the dirt bike he got when he was fourteen, and it never stopped.

Five years ago, on his thirdhand Harley, he'd cruised by Ride Custom Cars and Bikes, a massive auto supply store that was attached to a garage in the back that built custom cars and bikes. He'd heard of it, hell, everyone had. The Chaos MC owned and ran it, and the garage was famous, built cars for movies and millionaires.

But it was the flag that flew under the American flag on top of the store that caught his attention. Until that day, he'd never looked up to see it. It was white and had the Chaos Motorcycle Club emblem on it with the words "Fire" and "Wind" on one side and "Ride" and "Free" on the other.

The second his eyes hit that flag, he felt his life take shape.

Nothing, not anything in his life until that time, except the first time he took off on a bike, had spoken to him like that flag. He didn't get why and he didn't spend time trying. It just spoke to him. So strong, it pulled him straight into the parking lot and set his boots to walking into the store.

Within months, he was a recruit for Chaos.

Now, he was a brother.

Outside his apartment, he parked his bike and moved

from it to his truck. If she was in a state, Tabitha Allen wouldn't be able to hold on to him on a bike. If she was feeling sassy, which was usually the case, she'd put up a fight he couldn't win with her on a bike. So he hauled his ass into his beat-up, old, white Ford truck, started it up and took off in the direction of the address on the text Hop sent.

As he drove, that fire in his gut intensified.

She was in college now, supposedly studying to be a nurse. Cherry, the Office Manager at the garage who also happened to be Tack's old lady and Tabby's stepmother, bragged about her grades and how good she was doing in school. Shy had no clue how Tab could pull off good grades when she was out fucking around all the time. He couldn't say one of the brothers got a Tabby Callout every night but it was far from infrequent.

The girl liked to party.

This wasn't surprising. She was nineteen. When he was nineteen, he'd liked to party too. Fuck, he was twenty-four and he still liked to party in a way he knew he'd never quit.

But he wasn't Tabby Allen.

He was a biker who worked in a garage and auto supply store, oftentimes raised hell and kicked ass when needed.

She was studying to be a freaking nurse with her dad footing that bill, so she needed to calm her ass down.

This didn't even get into the fact that it wasn't a new thing she liked to party *and* take a walk on the wild side. Three years ago, on his first Tabby Callout, she'd been sixteen and her twenty-three-year-old boyfriend had roughed her up because she wouldn't put out. That was the situation where Cherry nearly got her head caved in with a baseball bat, and it happened right in front of Shy. It was a miracle of quick reflexes that didn't end in disaster. Shy liked Cherry, everyone did, the woman was the shit; funny, pretty, sexy, smart, strong, and good for Tack in every way she could be.

If you could pick the perfect old lady, Tyra "Cherry" Allen would be it. She had sass but with class, dressed great, didn't let Tack roll all over her but did it in a way she didn't bust his balls. She was hilarious. She was sweet. She was a member of a biker family while still holding on to the woman she always was. And, honest to Christ, he'd never seen a man laugh and smile as often as Kane Allen. He had a good life, and it wasn't lost on a single member of the Club that Cherry made it that way.

So, during Tabby's first callout, it would have sucked if Cherry was made a vegetable or worse because of Tab's shit. Not to mention, if Shy had to explain why he was at Cherry's back, watching her head get caved in with a bat, instead of taking the lead and protecting her from that eventuality, Tack was so into his old lady it was highly likely Shy would no longer be breathing.

How the fuck Tabby hadn't learned her lesson after that mess, he had no clue, and as he drove it came crystal that she needed to get one.

And he was so pissed, he decided he was going to be the one to give it to her.

Tonight.

Shy pulled up outside the house and he wasn't surprised at what he saw.

He knew that scene, lived it until he found the brotherhood.

In high school and out of it, the other kids had attached him to the "stoner" crowd, the "hoods," even though his affiliation with them was loose. He didn't connect with anyone in high school or after it, not in any real way, but that didn't mean he didn't find an escape. A place to drink beer and find a bitch so he could get laid. So he'd been in many houses just like this with cars and bikes outside just like the ones he saw now.

He still lived that scene but it was better.

It was family.

He saw a couple of bikes parked outside the fully lit and heaving house, and they pissed him off even more than he was already pissed. The bikes were older, the kids inside didn't have enough money for better, but still, they didn't take care of them.

If you had a Harley, you took care of it. You treated it like a woman, lots of attention, lots of TLC. No excuses. If you didn't do that, you didn't deserve to own it.

There were also a couple of new souped-up muscle cars, which meant whoever owned them put every nickel into keeping up the cool.

But there were more junkers and classic cars, the latter in the middle of restoration, all of it loving. Whoever owned them was taking their time, doing it right, saving up and taking care of their baby before they moved on to the next project in line to make their Mustang, Nova, Charger, GTO, or whatever cherry.

Those cars meant that not everyone in that house was a loser.

At least that was something.

Shy angled out of the truck and moved toward the house. Once in, he shifted through the bodies, ignoring looks from the girls and chin lifts from the guys. He was on a mission and wanted it done.

It didn't take long to find her. She was in the living room sitting on a couch, a cup of beer in her hand, her head turned away from him, her pretty profile transformed with laughter.

When he saw her it happened like it always happened. He

didn't know why he hadn't learned, why he didn't brace. He always expected he'd get over it, get used to it, but he didn't.

Seeing her hit him in the chest, the burn in his gut moving up to flame in his lungs, compressing them, making it suddenly hard to catch a breath.

He didn't get this.

She was pretty. Jesus, she was pretty. All that thick, dark hair and those sapphire blue eyes, her curvy, petite body, perfect, golden skin still tanned from the summer. Any guy, even if they didn't get into short women with dark hair, could see she was pretty.

It was more and he knew that too, had been around her enough to see it and often. Her face was expressive, she was quick to smile and laugh. She was animated. She was just one of those chicks it was good to be around.

She could get pissed off. She could get feisty.

Most of the time, though, she was in a good mood, but her good moods were the kinds of good moods that filled a room. Even if you were having a shit day, if Tabby Allen wandered into the common room of the Compound wearing a smile, some of that shit would wear off and your day would get better.

But she was his brother's daughter and that was reason number one not to go there. Further, she was too young and too immature. She did stupid shit, like her being with this crowd, drinking beer underage and laughing rather than home studying or hanging with kids from college. So regardless that she was fucking pretty, had a sweet little body, and could light up a room with her mood, he was never going there, but even if he could, he wouldn't, because she was flat-out trouble.

And yet every time he saw her, it somehow rocked him.

He ignored this feeling that he didn't want and didn't

understand, and his mouth tightened when he saw how she was dressed. Tight skirt, short. Tight top, cleavage. Lots of leg on show even if she wasn't all that tall. Nice leg. Shapely leg. Fucking great leg.

Shit.

And fuck-me high-heeled sandals that even if she was too young and his brother's daughter, the sight of them Shy still felt in his dick.

Damn.

He ignored this too and moved through the room, eyes on her, determined.

She must have felt his approach because she turned her head, looked up, and that burn didn't lessen at all when her unbelievable blue eyes ringed with long, dark lashes hit his.

He was not surprised when her smile faded, the animation left her face and she snapped, "You have got to be shitting me."

That pissed Shy off too. He fucking hated it when she cursed. Tack didn't give a shit, even when his kids were younger. Shy, though, detested it. There was something just very *wrong* about words like that coming from lips as beautiful as hers.

"Let's go," he clipped.

"Shy—" she began but didn't finish, mostly because Shy grabbed her beer, set it aside, then grabbed her hand and hauled her ass off of the couch.

Surprisingly, she didn't fight.

She followed.

Good, he thought. He wanted this done.

He got her out of the house, down the walk and opened the door of his truck for her. He was pulling her by her hand to get her close to the cab when she finally spoke.

"Shy, I keep telling you guys that this is not what you—"

He leaned in, nose to nose with her, and cut her off. "Shut it."

She blinked even as her head jerked. This wasn't a surprise. Brothers respected brothers, and one of the ways they did that was by showing respect to their kin. Chaos was Chaos, it was all family. Brothers, old ladies, kids. Shy had never spoken to her that way. None of the brothers had. Not to her.

"Get in the fuckin' truck," he went on.

Tabby rallied and started to say, "Can I just explain—?"

Shy interrupted her again. "Get in it or I plant you in it, Tab."

Even in the shadows of night, he saw her eyes flash before he saw her clamp her mouth shut. It was with jerky movements that she yanked her hand from his, turned, and climbed into the truck.

Shy slammed her door, rounded the hood, and folded in.

They were on their way when she tried again, her voice quiet. "Shy, really, those are my friends. It's all cool. Just a couple of beers. A few joints. I'm not smoking and I'm driving so I wouldn't—"

"So all of those kids are nursing students?" he asked.

"No," she answered. "They're friends from high school."

"You're not in high school anymore, Tabby," he pointed out, and felt her eyes come to him but he kept his angry ones on the road.

"You're right," she snapped, the quiet in her voice gone. "I'm not. That doesn't mean they aren't still my friends. We've had a lot of good times together. We're close. What? You think I should just scrape them off?"

He didn't glance at her when he replied, "Uh, yeah, Tab. They're trash. You aren't. Jesus." He shook his head. "I do not get you. I know your mom's a bitch, but for the last three years you've had Cherry in your life. It isn't like you don't have a good role model. Why the fuck you can't be like her is beyond me."

He heard her swift intake of breath before she returned, "Maybe it's because I should be like *me* and, by the way, Shy, Tyra would want me to be like me too."

The members of the Club called Tack's woman Cherry but Tack called her Red. His kids and everyone else called her Tyra or Ty-Ty.

"Anyway," Tabby went on irately, "they're not trash."

"They're trash," he stated firmly.

"They. Are. *Not!*" she stated loudly.

There it was. That gave him his opening.

"You want that life?" he asked.

"That life?" she shot back.

"Booze and bodies, booty calls and bust-ups," he explained.

"Um…*hello,* Shy. That *is* my life."

"So you want it," he concluded.

She ignored his question and pointed out, "It's *your* life too, you know. Nothing wrong with it. Never was, never will be."

A nursing student.

Right.

On this path, she'd never make it. On this path, she'd end up like those bitches in his bed. On this path, Tabby was pissing her college education away, and Tack might as well be pissing that money into the wind.

"You want that life," he said softly, "you think that's cool, baby? Then let's roll."

It was perfect timing because he'd flipped on his turn signal to turn into Ride.

"What the hell? Why are we here?" she asked, but he didn't answer.

He drove around the store and through the forecourt of the garage to park in front of the Compound. He didn't delay in folding out of the truck, rounding the hood, and yanking open her door.

"Shy, what are you—?" she started but stopped since he leaned into her, undid her seatbelt, tagged her hand, and hauled her out of the cab. "Dammit! Shy! What are you doing?" she clipped.

Again he didn't answer. He just tugged her into the Compound and straight behind the bar. He nabbed a bottle of tequila off a shelf at the back then pulled her in front of him.

"Ready to let go of that little-girl-beer bullshit?" he asked, holding up the bottle.

Her eyes went to it, then to him. He saw the confusion and he sensed her unease.

He ignored that too.

"Tab, asked you a question. You like to party. You aren't in high school anymore. You wanna grow up and learn how it's really done?"

She ignored him this time and asked, "Why are you being so weird?"

He pulled her closer and tipped his chin down to hold her eyes, now ignoring that it was starkly apparent she wasn't breathing and her body had gone still.

"Didn't answer my question, baby," he said softly and watched her swallow then lick her upper lip.

Jesus. Shit.

He'd never seen her do that. Definitely not this close.

The tip of that pink tongue on the perfection of that rosy lip.

Shit.

"Tab," he prompted, his hand squeezing hers.

"I want to go home," she replied quietly, being smart for a change.

"Too late for that," he muttered then moved away, pulling her with him as he moved from behind the bar, through the room, and into the back hall.

She tugged at his hand and called, "Shy. Seriously. You're more than kinda freaking me out."

Hopefully, in about two seconds, she'd be a lot more than kinda freaked out. She'd be scared straight and out of this bullshit she kept pulling.

Therefore, two seconds later, he yanked her into his room, tugged her to a stop and flipped the light switch.

The two women were still naked, lying head to foot on the bed, having, since he was gone, tangled with each other.

Briefly, he tried to remember their names.

He stopped trying when he felt Tabby's hand spasm in his and she gave a rough pull to try to break away but he just held her tighter and turned to her.

"Usually, we throw some back, get loose, in the mood," he educated her, lifting up the bottle. "I've seen the way you look at me, baby, so if you wanna just get naked and go for it, I'm up for that too. They're out but, we go for a while, no doubt they'll rally and join in. Sounds extreme but, trust me, you try it, you'll like it."

When he started talking, her eyes were on the bed but they moved slowly to him and he saw she was pale beneath her tan. Her eyes were also wide with shock and something else he didn't quite get, and her full lips were parted.

"What's it gonna be?" he asked. "You wanna loosen up or you wanna just go for it?"

"Why are you doin' this?" she whispered, and Shy shrugged.

"This is who you are or who you're headin' to be. Might as well quit fuckin' around, babe, and go for it."

Her eyes slid to the side then to him before she stated quietly, "This isn't who I am."

He looked her down and up and pointed out, "Short tight skirts, too-tight tops. I know it's not lost on you that I can see most of your tits not only through the shirt but spillin' out of it, Tab. Then we got your high heels, lots of hair, lots of makeup. You scream you got a wild side, baby. Quit fuckin' around. You been wantin' to explore it since you were sixteen. The time is right. The stage is set." He pulled her closer to him and lifted the bottle again. "Let's go."

When he said the word *sixteen*, she flinched and her hand jerked at his again.

Also, the look in her eyes he couldn't quite place came clear.

Hurt.

It sucked. He didn't like to do this to her, but he reckoned that emotion stark in her gaze meant he was getting through.

"Take me home," she said softly, and he shifted closer to her.

She swung slightly back, but her movements were wooden.

"Come on, baby. Don't bullshit me," he coaxed in a gentle voice. "I've seen the looks you give me. Now's your shot. You're hot, you like to have fun, you shouldn't waste this opportunity."

"Take me home," she repeated.

"If you don't want an audience or this to be a participation sport outside us two, I can rouse those bitches—" he jerked his head to the bed "—send them on their way before we get goin'."

"Take me home," she said again.

"Or we can let 'em sleep. Go to your dad's room," he suggested, and that did it.

With a violent wrench, she tore her hand from his, turned on her foot, and raced from the room.

Much more slowly, Shy put the bottle on the dresser, snapped off the lights, and followed her. He wasn't alarmed. She didn't have wheels and she was in high heels, there wasn't far she could go.

Surprisingly, when he exited the Compound, she was sitting in the passenger side of his truck, her head turned to look out the side window.

Yeah, she was ready to go home.

He didn't delay in moving to the driver's side, climbing in and starting her up. Tabby didn't look his way as he reversed out and headed toward Broadway.

They were well on their way through Denver to the foothills where Tack and Cherry lived, where Tab still lived with them and their two new boys before he spoke into the heavy air in the cab.

"You're a good kid, Tabby. Don't let your mother treating you like shit kick your ass. Get off that path."

"You're on that path," she whispered to her window.

"Babe, I'm not. I'm a man and I got brothers. I chose a lifestyle and a brotherhood. It's different for you and you know it. The bullshit you're pullin', the path you're on, no joke, even if you wanted the life, wanted to be an old lady, that wouldn't work for you no matter what respect we got for your dad. The path you're on heads you straight to bein' a BeeBee, and you know that too."

She didn't speak but Shy figured his point was made. Tabby knew BeeBee, everyone did. BeeBee had been banned from spreading her legs and spreading her talent throughout every member of the Club after she stupidly went head to head with Cherry. But even gone, she was not forgotten.

Back then, Tabby had been way too young to know BeeBee in any real way other than seeing the way BeeBee hung on and put out. But there was no way to miss her use to the Club, even for a teenage girl.

His point made, he also kept quiet the rest of the way to Tack's house.

He parked outside the front door and she instantly undid her seat belt and threw open the door. He turned to see she'd twisted to jump out and opened his mouth to say something, but he didn't get it out. He had no idea how she explained it to her father when a brother brought her home, but that was her problem, not his.

She turned back and all words died in his throat when he saw by the cab's light the tears shimmering in her eyes and the tracks left by the ones that had slid silently down her cheeks.

His body went rock solid at the evidence of the pain his lesson caused. Deserved, he knew, but it still hurt like a mother to witness. So when she leaned in, he didn't move away.

"You don't know me," she whispered. "But now, I know you, and, Shy . . . you're a dick."

Even with those words, she still lifted her hands, placed them on either side of his head and angled closer. Pressing her lips against his, that sweet, pink tongue of hers slid between his lips to touch the tip of his tongue before she let him go just as quickly as she'd grabbed hold. She jumped out of the cab and ran gracefully on the toes of her high-heeled sandals up the side deck and into the house.

Shy had shifted to watch her move, his chest and gut both ablaze, the brief but undeniably sweet taste of her still on his tongue.

The light on the side of the house went off, and he was plunged into darkness.

"Shit," he muttered before he put the truck in gear and turned around.

As he drove home, he couldn't get her tear-stained cheeks and wet eyes out of his head.

He also couldn't get her taste off his tongue.

THE DISH

Where Authors Give You the Inside Scoop

From the desk of Anna Campbell

Dear Reader,

When I first came up with the idea for the Sons of Sin series, which began last year with *Seven Nights in a Rogue's Bed*, I wanted to explore the effects of family scandal on my heroes and the women they fall in love with.

My first hero, Jonas Merrick, was all injury, anger, and passion. For my second hero, I wanted less of the wounded lion and more of the man who hides deep emotional wounds beneath a careless smile and a quick witticism. Someone a little closer to the Scarlet Pimpernel than Heathcliff! I also wanted to write about someone who becomes a hero in spite of himself, once he realizes that he alone can protect the woman he loves from men with much darker motives than his own rather murky purposes.

So Sir Richard Harmsworth, the dashing rake at the center of A RAKE'S MIDNIGHT KISS, was born.

All Richard's life, he's maintained an appearance of cool elegance. He's learned through bitter experience that emotional involvement only leads to disaster. When he sets out to retrieve the Harmsworth Jewel, the priceless artifact that proves his right to the baronetcy, he has no idea that he's embarking on an adventure that will change him forever.

Richard fights tooth and nail against falling in love with scholarly vicar's daughter, Genevieve Barrett, the jewel's current custodian. Even worse, innocent Genevieve is the one woman in the world who seems immune to his famous charm. To win her, he'll need to dig deep beneath his spectacular façade and unearth all those heroic qualities that he's convinced he doesn't possess. Qualities like courage and honor, steadfastness and self-sacrifice.

These two characters were such fun to write. I've always been a fan of the fast-talking romantic comedies of the 1930s and 1940s where the heroine was at least as smart as the hero and didn't give him an inch unless he worked himself into a lather to take it. I created Richard and Genevieve in that mold—I wanted passionate battles and battling passions! I hope you enjoy their bumpy path to true love and a happy ending.

If you'd like to know more about A RAKE'S MIDNIGHT KISS, please check out my website www.anna campbell.info. And in the meantime, happy reading!

Best wishes,

Anna Campbell

♥ ♥ ♥ ♥ ♥ ♥ ♥ ♥ ♥ ♥ ♥ ♥ ♥ ♥ ♥ ♥ ♥

From the desk of Debra Webb

Dear Reader,

Fall is around the corner and I'm already plotting how to decorate for Halloween and then Christmas. Yes, I said Christmas! Time really has flown this year. Here we are in case six of the Faces of Evil—RUTHLESS.

I'm certain you were a little stunned at the end! What in the world is Jess going to do? It's time for her to get her act together and face the reality of her situation—Spears isn't going to stop until he has her. There is so much *more* for her to consider now. And Dan, oh my goodness, is he in for a surprise! Jess will need Dan more than ever now.

Vicious is next, so brace yourself! Things just get more chilling from here. The pressure is on to stop Spears and no one is safe. As the next six cases play out, look for exploding tension, life-and-death situations, and even more heinous killers. That's the thing about the Faces of Evil: Each one is more evil than the last. So don't miss a single installment!

I hope you'll stop by www.thefacesofevil.com and visit! There's a weekly briefing each Friday where I talk about what's going on in my world and with the characters as I write the next story. You can sign up as a person of interest and you might just end up a suspect! We love giving away prizes too so do stop by.

Enjoy the story and be sure to look for *Vicious* next spring! Between now and then, I'll be sending you on a journey into Jess and Dan's past with a very special Christmas story. Watch for *Silence* coming soon!

Cheers!

Debra Webb

♥ ♥ ♥ ♥ ♥ ♥ ♥ ♥ ♥ ♥ ♥ ♥ ♥ ♥ ♥

From the desk of Kristen Ashley

Dear Reader,

I have an obsession with names, which shouldn't surprise readers as the names I give my characters run the gamut and are often out there.

In my Dream Man series, I introduced readers to Cabe "Hawk" Delgado, Brock "Slim" Lucas, Mitch Lawson, and Kane "Tack" Allen. My Chaos series gives us Shy, Hop, Joker, and Rush, among the other members of the Club.

I've had quite a few folks express curiosity about where I come up with all these names, and I wish I could say I knew a load of good-looking men who had awesome and unusual names and I stole them but, alas, that isn't true.

In most cases, characters, especially heroes and heroines, come to me named. They just pop right into my head, much like Tatum "Tate" Jackson of *Sweet Dreams*. He just walked right in there, all the gloriousness of Tate, and introduced himself to me. And luckily, he had an amazing, strong, masculine, kick-ass name.

In other instances, who they are defines their name. I understood Hawk's tragic back story from MYSTERY MAN first. I also understood that the man he was melted away; he became another man with a new name so what he called himself evolved from what he did in the military. His given name, of course, evolved from his multiethnic background.

The same with Mitch, the hero from *Law Man*. The minute he walked into Gwen's kitchen, his last name hit me like a shot. What else could a straight-arrow cop be called but Lawson?

Other names are a mystery to me. Kane "Tack" Allen came to me named but I had no clue why his Club name was Tack. Truthfully, I also found it a bit annoying seeing as how the name Kane is such a cool name, and I didn't want to waste it on a character who wouldn't use it. But Tack was Kane Allen and there was no prying that name away from him.

Why he was called Tack, though, was a mystery to me, but I swear, it must have always been in the recesses of my mind because his nickname is perfect for him. Therefore, as I was following his journey with Tyra and the mystery of Tack was revealed, I burst out laughing. I loved it. It was so perfect for him.

One of the many, *many* reasons I'm enjoying the Chaos series is that I get to be very creative with names. I mean, Shy, Hop, Rush, Bat, Speck, and Snapper? I love it. Anything goes with those boys and I have lists of names scrawled everywhere in my magic notebook where I jot ideas. Some of them are crazy and I hope to get to use them, like Moose. Some of them are crazy cool and I hope I get to use them, like Preacher. Some of them are just crazy and I'll probably never use them, like Destroyer. But all of them are fun.

All my characters' names, nicknames, and the endearments they use with each other, friends, and family mean a great deal to me. Mostly because all of them and everything they do exists in a perfectly real unreality in my head. They're with me all the time. They're mine. I created them. And just like a parent naming a child, these perfectly real unreal beings are precious to me as are the names they chose for themselves.

I just hope they keep it exciting.

Kristen Ashley

♥ ♥ ♥ ♥ ♥ ♥ ♥ ♥ ♥ ♥ ♥ ♥ ♥ ♥ ♥

From the desk of Amanda Scott

Dear Reader,

The setting for a story is as important as any other plot element, sometimes more so. Therefore, when I decided to pattern the heroines of my Lairds of the Loch trilogy after the Greek Fates Atropos, Lachesis, and Clotho (who became the ladies Andrena, Lachina, and Muriella MacFarlan), I realized that they'd need a setting equal to their creative "heritage."

I wanted the three to have gifts based on instincts that we all still share to some degree, but exaggerated, because in those days such instincts must have been stronger for survival. Shortly after that I began wondering if the story's setting might play a more active role of its own. You see, it had to be a defensible place. Their father, Andrew, the true chief of Clan Farlan, had managed to defend it for nearly twenty years against the treacherous cousin who usurped the rest of his vast estates and murdered his three sons.

The result is Tùr Meiloach (pronounced Toor MIL-ock), meaning "a small tower guarded by giants," but also referring to the estate's reputation as a sanctuary for "true" MacFarlans. Over time, the rugged land where the tower sits has acquired an eerie reputation that daunts most would-be visitors. Birds and beasts of the forest are said to be wilder and more vicious there than elsewhere, and men swear that bogs reach out to drown unwary trespassers. The mountainous terrain is replete with rivers too wild to ford; high, spiny ridges; and deep chasms with walls likely to crumble at a man's touch and bury him.

Legends abound of men, even whole armies, vanishing there.

Through various strategies, Andrew has succeeded in keeping Tùr Meiloach safe from invasion, but his primary goal is to marry his daughters to well-connected warriors who can help him win back his entire chiefdom.

Lady Lachina "Lina" MacFarlan, the heroine of THE KNIGHT'S TEMPTRESS, has the gift of foresight but doesn't know it and doesn't trust the odd sense she has that something bad is about to happen (such as being captured by rebels who have seized Dumbarton Castle). Nor does she recognize Sir Ian Colquhoun as her hero.

She agrees that he is a handsome knight of great renown but thinks he is too reckless, too impulsive, and never thinks things through.

Sir Ian can't resist a challenge and has thought since

Lina was eight years old that she is too calmly dignified, so her serenity always stirs him to unsettle it. He is not interested in marriage. Besides, he is wary of her wily father and his strange estate, but the lass *is* dangerously attractive.

Find out what happens when Sir Ian decides to rescue Lina and her friend Lizzie Galbraith from the "impregnable" royal stronghold of Dumbarton, and the King of Scots commands him to recapture it. Sir Ian's answer became the Colquhouns' clan motto, "*Si je puis*," or "If I can."

I hope you enjoy reading THE KNIGHT'S TEMPTRESS. Meantime, *Suas Alba*!

Sincerely,

Amanda Scott

www.amandascottauthor.com

Find out more about Forever Romance!

Visit us at
www.hachettebookgroup.com/publishing_forever.aspx

Find us on Facebook
http://www.facebook.com/ForeverRomance

Follow us on Twitter
http://twitter.com/ForeverRomance

NEW AND UPCOMING TITLES

Each month we feature our new titles
and reader favorites.

CONTESTS AND GIVEAWAYS

We give away galleys, autographed copies,
and all kinds of exclusive items.

AUTHOR INFO

You'll find bios, articles, and links to personal websites
for all your favorite authors—and so much more.

GET SOCIAL

Connect with your favorite authors, editors, and
other Forever fans, and share what's important to you.

THE BUZZ

Sign up for our monthly romance newsletter,
and be the first to read all about it.

VISIT US ONLINE AT

WWW.HACHETTEBOOKGROUP.COM

FEATURES:

OPENBOOK BROWSE AND
SEARCH EXCERPTS
•
AUDIOBOOK EXCERPTS AND PODCASTS
•
AUTHOR ARTICLES AND INTERVIEWS
•
BESTSELLER AND PUBLISHING
GROUP NEWS
•
SIGN UP FOR E-NEWSLETTERS
•
AUTHOR APPEARANCES AND TOUR
INFORMATION
•
SOCIAL MEDIA FEEDS AND WIDGETS
•
DOWNLOAD FREE APPS

BOOKMARK HACHETTE BOOK GROUP
@ WWW.HACHETTEBOOKGROUP.COM